Finding Bridie

Alan Baulch

About the Author:

Alan Baulch is a multiple genre Author as demonstrated by his latest novel 'Finding Bridie' and previous works 'Mind Trap' and 'The Tracer' together with his first volume of short stories entitled 'Love, Life and Fantasies'.

A British, London born retired former Businessman, IT professional and Foster Carer. At an early age heavily influenced by Dennis Wheatley, Aldous Huxley and further by the French writer Guy de Maupassant. Modern day favourites include Dick Francis, Patricia Cornwall and John Grisham particularly in style. He belongs to a Prose & Poetry group with the U3A (University of the Third Age) where he collaborates with other like-minded authors and writes both short stories and poetry.

He is currently writing the sequel to Mind Trap and lives in Lincolnshire.

By the same author

Mind Trap

The Tracer

●

Love, Life, Fantasies & Poetry

(Volume One – Short Stories)

Finding Bridie

Copyright © 2015 by Alan Baulch
All rights reserved.

1 3 5 7 9 10 8 6 4 2

Printed by Amazon

Available on Kindle

No part of this book may be reproduced in any form or by any electronic or mechanical means including information storage and retrieval systems, without permission in writing from the author. The only exception is by a reviewer, who may quote short excerpts in a review.

This book is a work of fiction. Names, characters, places, and incidents either are products of the author's imagination or are used fictitiously. Any resemblance to actual persons, living or dead, events, or locales is entirely coincidental.

To Janet

Chapter 1

"He's called again, you know!" Claire was scolding me, she had been my secretary for the past 15 years, making me better at my job and I loved her for it. She had a natural wisp of grey hair at the front of her heavily lacquered dark brown hair, which displaced whenever she became angry, mostly with me.

"I know, I know," faking my 'I'm really busy' expression, I put away my computer magazine with a wry smile.

"Why don't you want to see him, he keeps calling you it must be important?" She stood in front of my desk with another 'post-it' sticker to put on my computer screen, ready to join the two others already there and placing the folder she was carrying down on my desk with a thump, inside requisitions for my signature, normal for a Monday morning the latest 'post-it' stuck on top.

"Because I'm afraid I'll get sucked into his problems which have nothing whatsoever to do with me." I was being unkind not wanting to think about it, besides it is too hot in my office.

"How do you know if you don't call him back, are you scared of him?" She wagged her index finger at me, neck red with anger.

"I don't want to find out." Shaking my head as she left.

"He is not going to go away you know!" She

shouted backwards walking across the staff area where my twenty strong team sit, they were used to our spats, we were like an old married couple, and I doubted she would be interested in me. A divorced 45 year old was not looking for an old man like me, there was not a lad under 30 she did not flirt with and on occasions they would win the prize and be lucky enough to date her. 15 years ago when I hired her she had been stunning and could have had her pick, but back then, she was happily married. Now more mature she turned heads and knew it.

    A few minutes passed letting her cool down I signed the paperwork never something I enjoyed. I called out to her. "Claire, I have signed the papers you brought me in the folder." Watching idly, as she walked back across the open plan office coffee cups in hand, managing to swing her hips as she walked knowing she is being watched by a couple of my middle aged men in the team. She would prolong her anger at me while she made us hot drinks in the kitchen area next door to my office.

    Our council office building on three levels with a car park in the basement, is split into two, north and south by departments, we're on the north side and occupied half of the first floor, my office in one corner looking out on to the main street of the Kentish town of Maidstone.

    With constant space saving initiatives all departments were gradually turning into open plan areas, only a few of us managers had kept hold of our offices without having to share the space. The others without their own office constantly grumbled because they lacked privacy to surf the internet or look up personal items and private emails rather than actually doing their day job.

"Who is he anyway?" Claire placing the coffee cup on my desk and clasping both hands around hers, sitting down as she warmed them on one of my meeting table chairs, she's like a dog with a bone, her wide eyes waiting for information.

The telephone rang she grabbed it before I could. "Hayden Robbins office, can I help you?" She shook her head, not important making my excuses for ducking out of a meeting, knowing I would not want to attend.

"Come on, you haven't answered me," putting down the telephone on its cradle. I looked out of my window watching my boss run across the main road away from the building, papers under her arm off to her normal Monday morning update with our Director of Technology.

"He's my childhood sweetheart's father!" Not looking at her, still watching my boss as she disappeared under the archway leading to the main County Hall offices one of four buildings making up the campus known as Kent County Council headquarters. A good boss, a fit athletic looking woman who never tired of exercise, putting men like me into shame my stomach growing imperceptibly with each passing year.

"Quite a while ago then, I'm surprised you remember?" Tilting her head, wide- eyed in sarcasm, needing little reminding I am marching headlong towards retirement.

"We're all ancient," my poor attempt at retaliation, turning to face her, apologising to her the moment I said it.

"Oh dear, have you been a naughty boy?" She said walking out of my office with a smirk on her face and an extra swing of her hips making way for my first meeting of the day, the participants began automatically filing into my cosy warm office one or two following her with their eyes. I stifled a sigh, my working life a constant pointless round of meets, touching bases and updates they called them, I called them a nuisance.

Ignoring them, I grabbed the necessary papers needed from my desk drawer as they managed to squeeze in and around my table for four, one hard against the window and another against my grey filing cabinet with the two larger members already notably sweating opting for the outside positions. I pressed the latest yellow post-it note to my screen supposedly to deal with later and turned my chair around to make five at the table, each of us vying for paper space, the conference call telephone in the centre, we would need it today.

I went through the motions during the meeting, attempting to nod in the right places as well as agreeing with decisions made. Despite only 10 a.m., the hot day had started to produce odours amongst the people, my small office prone to hold its heat due to the south facing position. The large young man to the left of me already had sweat marks on his blue shirt under his arms and starting down the centre of his back and the day had barely begun. As the windows gradually clouded in condensation I pushed them open to let some real fresh air into the office, turning off the air conditioning by the wall dial without comment, too many bodies in a small office always ensured meetings finished quickly.

One of my methods was to make sure everyone is clear on what they were doing or going to do, ensuring I ended up with the minimum of work. I normally positioned myself as the co-ordinator. I found my mind wandering not able to concentrate on work at all, too busy thinking about a love left behind long ago, the post-its' weighing heavy on my mind.

Forcing myself to concentrate on the following two meetings, I became grateful when lunchtime finally arrived. I looked up from my desk out of the window at the grey early July morning, the temperature outside looked at odds with the heat in my office, the summer sun attempting to manoeuvre through the clouds showing a vast blue sky breaking through. Earlier, when I had started out for work, there had been a slight chill to the air, now I expected warmth out there and intended to sample it, mostly I liked my job including meetings in general, but sometimes a walk in town helped keep my sanity intact. I signalled to Claire, I was going out by putting on my jacket, not sure if I would need it, she waved, I'm fond of Claire Chandler she has a standing joke her initials are CC carbon copy appropriate for a secretary. I never had the heart to mention the joke was better when there were still typewriters and not computer's, she's a great secretary though, I am very lucky.

Walking down into the town towards the shops it always amused me at the number of people I knew, most acknowledging each other with a nod or stopping for a chat sharing gossip as office people do. Passing by a Weatherspoon's bar on a nearby corner with an open windowed aspect were familiar faces inside who would wave as I passed. Today I felt like a nodding dog nobody stopped although I knew quite a number of those strolling by who said 'Hello'.

I tried to dodge a canvasser needing my urgent opinion on a range of questions about holidays suggesting if I was lucky and answered them correctly, I could win one. I had done one of these before, providing I could take three other people I could go free, taking the slip the woman gave me a knowing look, I would see her again next month.

    Grabbing a red Leicester cheese salad with its little black fork, a BLT sandwich and a bottle of water at the Marks & Spencer food store in the centre of town. I decided to take a rare walk into the local park by the riverside to clear my head using the underpass by the river bridge to avoid using the main road and headed straight for the river's edge.

    Always fascinated by the narrow boat's, small vessels and prized yachts which suddenly appeared every summer, staying overnight for July's annual water festival only to disappear until the following year, floating gypsies, a romantic notion without much purpose drifting up and down the river.

    Passing swans and ducks would eye walkers with suspicion, with only the pigeons staying close in order to inspect what you had in your bag of goodies.

    Walking on, I crossed the bridge high above River Medway running through from the heart of Maidstone Town to other side where the park spread out before me. A ferry barge stopped to pick up six passengers underneath the bridge to join the same number already seated, the summer sun began shining through the clouds warming and brightening my mood. I watched looking down from the peak of the bridge as the 'Kentish Lady' passenger boat paused underneath for people to board as it made its way upstream towards Allington and East Farleigh.

    The lottery funded Whatman Millennium Park at lunchtime was full of people, the weather had brought them out in numbers, jackets slung over shoulders, woollens tied around waists, open neck shirt's, with sun hats and sunglasses making their appearance. The 18 acre site with the river linking it to Rochester and the Thames Estuary beyond running gently through, offered a tranquil place to clear any mind.

Today, play areas, treetop walks, skating park and the riverside arena normally used for staging open-air dance performances, bustled instead, with school mums in their groups, the younger children in prams not old enough for either play school or the main primary schools. Each being pushed around the park passing the time before the mums had to pick up their older children from their afternoon classes, students enjoying their free periods.

Revellers, spreading their fare on blankets on the grass, office cliques, energetic runners and the lazy, flat on their backs soaking up the daytime sunshine. Men from offices with their rolled up shirtsleeves, ties askew, sitting on inside out jackets their mission to enjoy the green and flowered space with the gentle trickle of water sounding through the summer breeze, at last the summer's sun shining through with little sign of clouds, most of the grey metal bench seats full. Spotting one in the distance, vacated by an elderly couple I quickened my pace, a short step past the picnickers.

People reading books and newspapers or listening to their music on their ipod's with joggers passing by, sixth form boys laughing their girl counterparts sitting in a circle chatting furiously about life as they saw it, talking loudly enough to attract the attention of the young men near them, some were alone heads buried in a magazine.

Taking my place on the vacated bench, I placed

my jacket carefully down beside me watching a solitary pigeon look up to me for its lunchtime scraps the imploring eyes and coos waiting for me to share the contents of my bag of food for crumbs ready to drop.

I relaxed taking in the cool pleasant breeze, my gaze downwards across the grass in front of me and beyond to the sunshine glistening on the water. I opened up the perspex container of salad, retrieving the black fork within and started to eat. The bird giving up in disgust as it eyed the unopened sandwich packet and crisp packet set out bedside me on the bench, I was sure it would return.

My thoughts quickly turned to the post-it notes and Claire's insistence to do something about them. Leaving my office, I had pulled the three messages from my screen, now removing them from my jacket pocket I laid them on top of the bench beside me.

The first message read:

'*My dear Hayden,*
My name is Desmond London, please excuse this intrusion but I need to talk to you urgently. I hope you remember as a young boy you lived opposite my home and greengrocers shop, you knew my daughter Bridie, you were quite fond of her as I recall. I know this is an unusual step after all this time but it is very important we speak.
My best regards,
Desmond.'

A week passed and I simply ignored the message, with e-mail's we don't want to read we trash them or they automatically get moved to the spam folder, we do it all the time, it's acceptable, always someone wanting something from you. I got 'spam' all day, every day in business hours as well as in my private e-mail, ignoring a post-it note from my personal assistant rated low although I wouldn't own up to it with Claire and yet I continued to feel guilty by ignoring it.

The second message went into a bit more detail:
'Hayden,

It is Desmond London again please get in touch quickly it is obviously about Bridie, I know you will remember your first ever love, my daughter? If you have lost my original message, we lived at my Greengrocers on the corner of Fenham Road Peckham in London. Please remember, I need your help desperately, she has been very sick which you may already know and I would like to explain to you what happened to her.
Very best regards,
Desmond.'

The urgency this time came through loud and clear, he gave the same telephone and mobile numbers to contact as before. Of course I remembered Bridie she was my angel, locked for most of my adult years in mind and heart since childhood, she was the comparison, the blueprint for every female I have ever met, he was right she was my first love. Her face clear to me even after all this time, a complexion darkened like a Spanish Senorita and a blaze of dancing freckles across her nose, she had a chipped front tooth once caused by her brother Joseph, after throwing one of his wooden play bricks at her.

Bridie had been devastated, distraught by her damaged teeth and hating her brother for it. She was a young teenager worrying how she looked to others. I remember eyes saucer like and bright green, her dark brown hair glistening in the sun and under the evening light, especially on my front porch, where we used to stand for hours cuddling, talking and kissing. The chipped tooth enhancing her personality. Soon to be moving home to Camberwell a couple of miles away I remember wanting to make the most of our time left together. Whether my memory is rosy as the reality, I found myself reluctant to find out.

The third message far more urgent and had caused Claire to push me into responding:

'Hayden, Hayden

I beg of you please get in touch it has taken me so long to find you I do need your help urgently. Please I am an old man without much time left to do the right thing by Bridie, please help me at least hear what I have to say and then decide how much you could help.
Let me speak to you please!
Desmond.'

The note, scribbled tailing off in a flow suggesting a rushed note. It made me feel guilty, but what could I possibly do for him, she's not my family I did not know them it had been some 45 to 50 years ago, I could not see what he expected of me. In my mind, I tried to find excuses for not getting involved and only one for doing so, curiosity.

Afraid it would stir up emotions best left where they are, dangerous with a wife and two children who mean the world to me, it could destroy us as a family, I'm scared it will alter my feelings for them and towards Bridie held sacred in my memory, this is first love stuff and very powerful. As a family, we have a good life I did not want anything to interfere with it.

Halfway through my cheese salad I felt a presence beside me, it was not the bird.

"What a great place Hayden, you know I read on the entrance plaque 1500 new trees had been planted prior to the place opening in 2001, incredible!" A shadow hovered above me.

"So I understand," looking up to see a grey thickset dishevelled old man who had to be in his mid-eighties wearing an old style rain beige Macintosh blocking my sunlight as he stooped over me, I stopped eating my salad.

"Hayden, I'm sorry if it appears I am stalking you, but I called again at your office and a nice girl directed me to the park suggesting I might find you here." Standing up I shook hands with him knowing who he was. Claire would have been pleased described as a girl if she had heard I suspected I was still a boy to him.

"Desmond, Mr London," it sounded strange after all these years he was familiar to me, I felt a young boy again scared he would talk to my mum and dad I nearly called him Sir, I pushed the thought from my mind.

"How did you recognise it was me you were after?" There were many like me throughout the park, grey balding aged men looking as if retirement the only way out of the drudge of working life.

"Your secretary Claire told me to look for a large tall man in a white open necked shirt with a navy blue stripe suit, crew cut balding grey hair with glasses, probably with a Marks & Spencer's green carry bag with your lunch inside and you definitely wouldn't be sat on the grass." I laughed how well she knew me, convinced Claire had told him more and he was being polite to me.

"I'm surprised she knew, I told her I would walk down into the town."

"She did ask as people came through the main door of your building if anyone had seen you. One young man said you were walking towards the park so she directed me here." I hoped it satisfied Claire we had met at last.

"I'm sorry I've not been in touch before now Mr London, Claire in fairness, did give me your three messages," exonerating her. "However, I am at a loss to know what I can possibly do for you because whatever it is, while I loved Bridie back then I was only 12 or 13 at the time and surely, you cannot expect me to rake up the past now. I have a family, a wife and children to consider." I moved my sandwich pack and drink gesturing for him to sit down beside me on the bench. The pigeon nearby perked up only to be disappointed once again. I reflected on how panicky I must have sounded. The group of boys stood up from the grass in front of us brushing themselves down getting ready to go back to school a couple taking an interest in our conversation. Realising what they were doing, ran to catch up with the rest of their pack passing the giggling girls vying for their attention, what was I afraid of?

"What a great spot for lunch and the view across the river is splendid, it's wonderful here," as he spoke his tone became serious. "Believe me I do respect you and your family and would certainly not wish to cause any unnecessary pain to anyone least of all to you. Please continue your lunch and be assured if there were anyone else I could turn to who I thought could help me better than you I would do it," Desmond seemed genuinely pleased to find me at last and I, despite my initial reservations happy to see him again after all this time.

He reminded me of a young boy starting out in life eager to face the challenges which lay before me and I ended up becoming a civil servant, another thought to push away or I will depress myself.

"Please Hayden call me Desmond, no longer do I think of you as the young cocky lad who used to be so smart and knew it all chasing after my pretty daughter, from what I have learnt about you, you have done well for yourself."

"What have you learnt?" Speaking too sharply, I must have sounded suspicious. "Be assured I have no money!" Immediately regretting my words and tone.

"Nor I, but it's your help I need, your support, not your money, another mind who has an interest in my daughters welfare at whatever level, your decision of course!" I could have kicked myself for my behaviour. Tough enough for him to ask for help from a stranger despite knowing him as a lad years ago, how did he know who or what type of person I had eventually become.

"The real question is what would you like it to be Desmond?" Opening myself up to him.

"Oh that's easy my dear boy everything you can give!" He laughed, but deadly serious, now he had found me, he would not let me off the hook now.

"I understand you're a computers man, clearly very busy and quite a senior manager, according to your receptionist when I initially asked for you at the County Hall's main building before getting directed to your one across the road."

"Yes it can be confusing, there are 4 buildings making up the County Councils Headquarters." I was posturing vowing to stop. "The main building is called Sessions House and is grade II listed, built in 1824. It has changed names a couple of times over the years. It actually started life as Old Sessions House so it's come full circle." I could not help myself it is my interviewing candidates for a job routine.

"Although I said I recognised you from the description your secretary gave me," he hesitated. "Forgive me even now in middle age I would recognise you anywhere, you have always had a distinctive bearing of style even when you were a young boy," his meaning complimentary.

"Thank you very much, kind Sir," bowing mocking myself offering him one of my BLT sandwiches, which he took. As if by magic the moment I opened the packet a familiar coo could be heard from underneath the bench, my friend the pigeon cocked his knowing head at me, I broke a piece of crust from my sandwich and dropped it Desmond didn't seem to notice.

"I need you Hayden I have been searching for you for months I will pay you for your time and help." His smiling face disarmed me, for him, outside of the family he remembered there was only one person who would probably have cared as much for Bridie back then as he did. Not having a clue where to start looking he was determined to find the one person then boy now a man who might make the difference he needed, I felt flattered and daunted by his expectation and faith he placed in me.

"How on earth did you find me, since I left home and married we've moved around quite a lot?" I could tell how pleased he seemed. "By the way whatever help you get from me is free, call it payback for the worry I must have caused you as a lad with your daughter." He laughed loudly.

"It's a deal. Initially I began checking the electoral rolls, first in many of the London Borough's. I then widened my search through the counties. Do you know how many H Robbins there are, literally thousands, I must have made a hundred or more telephone calls, then my solicitor an old chap and a friend of the family for many years, Victor Carlton, said I should have looked on Facebook, apparently, it's what they call a social media site," he started to laugh. "I swear he is almost as old as I am and he was tapping away on his laptop as he called it, on to the internet by way of using his radio." I found myself giggling at him.

"You mean wireless don't you?" Correcting him.

"What I said!" I let it go, grinning at him.

"And then?"

"He said he found you by virtue of checking the school you went to St. Francis Primary, I knew you had attended the local school and fortunately you'd put it on your profile, is this the right terminology Hayden?" I nodded amused at what was difficult for him to comprehend and what to me seemed commonplace, I dare not mention twitter I am having trouble with this one myself.

"Then what did you do?" I asked intrigued.

"You'd made a mention of a media business site called LinkedIn." I then knew how he had found me. "Well again we looked up your profile and this time it told us about you and what jobs you had done and where, listing out your experiences and competencies." He was quite pleased with himself and I thought I must remember to thank Victor Carlton should I ever meet him, at this moment I did not know how I felt about it.

"Desmond, I'm curious why on earth do you need me?" The frail old man sitting beside me made me feel embarrassed at my suggestion he had been after money, obviously hurt by my implication, I tried to make amends. "You have three other children if I recall and maybe other family too?" Unconsciously I watched my bird's lack of loyalty, begging for scraps at the next bench along the pathway and already joined by two more pigeons. I checked my watch nearly 3pm the sun at its height getting warmer time to leave the park. A boy rode by us on his skateboard zigzagging shouting to his friends ahead, his school cap turned back to front, school blazer tied around his waist, flapping behind him as he went by.

"You're right, of course and forgive me, it would work if anyone gave a damn, and it is a long story to tell." I was surprised at his anger. "All they're interested in, is their inheritance not Bridie, They call it their entitlement, I have worked hard all my life to provide for all my children and realise they don't give a rat's behind for their own sister or for each other." A disillusioned father spoke from his heart.

"Desmond, please don't upset yourself, come on let's go back to my office, we can grab some coffee and we can continue sharing sandwiches, Claire will bring us some more and we'll begin there, I'll clear some meetings so I can understand the problem better." Casting my eyes backwards my original companion eyed me with disappointment, I watched the bird spot a morsel dropped by a woman on a blanket, and I, forgotten in a wingspan.

Desmond visibly relaxed before my eyes; I made the decision to help him, not sure, whether I would regret it.

"You mentioned children Hayden?" Making conversation as we walked across the bridge back over the river.

"Yes a son Simon and daughter Carrie, they're great kids."

"How old are they?"

"Carrie's the oldest at 13 and Simon is 2 years behind at 11."

"Do you like them Hayden?" He had obviously thought about the question.

"What a strange thing to ask, of course I do, I love them." I was intrigued, the afternoon traffic created a buzz of noise around us we were out of the park walking up to cross a busy roundabout.

"I'm glad, you're lucky, you can love your children, but it doesn't always mean you like them," a tinge of sadness crossed his eyes. "You'll easily understand what it's like to deal with a very sick young girl and wanting the absolute best for her, are you happy with their mother?" He asked apologetically, his polite way of approaching my marital status and potential problems if Bridie and I become close once again.

I nodded, not wanting to contemplate his thoughts at this or any stage.

"How about your wife, tell me of her?" he pressed genuinely interested.

"Penny is a person of strong character it helps with the children as I'm as soft as butter, she works hard and is definitely the boss at home." Desmond smiled as a couple of joggers from my office nearby said 'hi' to me as they passed I waved.

"You don't like your own children Desmond?" Trying to remember their names and them as individuals.

"Quite frankly no, if you ever meet Joseph, Susan and Emma again you'll understand, I hope." Flashes of the past entered my mind, their faces miraculously appearing in my mind's eye, I could not remember ever playing with them as a child.

"Mrs London?" I asked tentatively, so far he had not mentioned her.

"Sadly Josephine died in 2001." He stopped there sighing deep in his own thoughts a memory too painful to discuss.

"Are you sure you're only asking about Penny to see whether she matched Bridie in some way?" Attempting to deflect his melancholy.

"Not at all," he mocked me. "Well perhaps a little."

"Penny is a real beauty and far too young for me, a great mother to the children." I said, meaning it.

"Come on, there's more to it, how did you meet her?"

"I met her about 20 years ago, at one of those seminars." He did not understand.

"What are one of those when it's at home," he reminded me of an old market street barrow boy convinced he was mocking me.

"One of those outings for business information gatherings, where people go out and meet people they don't really need to know or want to know, but sometimes it is important to get out of the office, have a free lunch and let the world know you exist outside your own environment , it's called a networking opportunity."

"Wow I want one of those!" He laughed at me.

"Surely you had a green grocery convention from time to time?" My turn to mock him and he took it in good spirit. "Awards for the biggest carrots and such?"

"Oh of course Hayden, we used to toss the salad or bowl the cabbages when we were bored," he laughed I had not felt like this since I was a child. It felt a pleasure to be around him.

"Ok I give up." I had a smile on my face I did like this man.

"Come on more of Penny, please," he insisted, as we arrived outside my office building.

"We sat next to each other at one of those seminars, she happened to be filling in for her boss and to this day she has this infuriating habit and I interrupted her doing it."

"Good God man what was it?" He faked alarm.

"She would keep fiddling and picking at her fingers, specifically her nails, pick, pick, pick was all I could hear." Frustration entered my voice.

"She hooked you and you didn't know it." He was smiling again at me.

"It was infuriating, she didn't bite just pick at them, after about an hour listening to the latest speaker drone on about how wonderful their particular brand of computer software was I heard this noise beside me, which led to her groaning about how her nails had suddenly split."

"So what did you do?"

"I smacked her hands, and she whelped like a dog, only the smack happened during a moment's pause from the speaker, the sound reverberating across the quiet auditorium, quickly followed by her not so quiet whelp, thus causing everyone's attention to be focused squarely on us," I recalled the scene. "We both giggled at one another, rose from our seats said a loud sorry and hurried out into the hall where we fell into each other's arms in laughter, the rest is history as they say." One of the best free lunches I ever had.

"You love her to bits don't you, Hayden?" He put his hand on my shoulder and squeezed as a father would.

"Yes, I really do!" I felt like hugging this man, he was easy to talk to and I really had known him all my life.

By swiping my identity card on the keypad of the building door it magically opened, I showed him up the stairs, past the kitchen area where Claire had previously made our drinks and to the left into my office.

I summoned Claire to suggest she cancel my afternoon's meetings. Already done she informed us, she knew me well and offered us coffee, I begged her for more sandwiches and she left smiling swinging her hips at Desmond who hadn't noticed, a grown up I observed. Claire happy and clutching my twenty pound note, pleased we had at last come together. My team members in the background craning their necks to see who my guest is or better, they walked past my office ostensibly to get themselves a drink from the kitchen to gain a better look.

"What do you remember of my daughter, Hayden?" He smiled broadly, as he thought of her.

"Someone warm and fun loving, my equal in every way," my mind rekindling the memories of her. "Intelligent in a common sense way, a dark, sultry look, I loved her back then Desmond, truly loved her with all my heart and to be honest with you I have never ever been as comfortable with someone since, not until Penny came along of course." I interjected, unsure if it were true. "You have the same way about you."

"Don't go falling in love with me young man I am far too old for you." We both roared with laughter.

"I guess these days you would call it having a soul mate, if circumstances were different, I knew we would have married," I struggled internally finding myself with a tear in my eye, wistfully yearning for a life lost, looking back is not a good idea.

"Sorry Desmond, I never ever believed you knew how strong I felt about her."

"I did Hayden believe me, but you were both so young not having lived any sort of life at all," he looked me straight in the eye. "I was wrong Hayden, I realise my stubbornness, a Victorian attitude and her illness getting in the way is my only defence." Genuinely saddened by the thought.

"All water under the bridge Desmond we were too young," Trying to be kind to the frail old man in front of me, he had more issues than I had to deal with. "If it was Carrie I guess I would be exactly the same."

Bridie would always smell of roses from her father's shop. Desmond had put her in charge of wrapping the flowers into bouquets on school nights ready for delivery and sale within the shop by day. At weekend's she loved to travel with him in his green Hillman grocery van to old Covent Garden to buy the flowers for her to sell in the shop at the weekends, it gave her pocket money. She loved her name, always getting a kick out of being London's Green Grocers and Florists as if theirs were the capital city's only genuine shopkeeper of fruit, vegetable and flowers.

She would design her displays, outside of the

shop on top of a table with artificial grass matting, and below making sure the spread of flowers would somehow, manage to touch the legs of those passer's by on the pavement, bursting from wooden water filled tubs, causing them to look down at them. A marketing technique designed for today's world not back then in the early 60's. The customers would normally bend down, pick a bunch of flowers from her display and pay their money to Bridie. A proper salesperson I remembered.

The soft fragrance of her shoulder fur topped black coat she wore in winter filled my heart; we used to huddle together in my doorway because it had a porch. I know she sprayed herself with her Mother's perfume. I never knew the name of it, but occasionally I have smelt it when near others and it always jogged my memory of Bridie, I am convinced it is Chanel. The time we used to watch television together on our sofa like grown-ups with my Mum and Dad sitting in the armchairs beside us in our living room on the top floor of our terraced home. I could see a part of her in the shape and mannerisms on Desmond's face, I felt glad he had asked for my help.

Claire tapped on my office glass window and brought in coffee and sandwiches, I had noticed the staff quizzing her about my guest, knowing she would be discreet.

"Are you OK Desmond?" Afraid he might be tired or uncomfortable in my air-conditioned office.

"Yes Hayden because I'm so glad I have found you, maybe we can find Bridie at last."

"Sorry Desmond have I misunderstood, have you lost Bridie, your notes suggested she might have been in trouble?" Confused I asked. "You mentioned in the notes she has been sick, I never knew, but I don't understand about helping to find her, is she missing?"

"Yes Hayden she is missing," he said.

"When, how, have you spoken to the police?" I asked, while opening up the freshly made sandwiches Claire had obtained from the nearby delicatessen, turkey and ham I discovered, pushing the opened packet toward him to share.

"Bridie's been missing for the past 50 years." His face ashen at the recall.

"What! She's been missing for 50 years and you've just decided it was time to do something about it?" I was horrified.

"No, no, I have confused you, I apologise." He was frustrated with himself.

"Desmond I think you had better tell me, starting at the beginning." I grabbed one of the sandwich packs to open.

Chapter 2

Monday afternoon still hot outside at about 27 degrees Celsius good for 4 p.m., the evening would be very pleasant. The air conditioning pumping hard making my office inside cool for the both of us. Desmond removed his tie and sat like me in his shirtsleeves. We finished the food and the hot drinks supplied by Claire in favour of cups from the water cooler in the kitchen.

"Bridie was 14 when she contracted consumption, the name my parents would have called it in those days." Desmond said ruefully, she was a little older than I was at the time.

"Wait a minute what's it got to do with Bridie being missing, do you know where she is or not?" My temperament lends me to wanting answers quickly.

"Well yes and no."

"Which means?"

"I believe I know where Bridie is, but she's lost to me." The man talking in riddles. "I have seen her once in 50 years three months ago in April."

"So she is not missing?" Struggling to understand.

"Physically, apparently Bridie was the person I met at the Maudsley, but I did not recognise her."

"Oh just around the corner where we, our families used to live." I recalled. "Why was she at Maudsley Hospital?"

"She was halfway through her assessment."

"What assessment?" It felt like pulling teeth.

"Her eventual release into the community," he drew a deep breath.

"What do you mean release, I thought you said she was lost, has she been in prison?"

"No, she has been in a sanatorium."

"Did she have a nervous breakdown or something?"

"No, she has been in asylums since you last saw her."

"You're joking? You're saying is she has been locked away in a mental institution for the past 50 years." This had the makings of a nightmare. "So why use the term 'lost' if you know where she is?"

"We don't know each other."

"What do you mean, is she your daughter or not?" Becoming frustrated.

"It is possible but she doesn't know me at all." He looked dejected.

"Isn't it to do with her mental state the fact she doesn't know you, and it would be difficult for you to recognise her after this length of time surely?"

"It's a good point I hadn't looked at it from her view." Thoughtfully considering how she had reacted to him.

"50 years is a long time Desmond, understandable yes?" Shooting in the dark.

"True but as her father I did expect something to click, anything at all, but nothing happened between us," his face full of disappointment.

"Ok tell me what happened when you saw her." This is not going to be easy.

"They told me it was her, I wanted it to be her, but I did not believe it." I worried who 'they' were, being concerned as an old man he might be 'losing it' having trouble believing how someone can be locked away for so long.

"Ok Desmond I give up, let's start again and this time you tell me how you want me to help you, because I am totally confused now." I needed to listen to him and not make judgements.

"I'm sorry Hayden; it's painful for me I have spent so long bottling up all my emotions. It's strange to talk about her to someone who actually cares."

"Tuberculosis, am I right?" Thinking about the last time I saw her, she was up at her bedroom window. "You had to take her away to hospital, I did try to speak to you if you remember but you were too upset, your wife and children were too."

"I know you did Hayden, I'm sorry." Shrugging it did not matter now, I watched a tormented man trying to prise out his story from his mind in some logical way.

"Take your time Desmond we have as long as you need." Looking at my watch, it drifting towards 5pm, my team getting ready to leave the office for the day.

"Do you know nowadays there is loads of documentation, reports and advice splattered all over the internet about Tuberculosis, for example 1.4 million people were dying from the disease in 2011, 50 years after Bridie first contracted it and can you believe there were 8.7 million cases in the same year worldwide. Back then she hardly had a chance, the Doctors were blind about treatments I know now and isolation was never the answer." The frustration in his voice evident. "A mental institution she didn't need Hayden." I felt his passion at the injustice.

"Are you saying you didn't agree with her treatment at the time? Attempting to keep him on track whichever route it was.

"No I'm not saying I disagreed, more like I never understood." All I could do was to listen and prompt him.

"She had been ill for quite a while, I hadn't spoken to her for a couple months before you took her away, I could only wave up to her at the window, have I remembered correctly?" Questioning my own recall I used to hold up signs to her from my own living room window, which faced her bedroom diagonally across the road, on occasions I would throw up a bag of sweets to her and ask how she was, Desmond never knew.

"Yes, you have, the Doctors tried to treat her at home, unfortunately she was not responding very well, they kept complaining about the lack of a clean environment and the cramped conditions of our home above the shop," guilt evident in his tone.

"Do you know each year 400,000 new cases are diagnosed and 40,000 die because of it, facts and figures, I remember the Doctors at the time giving us similar facts and figures, but none of it helped Bridie. They said if left untreated people generally die within two years. The medics who made the diagnosis said she must have had it for about a year already!" His pain and anger etched across a life worn face. "We were pressurised both by the medical evidence and our love for Bridie, we gave in and did what we thought would be best for her, how wrong we were." His shoulders sagged at the thought.

"Desmond you did what you were advised to by those who should have known, no-one has a crystal ball." He was battling with his anger at last telling someone it helped him.

"We should have been more protective of her we were very naive."

"It was a different age back then, in today's world I tend to challenge everything if I don't think it fair and I'm sure you do too?" he nodded. "Our society was very different when I was a boy."

"Of course you're right unfortunately it doesn't make me feel any better." One of my business colleagues passed my office and waved his hand in the shape of a phone receiver to call him, as I nodded to him Claire ran to stop him entering my office in an attempt to cover for me, good girl I thought.

"Desmond please, I'm not here to make you feel better much as I'd like to, the important point is to do what's right for Bridie if we can! Talk me through her case." Concentrating hard to share his burden.

"Normally it starts as an infection of the lungs, she was short of breath, fever, tiredness, weight loss, aches and pains in the bones were all of her symptoms, ignorant people such as me, laugh them off as the growing pains of a young teenager," Realising I had to stop him constantly blaming himself. "Initially it was thought to be flu bordering on pneumonia as she became more and more ill."

"Don't keep beating yourself up over it Desmond, it's not going to help you or Bridie, I'm with you now," confirming my support.

"It's difficult not to my friend." I felt sorry for him.

"What happened next?"

"This particular strain of bacteria grows over weeks and months slowly, gradually destroying tissue in its wake, someone sneezing or coughing around her would be all it took to catch especially when so many people suffer from hay fever allergies during the summer months. Can you imagine how many people came into the shop when she was working there and how many flowers were bought from her," his melancholy dragging him backwards into despair. "Even at the market where we purchased them could have been the cause, the mere scent of them would cause many to sneeze."

"She loved being in the shop Desmond I remember and her proudest moments was going to the old Covent Garden market with you for the flowers." Since then I knew the flower and vegetable market had moved to Nine Elms three miles away in November 1974 it would become a sad reflection of the change happening since her committal to the asylum. "Your whole family worked in the shop and lived upstairs it was surprising Bridie had been the only one affected, you must be thankful surely?"

"But why did it have to happen to her?" I doubted anyone would ever be able to tell him.

"Who would you have chosen?"

"Me I suppose."

"What good would it have done to your family, how would they have survived." Pausing for effect. "Desmond you have to face it, you were not given any choice in the matter however much you torment yourself."

"I appreciate what you're saying Hayden, really I do." I would have liked to tell him to scream aloud, but not in my office, he should have done it in the park.

"The Doctors finally said it was infectious and generally not good for her to be at home due to the overcrowding in our apartment. "Of course Josey and I felt guilty, four children six of us, we were limited for space." This was not easy for him. "The two bedroomed apartment above our greengrocers being full of vegetable dust from the shop below, with most of our type of produce dirty after being pulled out of the ground, it was not a good place to keep out bacteria," again blaming himself.

"Come on my friend lets agree you were providing for your family not intentionally making them ill." It is becoming a struggle within him.

"They were insisting she should go directly into hospital, somewhere isolated, we, my wife and I never wanted it, my wife Josey do you remember her Hayden?"

I nodded remembering the image of a beautiful bronze shoulder length hair of a slim woman wearing starched navy blue aprons and white high-necked blouses reminding me of the Walton's women on television. She always created the impression of flowing or floating from point to point, people enjoyed her serving them, she brightened the shop and the day alone, with a calm persona she was such a popular figure with the neighbours gracing her shop; I suspected she was responsible for the success of it drawing in customers dynamically towards her. Bridie had the same way with her as a young girl.

Although he had to tell me his story, I knew I did not have enough energy to prop him up continually, but I would do my best.

"Surely in today's world a course of antibiotic's and she would have been fine yes?" Trying not to complicate matters.

"Not quite, the condition isn't treatable with the normal antibiotics like you get for influenza, these days there are about four to six different types of drugs to take over a course of six months and it takes at least two years to clear the infection fully. Back in 1963 what chance did Bridie have, the right treatment was subjective in those days cost or not?" Not expecting an answer from me, mainly because I did not know enough about it.

"She did survive though?" I was beginning to have my doubts from the way he was talking.

"Oh yes but it wasn't the end of it, she developed pleurisy and the immune system could not fight back as it should have done in her case, this led to her condition becoming worse, much worse," he continued. "Given the time lapse of a year before being treated the infection had begun to spread throughout her body to the organs, bones and nervous system specifically in her case, the brain." He paused making sure I fully appreciated what he was saying I got it.

"Poor Bridie," It was all I could say, my head was spinning.

"The diagnosis today is called the life threatening term of Meningeal Tuberculosis. The problem is, once the bacteria is in the bloodstream it becomes rampant, in her particular case it affected the spinal cord and as I said the brain itself." His face contorted, beginning to assume a hollow effect, deep, way too deep, he was struggling to claw out every ounce of information he could for fear he would never remember it again, guessing him to be in his mid-eighties, it fully showed as he spoke.

"You're describing a severe case of meningitis with tuberculosis included, but it was treatable right?" I was horrified how this could have happened to the person I once loved. "You sound like a Doctor." It was impressive had it not been so sad.

"In the 1963, the standard treatment for TB would have been isoniazid and para-amino salicylic acid being prescribed lasting between 18 months and two years, along with streptomycin for the first three months." Once again, he paused for reflection.

"I have had 50 years learning about the subject, these days they adopt different methods and have different ways of attacking the infection, first and second line therapies for example taking isoniazid with rifampin plus others to start followed by ethionamide, cycloserine and para-amino salicylic plus others." Although amazed and impressed by his knowledge, this was going way over my head.

"The two-year course of treatment was new and expensive, there was a problem with the drug company trials and the cost meant the Doctors were hesitant to prescribe them especially while she was in the home environment and could not be properly monitored." Again, he drifted into his own melancholy.

"And then what?" Nudging him along.

"Being at home led to poor or only partial treatment, which in turn encourages antibiotic resistance within the patient, important as it happens in Bridie's case," he was sitting shaking his head

"You're saying they blamed you for Bridie's condition getting worse?"

"Yes."

"Rubbish! Sounds to me as if she didn't get the right or full treatment because someone was trying to save money?" I hoped this worked for him.

"Yes, but I should have offered to help pay the

costs," he said.

"Where you ever asked, Desmond?"

"No."

"Then stop thinking like it, you can't know what you don't know, you at your age shouldn't need me to tell you!" I was angry at his self-abuse.

"Sorry Hayden."

"There's no need for anyone to blame themselves for something happening 50 years ago it's today which matters not what could've been back then." In no mood to let him suffer any further. "And stop bloody apologising, you and I both know given the right knowledge and information and certainly in today's world we would have handled the whole thing a great deal better."

"You're right, I know now."

"But nothing is going to shift you from taking the blame is it?"

"Not much, no," he weakly smiled facing his own demons.

"So go on take all the blame you want, do you feel any better?" I shouted at him.

"No!"

"Good, now can we get on with it," I pretended to be very impatient with him and it appeared to work. He shrugged, his eyes looking to the skies.

"So some of the treatment has not changed in 50 years?" I tried to get us back to the points he was making.

"Except for the drugs trials various companies were carrying out at the time"

"Were you promised a cure?"

"A likely one if Bridie would take part, how many parents would refuse the chance to get their child a cure?"

"So you did?"

"Yes but it was all about the timing of when to give certain drugs, the amount of dosage, and what reaction each patient would have, unfortunately they couldn't monitor her properly at home."

"I see, you were tricked, the Doctors persuaded you to take her to a mental institution where trials were being carried out already." I started to understand. "She would be isolated too."

"Who better than mentally disturbed patients who cannot complain, to trial the drugs for the pharmaceutical companies. Naturally with any new mixture of differing drugs they can lead to complications for each patient, equating to additional drugs having to be used, together with some serious operations to cure the reactions of some of the new drugs taken." He said regretfully. "I believe they introduced Bridie to a host of concoctions without addressing the fundamental cause of her illness."

"Do you have proof this happened in Bridie's case Desmond?"

"I cannot be sure, there's no direct link in her medical notes not the ones I have seen and I doubt it happens with today's regulations with the freedom of information act. I know in my heart it is why Bridie has been in a sanatorium for so long, enough for her to become institutionalised and why I was not allowed to see her at all." It would certainly explain why she had been locked up for so long, someone was not about to let her tell her story to anyone, even if she could remember properly which I doubted, the operations would have seen to it.

"Desmond I don't know what to say, disgraceful." I truly meant it.

"In the 1960's, I had no way of having the

information then as I do now because of the internet, it was another age," his nature forgiving.

I felt myself fighting back the tears for the suffering my beautiful Bridie had gone through and for Desmond, who was intent on pouring out his very soul to me, I suspected it was the first chance he had to speak to someone about it, I thought of his other children and wondered what support they were giving him?

"We were desperate to save her me and Josey would do anything the Doctors said. They told us the Tuberculosis Meningitis threatened her life." I could see his mind recalling the pain.

"I'm so very sorry Desmond." As a father, I tried to imagine his pain; I put it out of my mind. "So you're saying after all this time she has still got Tuberculosis of the brain and cannot be cured?" I was eager to make headway, trying to work out how I could help him.

"Oh, she's cured alright although she now suffers from the side effects of what they did to her in the early days. God knows, how many brain cells she lost with the experimental drugs, operations, including a botched one leaving her partially paralysed for a time during one procedure causing fits, blackouts, mood swings, violent tirades and at times a complete shutdown almost to the point of death. The state of the individual and level of care left much to be desired and little room for complaint back in those days, no ambulance chasers then, today in this claim society I'm sure it wouldn't have happened." he made a hollow laugh more like a cough, echoing my sentiments.

"The final straw, before we gave in and agreed she had to get specialist treatment, suffering from fevers, headaches and seizures which were common place, Bridie became very frightened and confused without the proper care. We were desperately worried despite her begging to stay at home we agreed with the Doctors to take her to hospital, any hospital, but they said it had to be the sanatorium.

"The final straw?" he had this habit of going off on tangents.

"Oh yes she developed what they called Hydrocephalus." It sounded like Desmond and Josey fought hard to keep her at home and were finally pushed into agreeing to let her go having no choice at all with this latest development.

"Sounds like something to do with water, is it?" Ignoring his plunge into more despair.

"Right, its water on the brain, the upshot is it puts pressure inside the skull and could have enlarged her head, fortunately it did not, but it did create more convulsions, some tunnel vision and cause mental disabilities. Looking back at diagnosis's 50 years ago, they appear very suspect. We would certainly have questioned this now, back then, it became enough for her needing to go immediately to hospital, and because of her condition to save her life."

"I don't understand what the link is between Tuberculosis Meningitis and Hydrocephalus?" It sounded like two differing problems to me.

"Apparently it is a common complication or side effect and there are case studies where patients with both, underwent what they termed 'shunt' surgery. The need is determined for any long term survival of the patient." He knew her history well, I was learning quickly.

"Bridie had to undergo external ventricular drainage to remove fluid on her brain," he looked at me gauging whether I understood, barely I conveyed. "And because she showed a significant change or improvement in her neurological status within the 24 to 48 hours of the initial drainage, it was elected she have this 'shunt' surgery and she did according to her notes. Once done she improved enough to begin the process of getting well again.

"You were looking forward to her coming home on the news?"

"No, not at all!"

"Why not?"

"I didn't know we weren't told."

"How do you know all this then?"

"During the last three months since I have been given her medical notes."

"What?" Shaking my head, still trying to comprehend how he had managed to come to terms with what had to seem like the death of his daughter. "Was she well enough for her to come back home or not?"

"Once she left, we could not prise her away, from the sanatorium." Again, he dropped into a concerned expression. "To be honest with you Hayden, it was a relief, but we always hoped she would come back to us one day."

"She was being cared for properly do you mean?"

"Er well yes, but we no longer had someone who was shut away in a room for 24 hours a day to fetch meals for, keep the other children from getting too close and we found ourselves generally trying to concentrate on normal life for a change albeit we were one less in the family."

"You felt guilty?"

"Yes the business had started to suffer and we had mouths to feed."

"It must have been very hard for you and Josey?"

I could not imagine the trauma they went through.

"It was, however, there is the future to look forward to now if you'll help me." Suddenly he brightened, unburdening himself enough.

"Sorry Desmond I know you've lived and breathed this stuff but what is shunt surgery, some type of water drainage?" Ever felt there is a different universe out there and you are no part of it, well this was one of those times for me.

"Shunt surgery involves implanting a thin tube with a flow valve, which is called a shunt, in the brain. The excess spinal fluid is passed through the tube to the stomach and it gets absorbed into the blood stream." I shuddered at the thought and he laughed at the look on my face, I was gobsmacked and thought I was too old, to even think of words like it. "If you had it done you would actually be able to feel the valve as a lump under the skin of your scalp." Not something, I ever envisaged thank goodness.

"Where did they take her Desmond to begin the treatment what sanatorium?" I asked, recovering.

"They didn't I did, she would not let anyone take her away except me," his face crimson, overcome by the emotion he felt.

"Do you want a break Desmond?" Looking distraught his emotions on the edge.

"No, no," he was pushing himself to tell his story, dragging himself back and forth between moods of relief at telling me and the reality of Bridie's life which he felt responsible for, it was taking its toll.

"At least they allowed me to take her there," his recall vivid. "I took her in my old black car, Josey wouldn't come, could not bear it you see." I did, and I remembered his old car too. "Bridie begged me not to leave her there."

"Where did you take her?"

"Darenth Park Sanatorium in Dartford, they confined her there, it was a mental asylum."

"How was she treated?" I struggled to get my head around the problems she must have faced.

"There have been so many different approaches to her care and a multitude of theories for her cure they must have numbered at least 10 and those were the ones documented. I would guess the figure would be more than double if the truth were told, it's difficult to recall them all and certainly as a humble shopkeeper I was in no position to challenge their procedures, they were Doctors for God's sake, revered human beings, cream of the land in those days, no-one dared question them at all. After I left her I did learn they had fitted a catheter in her spine to drain the fluid off her brain." His face terrified at the memory.

"Who told you?"

"Her Nurse when I tried to visit her the first time and been turned away."

"They did the shunt surgery then?" Feeling proud of myself to get it right.

"Apparently, according to the Nurse who looked after her and her medical notes which confirms it."

"Wow! It must have been painful." I could feel the needle in my own back, it was not a feeling I needed.

"I didn't understand what could I do? Hayden I was helpless how could I take her pain away." He broke down in tears before me. I stood up and knelt before him as he buried his face in my shoulder I held him tightly.

Claire sensed a problem, and opened my office door. "Mr London may I show you to the washroom

I sure you need a break and I'll bring some tea when you get back." She led him away with his shoulders slumped, I mouthed 'thank you' to her.

I had to help this dear old man, I knew he needed peace in his life and he looked to me to give it to him, I hoped I would not fail him.

"Desmond was she coping?" I said on his return, he looked better.

"I don't honestly know they wouldn't allow me to see her."

"How come, you're her father and next of kin?" It did not sound right to me.

"It would not be good for Bridie they said."

"They did tell you how she was?" The injustice rang an alarm bell in my mind and I let it go, he had already settled into believing it was best for her, I had not the will to add further to his pain of recall.

"Oh yes she was not too well, she needed peace and quiet and would be closely monitored they said." He shook his head. "Not until recently did I find out what was wrong with her, the drainage left her with coordination and epilepsy problems in the early days according to her notes, following on she would have several draining operations or shunts, I could see why they would not let her out to come home." He suggested being too understanding in my view.

"If only I had known." Checking myself in danger of sounding like him. "Does she have coordination and epilepsy problems now?"

"It's not mentioned in any recent medical notes so I have assumed those issues went away as she got older." He looked at me directly. "Hayden, there was nothing you or anyone could have done for her, strangely Bridie acclimatised herself to both her illness and environment her intelligence appears to have increased at least from what I have read in her diaries, she's articulate and assesses situations very easily it appears." I had started to wonder how he knew if he was not allowed to visit her.

"She wrote diaries?" I guessed surprised he was even allowed to read them it would have been comic if it had not been so sad for him and her.

"I gave her some notebooks and pens when I first left her," I noted he was flagging in need of some rest. Throughout the years and despite being unable to see his daughter Desmond London would always leave at the sanatorium a steady supply of notebooks for her to write a diary. Each time he visited the sanatorium despite being refused any contact with her he would leave the notebooks either with the Nurses who would offer him encouraging words such as; 'she is progressing' or 'Bridie was having a good day' and 'we're sure the Doctors will contact you soon' they never did.

"Have you read them?"

"Not all of them, there are about 30 of them in all across the years, apart from her current one," he retrieved a couple of blue A5 notebooks from his small brown briefcase which I had not previously noticed him carrying, He handed me the first two.

"I used to write to her, placing a note within the middle of the notebooks, news of home, I never knew whether she got them or not."

"She doesn't want these let out of her sight, so I took a couple out without her realising when I saw her at the Maudsley a short while ago in April."

"You never saw her diaries the whole time?"

"No, but I have been overwhelmed by the paperwork since April, I have read some and will replace them the next time I see her."

"Do you know when it will be?"

"It is up to her Psychiatrist I don't have a date yet."

Skimming the first page, once again I pictured her face looking down from her bedroom window as a young girl all those years ago, the more I read the more I pictured how she had looked down on her father imploring him to take her back home, no wonder he was feeling so guilty.

"So she doesn't know you have these?"

"No, they said she hides them from everyone, but the staff know where she puts them, like she did when I saw her she forgets they're on show. At the Maudsley, one of the Nurses told me it is quite typical of most patients and they rarely bother reading them because most of the patients write some sort of journal or diary. Apart from any original thought which may occur from time to time they are mostly about what the rooms are like or the food, the staff or the latest new girl or boyfriend, having read several hundred of these type of notes they hardly bother anymore. To us they are more personal; as I get more I let you see them before I return them."

"Thanks may I take copies of these?" he nodded, I tapped on the window attracting Claire's attention who took them away for printing.

"What about medical notes?"

"I'm getting them in batches I'll forward them onto you as well."

"Of course anything to help me understand better."

"When you saw her again for the first time in April, how did it feel to you and more important how did she look to you?" I tried to picture my own feelings when I hoped to meet her again.

"At first I was excited, apprehensive and nervous at seeing my own daughter I fully expected her to shout at me for leaving her back then, what I didn't expect was the scale of distance between us, I didn't know her, and she didn't know me." It hurt him.

"But you did recognise her?"

"Quite frankly Hayden no, she had aged of course and I expected it, well no not quite true, what I did expect was some glimmer of my baby girl," he fought back the tears again. "To be honest I had hoped to see a picture of my Josey sitting in front of me, but I could not recognise a single feature, mannerism, look or warmth in her.

She was polite, courteous towards me and very cold, initially I could not work out what her Doctor had meant when he said, 'she had become institutionalised', but following our meeting I knew exactly what he meant. An aura surrounds the patients whether it's their reliance on others, a total lack of responsibility or not having to care about anything or anyone but themselves I don't know, but there is a vacant space behind their eyes, they talk to you, only they don't see you as a person, it's bizarre."

"How come you saw Bridie at the Maudsley Hospital why not at the Sanatorium in Dartford?"

"The lunatic asylum closed in 1988." This was the first time it registered with me she was in a proper mental institution and not a regular hospital.

"Did you ask her about the treatment when you saw her?" I asked.

"No, I was so amazed to see her after all this time." His face lit up with the thought.

"What was she like Desmond, how did she react when she first saw you?"

"The moment will be etched in my memory forever, let me explain how it happened." He was smiling. "I was asked to go to the Maudsley Hospital in April this year, along with Joseph, Susan and Emma by Bridie's Consultant Psychiatrist Professor Raymond Barnyard to discuss her long term care, at the end of the meeting my beloved three children decided to leave," his voice tinged with sarcasm. "I'll never forget Professor Barnyard's words to me." I was listening intently.

"Desmond, it's time he said and Raymond Barnyard placed his hand on my shoulder. Let me take you to see Bridie, she is looking forward to seeing you. Do you know Hayden, it felt like I was his son it felt so special and they were the sweetest words I could ever hear in my lifetime, I was finally going to see my daughter again after all these years."

"You must have been so happy." I said encouraging him.

"I said to him, oh God, are you sure?" the tears welling in his eyes as he remembered the years rolling back to the fateful day when he had left her at the sanatorium. "And she really is looking forward to seeing me I said?"

He became serious at the thought his facial expression shocked me.

"I have had three months since to think about this and I know Raymond Barnyard lied to me, he had no way of knowing how she would react to seeing me after all this time. Convinced my visit to her was part of a continuous range of tests, in order for the hospital to complete its overall assessment of Bridie."

Desmond described how he found himself

skipping even at his age as he followed Professor Barnyard rushing through the various light green corridors with the coloured lines on the floor showing the way. Finally, he arrived at the double doors marked Felicia Ward. The professor pointed to the plaque on the wall with a quotation he recognised from the British poet Felicia Dorothea Hemans (1783-1835):

The boy stood on the burning deck,
Whence all but he had fled,
The flame that lit the battle's wreck,
Shone round him, o'er the dead
Yet beautiful and bright he stood,
As born to rule the storm;
A creature of heroic blood,
A proud though childlike form

"He told me his team felt this quote represented the struggle continually faced by his patients on a daily basis. The Professor spoke proudly from his heart, you will like him when you meet Hayden he is a genuine sort." Clearly impressed with him.

Except he lied to you, I kept my thought to myself.

He described walking through double doors behind the Professor, opening up into a play area, where about 40 patients men and women were grouped together in two's, three's and four's. They were playing cards, dominos, chess, and quoits, reading or talking together, some sitting on the floor talking alone to themselves, others walking up and down the room.

Every one of them occupied but watching them in particular, Desmond noted they were almost standing to attention as the Professor moved amongst them acknowledging them with a smile or a wave; such was his presence as he passed. He would touch a shoulder, shake a hand, make a chess move, turn over a domino, give words of encouragement. He then sat down beside a woman on the floor with her back to a wall and gently held her hand as if to comfort her after hearing some bad news, she brightened up as he spoke quietly, barely whispering to her, he walked back and forth with the couple walking, first holding the man's hand and then the woman's.

"I was astonished, it was like following God it really was, on leaving the room they seemed to relax and all he said was 'truly fulfilling to see,' I tell you Hayden the man is good, a special person." Raymond knocked on one of the room doors and they heard a voice from inside quietly spoken suggesting he entered the room. Desmond nervously straightened himself upright, wiping his moist filled palms on his brown overcoat and wishing he had it dry cleaned before his visit. Pulling at his overgrown eyebrows, he was overwhelmed and about to set eyes on his daughter for the first time in 50 years it scared the hell out of him, what do you say to a daughter you left behind all those years ago, but he had waited for this day to come for so long.

"Are you ready Desmond?" Raymond nudged him forward telling him he would leave him now as Desmond recalled he was trembling. "You'll be fine, try not to worry."

With trepidation, he pushed the door open fully, and nodded to her trying to hold his feelings in check in case he upset her. His heart skipped beats furiously causing him to sway hanging on to the door handle.

As the door widened, the sun shone through the

window mesh, enhancing the painted room, the vision he had of his little girl came rushing forward into his mind, instead only to be replaced by the aged woman standing in front of him.

"She was all grown up Hayden, not my little girl anymore." I pressed him to continue, I could sense his mood dipping.

Chapter 3

As a sign of her age, she painfully attempted to stand up to greet him from the wooden chair behind the small white desk set against the left hand wall.

The room was devoid of colour the walls yellow, matching the sunlight, a steel grey bed pushed up against the far right corner and sidewall, it was dressed with white sheets and a grey blanket on top, the bedside cabinet itself a chipboard white with 3 drawers. A white sink, mirror above and a white toilet stood in the opposite far corner to the left underneath the high iron clad meshed window with five vertical bars promoting a prison feel to the hospital.

The furniture suggested the occupant temporary used only for patient meetings with relatives soon to be replaced by another occupant. Bridie's dress and the light through the window served to add life to the room, her dress tight across the stomach and she looked anorexic wearing pink bedroom slippers. Any personal effects were in a small dark blue hospital stamped bag she had placed on the bedside table.

She worried about personal presentation, pulling and pressing at her floral dress, predominantly yellow, doing up the bottom of three open buttons at the neck. He remembered a time when he used to measure her up against the doorway of the kitchen the way fathers did with their children and realised she had not grown much more than her then five foot frame. Struggling with his emotions he knew little of the person now standing in front of him, the years had treated her badly, he wanted to lift and cradle her in his arms unfortunately, and he no longer had the strength for it, and had lost his little angel forever. The woman before him seemed unfamiliar and distant in every way.

"Bridie, Bridie, is it really you, after all this time?" Stuttering to get the words out he could not believe this is, at last happening. She would not look into his eyes directly preferring to look around the room as he spoke. He took it as shyness after all this time. I felt for him as he relived the moment.

Her thick raven hair replaced instead with grey streaks longer than he remembered. Her eyes rounded by the lines of age, gaunt with the greyness like a prisoner's pallor complexion; there was sadness behind them as she too examined the old man in front of her. When young, she had resembled her mother whom he expected to see, at least some of Josey's style in her it disappointed him.

"Oh hello, you've come to see me father, how are you it's been such a long time," he had been surprised at the formality. The conversation stilted as if she had been working towards this moment herself and rehearsed the words. The coldness in the way she spoke made him shiver deep inside, not recognising her, with his other children, he expected this kind of attitude it was their way, but never Bridie. He did not know what to do or say she was a stranger to him.

Holding out her hand toward him as a queen expecting a bow and kiss, he shuddered at her light touch, her fingers like tentacles cold exploring his hand as if the human touch somehow new to her. He wrapped both of his hands around hers gently she jerked herself backwards forcibly from him and promptly sat down.

"I could not expect too much from my first visit, but her eyes were dull, she was an empty shell standing in front of me Hayden." His spirit dying within him.

"Did she show you any emotion at all?" He shook his head.

"No we were both awkward and unsure of what to do next. I also decided to sit down, and tried to connect with her as best I could." He spoke as if he were speaking directly to her.

"Your mother would have wanted to have seen you Bridie did you know she passed away some time ago?" He was not sure if she was listening.

"Your brother and sisters came with me today I wished you could have seen them." He detected a shudder, her head shaking not wanting to see them. Turning to me, he said. "I thought of this afterwards, if she was not really Bridie she wouldn't have wanted to see any of my family." A faint expression of dashed hope crossed his tired eyes and I guessed he had been clutching at straws.

"Never mind, they've left now." Noting she visibly relaxed before him, he attempted to hold her hands again across the table, and drew them back from him.

"How is the assessment?" Attempting to make as much conversation as he could, she shrugged.

"Come on have you no hug for your old Dad?" She looked at him in horror.

"Hayden she appeared older than I was, I asked her if this is what institutions have made of you, but she didn't understand." I guessed as much.

She stood up moving around the table shuffling carefully towards him, he also stood up and hugged her tightly feeling bones underneath the floral dress, but noticed she barely touched him arms down at the side, the coldness made him shudder.

I would later learn under the watchful eye of Professor Raymond Barnyard standing behind the mirror in the adjacent room, being puzzled over Bridie's lack of emotion toward her father, she was going through the motions, hiding something and it worried him.

It was too much for Desmond, who expected her to be pleased to see him after all these years, she might have hated him for leaving her at the sanatorium, but he had such high expectations of their first meeting. She did not look at all the way he imagined her to be at 64, a mere shell of who she had once been, it would take time to get the old Bridie back he thought to himself if it were indeed possible. She nervously bit her fingers and kept rubbing her arms as if itching.

"Did you notice any side effects from the early operations?" Breaking into his recall, he shook his head, not wishing to lose a moment of the memory in his mind. "Like her epileptic fits or coordination problems?"

"No, no sign at all."

They sat on her bed in silence for a short while, he with his arm around her shoulders which she accepted and strangely not asking any questions of him or about the family as he explained it was nearing the time for her to leave the institutions and so should prepare for her coming home.

"Your mother cried for you every day until she died, she loved you so very much." Again, he hardly noticed any reaction enough only as a politeness. "I so wished she could have seen you one more time and as I said Joseph, Susan and Emma were here with me today, they send you their love," he lied, distraught he had to do so.

Looking around the room, he saw notebooks and another hospital bag large and grey on top of the bed, recognising them as the ones he had been leaving each time when visiting. Losing count on how many, he gave her, but they were in three piles and guessed about 30 of them asking if he could take some of them to read? She became fiercely protective of them and refused emotion at last.

"They're mine not yours I don't want anyone to read them!" Standing defensively in front of the piles of notebooks protecting them, her eyes fired in defiance, never had he seen her so angry.

"Remember I gave them for writing down what you were doing for me." She shrugged. "Do you remember the notes I used to write and put inside?"

She looked at him blankly as if he was speaking a different language, he wondered if the notes were removed before having ever seen them, backing off deciding to 'borrow' a couple every time he visited or ask Raymond for them now being part of her rehabilitation back into society. He has to discover whom this frail woman is, hoping to find his Bridie inside somewhere.

She was barely interested in anything he had to say, all he could do was hold her hand and say how sorry he was, with her completely silent, she seemed to shut down as if talking had become too much, he sat awkwardly beside her on the bed as she was guarding her notebooks. Out of his depth, he placed his hand on her shoulder she did not move.

A Nurse knocked and opened the door calling time on Desmond's visit suggesting he made his way back to Professor Barnyard's office before he left. Kissing her on the cheek Bridie again pulled away from his touch, dismissing him as she left the room, asking the Nurse what was for afternoon tea oblivious of the upset she caused.

Following the Nurse, he watched her walk down the corridor realising she had left her belongings behind, he took the first two of the notebooks unseen hiding them behind his back. She rushing too interested in her afternoon tea and wanting to get back to the groups in the main lounge.

He looked once more around the room no more than an empty shell with a few sticks of unfeeling furniture like the person his daughter had become. He took a quick look into the grey hospital bag she had left behind, and apart from toiletries, there was an opened pack of chewing gum and a folded piece of paper, opening he read the words loudly:

M

Will always love you
B x

He heard a noise from outside of the room further down the corridor, a girl shouting. 'I must go back, I must go back' Desmond thought Bridie realised she had forgotten to say something or wanted to be with him some more. Instead, she pushed past him through the door and grabbed the hospital bag and scooping up the diaries pushing them into it as best she could.

"Have you looked inside, have you, have you?" her insistence unnerved him he shook his head in a lie. "Good, Good, bye then," stammering as she continued putting them in the grey hospital bag, placing the blue bag into the Nurses arms telling her she could carry it for her, marching off again muttering about missing her tea. The most emotion he had seen from her since they first met.

Outside of the room, he encountered a patient, a man in his seventies unshaven with a red check shirt; his hunched shoulders had a grey cardigan around them like a cloak it had holes in the sleeves, spittle dripping from his mouth, which he wiped with the back of his hand. It was important to the man Desmond saw him. He pushed out his hand toward him, grinning gap toothed and unshaven, Desmond shook his hand tightly, the man giggled and ran off back to the main relaxation area his mission completed. Desmond wondered about the man, he had been older than Bridie and wondered how long he had been there. He pushed the thought from his mind and wiped his hand of the man's sweat one patient is more than enough to worry about.

"What did you think of her Desmond?" Attempting to get him back in focus.

"Pity more than anything, she was a stranger to me, I could see what these places had done to her, stripping her of any functional mind." His thoughts not far from the old man. "Seems to have trivialised everything perhaps it's what these places do to people making everything simple, black and white and although she was cold toward me I still loved her, she has to belong somewhere why not to me, I'm looking for the same person who used to go and buy flowers at the market with me." He refused to get emotional again, the pain too difficult to bear.

"What if your Bridie never returns?" He had to face the possibility. "I'll take what I can get."

"Even though, this one may not be Bridie?"

"Yes, she is or was surely someone's poor daughter," generously put I thought.

"You don't believe it was her, you said she was missing, do you feel this way given you've had time to reflect on it?" I had to ask.

"I didn't recognise Bridie in the woman I met, no! My daughter is, was, a warm, loving generous being, the same as her mother, but not this one who was cold as ice and putting on a show for me."

"I see." Words failed me.

"In her short life with us from a baby to a teenager one thing which never passed her lips was the word father. The other children liked to use it, to them it was posh somehow but Bridie was different she either called me Dad, Daddy or her favourite was 'Papa' and I adored it, it was so lovingly said always," he was close to tears again.

It was nearly six o'clock, the air conditioning not working so hard, it would be pleasantly warm outside, most of my team had left for the day, Claire was putting on her coat, hair in place and getting things together ready to leave for the day. I recognised a young man from the technical department hanging around, another lucky soul I thought.

I raised my hand to my ear in a sign gesturing a phone, she nodded and knew it meant for her to call Penny at home to say I would be late. Claire could handle Penny far better than I could. I intended to drive Desmond home allowing us more time to talk Claire handed Desmond back the two diaries and kissed him as she left for the day arm in arm with her new young man.

"Look Desmond most of my team have gone home and the security people will be kicking us out of the door soon I think it's time to take you home my friend." By now, Desmond looked shattered, bearing his soul had put a great strain on him, although he insisted on getting the train we were soon in my car travelling along the M20 motorway to pick up the main A2 road leading to Sidcup and his home in Kent.

We drove in silence for about ten minutes the traffic busy, but knew of one question I had to ask him and all afternoon been afraid to, unfortunately now was the time.

"What did Raymond want when you went back to see him?"

"A debrief really, he had been watching us, he too noted the lack of emotion Bridie had shown toward me, I hope it doesn't affect her release, I do worry what tips the balance." A father clutching at straws.

"I guess they've gone beyond a simple reaction by now, given the testing they would have to do."

"I'm sure you're right."

"Desmond you know I have to ask, what is it you actually want me to do for you, you tell me you need my support, someone who shares your interest and the well-being of Bridie, beginning by saying you wanted help in finding Bridie, clearly she's in the Maudsley Hospital. Please believe me when I say you have my support unreservedly, but what is it you think I can do for you?" I braced myself for his answer.

He took a while to speak, so long it fact I thought he had actually fallen asleep this was not a question he had considered lightly about giving an answer to.

"Sorry Hayden, to put my requirements into actual words or need has meant me coming to terms with my own capabilities or inabilities if you will. I am an old man and I don't have the strength to fight for the truth and I was hoping you would do this for me." I nodded in support though unclear where this was going. "I believe I haven't found my Bridie yet, whoever I met at the Maudsley Hospital was not her and on reflection knew in my heart. One problem is I find myself bluffing when I talk to Raymond because, if I start arguing the case against the person who is being assessed, and if it turns out to be Bridie she might never be released. If it's not her then the person is either a fake, it's an institutional cover up or I'm seen as mad or at the very least an old man with dementia and therefore liable to be locked up myself and put beside her." He smiled at the thought although he was deadly serious.

"You realise there's an end game to all this too, when she has completed her assessment they will want to release her to you?" Doubting he would cope.

"I know this, I don't know who the person is I am getting, especially if I don't believe it's Bridie."

"You want me to prove who they say she is?" I was getting it now.

"Yes, you'll get access to her medical notes, her diaries and be allowed to speak to whoever you wish on my behalf, whatever the need you have my permission to go and get it." It could work.

"What if I find she really is Bridie, what then, will you believe me?"

"Reluctantly I will, no I'll rephrase, I'll happily accept whatever you say, providing you're part of my journey with her too as my dear friend." It was a big ask and one I would have to consider carefully.

"What if it is a cover up and she can't or won't be found?"

"Then they'll be a reason why."

"And you want me to pursue this for you?"

"Yes."

"Have you considered at her age she may actually be dead Desmond?" The pain etched across his face.

"Show me the burial or cremated record then I'll believe it." He was stubbornly defiant.

"Ok I want to help you and need to talk to Penny and the children at home." Unlikely to be an easy conversation.

"Hayden, I need to rest in peace, I don't have long in this world and want to put things right." He put his frail hand on my left arm as I drove. "Please, please find my Bridie, the one so vivid in my memory I beg of you." He had me with his first post-it note reinforced in the park he did not need to beg.

"Are we here yet Desmond?" I interrupted him, crawling along a row of houses.

"Yes, yes third one on the left."

Before we left my office, Desmond had given me his postcode and I had keyed it into my satellite navigation system in the car, it had been guiding me quietly as he spoke and accordingly it told me we had arrived at our destination only we had not quite. He pointed the way and with the sound of gravel against my tyres, I drove up to the doorway of his charming bungalow.

Refusing his offer to go inside we agreed to see each other on Friday to allow me to discuss this situation at home and consider what level of involvement I could afford or wanted to give. I could not quite work out whether Desmond was pleased about seeing me or had realised, he had taken on one more burden.

I suggested I would come to see him here in Sidcup, in order to determine our plan of action together and talk some more. As he stepped out of the car, I hurried around to him and we embraced like lost souls who had once again found one another, for me I knew my life was set to change forever.

Turning up for work the following day was an anti-climax for me I could not get myself into anything work related. Annoyed at myself for not bringing up Desmond or Bridie with Penny last night being too much of a coward, I was not proud of myself, deciding to go out I could not face work this morning.

"Claire I'm going out." Shouting across the office it was 9.30 a.m.

"But you've meetings all day," she argued frustratingly raising her arms in the air, causing the rest of my team to laugh.

"Cancel them!" Tuesday morning I classed as a light day in terms of meetings, catch-ups no more, decision less where the time could be best spent doing something far more productive.

"Where can I contact you?" I avoided answering her for fear she would persuade me against going out. There was always a good reason to stay in work.

Claire's voice trailed after him, she watched the back of her boss disappear into the lift at the far end of the floor, she felt his torment having worked with him for several years and knew his mood swings this was a bad time for him. She waved his blackberry mobile at his back as he deliberately left it behind.

I dashed down the three flights of stairs to the

office car park rushing to avoid contact with anyone who could drag me back to the office. The air conditioning pushed out cold as my car engine fired up, I negotiated my way out of the tight exit, always a challenge getting in and out of the car park, and many never quite made it. Evident when walking around the car park, the scratches, the paint, matching the corresponding dent or scrape on the offending car with the walls devoid of plaster telling their own story. Driving London bound from Maidstone up Bluebell Hill past Cobtree Golf course remembering when I had the time to play in the early mornings before the office, now travelling to meet the busy M2 Motorway.

On past Buckmore Park the Go Kart circuit on the left and high above past the Rochester aerodrome to the right, where once a girlfriend before Penny had surprised me for my fortieth birthday purchasing a single flying lesson which had left my airline pilot dreams as a small child in tatters. I had shaken with fear at every twist and turn in the light aircraft. I was not impressed when the instructor made me point to our home from the sky only to weave and dive towards it. Flying with a joystick between my knees the instructor's hands firmly off his half wheel egging me on, vowing I would never attempt to fly myself again.

As I drove discarding my neck tie and opened the top two buttons of my shirt I sat back to enjoy this Tuesday's hot balmy July summer, my route taking me through Greenwich then Lewisham through New Cross. Places in the suburbs of London I had not been near for years, pulling up in Peckham to a much coveted, resident parking space allowing no more than an hour's stay in Friary Road. My destination was in the adjacent road, Fenham Road, where I had spent the first 13 years of my life, I was born only a mile or two away in Camberwell at St Giles Hospital.

Getting out of the car, looking around at my childhood playground it took my breath away, familiar yet changed, now somehow smaller and modernised, but not much.

Standing on one corner the smell of the Tandoori Curry house, which did not exist when I lived in the road, stretching the nostrils with the aroma's from the far east of Asia. I decided to walk on the left side to the end of Fenham Road and back again. Looking over at the opposite corner once the London's family home. Men hard at work drilling and hammering as the building was being prepared for people to live in.

The terraced road like many others throughout London in the 1960's had their share of couples, families, old and young alike mirroring society and this one, boasting on one corner its own Greengrocers selling fruit, vegetables and an array of flowers was no different. On the other corner a blue coloured mini-market Grocer shop for tea, coffee, tinned meats, biscuits and a variety of cleaning products and toiletries, both also served Friary Road where it crossed Fenham Road.

Today, the Grocer's corner shop, where a friend and I painted the whole front of the shop for ten pounds with a couple of blue paint tins and brushes old Mr Jarvis the owner, had not sold, now occupied by the Curry house I could smell. Instead of the blue, it now has a façade of black with red letterings and arched darkened windows accentuating the dragon displays painted on the glass to enhance the mystique of the restaurant.

Sadly, the Greengrocers on the other corner, once Bridie and Desmond's home, where a vibrant part of the surrounding community and meeting place for many existed, stood a mere façade of what was left of the old building. A history perished as part of the rebuilding on this side of the road. How many memories this corner of the world held, including my love for Bridie.

The large company sign, informing of the intended six apartments nearly completed and soon to become highly fashionable rental properties amazingly occupying the space of the shop, the garden, the goods storage and a small garage used for the London's family home, delivery van and Desmond's black Austin Seven where Desmond's Greengrocery business once traded. Offering proudly its produce on the tables outside the shop on the pavement all draped with artificial green grass like skirts and Bridie's flowers for all to admire. Standing opposite after all these years, staring at what was left of the building back then, with those walking by giving me odd looks.

I heard work continuing inside the boarded up exterior of the London's old home, my eyes stretched up to what would have been Bridie's old bedroom, looking for the window now brick filled and painted half hoping, expecting her to gaze down at me waving from another life, we once had.

I began walking up the road where the window boxes used to adorn the outside of each property, brick walls and gates proudly holding in a ground cover full of flowers and ornaments now replaced with satellite dishes and huge recycling bins in green, blue and black.

Most of the wooden gates no longer attached or a

black wrought iron one in its place. The road and pavements outside the houses once a child's playground, where hopscotch, marbles, football, tennis or cricket played a major part in our growing up process. Interrupted only by the odd small delivery van, the coalman's handcart, milkman's float and a growing number of bicycles, my own father had his own motorised bicycle with a two-stroke engine in the back wheel, a Cycle master nicknamed his 'Pop, Pop' he was a menace on it.

Games played as the competitive fathers got involved with their children, giving their offspring the benefit of their vast sporting experience, typically showing off and falling flat on their faces, pretty much the same as today, I am the same with Carrie and Simon.

Now each day, the tenant or owner battles to acquire a precious parking space as near as possible to their front door, locals strive to dodge the oncoming traffic and children are nowhere to be seen, such is the progress society has made.

Back then, everyone talked to and knew each other, memories of a street party for the Queen's coronation on the 2nd June 1953, I was too young but what I could remember was everyone waving flags. At the time, the road full of young families with perambulators dressed in frills and lace proudly showing off their occupants to the world. Mothers felt safe in the knowledge their charges would remain unharmed, a baby would adorn the pavement for hours outside each of the terraced houses making gurgling noises knowing others who they would later meet and grow up with, were a step or two away.

Visitor's faces would appear under the baby's personal canopies attached to their pram to say hello while each baby would make their individual gurgling noises. The odd ball would land inside the pram sanctuary from the children playing in the road and nobody bothered, any child playing too rough gained a 'clip round the ear' by anyone who passed and no one cried 'abuse' instead thanking them for correcting the child. Today's blame culture might play out the scenario quite differently.

Local people would, on walking by pass the time of day speaking to each child in turn looking up happily expecting all different shapes and sized faces to peer into their external bedrooms and screaming with delight when tickled under the chin by the hand mysteriously appearing from nowhere. In these troubled times, we are more likely to be arrested by the police, I doubt anyone bothers or dare to do it anymore. The boys grew up as I did with the girls playing in the road without fear of people or of traffic bearing down upon them.

A little older and boys became the local paperboys humping broadsheets in their huge grey sack the bag overwhelming them each day where forcing the papers through the thinnest of letterboxes became a game, their counterparts became Saturday girls ringing the tills at the local Woolworths store. Sadly for our history no longer operating, all proudly dressed in their speckled pink and blue-collared uniforms with proudly sporting their name badges.

Meanwhile another cute batch of children were growing up while those further on in their path playing an altogether more grown up game of studying, working and starting families producing their own babies.

As grown up life took hold some stayed behind

on the street, while others moved away, some died and gradually the inhabitants of the road changed imperceptibly mirroring the many faces of society. The smell of curry now infiltrates gently into each house according to the wind of the particular season and proximity of the home to the corner ensuring each household buys a takeaway at least once or twice a month.   Where once the fragrance in Fenham Road had been Bridies fresh flowers spreading their scent from the London's Greengrocers corner shop, no man in the road ever forgot to buy his wife flowers at the end of the week.

The competing road housed a newsagents, launderette, all long gone, the frontages still there, although now behind the façades were living rooms.

Once, firm friendships and alliances were formed, memories built and a fondness for people and place staying for all eternity, a lifetime at least. All the kids used to go to the local Catholic school wearing the brown uniform highlighting St. Francis of Assisi on the blazer badge both sexes wore or the Peckham Road Primary now called Harris Primary Academy, brandishing navy blazers with a red emblem, a healthy rivalry between the two schools existed.

Both schools although very near home never allowed us out during school break, death's door excuses only. Boys and girls used to sneak out to the bakers nearby for any pies on offer or the sweet shop for an old penny bag of broken crisps if we had enough pocket money left.

Avoiding the green speckled sausages and the lumpy mashed potatoes and ghastly semolina pudding with a floating blob of strawberry or raspberry jam dished up at both of the school's lunchtimes became an art with bad throats, potato allergies or some becoming vegetarians overnight, although most of us not understanding what it meant at the time.

The local baker knew the children well, by the time the boy or girls of the road were trusted with going for the family's hot cross buns early on a Good Friday morning they knew they could rely on the baker to give them an extra bun to eat on the way home. Hot cross buns were once a yearly event, these days the supermarkets brandish them all year round. Where is the fun? It was an honour for each young person to bring them home, for a short time, they felt important and if ever they escaped the lunchtime school menu, the Baker could always be relied on to supply a fresh warm crusty roll to them.

Every young child up to a certain age had to be in by the same time at night and everyone followed the rules, the saying at the time I recall as "woe betide you" if you stepped out of line.

As I walked further up the road, I found myself smiling, my childhood was very good, I only remembered the happy times and they had gotten better with Bridie by my side.

Throughout the years of growth, there was a certain romance in the air with fresh cakes, sunshine, the sweet scent of flowers, snow and winter fires with hot chestnuts roasting, obtained from London's Greengrocers. For those tasting the magic it was the greatest feeling, but to lose a love of life hurt to a depth, which can build across decades and I knew it had happened to me with Bridie.

I was a few steps from my old home at no.63 with my parents and older sister we had occupied the top floor of this back street 1920's Terraced house.

Our home comprised of the main room acting as a lounge by day, by night mum and dad's bedroom, my sister and I shared a bedroom. She used to scare me, pretending someone was up the chimney, a Sir John Bayswater and if I did not go to sleep his body would crawl out and get me at night, I slept always. Years later, I still think of it and Googled it once, he did not exist of course, but the mere threat beat any sleeping pill. A few steps down from our room led to the kitchen and onto a scullery these days it would be called by its posh 'Utilities' room name. We would lay the tin bath down at weekends filing it up from a water heater called the Copper we each took turns using the same water. Mum always went first followed by my sister and then Dad followed by me always the last, I remembered the water got extremely grubby by my turn although it was normal back then, Dad and I had to empty the water away together. There was a toilet with a wooden bench acting as its seat where we used to tip out the water and once I had the company of a mouse staring up at me as I read news snippets of the newspaper cut in squares used as toilet paper, never quite reading a full story.

Uncle Bob and Aunt Clara lived on the ground floor. I remembered them fondly they always had a roaring coal fire. I doubt I have ever been as warm since those days, sitting in Uncle Bob's armchair by the fire. He somehow managed to produce the most delicious buttered toast ever, with the mark of the metal fork in a U shape on both sides every time, I used to visit them once a day and although not related to them at all I loved them dearly. As a family, we were rapidly outgrowing the place, which is why we moved to a three bedroomed maisonette in Brunswick Park, Camberwell, right opposite my birthplace, St. Giles Hospital, at last my sister and I had a bedroom each. It impressed my parents as the park dated back to 1847, then called Brunswick Square and named after King George IV's marriage to Caroline, daughter of the Duke of Brunswick. Mother thought it a posh place to live and made sure our old neighbours in Fenham Road knew it.

Bridie's Dad discouraged us constantly, we so loved each other back then, the early sixties a magical time for us both.

Progressively during my final year there, she became more and more of a recluse because of her illness, staying in, more than she went outdoors, and Bridie's father told me she wouldn't be able to come out for a long while as her condition was becoming much worse.

I remembered him telling me the illness she had could be catching, contagious he said, so I should not go anywhere near her. Although I used to wave at her as she sat by her window above their shop, disappointingly, I never saw her again to speak or to hold her again.

I came home one day only to learn, she was in hospital, I tried to speak to her father afterwards but he always became too upset. Her mother was no better, Joe, Sue and Emma, her brother and two sisters told me to shut up and go away as it was none of my business, I remembered not liking them at the time.

Not long after we left Fenham Road, my mother heard Bridie had stayed in the hospital on a permanent basis only then did she begin to be a fond but distant memory, I missed her and had to change schools, my world turned upside down. I did not realise at the time how long she would be in there for.

No.65 had its own memories, Mum used to argue a lot with Angela's Mum next door. I grew up with Angela, prams side by side, in the 1950's outside our terraced houses on the pavement without a single worry.

I too vaguely remembered faces at a young age peering into our prams and making us laugh. Mum used to say I would marry the girl next door and although Angela and I were friends, I only ever loved Bridie on the opposite corner. What happened to Angela I wondered?

Walking on, I recalled the brown and white boxer, a dog I adored belonging to one of the neighbours, always at his gate asking to be stroked, spittle always swinging from his mouth, trying to attach itself to your clothing, I guessed it was at no.33 although the gate was long gone. I came to no.17 and remembered my old pal Paddy Brennan, he was part of a loud Irish family, we used to get up to all sorts, banging on doors and running away we used to do a paper round together. I wondered what happened to him.

Crossing over the road, the Harris Academy taking up the block I walked back towards the middle road, which I recalled led to the baker shop even now I could smell the finest Good Friday hot cross buns you have ever tasted. I had forgotten about the woollen shop, Mum was buying wool in there and knitting one of us a jumper, pullover or cardigan, now left with the façade, the shop inside someone's living area.

Walking on back to the car the metal fencing around Desmond's old plot prevented me from going near to the building, occupying most of the surrounding pavement and next block. From there, I looked back down the road wistfully, where I had spent the first 13 years of my life, no.63 with my old Mum and Dad and my Sister. Angela at no.65 and Bridie the Greengrocers daughter at the corner shop, they were my life, apart from school I knew of little else, I craved for those days again but it was time for me to go back to the real world.

Driving slowly away from Peckham following the route I came on back to Maidstone knowing it was time to meet the people involved in Bridie's past and then to read her diaries.

Desmond needed help desperately for his daughter. Someone I, more than fondly remembered as a young boy often wondering what had happened to her, but it was 50 years ago and very dangerous opening up childhood memories securely locked away in the back of my mind. Bringing them to the fore had a way of distorting a past best left alone.

Chapter 4

I was only out of the office for three hours and soon listening to Claire with an annoyed edge to her voice telling me what meetings were rearranged and to when, slamming down my Blackberry on my desk. I hardly listened knowing a simple check on my outlook calendar is all I needed on the very mobile she almost broke.

Claire was brilliant during the following week, she arranged for letters by Desmond allowing me to view all of Bridie's medical records on behalf of the London family and to speak to whomever I chose to about Bridie. With his permission, I intended to build my own impression of her life since I last knew her, so fresh in my memory it was hard to believe it had been so long ago, I started to look forward to the investigation.

"I have made an appointment for you to see a Mr Barnyard at the Maudsley Hospital the one doing the most recent assessments of Bridie he is her psychiatrist and a Professor so you mind you treat him with respect." I cringed at her reminder to me knowing, I was not the best at respecting positions. "Following the Maudsley Hospital you're due to meet an Andrew Bartholomew at the Darenth Park hospital in Dartford. He is one of the resident consultants, fifty years is a long time, he is only a young Doctor and would not know Bridie at all, however he can help with medical records and then there is Sir James Carew, Chief Executive officer at the Cheadle Royal Hospital in Manchester. It is where she went after the Darenth Asylum closed in 1988. The Cheadle Royal is a private care hospital."

"Thanks Claire you've been great." I said and meant it.

"Something you may find interesting, Andrew Bartholomew is the son of Professor Cedric Bartholomew who did treat Bridie," she was pleased with herself.

"Is his father alive?" I did find it interesting.

"Sadly no, oh and I have booked lunch at Angelo's tomorrow at noon, 2 hours both for you and Penny." She said wagging her index finger at me as she started to leave my office.

"Why?" I worried about a missed anniversary or worse her birthday.

"It's about time you told your wife what's going on!" Claire gave me the stop procrastinating look, arousing my team's curiosities.

Telling Penny was my dread, how do you explain an involvement with your first love without hurting the one you are with now? I was not looking forward to it. I knew Penny would be upset and not want me to get involved, it's not every day a first love reappears and with so much baggage, especially one requiring a great deal of help.

I kept looking at the copied diary notes on my desk afraid to begin reading them knowing once started I would be hooked forever. I decided to get on with some actual work, answering E-mail's, showing up for meetings and walked around my team, discussing their work and generally made sure they were ok, some wanted a chat others said they were happy, these were the ones I worried about.

I decided we would have an impromptu meeting

in the open plan area letting them know what was going on with me and how I would need them to continue their work despite my absences. Several offered their help and one or two of my longer term and closer colleagues offered sympathy, most did not relish my task of telling Penny. I was pleased because now, I had no need to sneak in and out of the office.

Wednesday two days since Desmond turned my world upside down.

With a panoramic view of the first floor north side, I had the prized possession of three small external windows enabling a view of the traffic and pavements below. I recall my office was full when 150 Gurkha's from the nearby Maidstone Army Barracks paraded through the town to celebrate a tribute statue unveiling.

Luckily for me during a past major information technology project, I had the opportunity to build this office to help with the discreet nature of the work at the time or so I told everyone and retained it after completion.

Designed to be small enough to side step any sharing arrangements while not using enough space to be deemed big enough to make it worthwhile to pull it down and fill with additional staff. I made it functional for myself by adding a printer with a book case for it to reside on, an office speaker phone and besides my larger than average desk, a small table and four chairs to hold small meetings to appease those who were annoyed about my having an office all to myself.

If the managers asked us nicely, Claire or I would graciously grant them use of it for meetings or 1-2-1 staff assessments, not too often of course, but enough to make it a valuable resource, ensuring it would remain my office, I had acquired a certain status because of it.

Claire and I worked to promote and maintain my status within the organisation especially as she was a confidant with many if not all the managers and council members. Everyone wanted her working for them she had an inner power, a steeliness approach to life and knew she could say anything to me and anyone knowing I backed her, she completely had my interests at heart, and we were genuinely great friends.

Receiving a summons from my boss Georgina when I had arrived for work, hearing from the other managers, I had been cancelling a number of meetings recently she wanted to know why. She understood my situation with Desmond and clearly knew some of the story already so I told her the rest. Although very understanding as expected she impressed on me the need to balance my work as well. Silently, I thanked whoever told her in my team sarcastically, although on reflection the person probably did me a favour, now everyone knew. I was not used to my private life being so publically on display hoping no one would stop me the next time in the street and asked questions should I walk into town, I doubt I'll do it for a while.

On my return to the office, Claire reminded me about my lunchtime date with Penny at Angelo's; I looked forward to the food, they do the finest pasta in the world, but not telling her about Bridie. This morning, Penny had started the day in a foul mood as Carrie omitted to tell her about the fairy costume required for a part in Cinderella her latest school play. Apparently, there were four children playing the part of the fairy Godmother, Carrie being one of them wanted to look the best, she had also committed Penny to provide a cake for the school summer fete held in the school grounds at the weekend. I found it funny Penny was not amused.

Today's lunch with my wife was always going to be a tetchy affair, her consuming thought always intrigued me, she was either looking forward to a surprise which I had to quickly dampen down or a disappointment which was usually in me with no middle ground in between. Wondering why she had needed to drive the thirty minutes to Maidstone from Ashford where we lived to eat when there were perfectly good places at home we could go to in the evening meant she was frustrated to start with, what I had to tell her would not be conducive over a candlelit supper for two. Penny was not an occasion person and did not like surprises stating emphatically she could not understand what all the mystery was.

Angelo's is an authentic trattoria Italian style restaurant, with pictures reflecting Sicily's lifestyle, Rome and the Vatican City. We met outside and entered together, Penny always managed to be taller, despite her being a few inches shorter, her latest shoes tipping the balance. The restaurant half full with more people following us inside the building.

"Hi honey," I ventured although Penny never wasted time on small talk, barely waiting for us to sit down.

"So come on talk to me, you got the promotion you've always wanted and you've booked us a holiday when do we go and where to?" I sighed, today would be disappointing for her.

"Let's at least have a drink first and study the menu," we had been ushered to table four by a black suited manager, who immediately began fussing over Penny who as always looked beautifully stylish. Always ignored in favour of my attractive leggy blond wife, who today looked exceptionally younger than I did, is normal. I felt our age gap of 17 years to the full, imagining the staff wondering whether I am her father or not.

The manager advised who would be serving us, as I eased myself into the high white leather back chairs arranged around an authentic circular oak table, I could see her mind working, what she could spend my pay increase on, such is her materialistic view of life. Within second's Ruth, mentioned to us by the manager appeared from nowhere holding an order pad, I ordered a bottle of Chianti for us both, sparkling water for Penny and still water for me. We sat in silence as we chose our lunch from the huge cardboard menu both disappearing behind.

When the drinks came, Ruth asked if we were ready to order, I chose the Lasagne Fresco my favourite, homemade pasta ribbons, layered with tomato sauce, Ricotta and Mozzarella cheeses, ground veal and mushrooms. Penny opted for the Sicilian Pizza, Italian sausage, spicy Capicola ham, Salami, Fontina, Mozzarella, Parmesan and Oregano, my mouth watering at the thought.

Penny didn't do emotion, she was more about how she looked to others and boy, she certainly knew how to spend my money, always immaculately dressed in designer clothes, right now despite her being 47 she looked more in her middle 30's, she still made young men's heads turn, her and Claire a pair I thought. I had to admit when it was necessary to show Penny off at business events it had worked to my advantage my typical trophy wife and those I needed to impress would fawn over her unreservedly. Unfortunately, together we had no substance to our marriage except for the children. Our standing in life, our popularity and the type of friends we had were all we seemed to be about, it was how we presented ourselves. Our children only had 'sleepovers' with friends who were the 'best peoples' children according to Penny and only to be used as a future tool to further our standing within the community.

"We're both driving Hayden, very unlike you," she watched me pour the red wine for us both, she picked at her fingers.

"A glass of wine is unlikely to matter I think we'll need it." I said apprehensively.

"This is not about promotion is it? You're starting to worry me now you've lost your job haven't you?" Panic was rising in her voice a half grin on her face. "Oh God I'll be penniless, I'll have to move, I'll never live it down, what have you done to me?" her face contorted in terror of the unknown as her world about to collapse, everything always about how it affected her, she never saw us as a couple always her with me lagging behind, which I invariably did.

"Penny listen to me I have not lost my job but it is serious!" I was in no mood for hysterics.

"What have you done Hayden, for God's sake tell me," Penny always thought the worst of me. Her first option always criticism.

"Desmond London came to see me." I said, finding a way to start.

Our food placed in front of us, we waited as the black suited manager, topped up our wine glasses.

"Who the hell is he?" Her voice was shaking barely able to control herself.

I took my first mouthful, it was delicious, and trying to ignore her, used to these episodes or tantrums, drama queen is the term. "Instead of filling your face tell me!" She almost spat in anger insulting me with ease.

"Penny please can you try to keep your voice down," It rising in pitch. "You should eat something mine is delicious."

"Don't play with me Hayden!" Her anger at boiling point, her face crimson, someone laughed at a joke in the background, she turned and glared they didn't understand why.

"The father of a girl I used to know." I found myself playing with the salt and pepper pots, her voice at a screech, only playing with her food.

"You've got someone pregnant, my God?" I caught the anger in her tone. "How could you do this to me, and at your age when did this happen?"

"For goodness sake Penny, keep your voice down!" I said once again, this was not going well and she ready to leave the restaurant the perceived embarrassment getting the better of her. I never quite understood how her emotions could switch in a split second from loving to hate it was quite brutal at times, throughout my life I walked on eggshells around her. "Why don't you calm down and listen to me for once!" I was getting annoyed myself.

"Don't you take this tone with me, it's not me who's been messing around," she was talking herself into a frustrated state.

"Penny will you shut up and listen to me!" Attempting to gain some sort of control of the conversation her readiness to judge me was crushing. The food was getting cold and around us the audience growing.

She downed her glass of wine in one gulp, poured another and immediately waved for another bottle from the waiter, telling him to leave it on the table she was prone to sulking heavily. For a few blessed moment's we ate our now lukewarm meals in silence, the next few minutes busy with buttering bread rolls, thankfully we were left alone by the serving staff, who sensing our mood quickly disappeared, Ruth had long gone.

I told her about Bridie, how much she had meant to me all those years ago and why Desmond had asked for my help.

She had absolutely no intention of apologising for her accusing me of getting someone pregnant Penny never big on apologies.

"What's it got to do with you," she responded unsympathetically and became condescending. She was not going to discuss or have a reasonable conversation; the only thought was to make sure she came out winning any argument no matter who was right or wrong. "So you're hooked because of a teenage crush you had on someone 50 odd years ago, tell him to take a hike." Her mood darkened with every word stabbing at her pizza with me in mind.

"I'm not going to do that, besides he is an old man and is extremely worried and afraid of what's going to happen to her." The Lasagne tasted good despite cooling rapidly unlike Penny I mused.

"And how is it your problem, may I remind you of two children and myself at home who also need your attention, not some dream girl you've invented in your head, oh and by the way you must realise she has to be an old woman now anyway, as old as you certainly." Her voice cutting trying and succeeding in hurting me, it was her winner.

"I cared deeply for her once," I was not prepared for this type of reaction, she was totally without understanding, if it could not be for me at least for a father worried about his daughter. I drank my wine feeling defeated, which she would always managed.

"Rubbish if you had cared so much for her why haven't you tried to find her before Desmond London came to you?" I found the point irrelevant, even throughout the mist of an attack.

To her it was a good argument her attitude serving only to push me into deciding to follow it through with or without her blessing.

"I had no way of knowing she had been as ill or locked away for as long as she has, Desmond's own children are pretty useless they will not help him, with nowhere to turn he came to me." I tried to rationalise with her.

"What do you think you can do for him, hold his hand while he sheds a tear for the daughter he lost all those years ago, grow up and stop trying to be nice to everyone," she was turning the screws and enjoying it.

"I'm not sure what help I can be to him, but I have decided to try," my mind made up.

"If you're going to get involved with her we will not be waiting for you at home!" Her anger at boiling point, unless she is instigating the help herself and then getting me involved she could not contemplate me doing anything, which had not involved her.

"What is that supposed to mean?" Yet another threat she was going to leave me, I had grown tired of these threats, they happened at least once a month.

"It means if you think I am going to sit around

wondering if you might fall in love again with your teenage nutcase of a sweetheart leading you to breaking your own children's hearts and mine, you're mistaken!" Her voice getting louder and louder, the restaurant was full and our conversation was open to all. "Two old people doddering along together, I can picture you both now." She made a hollow laugh.

"Penny I would not do it to the children or you." Not recognising her picture of me. "How about cutting out some of the hurtful remarks Penny, they're unnecessary!"

"What would it be like Hayden?" Ignoring my comment, she was in full flight now, the audience in place. "Do you want me to be her friend? Would you want me to have her come to stay with us? How about cosy chats by the fire, or can she be an auntie to the children, or their nanny, get real!" The outburst amazed me, but it was typical of her mentality.

"I don't know what I want or what it would be like, why are you being like this?" I wanted to feel good about helping Desmond, not guilty because I was being unfaithful to her in some way. Conversations like this with Penny always drove me further and further away from her.

"Let's call it self-preservation, call it what you like, don't involve us it's your past not ours, once you're done with this rubbish let me know." She showed every sign of jealousy and it was not pleasant.

"What if I can't let it go?"

"Make your mind up time, her or us," her ultimatum crystal clear including the children as well, the audience almost applauded but for the embarrassment it would have caused.

"Why does it have to be an ultimatum?" I did not remember finishing the meal I had ordered. Penny had walked out of the restaurant my question trailing behind her. A well-timed dramatic exit having only half eaten her pizza leaving me to get the bill and face the stares of the restaurant audience and to look forward to what would likely be a very frosty evening later at home. It would be a while before I went into Angelo's for lunch again.

My return to the office saw me going through the motions to get by until it was time to pack up for the day. I was in a bad mood all afternoon and Claire having taken the afternoon off work luckily was not around to get the backlash. I found myself not in the least hurried in my drive home my normal rapid keeping pace on the motorway turned into a holiday crawl on the inside lane, I had no wish for another argument, I arrived at my house and parked the car on the driveway venturing into the house as quietly and slowly as I could.

To my surprise, Penny had arranged a dinner party at short notice. Not talking to me of course, except in short orders like, 'pour the drinks dear', or 'take out the plates please', or 'top up Barbara's drink dear'. All in her steely tone which had been perfected over the years since we had been together and used at such times when it was impossible for me to retaliate, unless I wanted to end up looking the jerk. She had this way of placing me on the back foot, it made me want to walk away many times but our life was about being on show saying and doing the right things in public. It was a shame she did not remember to do it in the restaurant at lunchtime.

As the evening dinner progressed, while our friends appeared oblivious about the earlier lunch the conversation strangely shifted to old flames, and how important they were to us now.

Unconsciously, her chosen people wholeheartedly agreed with her point of view, being her dinner guests of course they would, although I detected one or two had stronger feelings on the subject than they would let on to Penny. She had an unpleasant smirk across her face I did not like, this being her subtle demonstration, telling me to give it up and look how everyone is on her side. It did not work and for once, I could tell she realised her mistake and knew she had taken things a little too far.

Initially I was not sure what I expected from Penny when I told her, I am certainly clear about what level of support I could expect to get now. It made me consider the steeliness in her voice, the controlling attitude to our life on her terms, never presenting us as a couple only her and myself a few steps behind, is this what I wanted for myself, someone too controlling an unhealthy attribute in anyone. I am unsure if it is what I want anymore, since I had met Desmond again it has made me re-evaluate what is important, what I have, is not it.

In the morning, we barely spoke, as she laid out breakfast cereal for the children and toasted some sliced bread, normally she would sulk for quite a while until I apologised to her and begged forgiveness.

It always happened and each time she somehow gained a little more control over what I did and what I thought, I didn't like not being an equal in my own household something I strived for in all other parts of my life. This subsequently led to the many arguments we had. It will take some time before I gave up more of my soul, which I knew would eventually happen again, because she would not come around in a million years, I hate my own weakness where she is concerned.

Thursday saw me doing my normal day job and I happily immersed myself, consciously, I was aware of the two copy diaries sitting on the left hand corner of my desk, I put them in the small black carrycase I normally put my homework papers in.

Claire brought me tea. "I have a couple of parcels on my desk for you, I'll get them," swinging those hips again she returned and thumped the parcels on my table. "Go on open them." She pulled one of the chairs away from the table and sat down.

Four more diaries and a thick pack of Bridies medical notes with the word 'COPY' in huge bold letters on the front page.

"What?"

Pushing my office door shut, which always alerted my team to something 'going on' likely to be about their jobs, their pay, or criticising their work, apparently I would think of nothing else, I laughed knowing exactly what she wanted, my mood brighter than it was yesterday afternoon.

"Well how did it go?"

"How did what go?" I asked innocently, playing with her.

"You know very well what I'm talking about, your lunch with Penny yesterday?"

"Oh that, ok."

"I'm not leaving this office or allowing anyone in until you tell me all." I told her all about the disaster.

"I can understand how she would feel this way."
"Well I don't, she should trust me more."

"Come on how would you react if she got involved with an old boyfriend and had to spend time either looking for him or making sure he was being supported properly?"

"Not the same thing at all."

"Yes it is and you would not like it."

I acknowledged it and instantly felt guilty.

"Tread carefully Hayden, this could harm your relationship big time."

She is right of course, what was unusual, relationship or personal discussions between Claire and I, were usually taboo. It being part of the reason we had become great friends we made no judgements on each other's life, but I had involved her in the whole process and the help she gave me was tremendous so I knew indirectly I had invited the comments she made to me.

The evening at home, was quiet with little conversation between Penny and I, she had decided to move into the spare room and she was caught wrong footed when I told her I would pack a bag and stay at Desmond's probably until the following Tuesday morning. I realised I needed a break from her and she from me.

I rang Desmond and suggested I could stay the weekend in order to get as much information from him to help me; he seemed pleased with my decision and vowed to make up the guest bedroom.

Penny's reaction as expected 'I could please myself'. Shrugging her shoulder's she went to bed. In the morning I woke up late, no going into the office for me today, she and the children had left already on the school run.

Today Thursday, I would drive to the Darenth Hospital the site where Bridie had spent her first 25 years locked up in the old sanatorium there.

My journey to Dartford had taken me an hour, I pulled up in the car park of the Darent Valley Hospital, no trace of the Darenth Park Sanatorium existed anymore closing in 1988, apart from photographs in the main lobby displaying them as part of the history of the site dating back as far as the 1800's.

Although no longer classed as new, the Darent Valley General hospital opened in September 2000 and been designed to become more compatible with a variety of patient illnesses and requirements of the local community. The hospital corridors like many others painted light green, the helpful floor markings and guides on walls and hanging from ceilings took me to the first floor and neurophysiology department.

The plaque on the green door read "Andrew Bartholomew, Consultant Surgeon, I knocked on the door and entered to the sound of "come" from within and a young tall, thinning blonde haired man held his outstretched hand to me in greeting. I noticed his 'soul patch' a small piece of beard hair beneath his lip just above his chin, a young man with a fashion statement I thought, a member of my office team had one too.

"Thanks for seeing me so quickly Mr Bartholomew, I do appreciate it." I shook his hand. His office no bigger than a store cupboard, his table with a typist chair underneath full of patients notes on the seat, the floor was no better, a white board displaying his ward round rota and patient medical highlights, I felt I was intruding into his confidentiality with a dozen or so patients.

Even with a window, which did not open it became claustrophobic. It had a wall fan attempting in this July heat to cool the office, no air conditioning, a coat stand somehow furnished the rest of the room with a stethoscope hanging from one of the pegs completing the picture of a very busy young man. A couple of cushions placed on the larger than average window sill unwittingly providing additional seating which he used instead of the typist's chair and told me this was where he also slept when on call. He removed a stack of blue files from a chair in one corner and put them on the light brown metal cabinet fighting with the pile of magazines ready to spray themselves across the office floor somehow he balanced the papers on top and offered the chair for me to sit down.

"Welcome Mr Robbins, I gather you have questions about your friend's daughter Bridie London?" I watched the tuft of lip hair rise and fall as he spoke.

"Yes I'm after any records you may have which relate to Bridie's stay at the Darenth Park Sanatorium or Asylum which stood on this site." I offered.

"It's a big ask as the NHS have a policy only to retain medical records to a maximum of 30 years, but there are individual hospital policies and within departments where the keeping of records drops down to any time between 6 years to 20 years. What everyone agrees to is medical records are kept at least 8 years after a patient's death unless it contributes to historical events."

"Do you mean like a plague?" The thought made me shudder.

"Exactly, this isn't relevant in your case as Bridie is alive, although the rule of thumb for mentally disordered persons, are those types of records are generally kept for 20 years."

"What happened to the patients records, once the asylum closed?"

"Mainly the records would follow the patient, although where they cover 50 years or more it's likely the ones over 20 years would have only summaries and or microfiches of significant elements of the patients background as it affects the latest care." He shook his head. "Quite where you could find a machine to read the microfiches these days is anyone's guess.

"What's wrong?" Noticing his frown.

"I speak from an impression this is what is supposed to happen, whether it does I'm not so sure, besides the worth of patients records kept for so long would be unlikely to be helpful to any patients even if they were alive." It was a fair point. "Administratively it must be too costly for the NHS."

"Anyway given Bridie's father has authorised for you to be fully informed. I'll try to help answer any questions you may have although as I told your secretary, it was my father Cedric Bartholomew who was the Consultant Psychiatrist at the Darenth Asylum back then who actually treated her and sadly he is no longer with us." He reflected on his father.

"I'm sorry and yes I was made aware of your father being her physician I have been sent a thick medical file which I will work through very carefully and yes, the earlier parts do look to be summarised, so please bear with me Mr Bartholomew." I warmed towards this well-educated young man.

"Please call me Andrew, from what I know Bridie was initially diagnosed with Tuberculosis and then developed the brain meningitis strain according to the notes I have read of the case."

"It's Hayden, forgive me Andrew, but I'm here to get a feel of what Bridie's life was like, apart from her medical records, which are comprehensive, honestly I could not profess to understand all the jargon in them. I am more interested in how she felt about her illness, the others she met, was she lonely, what she was like as a woman growing up in an institution, did she miss her family and what friends she has made while she was here, sorry in the asylum." Images of Bridie as a young girl kept drifting in and out of my mind, I continued.

"I'm after finding out who Bridie is as a person, you know from what Claire my secretary has told you she is currently in the process of being assessed at the Maudsley hospital in order to determine whether she's fit to return to society. There is the question of whether she could or should be released to her aging father." I had my doubts whether Desmond could cope, but I was not going to affect the process if I did not have to.

"Difficult without speaking to, treating or knowing the patient personally and importantly I have also developed my career into another strain of medicine so you'll appreciate where my father was indeed the expert in his field of Psychiatry I am not."

"Yes I can see how it would be a problem for you, I'm clearly asking too much of you which I apologise for, I had hoped maybe your father might have said or referred to her in some way." It was frustrating and impossible for him I began to feel I had wasted his time.

"My father would rarely talk about his patients and I cannot remember him speaking about an individual case when I was growing up, he would have had so many patients." He was troubled as he spoke to me and believed it was because of his lack of being able to help.

"Andrew I'm sorry to burden you with this, I shouldn't have taken up your time I can see you're very busy." Looking around his mountain of paperwork, I stood up to leave.

"Please don't go yet, I'm intrigued and I'll try to help. May I ask why you're involved after all these years, Darenth Sanatorium closed some 25 years ago and frankly I'm surprised she is in any institution or why this case would come up after so long?" The story had him hooked.

"Her father sought me out because I was once Bridie's childhood sweetheart and he is getting no support from his own children and to be honest given different circumstances occurring between Bridie and myself she might not be where she is or has been up to now." I found myself adopting Desmond's guilt, I shrugged it off it would serve no purpose.

"You must have made quite an impression on her father as a young boy." Andrew appeared to be wrestling with a problem on his mind.

"What is it Andrew, if you want me to back off I will?" I had no wish to create issues between us.

"No, no, not at all," Andrew seem to relax and whatever was troubling him he had made up his mind. "Look Hayden, my father wrote several journals of his time at the asylum, but they would be only his feelings and thoughts, impressions.

Psychiatry is a subjective field of medicine working with individual minds means there is no stock right or wrong answer, his experience taught him this and because of those years at the coalface, he had this desire to pass on whatever information he could, specifically to me hoping I would follow in his footsteps." I could see he was saddened at his perceived father's disappointment in him.

"Every Father's wish," I interrupted. "My father wanted me to be a Blacksmith."

"What shoeing horses and the like?"

"Do you know everyone says that to me," I laughed. "Unfortunately nothing quite so glamourous, he made railway lines." It was Andrew's turn to laugh.

"I'm aware father encouraged his younger patients to write diaries of their time in hospital, it helps for them to read back experiences in their convalescence. Unfortunately this hospital is not a mental facility, it doesn't have the same benefit of skill bases for structuring the mind's thought patterns or behaviours which were needed in Bridie's or my father's environment. Nowadays, it's about emotional intelligence, do you know if she wrote diaries?" My own council provided courses on the subject.

"Yes she has about 30 of them, I haven't read any of them yet, but I am told by Claire today we now have copies of the first twelve." Raymond had been busy. "Can I see your fathers journals it would be helpful to get a view from a grown up's perspective," I could see he was tormented by letting others view his father's work it would be an unexpected bonus for me.

"I wanted to document his life through his journals at some point," his inner struggle within swaying him in my favour. "Hayden, if you promise to guard them with your life I'll let you take them away to study and please try not damage them in any way or write in them. It is literally all I have of him, his work was his life and as such, he had little time for family. Being a Doctor myself I understand the pressures he must have faced and how the family needed to appreciate how much of a difference he made to others," Surprisingly, he opened up the locked metal cabinet beside me and took out six leather bound journals. They had a dusty, brownish look to them as if not touched for quite a time.

From another drawer he retrieved brown paper and string, miraculously clearing a space on his table and began lovingly bundling them up finding an old shopping carrier on the floor, placing inside two perfectly formed separate journal parcels each containing three.

"Andrew, I cannot thank you enough, this is way more than I had hoped for." A sense of excitement ran through me and knew Desmond would be pleased at my efforts.

"Incidentally, in case these don't contain the information you need I do have a mountain of papers and course notes of his at home in my loft we could look through." He smiled, I was conscious of him glancing at his wristwatch he was late for an appointment. Being absolutely delighted, I felt it was time to go before he changed his mind.

"My thanks Andrew be assured I will take extreme care of these," I clutched the heavy journals under my arm so tightly it hurt. "I may yet be back for the other notes as well."

"One other thing Hayden, before you go I suggest

you have a chat with our old gardener, he is full of tales of the old days before the Asylum was totally demolished on this plot. With the gardens needing to be tended during the intervening years with housing and industrial units being built on the site, he was retained by the contractors who eventually built this hospital and then rehired by Darent valley so he never actually left here."

"Do I need to ask anyone for permission to talk to him before I go and see him?"

"No, he is employed by the hospital, if someone complains refer them to me, he might be able to help you on how life was back then and may also have known Bridie herself."

We shook hands with my promise to update him on my progress and the continued safety of the journals. I almost skipped out of his office buoyed by the journals I could not wait to read, under my arm, they were heavy so I expected a lot of information to be in them.

Nearing lunchtime the hospital restaurant on the same floor as Andrew's office was the ideal time to have a break and to ask where I might find an elderly gardener called Harry Bates.

The hospital receptionist, who happened to be sitting on the next table to me eating her lunch out of a plastic box, was eating a homemade tuna salad. She directed me to the rear of the hospital grounds.

I followed her directions out of the main hospital building following a pathway where two large aluminium sheds stood, both had open sliding doors, the left one had garden tools spilling out in front of it together with a huge Hayter Heritage garden mower tractor standing proudly at the side a rich man's lawn mower. In the right shed through the open doorway, I could see the lights were on and there an old man dozing in an armchair fit for a king.

Chapter 5

I looked through the opening trying not to disturb the man inside, the shed appeared good enough to live in, a wooden bed occupying the far right corner, I trod on something which crunched, probably a biscuit packet it was not the cleanest and it disturbed his sleep waking with a gruff sound.

"Who is there? Who are you? What do you want? What are you doing in here?" shouting, attempting to focus by putting on his Lennon style glasses where upon he eyed me with suspicion. The level of his voice suggesting he might be partially deaf.

"Apologies Sir, I didn't mean to startle you. It is Harry isn't it?"

"Mr Bates and you haven't answered my questions," he got up with a groan evidence of a worn out back and walked out of the shed ahead, expecting me to follow. I could see his rugged leathery features clearly borne out by many years working outside, his shoulder's broad where in his youth he would have occupied his time with many visits to a gym.

"I'm here to help a friend of mine who happens to be the father of an ex-patient of the Darenth Park Sanatorium which used to be on this site. I've been trying to build up a picture of what life would have been like for his daughter in the old asylum and I'm told you were here in those days as a young man and may be able to help me."

"Who told you?" Still eyeing me with suspicion,

he started to walk across the grounds towards the perimeter wall of the gardens I had no choice but to follow.

"Andrew Bartholomew." I hoped he liked Andrew.

"I knew his father fine man, treated me fair always," he stopped shouting, lowering his voice as we moved away from the hospital building. "What name?"

"Hayden Robbins," I outstretched my hand, which he ignored.

"No you fool the daughter." This was getting difficult.

"Oh Bridie, its Bridie London," I watched his mind search his memory hard.

We walked in silence except for the burp and the thump to his chest as he did so. The old walled entrance appeared in the distance the unused wrought iron gates locked I pointed this out to him, as we walked towards them.

"Yes, the newer building layout redirected the entrances to be more conveniently positioned for the main roads and newly built car parks." He held onto the prongs a feature of the old gates.

"This is a massive place to upkeep do you do this by yourself?" I was trying to engage him in conversation.

"When I first arrived here there was 164 acres, when they demolished the sanatorium they put houses over there," he said pointing somewhere far away in the distance. "They put business units over the way too," pointing in another direction.

"You've been here, since the early sixties Andrew tells me?"

"When they built this new hospital, they sacked

two of my helpers saying there was less ground to maintain so less people." It had clearly been an issue for him, he bent down as we walked to pick up the odd twig or crisp packet dropped by a picnicker.

"Is there less ground?" Ready to be as empathetic as possible with him.

"Yes, they took 100 acres and made it into the Darenth Country Park."

"So they were right?"

"I suppose." I became lost, he did not seem happy with the thought.

"Hayden is it?" he became serious as we came upon an old preserved wooden bench the plaque on the back of the seat had the words "In loving memory of Ellen Amelia Thornton missed forever 1915 – 1985." I wondered about her perhaps a past asylum patient or better, a mother much loved I hoped so. We both sat down proudly on the dedicated bench. Harry looked around covertly, to see if anyone could hear him, the bench cold, he put the crisp packet and twig in the bin by the bench.

"Yes Harry." I took the plunge his suspicion of me appeared to have evaporated.

"I remember Bridie when she first came here very pretty girl, you'll appreciate back then I was a young apprentice gardener I joined the hospital in 1961, 17 I were, he spoke like I expected a yokel to.

"You can remember her so clearly?" I was surprised because by my calculation he must have been pushing 70 years old, I was surprised he still worked here at all.

"I remember most of them as they came and went the boys as well, I would watch the same scene play out daily certainly during my first two years. I remember her particularly because I vowed not to watch ever again." His bright blues eyes glistened at the recall. He rose intending to walk on expecting me to follow. "You'd like to think you could get used to the misery, but it is heart breaking."

"What happened when she first arrived at the asylum Harry?" His stride purposeful, I double skipped to get in line with him and me the younger one.

"I was the one who cleared the rubbish, leaves, mowed lawns and dug holes for the senior gardener at the time so I was mainly in and around the entrance as it was important for the initial impressions of the hospital as people arrived," he nodded toward the gates. "I have worked for the Darent Valley Hospital and the previous Darenth Park Hospital the mental asylum on this site for as long as I can remember but those earlier years will stay etched in my mind forever."

"Was it a children's asylum? How many children were there in those days?"

"When the hospital was full to capacity it housed approximately 1800 although 300 of those were said to be on licence to work outside of the hospital or go home at weekends to re-acclimatise to home life more men than women, a carryover from the war years. By the 1960's children were introduced, there were men who would help me carpenters, builders too, problem was supervising them, they would harm themselves and have many accidents it had to stop, they were frightening the children. There was a school for them I remember, some of the patients were in for the long haul and sadly some didn't make it, fortunately the majority returned home quickly." He placed his hands on the metal of the old gates as if they would give him inspiration, an army of people must have passed through these over the years.

"How many stayed longer Harry do you know?"

"Yes they calculated it once it was about 4 out of 10 patients who had been there 25 years or more."

"Including Bridie," I observed, we left the gates behind continuing to walk the grounds, from time to time he would curse under his breath at the litter left by staff or visitors. The path winding its way up to and past the hospital front doors.

"No-one calls for mental patients to be able to leave an asylum, people are too scared of them on the outside. Even families shy away from wanting them back in their environment."

"But some do leave, or the asylums would be overrun surely?"

"Most end up in a body bag through self-harming, get old or get sick like in any hospital." Someone dressed in a white coat said 'hello' to him passing us by.

"If a patient is cured they should go home."

"You would think so but it's not the case, it depends what they're in for."

"I don't follow?" he pulled a broken branch off a small tree. "You talk like they were prisoners."

"People get put in sanatoriums for a reason and mostly not because they've gone mad one day it's because they've done something wrong, attacked or hurt someone. I'm not forgetting those who are genuinely sick of course, but how many court cases do you read of where murderers, rapists or abusers get off because they're not of sound mind either at the time or permanently and many get off on a technicality."

"I have seen quite a few, of course I have," he decided to sit down on another bench this one had no plaque, we watched the doors of the hospital open and close automatically as people passed through them.

"Exactly, where do they send these people for assessments?" He continued not waiting for an answer. "They lock them away in sanatoriums or the mental wings within prisons for assessment. The danger is when people complain prisons are overcrowded it's these people who haven't been sentenced for any crime who get released only to inflict more harm in the community and suddenly everyone is furious." To an extent, I had to agree with his cynicism, we were on our way again.

"So what makes a sanatorium push to release their patients?" It dawned on me I am talking to the gardener, a well-healed experienced and knowledgeable one, but a gardener all the same.

"Cost, pure and simple, when Darenth Park closed down in 1988 it was not for the welfare of the patients. They had to get rid of 1800 of them over the preceding year or months to prisons, other sanatoriums, some hospitals, nursing care homes, hospices and in some cases children's homes, if not they would be sent home or put in special housing. It becomes someone else's problem not the hospital's, why because of cost, they needed the money from the land to build houses, businesses and a better cost effective hospital and a park for the community as a whole, who cares about displacing mental patients, they don't vote, let others pick up the slack." His anger at the injustice quickly bubbling to the surface, showing in his rapidly colouring crimson face.

"What of Bridie?" We walked behind the hospital, past the laundry and the appliance store, inside I could see walking sticks and wheelchairs.

"Bridie was one of the last ones to leave the sanatorium in 1988." Sadness entered his voice. "I knew Bridie from her arrival she made such an impression on me for all the wrong reasons I decided to find out who she was and watch her progress however long she might stay with us." It must have affected him when the sanatorium closed, his ever watchful eye no longer needed.

"What were the wrong reasons?" he banged his hand on an air conditioning unit not working attached to the side of a porta cabin as an extension to the orthopaedic unit, temperamentally it stuttered into life, clattering destined to die again very soon, probably waiting for Harry to turn a corner no doubt.

"I remember a bright spring April day the staff, patients and visitors normally took the opportunity to explore the hospital, have afternoon tea and cakes or picnic with family and friends within the grounds, blankets laying spread out on the grass, boxes, baskets containing the food and crockery used as makeshift seating. Unwittingly the young teenage girl and departing gentleman had acquired a large audience, who were watching, listening in silence to the cries of despair at her being left behind alone to face what lay ahead." We crossed a staff car park to the rear of the hospital, we seemed to be going further and further away from the entrance. We found yet another nameless bench to sit on and I suspected Harry to have positioned them around his daily walk checking on the grounds. I noticed others seemed to be doing the heavy work for him and he supervised. One young lad carrying garden tools back to one of the sheds told him what planting he had done.

"And this was Bridie London?" We were heading

towards a gate, the lad disappearing.

"Yes, I didn't know her name at the time, but her cries served as a reminder of when most of them, as patients, arrived with thoughts of what will become of them, being emotionally distraught, most with an overwhelming feeling of sadness and terror combined. I have watched their fear taking hold very quickly many times, with a sense of loss, family betrayal, being cursed by their illness, panic, anger, frustration and despair left alone having no control over their individual lives." Harry Bates paused, ensuring I fully understood the picture he was painting, the years indelibly ingrained in his mind.

"How did you as a gardener know all this?" We arrived at the gate he tested and pulled at the Chubb lock attached on the end of a thick chain.

"Eyes and ears laddie!" he adopted a mock Scottish accent and laughed aloud, leaning on the five bar gate separating the hospital from the patients and visitors from the business side where storage, equipment and offices led to the grounds and Country Park beyond. Laddie I thought I could only be five to ten years younger.

"Over the many years I have met most of them, the majority get bored wanting to explore the grounds, I used to take them for nature walks explaining what plants we had or the type of trees grew here. The patients used to pick out hiding places, there were many searches or hunts for missing people and I knew the grounds better than most." We walked around the edge of the grounds perimeter, I was not stopping him do his job.

"Not all of them I hope." My attempt at humour, it failed.

"No, no most wanted a chat, a cup of tea or a biscuit, something different from their daily lives of shuffling along corridors waiting for their next set of pills to keep them in a zombie type of sanity the hospital staff expected from them. I was a release for them and they talked to me." His face lined with the memories of those days.

"You should have joined the medical team." I could see the back of his two sheds in the distance becoming closer.

"No fear, I wouldn't have coped." I doubted him he is a very astute man.

"What of Bridie's arrival?" Bringing him back to my reason for being here.

"The leaver, who I later discovered was her father."

"Desmond London." I interrupted out of breath with all this walking, the afternoon was closing in and it was getting chilly.

"Anyhow, he became guilt ridden rushing toward his parked vehicle with one eye on the exit as if attempting to escape. I knew his heart was racing, beating, pounding within his chest to the sounds of screams, begging cries, ringing in his ears across the grounds, causing attentions to be deflected from day to day lives, I know because seeing so many it affected me in exactly the same way and I wasn't their family."

"Did you think of them as such?" The sheds were getting nearer.

"Pretty heartless if you didn't, besides no-one could cope in the environment without some compassion." Harry is a grand old chap I thought.

"Nurses pushed their patients faster along the paths because of the noise. Doctors, sitting with patients, on benches adorned with plaques of past inhabitants of the asylum concentrated on them a little more intently. Picnics set out as visiting relatives, ignoring the cries purposely busying themselves taking the opportunity to enjoy the sun filled day with their loved ones, who are also locked in a prison of care for mental health, guilt shuddered through the scene as each scream rang out."

"I'm so amazed Harry at your sense of all this going on around you."

"Gardeners have souls too you know!" he stooped in his tracks and looked directly at me. "Besides I've had years of practice."

"I didn't mean to…." I felt myself getting uncomfortable.

"I know you didn't," he dismissed my comment and continued. "Everyone was thankful it isn't they who were being punished on this day, sadly I have seen it a million times it's the reason why I used to take the trouble to learn their names. I tried to treat them as friends and gradually as I became older they could pass as my children and now grandchildren, throughout the years watching their progress I always hoped they left the asylum better than when they arrived."

"And the wrong reasons for Bridie?" We were standing outside the sheds.

"Ah yes, Bridie came to us a very sick girl, but she was not in the true sense."

"You mean mentally?" Desmond had made such a comment to me.

"Yes, we all knew it, Doctors, Nurses and patients alike, even the bloody gardener knew?" A wry smile crossed his mouth.

"Why was she not released?" I felt I was asking too much of him.

"Well at first, she was sick and needed to be isolated, she had many operations and her medication I heard didn't work apart from no other hospital had the facilities to treat her. She would get into difficulty health wise, assessed several times and gradually over time became part of the place, except in the beginning, she never complained about being here, her family typical of others I see who visit most have resigned themselves to her being here and the years roll by mostly accepting the way it is to be." We went inside the right hand shed.

"But you never saw her family again?"

"Strangely, unlike others she was not allowed to see anyone connected with her past, but her father Desmond you say?" I nodded. "He would walk the grounds, it wasn't unusual, other families did the same to be near their children, but a few wouldn't be allowed any contact."

"My God, sheer apathy on the part of those in authority?"

"If you like," he shrugged there was a ledge with cups and a kettle on the side.

"Did most of the patients know you?"

"Of me, not necessarily know me, I was a young man in those days and the girls used to like chatting to me, and the guys wanted to work outdoors like me." Pausing thinking of the point he needed to state. "I needed to be careful, these youngsters were ill, no matter how they behaved, I had a role to play in their guidance not officially of course I remember Mr Bartholomew used to give talks to all the staff on the importance of how we talk to or react to the type of patients in our care." As I listened, he had me believing in the team ethic Andrew's father had tried to impress upon them, he added. "I learnt so much from him."

"He seems to have played a large part in Bridie's life."

"Cedric taught me a great deal, not about any specific patient, more about what to look for, patterns of behaviour, changes of temperament. We used to talk over a beer in the summer and hot rum in winter. I would watch both the patients and families highlighting any issues for them. I believe I did help them from time to time, at least he used to say so, you see he made me feel I was part of his team, even though I was a humble gardener," he had made his point very clearly to me. "How I gained the practice."

Harry spoke sadly of the girl's father leaving haunted by his guilt. I pictured Desmond as he recalled the moment.

"Tears flowed freely down the departing proud man's cheek bones embarrassed by his weakness and feelings, tormented because of the beautiful daughter he had left behind." He paused trying to recall the scene from 50 years ago.

"With a furtive backward glance, raising his arm, he made a half wave back to the second floor window where she stood only to bring a new wave of screams heard through the open window, a soul clearly distressed by his leaving. I could see it destroyed his own mental state at the same time as serving to hasten his departure, without knowing, it would be a very long time before he would be allowed to see his daughter again, let alone take her home" Harry stopped his own emotions picturing the scene and turned towards the whistle of the boiling kettle.

"Driving away, her screams reverberated around

the sanatorium grounds bouncing off the building walls increasing the intensity of her sound. Her father knew, at the delicate young age of thirteen, he was consigning Bridie to a life of misery and by her desperate sounds he realised, she knew it too," Harry had turned his gaze from the departing car to study the young girl at the window.

Harry painted the picture he saw before him, for what seemed an age she stood arms spread high against the window now closed for fear she could jump, the palms of her hands, arms and body pressing firmly onto the glass, her face soaking the glass with tears as she pressed her face hard against it.

With her father disappearing from sight she had fallen silent, an air of resignation befell her he shuddered at the misery etched in his mind for life, grateful to share these thoughts with someone who would understand from the family perspective. He recalled she stared hard at the wrought iron gates closed once her father had driven through them, willing him to return, her tear lined cheek resting softly on the pane as she sobbed desperately.

With Harry watching, a kindly Nurse he recognised as Rhona Jackson approached from within her room placing an arm around Bridie's shoulder's, no longer could he hear the sound of her cries instead saw her sob visibly into the arms of her comforter. Silently he blessed the Nurse with her and wondered, as he always did, what would become of the frail girl so stricken with sadness.

"How dreadfully sad it must have been for her." It was all I could manage to say.

"The sanatorium contained many, many rooms, I used to call them patient cells and try to recall how many faces I have known so I never forget them, watching them peering from their own windows lonely for sight of their families throughout my time here. I constantly re-enact the same scenes time and time again in my mind, even waking me up at night." He broke down in front of me I knew he was not just the gardener, but acted as a watching carer over the many poor souls continually arriving at the asylum, gradually taking on the father's role when he was able.

"Please Harry enough for now I have no intention of upsetting you, how did you feel when the asylum closed down?" I was conscious I kept pushing him for a glimpse of a past long gone. He offered tea, which I accepted.

"On the one hand, I felt tremendous relief, but on the other it was terribly sad, especially as a good many went to prison where they shouldn't have, the problem for me was no-one who left were cured just relocated and I had no opportunity to find out how anyone was getting on whether released or not."

I appreciated it must have been very hard for him, I decided I would include him as much as possible on my journey so he would have the chance to follow through on at least one patient he knew.

"My job was to continue looking after these grounds and I have retained every memory because I have never left. I know where all the bodies are buried and where the ashes are scattered literally and now I don't know what I am still doing here," his voice tinged with sadness for those children he had seen come and go at the asylum. "I watched them pull down the asylum piece by piece along with the memories of those children who hadn't made it." He remembered them all, a huge burden for anyone to carry around.

"No, I have to continue I am no longer a young man and had to tell someone once and for all to free myself of the burden I carry in my heart, I thank you for this opportunity." He held my hand and shook it firmly bringing a tear to my eye, it fed his own sorrow of loneliness, a great many girls and boys used to speak with him, he had befriended many over the years making them tea or providing biscuits attempting to offer some sanity into their sad lives. He felt an important part of the establishment, discussing people he observed with the main Doctor who actually listened to him. There were those well enough to return home, but also those who never quite made it out through the front gates ever again. He told me how he regularly visited the memories at the adjacent church graveyard where the forgotten young men and women found peace, some days the parents or relatives of those buried or had ashes scattered would come for an hour or two to talk to someone who knew their child, he felt privileged to help them.

Other days the weight of sorrow played heavily on his mind becoming too much to bear and today was one of those days. During those years before the sanatorium closed, he had lived many lifetimes through the eyes of the children he had known and befriended wondering at the time how long he could continue in the job.

"Do you have news of Bridie? Where is she now? How is she?" His eyes lit up at the thought of her.

I told him the story of Desmond, and the places Bridie had been in since she left Darenth up until the Maudsley hospital and Raymond Barnyard's assessment Harry was disappointed I had not yet seen her for myself.

"Bridie once had a particular friend did you know a girl called Maisie?" I was pushing him again. The tin of biscuits surfaced and helped myself as I clutched my mug of tea, feeling a chip around the rim as I drank.

"Maisie Belling yes I did, strange girl she was a mental patient of course, they were like twins, lookalikes which they played on, inseparable. There were others, a Florence and a Deborah they all practised looking like each other," his memory working well.

"Why do you say a strange girl?"

"Later they became great friends I am told but going back to when Bridie arrived I looked around the grounds and most busied themselves weak attempts to ignore what had happened, except one young girl who had watched the same scene play out as I did many times in the few months she had joined. Her face was smiling as if she enjoyed the pain the new girl was going through, it disturbed me. She looked across to me attempting to connect in some way as a kindred spirit which I always ignored looking away from her not wishing to get involved, after all I was the landscape gardener, I had spotted her looking before and felt she actually enjoyed it, Maisie used to befriend all the newcomers.

"Do you know what happened to her when the asylum closed?

"Maisie went to prison the rumours were she had killed one of the Nurses in the past, given the sanatorium was regarded as secure with the amount of patients being rehomed it was safer in the short term to push them toward a closed prison."

"Which prison do you know?" Thinking I will try

to find her.

"Broadmoor I believe."

"It must have been dreadful for her the poor child," I winced at the thought.

"A woman nearly forty and a probably a murderer don't forget," he was quick to point out the reality, it was hard for him to show her any compassion and offered more biscuits, declining, I felt like one of his boys at the sanatorium.

"You know I watched Bridie grow up but the last couple of years I never saw her much and never saw her go either. I remember once a couple of months after she arrived she had turned up outside of the main gates," he fondly recalled the moment.

"Hello, Bridie isn't it? What are you doing out here, are you lost?" He lost himself in the memory telling me. "A sad girl in herself she was, but intelligent and if I do say so myself, quite sane." He continued as he recalled the conversation.

"I'm ok, just walking it's my first time outside the building, I am feeling better now I often watch you digging and mowing the grass from my room." She said looking around her to check if anyone was listening.

"I'm about to close these gates, I keep leaving them open, as I am nearly finished my work outside why don't you walk back inside with me?" Scared he might have to drag her.

"She knew I clearly hadn't finished because I had dug quite a long hole ready for rows of plants. I should have closed the gates it was a mistake, but I didn't expect her or anyone else to be outside the sanatoriums boundary." It troubled him even now after all this time.

"I don't want to cause you any trouble Harry," he recalled her saying it was the first time she had used his first name. It embarrassed him.

"What was she like toward you Harry?" I said breaking a spell she obviously had over him as he recalled her deep in his memory.

"She was always lovely, sometimes a bit flirty and most times depressed like a cloud always following her overhead but inside she had a heart as big as a sunflower anyhow I gestured for her to go back through the gates when we began to hear voices and footsteps running up to the gates." He started to smile. "She noted Doctor Bartholomew and Nurse Sophie were both panicking and told me so, I remember we laughed about it afterwards."

"There you are," they expressed with some relief. "We thought we had lost you Bridie."

"Bridie and I shared a special moment she held my hand tightly asking, if I could be allowed to walk her back to the hospital. With both Doctor and Nurse reluctantly agreeing we walked slowly and she talked about my strong hands being like her fathers, his too, were never clean because of his greengrocer business, she swung our hands as we strolled the Doctor and Nurse walking about 10 paces behind us." He paused and said very seriously. "I adopted her then and there Hayden, as if she was one my own and looked for her every chance I had, and when she hooked up with Maisie I used to make them both tea here in this shed, right where you're sitting."

"So Bridie was let out alone, I thought they panicked?"

"Gradually as they got older they were trusted more, the last few years I used to get visited more and more by the 30 to 40 year old women as they had become."

"Who come to see you?" I was getting a little confused.

"I meant Bridie, Maisie and sometimes Florence and or Deborah would come, they grow up you know!"

"Of course I keep imagining 13 or 14 year old girls not grown women."

"It became very difficult for a middle aged man, being surrounded by flirtatious women." I could tell he would have revelled in it.

"Who was that?" I joked.

"Me you fool!" He laughed.

"How were Bridie and Maisie together as women?"

"They used to play tricks on everyone, to make people guess who was who as they were so alike. I was one of the few people who could tell them apart, no matter what disguise they used and Maisie was always trying it on me, more important to her somehow. I always felt when it never worked she avoided contact with me especially in the last couple of years and she kept Bridie away as well, which saddened me."

I could tell he was getting tired and promised him I would come back and give him an update and bring some photographs to show him, he told me to hurry as he may be retired by the management soon. With the impression, I had acquired a new friend I would make sure to include him in my search for the real Bridie.

Chapter 6

When I left Harry, I called Desmond to let him know I was on my way to his home and would be arriving late evening a day earlier than suggested. The detached bungalow was sprawling, it surprised me the grounds spread for at least five acres I imagined a home full of children once having lived here.

Desmond took me on a tour and destroyed my illusion of his home once being a child filled home, he had purchased the bungalow from a young builder who renovated it after many laying empty and moved in when he retired shortly before Josephine had died and his children long ago had left home. The added conservatory across the back of the whole length of the bungalow split into two, one third a lounge area and the rest a swimming pool. We sat together on the floral armchairs watching the glistening of the pool waters from the other side of the glass partition, a woman's touch no doubt.

"You have a lovely home Desmond, have Joseph, Emma and Susan been here?"

"Oh yes they have keys, but they refuse to enjoy it themselves believing it to be a waste of money especially now I am alone," from what I knew of his children I could see Joseph saying as such.

"We spent most of our time in this conservatory, Josey and I, we loved to relax and have tea after a swim." I sat looking at past photographs of his beloved wife and his four children this rambling home and gardens filled with flowers a clear influence by his late wife. We sat talking for many hours of his life, when he gave up the shop, he filled his home with his memories and I felt very comfortable in his company.

We adjourned to the living and dining room the conservatory becoming colder, as the warmth of the July afternoon began dying down to a cool and breezy light pleasant evening.

Before long we were sitting at his dining table full of papers spread over it, pushing aside them to make space for the sandwiches he had prepared in advance for me. I looked at the piles of papers and I hoped he knew the order of them, to me it looked chaotic. Every scrap of words about Bridie spread out in one place.

Returning with our coffee's he gestured for me to push more papers aside and help myself to a couple of coasters for the coffee to sit on the table with. Once he placed the coffee, he spread out his arms as he sat down.

"Josey and I never knew any of this Hayden reading the medical notes I cannot believe the catalogue of wrongs done to her." Desmond felt as any father would, somehow he had failed Bridie I needed to help this man and quickly. "Every time I read something in her diaries relating to her medical state, I traced the time in the medical notes and it appears she had so many operations I cannot tell whether they helped her or not." His shoulders hutched in despair.

"Desmond, I may have something which will help," Having left Andrew's fathers journals in the car, I retrieved them placing them on the table on top of the papers. "This is a piece of the puzzle you don't have Desmond, Cedric Bartholomew's journals during his time at the sanatorium. I promised with my life to Andrew I would look after them." He beamed at me I had begun to help him.

"My God, I knew it was right getting you involved I doubt he would ever have given these to me." With tears in his eyes he gestured for me to eat, placing his hands on the journals in front of him, he was revitalised.

He mentioned meeting Cedric on several occasions and as I spoke to him of Harry Bates we laughed as he too had sampled his tea and biscuits over 25 years ago and looked forward to seeing him again.

"Desmond I don't see why she went to an asylum and not a normal hospital?"

"The Doctors told us it was contagious, segregation, seclusion was the key, these days the word would be isolation. She had been ok in the morning, although we kept her locked in her bedroom as the Doctors advised; we used to talk to her through the door offering encouragement. Our other children thought it a great game, they used to play guessing the colours or clothing they had on or what objects were in front of them," he recalled wistfully. "She appeared to be getting better when suddenly, she had an epileptic seizure not uncommon with this disease, but it was the first time she had ever suffered one in front of us. We were helpless and unsure of what to do, it brought home to us how medically ignorant we were," tears began rolling down his cheeks as he recalled the incident and the start of his journey to lose a daughter he could no longer stem the tide of his emotions.

"Please Desmond try not to upset yourself, take your time and know I will help you in whatever way I can." Unsure of what I could do, the man in front of me needed my support and for my past love of Bridie, I owed it to her. I spoke to him about Penny being happy for my involvement, a lie yes, but necessary in the circumstances.

"Hayden, you've no idea how violent the seizure had been, it frightened the hell out of both of us, today people watch it all the time on television in reality shows or soaps and know instinctively what to do. Back then we didn't have a clue, she choked on her tongue and the Doctor's said at some point during the seizure she may have been starved of oxygen such was our lack of knowledge of what to do," the despair clearly evident in his voice.

"Desmond, you should not blame yourself." I knew he did.

"You try living with this for 50 years and not do so it's impossible," his anger rising at the frustration of his own inadequacies. "To see your own child in such torment, violent, unstoppable we could not bear it, we were powerless, useless and it broke Josey's heart, she needed help desperately, this was why we agreed so readily for her to go into hospital." His face ashen at the thought, age catching up with him.

"What happened next?"

"The Doctors suggested we would no longer be able to cope or contain what was happening to her at home, they were right we knew it, they advised, no they insisted it was in the best interests Bridie went into hospital and told us we also risked contaminating ourselves, our other children and possibly our market produce. These days the thought process would be highly questionable but back then, you tended to believe everything. We had visions of our shop being the hub of infections for everyone spreading for miles. Stupid of course, but then we didn't understand."

"I was going to say it's a load of rubbish." A different century literally.

"Quite, bullshit actually," he smiled for the first time since I had arrived. "Josey was worried about the children, customers and the business and we needed to be solvent for Bridie to have the best care so we consented for her to be put into a home for adolescences suffering this kind of trauma, little appreciating we were consigning her to a mental asylum." I started to wonder whether consigning her there was more about having a drug trial candidate, did it really happen back then? Perhaps I am being too cynical.

"How did Bridie feel about this Desmond?"

"When the initial seizure happened, she realised she couldn't refuse to go into hospital anymore, but was scared."

"You said initial seizure, there was more than one?"

"Three more before I finally took her to the asylum in the space of a week."

"When you took her what was it like?" I knew of course, Harry had told me what he saw unfortunately, Desmond had lived it altogether differently.

"She hated it and begged me to take her home immediately I couldn't of course, so I suggested she wrote an account of her time there in the form of the diary notes." He held his head in his hands.

"I'm so sorry Desmond." I could only imagine

the heartache he had gone through.

"Desmond, do you have pictures of Bridie, when she was living at home and when she was at the Darenth Park sanatorium, like before and after types?" His mood lightened, I was on the case.

To my surprise, he did have a couple in his raincoat pocket, and rummaged in a sideboard drawer and found two others. I cleared the table of the cups and sandwich plates washing them up in the kitchen overlooking the vast garden at the back of the bungalow, a dream full of flowers I gauged Bridie would have loved this. On my return, he placed the four in front of me and my heart skipped a beat, there were two photographs in black and white crumpled being in his coat and two in colour. He passed me a magnifying glass to use. My Bridie was as I remembered a fresh faced teen looking completely in love, smiling through her heart I hoped it was for me. The black and white picture showing it was bright day of summer. I could see the shadows the sun created around the images in the background, she wore a white school blouse, dark skirt, ankle socks and black shoes, her dark hair shining in the brightness at shoulder length, she must have been ill when it was taken and no-one had realised. She was sitting on what appeared to be a dark tartan blanket laid on the grass, the backdrop was an oak tree in the distance, the sun attempting to break through its branches, I guessed it was taken in a park during a family picnic outing she was smiling at the camera lens, clearly happy.

I asked where the picture was taken, Peckham Rye Park, I knew it from my childhood Desmond even found the old Kodak Brownie camera he had used.

Initially I thought the second picture also black

and white was a school one as it was with a group of girls. Closer inspection showed the girls, young women in their 20's together with what appeared to be a white laboratory coated Doctor, a darkly dressed Nurse perhaps a sister with all the girls wearing a grey tunic or dark uniform, difficult to tell on a black and white image. Out of all the girls in the picture, I judged ten were smiling, five not looking at the camera and the rest appeared miserable and did not want to be there. I noticed the background façade of what appeared to be the Darenth Park Sanatorium. Desmond confirmed it.

I asked about the white coated man and Nurse in the picture and became interested to learn he was a young Cedric Bartholomew and Rhona Jackson, I wondered if Andrew had a copy and vowed to give him one.

Bridie was harder to recognise in this photograph, there were at least two or three girls who could have been her within the three rows seven at the back must have been standing on a bench, seven freestanding in the middle and six seated at the front. I pointed out the likenesses to Desmond.

"Yes, I agree, the one on the far right of the second row is Bridie, the girl next to her is a girl called Maisie they were inseparable at the Darenth so I understand." They could have been twins, Harry had been right.

I looked hard and instantly recognised her, normally when photographs are taken people are usually a 'picture' of health not so in this case, looking closer through the magnifier her illness had taken its toll, although without the benefit of colour I could see her likeness with the first picture. Studying the other girls, particularly Maisie I am amazed at the likeness between them.

He gave me a third picture, a colour photograph, this time there were eighteen women in the frame, they were in their late 40's. The background cold and pale green, it shocked me my brain seemed to be able to cope with a teenager becoming a 20 year old but then to double her age in an instance took me completely by surprise.   Desmond explained this one taken outside the Cheadle Royal hospital, the walls full of ivy growing high above them. Once again, I could not recognise her, Desmond helped by pointing her out to me, two rows this time Bridie being the second in on the left of the front nine.

"Desmond did you instantly recognise Bridie from this photograph?" I doubted myself and had to know if it was just me.

"No I wasn't able to; she was pointed out to me by one of the warders." I wondered if he had followed the same habit by visiting the Cheadle Royal to be near her.

"Why didn't you see her there Desmond?" A pained expression spread across his face, surely the regime at the hospital is different, he should have been able to see her at last.

"She refused to see me," my turn to shake my head.

"Please let it go." He raised his hand to me, too much for him to discuss, I dropped the subject but I became suspicious as to why.

"Where's Maisie her friend in this one?" I searched for another likeness.

This time it appeared to me Bridie had changed beyond recognition, certainly from the first two photographs surprisingly because this one is in colour, but it would serve no purpose if I pursued this.

"She's not in this one, she wasn't sent to the Cheadle Royal but to prison," he dismissed it, naturally being only interested in Bridie.

I noted there is a drastic change in her to the original picture. She looked pale and gaunt looking giving off a child-like aura. Finally, the fourth picture showed her at her current full age, no compliments to be paid life had been unkind to her. It disturbed me, looking closely at the fourth picture a single figure taken in the courtyard of the Maudsley Hospital the photograph given for Desmond to keep now he was part of her assessment, I instantly recognised the same person from photograph three. Once again, it was like there were two different people from the first two pictures to the last two. I tried to gauge what I felt for her, I wished to God I knew, something bothered me as I looked closer.

While I made myself comfortable in the bedroom he had previously prepared for me, Desmond clutched the first of Cedric's journals he sat away from the table in one of two armchairs placed in the bay of the window and starting turning its passages, ignoring me when I returned from the bedroom becoming mesmerised by its contents. I sat in the opposite armchair and began looking at each picture with a fresh eye through the magnifying glass. There was a likeness in all of the photographs but the smiles were not the same in the last two the eyes themselves were no longer smiling,

"Oh God Bridie, why on earth did you have to come back into my life, I put you in a make believe box in my mind, literally dead and buried and now you've been dug up and very much alive." I spoke aloud my thoughts frantic I had to get some fresh air.

"I'm so sorry Hayden I am obviously causing you some of your own pain." I nodded to him unable to speak gesturing to the garden where I escaped to, not realising he had heard me.

I sat alone listening to the cool breeze bouncing off the trees at the bottom of Desmond's garden where the outside lights placed subtly within the surrounding bushes.

"It was Josey's idea to make the garden an extension of the conservatory I miss her so much which is why I must make sure Bridie's future is secured before I die." He was troubled as he joined me putting down the first journal. "Six months ago, end of January almost February, the winter nights made way for the oncoming spring days closing from the increasingly fresh sunny days. The skies developed a moody overcast as they darkened above bringing a cold shiver in the bones informing those looking forward to spring that winter was still here. I sat where you sit now a lonely old man feeling the evening drawing in on me as if I was waiting to die without any possibility of seeing my Bridie ever again." Telling me, he had considered suicide.

"So what happened?" The picture of doom very clear.

"Raymond Barnyard happened and I shall be eternally grateful to him."

It had been one month since the London family sat down with the Consultant Psychiatrist at the Maudsley Hospital, Denmark Hill in London. Desmond had originally received a telephone call from Raymond Barnyard his daughter was about to be transferred into his care and there would be several months of assessment of her. He should not raise his hopes as to any likely outcome. As her father, he should be aware this was taking place. It will be several months until he would contact him again however, he will then suggest a plan for her ongoing care.

Prior to this and not since the reading of Josephine London's last will and testament in 2001 and with the exception of Bridie who had been in a sanatorium, had the family all been together. The family consisted of Desmond London, the mother Josephine now deceased, three daughters including Bridie, with one of his other daughters twinned with his only son.

The subject of their meeting was to discuss Bridie London's release from the mental asylum process.

"Do you have any other family either side, brothers, sisters of your own?" Desmond had not mentioned any extended family.

"Yes I do and Josey had a sister who was very supportive, sadly, passed away about eight years ago. On my own side I have a younger brother whom I have not spoken too for about forty years, pretty soon after he married, a family member in an insane asylum was not good news for a couple looking to better themselves, the stigma perceived harmful. On the plus side, brother Thomas's wife felt her husband should have a share in the Greengrocery business despite it being passed down to the eldest son for the last few generations. Thomas conveniently forgetting to tell her about the sum of money put into trust for him instead which he squandered the moment he became of age." I laughed.

Desmond London's eldest child and daughter Bridie had faced back in 1963 the worst crisis of her young life when she developed Tuberculosis, forcing her father to remove her from their family home and greengrocer business at Fenham Road in Peckham, a suburb of London. The advice provided to them by their family Doctor, given her illness and the epileptic seizures, being so acute warranted her immediate hospitalisation. This took the form of isolation from the other members of the family especially her brother and two sisters, the customers and produce of the business. The only place to have the correct facilities at the time in order she may get better was the Darenth Park Sanatorium at Dartford in Kent, where he was to take her as soon as possible with little more contact with other people.

She had been unwilling to leave her family, making him forcibly remove her and take her to the sanatorium himself. A part of him died on the day he left her there. Desmond London has not been the same person since, and as her father, he felt responsible for Bridie's circumstances and his wife Josey's feelings who had been powerless to stop her husband taking her, watching her growing eldest daughter and best friend disappear from her life. Gradually the loss of her daughter slowly destroyed her, progressively causing her to be both physically and mentally ill and this led to her giving up on the will to live. Now at 83 and becoming increasingly frail himself, fifty years had passed since Bridie was hospitalised, Desmond felt it was time he brought her home knowing it could bring with it a mountain of problems, he had to try his wife Josey would have known what to do, he was sure of it.

Josey would spend hours and hours in Bridie's old room sometimes sleeping in there, nothing allowed to be moved or touched, she would remember how they were together, the day they had painted the walls of her bedroom in terracotta and the ceiling white, they had shopped to get transfers and border paper for around the walls for additional colour. They begged and begged Desmond to clean up the mess they had made which he did and laughed loudly as they washed each other's paint filled hair. Josey was the happiest of mothers she loved Bridie with her very soul, sadly, once Bridie was taken from her, Josey was left only the photographs of her first daughter growing towards being a healthy teenager and the potential of the woman she knew she could have been, the albums being little comfort for her heartache.

Josey would sit and stare out from Bridie's first floor bedroom window for hours longing for her to walk around the far corner of their road. She used to bounce happily along the pavement, swinging her satchel by her side and waving glad to be back home once again after finishing her day at the secondary school she attended daily. She dressed in her brown school uniform with her brown shoulder length hair, held in place by the Alice band flicking up and brushing on the shoulders of her brown school blazer. They had purchased the band together at the local Woolworths store on the high street.

Josey knew it would never happen ever again and many times she would cry herself to sleep at night at the window resting her head on Bridie's white painted dressing table, although she died of a stroke quietly slipping away in her sleep peacefully the hospital had said, but Desmond knew differently.

"She had come to accept our daughter would be forever lost to us. The bitterness across the years enveloped Josey," he suggested sadly, several times he had attempted to visit Bridie or at least get his wife in to see her in the sanatorium without success. Legally, the staff at the asylum informed them they could, only to be stopped from ever seeing her which Desmond never understood, ignorant of the law and his rights and having barely enough money to feed what was left of his family he could not afford the basic advice of a solicitor. For several years, the sanatoriums excuses were Bridie was either too ill, too violent on a particular day or it was not appropriate at this time to see her. His beloved daughter had become a mental asylum patient entrenched into institutional life. In 1975, Bridie London was detained 'sectioned' under the Mental Health Act giving him less rights of access than he ever did.

I listened to his story amazed this could happen in what I believed was a modern day tragedy.

In the early days, Desmond tried to involve his local member of parliament to force the medics to give him access, but to no avail. However, he gained parental rights to see her, only for Bridie to apparently, refuse to see him, the sanatorium continually sidestepping him.

With no reason offered why they could not see their daughter and further destroying his fragile wife who never expected it to turn out like this when she reluctantly agreed for her to go. Josey never recovered, she died from a broken heart yearning for her lost daughter to come home with the years of waiting finally taking their toll. Now the Consultant Psychiatrist at the Maudsley hospital was giving him the option of bringing her home late in life, hope filled his heart, he was determined to move heaven and earth to make this happen for Josey his dear wife's memories sake. He had to, needed to, find a resolution to the problem faced. At first, there appeared to be no one he could turn to until it occurred to him there might be someone who could help him.

"Are you listening Josey, what do you think?" he shouted aloud looking up towards the sky. "Good idea? Let's at least try shall we?"

Listening I realised he was talking of me, not to me he continued.

Desmond felt his children only stuck around him because of their mother and the prospect of money with their unshakeable belief they had loads of it. The business handed down through the generations from his father and his father before him, Josephine who had come from better stock, was from a middle class banking family who had promptly disowned her when she met and married a barrow boy as her father called him on more than one occasion to his face. She did have some money an aunt had left her, but it was only a small legacy so money was always tight. The green grocery business was profitable enough to keep the family living well, but like all shopkeeper's he continuously lost business to the growing supermarket chains, which as we know now, caused many local shops to close down. The freehold of the building they owned and not the business making the real profit.

Josey's will was read 12 years ago when all her worldly possessions were transferred to him for Bridie's future care. His dear children, Bridie's brother and two sisters at their mature age were very angry and not concerned or unhappy at their mother's passing or bothered for her beneficiary dear, dear Bridie.

During the past 12 years, a once a year phone call

to their father and a 6 monthly call checking on Bridie at the Darenth Park sanatorium and later to the Cheadle Royal mainly to see if she was still alive. It always reminded him and established his children were in need of their inheritance somehow Bridie had robbed from them of whatever the value it might be. This impromptu family get together was not the result of any family love between the London's, but because of the Consultant Psychiatrist Raymond Barnyard's telephone call requesting a meeting to discuss Bridie London's potential release. Officially from the Cheadle Royal Hospital, originally named the Manchester Royal Lunatic Asylum a psychiatric hospital, via the Maudsley Hospital in London, for potential release assessment.

Bridie had been in one other place since he first left her at the Darenth Park Sanatorium 50 years ago the Cheadle Royal. Not once had he seen her, she moved from there from Darenth in 1988 after 25 years, spending the next 25 years at the Cheadle Royal only to finally end up at The Maudsley Hospital in London.

During the early part of the 25 years Bridie spent at the Darenth Asylum, he had stopped seeking appointments with both her and the Doctors or Nurses providing her care. Given his lack of success in not managing to see her by deciding he would simply turn up each day, each week or each month unannounced, usually around midday and walk in and around the grounds of the asylum to be near her he felt better in himself.

He imagined her walking beside him chatting about the friends she made or the activities she had taken part in, initially he hoped to catch a brief glimpse of his beloved daughter, but as time passed by and knowing he would be unlikely to recognise her, held out the faint hope she might know him. He watched patients with their families realising he had missed all her growing years. As time moved on, he became unsure whether he would recognise her at all. Once or twice he caught what he thought was a fleeting glance at someone who might be her which only served to torment him further.

I suggested he took a break from telling the story but he was insistent, I made us some coffee and we moved inside out of the beginning chill of the night and sat again in the bay window armchairs.

On occasion's he would chat to the young gardener Harry at the sanatorium growing older with him, with his every visit they used to speak of the patient's being allowed to walk the grounds mainly during the mornings when no visits were allowed. He would describe Bridie to him as a thin waif of a girl now woman, well in herself but deeply sad and lost in her own internal world. Several times, he would turn up in the mornings, but never saw her and often turned away by the security guard or Nurses.

When she moved on to the Cheadle Royal he could only manage every six months, his daughter would have been a middle aged woman by then and unlikely to recognise him as her father, the atmosphere of the place not the same. Gradually, guiltily the visits slowed to a stop. Desmond was desperate to see her and at times had tried to insist on it, there was always resistance, a well-worn answer quoting the rules and regret about the patients not up to it, needing rest, and mostly the patient didn't want to see him, perhaps another day he could try which never came.

It became more and more difficult for Desmond to be near her each time tearing at his wife Josephine's heart when his visits continued to prove fruitless with little chance of seeing her, they both decided he should stop trying, time and with his age getting the better of him, the guilt overwhelming especially when his wife died.

In February, six months ago, Bridie transferred to the Maudsley Hospital in order for her assessment for potential release, but as it turned out it became more about them assessing Desmond for his suitability to care for his daughter while she was rehabilitating or re-establishing herself into society. The fact she had never established herself at 13 years old, apparently irrelevant.

Raymond Barnyard assured him he would do all he could for Bridie, in order she would finally come home.

"I was overjoyed, but as the days turned into weeks and weeks into months and despite my calls resulting in being told her assessment is progressing satisfactorily, I began to feel it was the same old story." I could see how it would.

"I'm so sorry Desmond," feeling his desperation.

"So I was surprised when I received a call from Raymond Barnyard's secretary, asking if I could attend a meeting to discuss Bridie's progress and the future." He gladly accepted, pleased to have an excuse to be near her once again.

Raymond Barnyard, Bridie's physician had played it well bringing the London family all together in one place on the premise at one time or another all of Bridie's next of kin had made contact with the hospitals as stated in her notes, so felt they should all be party to the decisions made about Bridie. Desmond and Josephine London had four children, one son Joseph and three daughters Bridie the eldest, Emma and Susan. Her physician had picked out the details from Bridie's file.

Desmond could never tell his other children, but realised he disliked them intensely for the money grabbing vultures they had become. They continually borrowed money under one pretext or another and despite their assuring him to the contrary, they never had the slightest intention of repaying the money back to him, when challenged their cry always how they were entitled to it given the money spent on Bridie over the years. When young, his children were never satisfied and as people, they were very cold emotionally. Both Josey and he had known this from their early age and no amount of different ways of upbringing approach toward them ever changed, it was evident in their daily lives now and how they were about Bridie.

Chapter 7

On Friday, I woke to the smell of hot coffee and toast.

"I wasn't sure what you ate in the mornings I have cereal if you wish." I guessed he did not have many visitors.

"How did you find the journals are they useful to you?" Not having read them, I was curious, Desmond having taken them to bed the night before.

"There was, is, a good deal to read and most is not to do with Bridie, but it is interesting because it reminded me of the feel of the environment at the time, some of it confirms what is in the medical notes and there are links to Bridie's diaries. It completes the information overhaul, I am grateful, but I haven't finished them yet."

By mid-morning, we were sitting outside the day bright and sunny and Desmond continued with his story.

Walking up to the classically designed white main entrance of the Maudsley Hospital, the façade based on early 19th century brick, surrounded by black painted metal railings and lawns, containing the hospitals incumbents within the local conservation area. The former military hospital opened in 1915 only to close and reopen again as a Psychiatric hospital in 1923. It uses the resources of the Kings College hospital's Institute of Psychiatry opposite on Denmark hill.

When Desmond arrived at the Maudsley Hospital they were expecting him, the receptionist told him the Professor's other guests had already arrived and directed him through the double doors to her right and by taking the lift to the second floor, he would be met by Professor Barnyards secretary who will take him on to his office. A pretty, fair-haired young woman wearing a white laboratory coat introduced herself as Michelle and led him through to a waiting area where four people were sitting either waiting for someone or had an appointment with one of the Doctors or Nurses. He followed as she took a left down a corridor where stretched ahead of him he noticed a patient ward, with the sign 'No admittance without authorisation', the double door fronting the ward with wire meshed windows and a key entry pad, suggesting the patients inside were not going anywhere.

Inside the Professor's office, Desmond London's three agitated children, grown up's of course, seated in a semi-circle in front of the mahogany desk complete with a faux leather green pad insert. The room dominated by bookcases lining all four walls filled with volumes of journals and medical books claiming, apart from the windows, every inch of wall space, his desk sat proudly in the centre of the room overflowing at each side with case note files, lending presence to the man occupying in this busy mental health training hospital. His role today after many years of practical experience was as a Professorial Consultant Psychiatrist managing more the families of patients rather than patients themselves and for the overseeing of the assessments for potential release patients.

Barely acknowledging their fathers arrival, son

Joseph spoke to him first.

"Do you know why we've been summoned here today, father?" His son's belligerent attitude tearing sharply at his heart, a face contorted with anger. "Patrice I can tell you was not happy with me wasting time coming here, we have things to do!"

He doubted if Joseph loved her, surprisingly, she had dutifully provided him with twin daughters, whom Desmond had seen twice since they were born, once when he was coerced into paying for their christening, the last family gathering before Josey died and secondly at Josey's funeral. His son would on occasionally be short of funds and although their private schooling had been paid for by Patrice and her family, he was expected to chip in for uniforms, books and the odd, must have school trips, Desmond remembering Namur in Belgium and Innsbruck in Austria as being two of them.

They were nearing their teenage years and had no permitted contact with him their grandfather. Joseph had studied art as a profession becoming an expert in his field, in his early days he would work for high-end auction houses, occasionally lecturing at universities where he met Patrice. While being knowledgeable, his work was commission and contract based, Joseph, a lazy individual hardly earned enough to survive and borrowed heavily off Patrice's family who watched every penny he spent, which is why he always came to his father for money.

One day his luck changed when one of his contacts suggested when Buckingham Palace opened their doors to the public in 1993 he became a tour guide, his professional expertise and lecturing while making him a good fit for the role, made him absolutely intolerable in his personal life as he believed himself of noble birth by association. He made Desmond feel as a greengrocer he somehow let his son down. Despite this fact, he continually went to his father with his hand out. Desmond longed for the warmth of friendship an only son would be able to provide unfortunately, it always met with coldness.

"I suspect they want money, why not send us a letter," his daughter Susan who he noted now had blond bleach coloured hair and had not changed from constantly bitching about money or the lack of it as usual. "Better yet don't bother us at all, its cost me to travel here today who is going to pay for it?"

"Shut up Susan it must be serious otherwise the hospital would not have called us in together, we've all paid to get here." Desmond had become angry with his daughter, she was another with delusions of grandeur a cook in a primary trust school, somehow turned her into the headmistress, concerned about her size the office chairs were groaning under her weight.

"When is this Barnyard fellow arriving, I cannot waste all day." Doing his best to ignore his son's frustration, Desmond frowned at his other daughter Emma who had turned up with red hair today and it was very short man like, she was his youngest child, he always thought well of her especially as she had been stuck with Joseph and Susan as her role models when growing up. He understood her to be a secretary for a Retail Company Executive, smiling to himself wondering whether she was a checkout assistant, as if on cue, the office door opened sharply.

Causing his guests to jump with a start, the tall,

lean, rugged looking Professor Barnyard opened his office door sharply and entered with a deliberate flurry running his fingers through his full head of tussled grey hair, adding the sense of dominance, he had purposely cultivated throughout his career. It being one of his true pleasures in life, as he brushed past them towards his paper filled mahogany desk.

"Please, please don't get up," he sarcastically noted, three of them did not intend doing so, he took the hand of the one riser. "Desmond how nice to see you again it's been some while, I trust you're well?" He had first met Desmond some six months earlier, although older, he reminded him of the TV Detective Columbo for his mannerisms and dishevelled look. He gauged he would have been a very handsome man back in his youth, Raymond had first met him when Bridie London first transferred to the Maudsley Hospital for assessment from the Cheadle Royal sanatorium in Manchester as a likely forerunner to cancelling her past sectioning, following closely, if she passed his assessment, by her release into the community. Desmond wore a familiar old light brown raincoat worn by the detective with curling collars of aged cloth characterising him, endearing him immediately to Raymond.

"Do you know this man?" Annoyed, Joseph demanded from his father who nodded at him.

As a naturally brusque person, Raymond Barnyard did not do small talk and this occasion no different, not waiting for a reply. He adjusted his red tie in a framed picture glass mirror on the wall straightening it to his white collared light blue shirt and adjusted his cuffs facing a picture of himself and past Health Minister when a new wing of the hospital opened. By looking in the glass taking his time he was able observe and assess the London family closer than they would have appreciated. It caused the group to crane their necks trying to identify the politician in the picture.

"Welcome ladies and gentlemen to the Maudsley Hospital, you may be aware this is a teaching and assessment centre for the mentally challenged, specifically for your daughter," he nodded to Desmond then looked directly at the three he assumed were his children, the likeness between the three but not so with the father, a matter of age he told himself. "Your sister Bridie came to us some 6 months ago, perhaps Desmond you could introduce me to your family, as I understand it they've never ever been bothered to try and see how Bridie has been doing at Darenth or at the Cheadle Royal and certainly not here. Apparently between you we have received the odd telephone call," he looked down at some paperwork he had brought in with him as if checking his facts. "It doesn't sound as if you care very much for your sister?" The effect made the three people he was assessing squirm, one with embarrassment and two with rage, interesting he considered, his psychiatric hat on.

"How dare you make assumptions," Joseph exploded. "We didn't realise she was here anyway."

"Ah, you do care? Good," He looked toward Desmond for the introductions and noted he returned a smile. It became enjoyable to watch them fidget as he learnt their names.

Desmond stifled a grin and made the introductions defining Joseph as his only son and his two daughters for the Professor the greying lack of hair for Joseph with Susan currently a blond and Emma the youngest a deep red.

"Well, we cannot all be natural can we?" It amused him to antagonise, their father was enjoying himself he noted, stroking his full head of grey hair. "Or be blessed with attributes greater than others," he probably went too far today he did not care.

With his experienced eye he observed the three closely, Joseph, a pompous oaf full of his own importance had positioned himself at the centre of the family group. Determined to dominate his two younger sisters, a slim man smartly dressed in a blue serge pin-stripe suit with smart white tailored shirt with a red, maroon and yellow crossed tie purporting to be an old school tie, which Raymond took as an attempt to suggest his education to be more than what it is. A reddish tinge to his cheeks and darkening veined nose told him Joseph was a heavy drinker he put his age in his early sixties. He surmised a henpecked husband with children who took little notice of their father he constantly twisted the ring on his finger nervously.

Susan, a dyed blonde woman desperately clinging to her youth and failing, she too dressed well and wore a tight iced lemon dress surrounding a much fuller figure than she would have liked, the brownish fingers on her right hand suggested a smoker, she fidgeted in her chair her habit drawing her in. Her clothing gave off an associated odour of stale musty tobacco. Although the twin of Joseph he had thought her younger than him in her late fifties, she had the etchings of life engrained in her face as only a smoker has, her face taut from years of dragging in the smoke through her cheeks. With the ring on her finger, he doubted she had a happy marriage being quite an upright person and starched as an individual, he gauged no children.

Emma on the other hand dressed dishevelled like

her father more a hippy of the sixties in a floral skirt and baggy tee shirt, beads hanging from her neck she appeared a generation younger than Joseph or Susan, a bored individual in her middle fifties and judging by her demeanour not interested in being there. Rings on all fingers and not one suggesting a wedding had occurred, from her demeanour she suggestively gave the impression she would be likely to enjoy a woman's company more than a man's, he doubted Desmond knew or considered it. She had a hard look to her red hair short and greased pressed tight to her head.

"I called you all here today obviously to discuss Bridie, her progress, her wellbeing as well as her future," speaking in bullet points he felt like the headmaster talking down onto his classroom of pupils, it was not lost on the angry twins. "As you may be aware she was transferred to us from the Cheadle Royal Hospital in Manchester where she had been a committed mental patient mainly on the basis of her history of violence, unmanageability and previous ill health which began her life in these institutions, as an individual she has been selected for assessment." He had the attention of the group.

"How is she Mr Barnyard?"

"Desmond, she's good, probably better than good, I wondered who would actually ask," Studying the boiling point of the two 'angry's'. "It would naturally be her father."

"So what are we doing here then?" Joseph spoke impatiently he disliked this greying mop haired lanky medic, who was patronising him. "How much do you want?"

"I don't understand do you mean money?" The Consultant Psychiatrist looked at Joseph in disgust.

"Mr London, Joseph, let me be 100% clear we want nor need any money from you or your family."

"Want do you want?" he emphasised the 'do'.

"To tell you she's free to go," he paused waiting for a reaction. "She's all yours ready to go home with you, today if you wish."

"What now? Your joking she is sectioned right?" This time it was Susan, Barnyard noticed the nervous twitch above her right eye. "I thought you said she had a history of violence and what was it, unmanageability, how can she leave with this record are you telling us she has been rehabilitated?"

"Yes, she can go home and hopefully welcomed into the bosom of her family," it was like watching a horror movie their faces an absolute picture.

"She can't leave, she is, has been institutionalised for, for, for what 50 odd years, well let me tell you she's not staying, definitely not with me, No! No!" Blondie huffing, puffing and had started to stutter at the very thought of it.

"Nor me either, I have got a family," Joseph stated horrified at the mere thought. "I cannot let a women like her loose in my home with the children it would not be safe, I will not allow it, no, no, no." Raymond achieved the desired effect.

"It's your sister for God's sake, what's the matter with you both," Desmond looked towards Emma his younger daughter for some support.

"I suppose we could look at the possibility," Emma found herself hesitating her father's imploring eyes willing her to agree to share the responsibility, she was quickly cut short by the other two.

"Oh, you play along, you only want to get the money Mum and Dad's has already paid and is paying for her care." Blondie unmoved by any sentiment required towards her sister Bridie, she shifted her bulk on the chair it made a rasping noise she ignored it.

"Not fair, I merely feel we should discuss this rationally." The beads swaying from one side to another on her head causing Emma to hold them in place.

"Isn't it, you're soft in the head, do you really want a stupid, dribbling mentally retarded 60 year old woman living with you, I don't think so." Scratching his balding head Joseph was getting frustrated at the way the meeting was going, he wiped sweat from his brow.

"Bridie London is your family or am I mistaken?" Barnyard pressed another button with Joseph and Susan his two angry people. "Besides because of our assessment she's eligible to be de-sectioned as it were, as siblings it is your responsibility no?" He tried not to show his enjoyment.

"No it bloody isn't," Joseph maintaining the role of speaking for the group wiping his hands on his trousers. "If anyone's responsible it's father not us he has the money not us."

"Forgive me Desmond are you not 83 years old?" Never had Raymond known a family outwardly talk so much about the money they wanted, needed or expected to gain. As well as a blatant disregard for other members of their own family, turning back into their conversation like Emma he too was becoming bored with this group.   "By the way she is 64 and certainly not stupid."

"Whatever," Joseph pointedly replied to Professor Barnyard. "There is no way I am going to look after my insane sister."

"Is this really true, she is well enough to come

home?" Ignoring Joseph, a first sign of hope for several decades filled Desmond's heart he was excited if it were.

"You're too old to look after her," chorused Joseph, Susan and Emma. "Don't even think about it."

Raymond had forgotten the one person who did care he had his fun, now he needed her father's hopes to take on a sense of reality.

"Desmond reluctantly they're right and she's not quite ready, we've a lot more work to do with her but I believe she will be ready soon," he offered.

"Well someone's got to look after her and we cannot let this opportunity pass to free her from the life she has had." Desmond sadly looking from Professor Barnyard to his children. "Josey, your mother would never forgive me if I didn't try and if I don't who else will?" He dared them to speak.

"Spoken like a true father, yes it is true Desmond although she's subject to the clinical commissioning group of South London, who are the governing board but they will act on our recommendations." He wanted it to work for the old man in front of him.

"Your recommendations influence the board yes?"

Raymond decided to be careful of his promises the old man was looking frail, his adult children no help to him whatsoever.

"Of course, but let us concentrate on Bridie herself, sadly, she has lost her youth and some of the spirit. Maturing over the years has helped her come to terms with what has happened. Particularly how the initial illness sent her down a spiral of mental distress." He paused for effect. "Ultimately, it will be her decision to return to society, including where and whom she wishes to live with."

"Huh, like she will have a choice!" Her brother sneering at the group in triumphant pose. "At least she's not ready yet, but more money will be spent on her, our money!"

"Rest assured, Mr London we will not be charging you a penny," the formal reference agitated Joseph even more. "Oh, and she does have a choice Mr London, she will be free to live however she pleases, we of course have to be sure it is in her best interests and cannot harm her progress for rehabilitation, before we release her from her original committal."

"What do you mean Mr Barnyard?" Now concerned for his daughters welfare realising he could not cope if she had behavioural issues.

"Initially in 1963 because of Bridie's original illness she was voluntarily committed to the Darenth Park Sanatorium in order she, like others could be isolated, you would have been consulted Desmond at the time, however according to her notes in 1975 she was officially sectioned and deemed a danger to herself and society." Barnyard was puzzled. "Clearly we don't know the full story, but for Bridie's sake we need to unpick her past in order she may have the best chance of a future. We have to investigate further, although our assessment will help release her from the sectioning.'

"So is she ready to be released or not, Doctor?" he ignored the impolite reference to his status by Susan and worried about his chair surviving its ordeal, a creaking sound testing its robustness.

"Of course she is, but as I have outlined she will need considerable help and we together have to make sure she gets it."

"Who do you expect to do this unpicking, Professor?" it was Emma's turn to ask a question.

"We can help of course however it should be someone who knew her and can relate closely to her past and generally means by her family commitment." He doubted red hairs commitment.

"This is a load of rubbish, all very grand and noble getting mental patients back into society the truth is, more likely because of Government or the social services cut backs!"

"For God's sake Joseph this is your sister we're talking of, your own flesh and blood," it was Desmond's turn to get angry with his son.

"Actually Desmond, your son is not altogether wrong, we cannot afford to keep her in this facility any longer than necessary. There is extreme demand and pressure on this hospital, which is primarily a teaching one, the alternative is to ship her back to Manchester, to the Cheadle Royal. A government led nationwide assessment of all mental patients in hospitals and prisons to free as many people as possible had to take place. Cutback of funds, lack of facilities, space, trained staff and the cost to the taxpayer are all factors, prisons and hospitals are full to bursting. In turn forcing assessments to be undertaken across the whole country and luckily Bridie looks, or at least appears as if she could be made ready to go home, particularly as she has a family who can take care of her, I admit financial considerations are a huge factor in the decision making." He looked directly at the three siblings.

"There I told you so, there must be funds available in cases like this surely?" Smugly Joseph knew he had been right.

"Well yes there is, there is another factor including whether you are the right people to take on this challenge and whether it is right for Bridie. The health service is not a bottomless pit full of money, the financial state of the country affects us too."

"Good then social services can provide for her in future, give her a house or apartment and some money, instead of taking ours all these years." Raymond realised Desmond's son was trying to duck the issue.

"Not true Joseph I have helped you, all of you, over the years," Desmond scolded his son again.

"All I know is, at last we can have a share of the money it's been costing or will cost for Bridie." The brother folded his arms, making it clear he had his say. "We've had to beg for money all our lives."

Raymond bit his tongue, not liking the treatment being given to the old man by his children, unfortunately he had learned over the years having seen the same situation play out many times to keep quiet when the dirty laundry gets aired within a family.

"Any money I have is for Bridie's care you all know your mother wished it and so do I." Desmond was once again arguing with his children over money, he was saddened because of it. He was sick of having to defend the help he gave to his daughter their sister.

"Mother's dead Father many years ago and you're not going to live forever, we're not going to live forever either so it will be left to us to foot the bill for her future care if social services don't take on the responsibility," all three nodding agreement.

"Don't you all see, all I am trying to ensure is my daughter Bridie, your elder sister has an opportunity to improve her quality of life after fifty years locked up in an institution, a life you have all taken so much for granted," Desmond was begging them.

"It was never our fault Bridie became sick father," Susan spoke solemnly. "Our elder sister was taken away from us too, what sort of childhood do you think we had? Our sister gone, mother a shadow of who she could have been, certainly not the mother I wanted and you were no better, all you both cared about was Bridie, your darling girl, well you had two others girls whom you took no notice of." Raymond watched Desmond's ashen face as she continued her hate filled words. "Your three other children needed both your loves not just Bridie." Emma and Joseph were nodding their agreement.

"Desmond, you ok?" Raymond horrified at their outburst to their father, privately he would hate it directed at him, more so as they did it in public.

"Yes, yes I'm fine Raymond, thank you," he had not expected such an outburst in part he knew to be true. He knew exactly where he stood for their support, nowhere.

Mercenary bastards, Barnyard thought.

"Besides if she's well enough to be released she's well enough to get a job and fend for herself in society, isn't she Doctor?" Joseph in full flow himself callously sensing they were winning their arguments. "Why do we need to worry about her at all?"

"Oh, let me see, I know, the little matter of it happens to be your sister we're talking about," The coldness demonstrated disturbed him, Desmond London felt ashamed of his three children and looked to Barnyard for support.

"Your sister will require a great deal of support as she acclimatises, 50 years out of society will mean she will struggle to cope with the basics of living for several years to come, like supermarkets, traffic on the roads, mobile phones and clothing to wear." Barnyard stressed. "Everything you all take for granted."

"What skills does she have, she must have learnt something in her sad little life, she can work, get a cleaning job at least?" Susan was deadly serious.

"Are you not forgetting she's also a pensioner?" Raymond pointed out.

"So are we, well we're marching towards pension age and Emma's not far behind us," Joseph stated.

"Oh bloody hell, so she can't work anyway, well she must be due a state pension?" Susan looked at her father shaking her head. "She could go on social service benefits and I dare say she could be homed by them as well."

"Do you have any understanding of the traumatic life Bridie, your sister has been through?" A rare occurrence Barnyard was furious with them he did not wait for their answer. "Her whole life, first as a young child and as a teenage girl through illness, Tuberculosis Meningitis which affects the brain happens to be the worst strain of the condition possible and in those days touch and go whether she would live or die, this much away from death or at the very least a vegetable." He demonstrated by the quarter inch gap held up to them between his right thumb and forefinger. "Nowadays with antibiotics and the right mix of drugs, correct diagnosis of the condition means generally a recovery period of a month maybe two, it cost her 50 years of her life for God's sake don't you people understand?"

"She couldn't have been ill for the whole length of time surely?" Emma queried. "And it's hardly our fault."

"You're right the wrong medication led her to develop mood swings and also led to many operations which she should never have had. The pharmaceutical companies in those days paid for guinea pigs, new hospital wards or refurbished ones, new equipment or a freeze on drug costs and all with little control over what happened to each patient, the mental insane were deemed expendable. Some mystery surrounds her violent episodes, which led to a restriction on visitation rights and for the level of family contact permitted. My guess is she was operated on needlessly in the early days and stages of her illness, which would have had a lasting effect on her overall health." Raymond Barnyard watched Joseph stifle a yawn and became angry determined to make them pay attention. "It may not have been your fault, but it was not hers either."

He smiled assuredly at Desmond and continued.

"One of the reasons we believe she became so violent and sectioned in 1975 being described as 'out of control' is she was raped in 1972 and badly beaten by a trusted male member of staff to within an inch of her life?" It had the desired effect on the group. Desmond decided not to tell Hayden of her rape.

"Oh God my poor Bridie, did they catch who did it? How could this have happened?" Desmond started to cry for her openly.

"For goodness sake father pull yourself together it was 35 to 40 years ago she would have gotten over it by now," Joseph demonstrating his coldness of thought.

"According to her notes the authorities knew the person involved but had no proof so were unable to do anything about it," he paused for effect gauging their full attention somewhere in these cold hearts, maybe there was some compassion although he doubted it. "The person was only suspended for three months and on his return moved away from the particular wing or area where she was and his employment was to be closely reviewed. Soon after his return to work the person thought to be responsible was found stabbed to death and her friend Maisie told the authorities Bridie had been avenged."

"She wasn't convicted of the crime was she?" this was new to Desmond who shuddered at the revelation. "Why wasn't we told?"

"I honestly cannot answer Desmond, following this incident there isn't much recorded about her except the odd skirmish or fight which is a normal occurrence in such an institution of our type and no, she wasn't convicted of any crime." He looked around at his own environment gesturing with his hands claiming his part of the institution he worked in. "The next milestone for Bridie came some 16 years after her rape and 13 years after she was sectioned, at the time she would have been 38 years old."

"What happened to her then Mr Barnyard?" Only Desmond was interested.

"Darenth Park Sanatorium her home for the past 25 years was to close it was 1988," Barnyard referred to his notes. "The problem for Bridie being sectioned already and believed to have been involved in the rapists death meant the authorities had to make sure she was transferred to a maximum security hospital. I understand from the notes Desmond, you offered to support her privately, financially in part, which stopped her from being imprisoned and this is where the Cheadle Royal came in, however, there were conditions set out, one stipulation was 20 years had to pass before visitation and parental rights could be re-established. At which time she would be assessed as to her mental state and unfortunately you signed to safeguard her from the horror of prison life, misguided though this was at the time, because I believe you were hoodwinked."

"I don't remember, at the time I would have signed anything to make her better."

"Can we make a claim?"

"Shut up Joseph," he had about enough of his son's attitude. "I thought I was doing the right thing by her."

"I don't doubt it Desmond, but your signature meant all the treatment and the operations caused by the pharmaceutical companies I have previously mentioned, the rape attack, together with the murder, yes, the murder of the perpetrator and in fact anything during the previous 25 years would be covered up. All information unlikely to come to light for yet another 20 years providing enough time for, in particular, the Darenth Park Sanatorium's medical and administration staff to have long since retired," he was disgusted at his own profession for acting in this way.

"But we could sue them couldn't we?" Joseph's eyes lit up like pound signs, ignoring his father.

"I doubt it, Desmond you felt this would assist her own rehabilitation, which it may well have done, but what you in fact did is sign away your rights as a parent. I am sure you now realise the past 25 years has seen an enormous shift in both the law and attitudes of society generally. The rights of the individual has fundamentally changed certainly in European terms and mean these type of conditions wouldn't be allowed today and part of my journey in assessing patients such as Bridie move a long way towards rectifying such anomalies. The past five years have seen several assessments of her until she came to us six months ago for a full release evaluation. We all agree she is now ready to make her own place in society and needs your help as her family."

"Don't think I'm going to be her Nursemaid, I agree social services should pay," Desmond despised Susan for her comments.

"Bridie was one of the lucky ones Desmond," ignoring the others and only speaking to the father, if you had not been subsidising her care she would have certainly gone to prison automatically as many others did who had no means of support or family."

"We could have had the money."

"What of her friend Maisie? Desmond ignored his youngest daughter.

"I believe she had been the unlucky one and went to prison, she had no family to financially support her, I appreciate it's a shock for all of you, but if we pace ourselves during the coming month's we can make her ready for release. It can work believe me I have seen it before," he emphasised optimistically believing, hoping the London family would come around once they thought carefully about it. "She will require much care for at least two or three years, to be able to join society again."

"Are we done then?" Emma had turned angry. "Is this what I have wasted my time coming here for, at the very least I expected her dead and I would get some money, well I'm not taking her in," looking directly at her father she stood up and made for the office door. "Don't you dare look at me all righteous, where were you when I was young? It was always Bridie you had four children not one."

"Goes for us too, she has been enough of a parasite on this family it is time to stop," Joseph followed Susan as they made to catch up with Emma.

"Despicable all of you, I am ashamed of you!"

"Emma's right father, you had four children not one, we've had to fend for ourselves she has had her life handed to her on a plate, without a worry in the world." Joseph ushered Susan from the office.

"She needs our resources more now," they had not heard him, closing the door behind them. "I'm so sorry for my family Mr Barnyard, truly I am."

"Sadly Desmond I see it all the time, we'll try and work out a plan together," pausing for thought he observed. "You're going to need some help you know, long term help and it's not going to be social services. You must find someone who is able to provide the type of support she or you need."

"I know."

"Dare I say it Desmond, it has to be someone who is going to be there for her long after you're gone at least until she can reasonably survive on her own. Until she is out there we'll never know the timescales." Raymond was concerned for the burden he was putting on this fragile old man.

Desmond once again described how he first met her again even though he had already told me, a sign of his age I guessed. He had made his way back through the corridors and back towards Raymond's office, unsure of how he should view his visit.

"How did you find her Desmond?" Raymond

Barnard offered him a chair as he peered over his mounting paperwork.

"Strange, cold and distant and I did not recognise my daughter at all to be blunt." It greatly disturbed him.

"Perfectly normal I'm afraid, her illness, the operations, the year's she has spent institutionalised leave their mark, initial hope of returning to family life quickly turns into despair and the acceptance and habit of what life has dealt. She's unlikely to be thrilled by promises of a better life she had long forgotten, she is a different person than the one you knew." Desmond recognised the Professor was trying to provide a positive outlook, it was difficult when he realised he desperately needed support having already written off any help from his children.

"She's unrecognisable, not a spark of the person I knew." Despair clouding over him, far quicker than he realised it would.

"There's a lot of work we have to do to bring her back to you, reminding her of the past will be some of it, as I stressed before you need help, I see you have a couple of her diaries suggested initially by you, you'll find they make interesting reading."

"You've read them?" Desmond found himself disturbed at what he saw as a breach of his daughter's privacy, dismissing the thought he responded. "Can I have sight of her full medical record's I need to understand what I'm going to be dealing with?"

"Of course, I'll get my secretary to bundle a set of copies up for you, it will be quite an expansive pack for you so may require several bundles."

"I expected support from within my own family,

but it's not going to happen, unfortunately." Barnyard nodded sympathetically noting the attitude of his children.

They agreed to meet again in two weeks, the idea once again crossed Desmond's mind if he could find the person he needed and wondered how he would find him and worried if he would ever get his daughter back in mind and spirit. He was pleased he had at last begun the journey for both himself and Josey's sake.

He decided instead of going back up Denmark Hill to its train station, which would take him to London Charing Cross in order for him to get a connecting train back out to Sidcup where he lived, he would walk down the hill towards Camberwell Green. It was a few years since he had walked this way, at the bottom of the hill he realised Church Street ran across the junction leading him to Peckham Road which would take him near his old house and greengrocers shop, he turned, walking toward Peckham.

A short walk down on the left by the bus stop was the old public house The Stirling Castle, his own father used to drink at the place often. Much changed since he last remembered the place, summer tables and chairs with umbrellas adorned the pavement. He assumed they were out there for the smokers who needed their fix. He walked in and instead of old brown wood and red flock wallpaper of the past, the atmosphere was one of bright airy décor, comfortable seating and the tables announcing food available by the display of menu's on top of them. He was able to sit at the bar and ordered his father's bitter, a pint of old Courage's Directors.

Drinking slowly, he wondered what his father

would have made of the place, three generations of sons had held the Greengrocers business, but it had died with him when he retired, Joseph did not want any part of it. He sometimes felt only Bridie had any interest in taking on the business. He sighed it was not to be.

He walked from the Stirling Castle and took a left a couple of streets downwards into Benhill Road; unwittingly he was taking a shortcut towards Peckham and his old home in Fenham Road. He remembered another old haunt of his this time it was the British Lion Public House where many a night he spent drinking, dart playing and being part of the local football team so named after the pub itself, players picked on the basis of owning a set of boots rather than any skill they had.

As he strode down the street, to the right he passed Brunswick Park with Tennis courts, children's play area and seating for the local residents, Victorian houses fronted the park with St. Giles Hospital to the left hand side. Something triggered in his memory, his children were all born in the hospital and so was the person who he was looking for, was his memory playing tricks with him or did he recall the boy say he was moving close to the hospital where he was born. The boy and his family moved shortly after Bridie had taken ill, but he remembered his mother had told Josey they had moved to Brunswick Park.

Forgetting about the British Lion, he walked across to the Victorian houses dominating the park, each comprising of three apartments. He decided to ring one of the middle terraced houses in hope.

Never heard of them replied a middle-aged man with his small barking Yorkshire terrier at his side.

He tried another, and then another, finally a young woman opened the next door and also had never heard of them but made a suggestion to try number 8C where an older lady may remember the family.

It took some time for the old woman to answer, dressed in what appeared to be her night clothes she lived at the very top of the house she complained to him about the flights of stairs she would have to climb to get back up to her home again. He was in luck she did remember the family with some fondness. The mother had died, with the father who is also dead now, moving locally into a social housing apartment. Of their two children the girl married and went to live in Colchester in Essex, the boy also married much later and went to live in Maidstone in Kent where he worked, this was all many, many years ago she could not tell him what happened to them since.

Thanking her, his depression lifted with a jolt, although a small piece of information it was a start, he knew he would find him now, he had been lucky. Striding back towards Denmark Hill train station with renewed purpose, he would walk back to Peckham another day, for now he knew he was going to find him and hopefully in time to save Bridie from spending the rest of her life behind bars.

On the train to London's Charing Cross, he removed the diaries from the inside pocket of his raincoat, they felt old, he looked around to see if anyone was watching him, they were like gold dust to him precious beyond words, although probably not to anyone else. He was being paranoid turning back to the diaries and ignored everyone else sitting in the carriage. The pages were browning with age, some were sticking and stained with drink, perhaps tea he imagined, these were the early ones, 50 years old notebooks hardly built to last in those days, the pages already loose.

He gauged each diary covered roughly a year or two. Most of her notes inside were ramblings, what she had eaten, how she made her bed, her washing and teeth brushing filling most of her days, remembering the stack of notebooks from her room there were only about 30, either some were missing or she had not been writing all the time.

In them, she described unwittingly the very basic level of accommodation, bare walls, little conversation with others, her sickness, how she felt about him leaving her.   The carriage was filling up as each station came and went he struggled to hold back the tears in his eyes, he was living his young daughters life. There was a moment she had thought he would come back for her, she had cried herself to sleep, he became saddened by the loneliness Bridie must have felt. Initially some were about the boy left behind and jealousy over her rival for his affections, she described her Doctor and Nurse together with other girls she had met along the corridor where most had rooms of their own. He noted her handwriting was very poor and the spelling of words quite awful, it never mattered, he felt closer to her now than he had ever done.

The train idled into Charing Cross with his connection minutes away on a far side platform, his treasures firmly back into his raincoat's inside pocket, he had once more found his beloved Bridie, strange as she was, determined not to stop until she was at home with him, he would not fail her again.

Sitting down on the train gently pushing to its final destination he felt a pang of pain in his heart, he had experienced such a pain before and having ignored it then he would do so again. He had been on the go all day he told himself and should not have had the bitter in the pub, he was fooling himself of course, but there was no way he would be stopped from getting her released whatever the cost. Knowing he needed to rest, he closed his eyes for the minutes it would take the train to stop having pulled into the station and to let the hurrying crowds alight the train before him. Such was his tiredness a platform guard woke him up, the train was ready for its return journey.

By the end of the weekend, Desmond had unburdened himself to me buoyed by Andrew's fathers journals, he would pick them up at every opportunity knowing I would be leaving with them at the end of my stay I had promised Andrew I would look after them and it meant keeping them with me. My own bedtime reading, the medical notes easily sent me to sleep on each of the three nights I stayed with him, they raised more questions than giving me answers. It felt natural to be with him and I felt a part of his family.

Driving directly in to the office on the Monday morning, I couldn't stop the feeling of a sheer waste of lives and the unhappiness caused to not only Bridie, Desmond and his wife, but what of the other 100's of children how many of them had a similar story to tell.

In the office, Claire became interested in how my weekend had gone with Desmond and how Penny was. She had framed Bridie's young and old portraits for my desk. Desmond had given me copies of, Penny, Carrie and Simon no longer centre stage. I looked at the snapshots of Bridie, as if they acted as a point of reference, they touched my heart. Something nagged at me the more I kept looking at them, something was missing or wrong in the pictures, I let it go for now although it troubled me. I worked hard all day pushing it all from my mind except Claire had arranged for me to visit the Maudsley tomorrow.

Chapter 8

It's Tuesday morning and I find myself standing outside the Maudsley Hospital knowing Bridie was on site I felt excited and scared at the same time, my emotions all over the place, I waited for Professor Raymond Barnyard to collect me in reception. The hospital atmosphere relaxed and peaceful the sound of piped music pleasantly filtering intentionally my the mind similar to the 'tranquillity' compact discs everyone used to buy to help them sleep, I recognised the whales calling it went with the territory I suppose.

"Hello you must be Mr Robbins Bridie London's apparent saviour!" I shook his extended hand he was making fun of me. "Come, come walk with me into our courtyard it's a bright sunny day." He picked up his pace and expected I keep up with him.

"Does Bridie need saving Mr Barnyard?" His hair had a mind of its own which he made a determined, but unsuccessful attempt to control.

"Let's hope so Mr Robbins but please its Raymond." I bit my tongue Desmond spoke highly of the man I am not going to argue with Bridies lifeline.

"Please it's Hayden," I found myself bowing playing his games Desmond said he was quite fond of, the courtyard we entered a discreet place, overshadowed by buildings on four sides with entry or exit doors on each, the wooden benches with plaques of remembrance together with handy bins for the smoking fraternity. In the centre a small waterfall, not working surrounded by pot plants donated by the living in thanks presumably for their cure, someone had thrown in an unwanted fishpond lily I was turning into a cynic.

"What can you offer us Hayden, why would Desmond think you're worthy enough to help his daughter after so long? Coffee?" he marched off waving to me as I looked at his back disappearing into one of the side doors only to be seen walking down a corridor through the windows travelling toward a kiosk without waiting for my reply. Did I say yes? I could not recall.

"I guessed a white no sugar man on the strong side," Placing my drink in the middle of us sitting on the bench on his return, he was right.

"Are you talking of me, you or the coffee now?" We both laughed the ice broken.

"Ok let me tell you where we are at, assuming Desmond has told you of the meeting we had with his son and two daughters?" I nodded with some undisguised pain.

"From our point of view it didn't go well. Our aim is to rehabilitate Bridie into society and so far our assessments have been positive enough for us to consider her being ready to leave mental care."

"Is it likely?" I was looking for honesty not the optimism of her father.

"Only partially, she comes with a certain degree of baggage from the reports of her time at the Darenth asylum and the Cheadle Royal, both institutions being designated as secure facilities. She would have been held in such places because she can and does cause disruption and in some cases caused physical harm to staff, other patients and herself." He studied me carefully, I felt him assessing my reaction.

"So why let her out at all?" My question a valid one.

"We are required by policy to assess mental patients constantly but in Bridie's case and many others we've failed to do so, in her case she's been locked up for 50 years which is unacceptable unless we deliberately want to throw away the keys."

"Surely the easiest option, why bother in Bridie's case specifically?" I could tell he did not like someone questioning him.

"We certainly have enough patients to pick and choose from, but her case is particular important because we feel an injustice to her and her family has taken place."

"Who is we, and how so?"

"The CEO of the Cheadle Royal and I, he recommended her to us." Interesting I wondered if Desmond realised someone else was batting for Bridie.

"Do you have jurisdiction over a private facility such as the Cheadle Royal?" Knowing she had stayed there, I looked them up on the internet.

"Oh yes they have to conform to government dictates like the rest of us especially as her care is partially funded by the state." I nodded to him as if I understood, but this was not my world so in truth I did not, however, for her sake I would run with it.

"What you're saying is if Bridie fails this assessment this is the last chance she will have to belong to society and she'll go back to the Cheadle Royal?"

"It's possible if they'll have her back!"

"What do you mean if they have to have her back, why won't they?" This started to worry me. "Where would she go if her assessment doesn't work out?"

"Into a secure facility like Broadmoor or Prison." It was a sombre thought.

"Does Desmond know this?" I suspected his sanity could not take it.

"I haven't told him of this potential outcome."

"Good let us keep it that way, otherwise it would kill him." I was deadly serious, having spent the weekend with him getting her release had become an obsession with him, anything less, even a suggestion she might fail the assessment would destroy him.

"So where do the family or me, come into the equation?"

"If she's going to survive on the outside we have to see her respond effectively to both family and friend's full support behind her, this will be needed for several years."

"Scary!"

"It is Hayden, Desmond is an old man in his eighties, his children are a cold bunch of bastards and quite frankly you're no spring chicken with, as I understand it, your own family to support. I don't see her having a cat in hell's chance if I am honest."

"Thanks for the vote of confidence," with more than a hint of sarcasm in my voice. "What about Bridie does she realise this and how does she feel about it or doesn't she have a choice?"

"Cold, steely dismissive of any facts is the only way I can describe her, from my discussions with Desmond who did not recognise her from his remembered description of being a kind, loving gentile person, the years have clearly taken their toll on her as I am sure you will see when you meet her again." I visibly started and felt a nervousness envelope me. "And right now, please don't tell her but no she doesn't have choice."

"Your joking I wasn't expecting to see her," my heart skipped a beat I felt my face redden, like the young school boy I had once been, when I last set eyes on her. "I remember her as Desmond does, so the coldness is quite surprising."

"It was to me until I met Joseph, Susan and Emma she's exactly like them." I was surprised.

"Raymond I can assure you she was never like them at all." Pleading to him in case it affected his assessment of her.

"Then all the more reason to bring her back to resemble her old self to be recognised by you and Desmond before our assessment is complete." What if she is lost to us, I started to doubt our capabilities.

"I don't understand I thought she was ready to be released." Sure Desmond had suggested as much.

"Or be sectioned again," he looked at me strangely and I felt I am missing something. "You don't know do you? Desmond hasn't told you has he?"

"What hasn't he told me?" Getting frustrated.

"In this country we have a number of mental health patients of a certain age who have been locked up for most of their lives in one institution or another, however they got there." It is recognised by the government the health service failings of the 1950"s and 1960"s must be dealt with." This news to me.

"Surely this would be public knowledge families would be complaining." He shook his head.

"There are less than a hundred patients who fall into this category throughout the United Kingdom, through time the problem is dwindling and probably in twenty years due to illness or death from old age the problem itself will go away. The practice in the last forty years has been so much better." No wonder it has not been newsworthy, with the authorities hoping it would go away and soon doing so.

"Are you saying you've identified all those specific patients?"

"Pretty much yes, there are a small number in private care such as Bridie which will continue while funds are available, however some are in prison and some are in public funded nursing homes not receiving the care they deserve. The majority have no family or have been disowned." A stark reality of asylum closures across the decades. "With most they don't have a Desmond and now a Hayden to fight for them." He smiled.

"Are you saying choosing Bridie is not quite as random as you've suggested or for her own well-being." He just stared knowing I had touched a nerve. "What you're saying, it's not about those who could live normal lives you choose, it is those with families who could cause the most embarrassment for the health service."

"There is an old 19th century ex workhouse currently being renovated in Abington, Oxfordshire. The vast estate, once held some four hundred children, until recently, it has been used as a storage facility when a planning application to build houses, hotel and a shopping mall was submitted, for once, some initiative was shown with a deal being struck for a single three floor wing of the workhouse to be used for these patients. The application recognises the need to take care of the hundred patients and in the meantime the rest of the workhouse will be revitalised, They will be given funding based on the numbers still in care until quite frankly they die, then a further regeneration will occur. I think the word is progress, Bridie is lucky to be supported, funding some private care because should her assessment fall short she will almost certainly end up in the old workhouse albeit modernised."

"So all the problems will be contained in one place?" I was shocked.

"Yes, so we need to work at getting Bridie out of here and back with her family or friends." He gestured towards me. "Let me take you to her then we will talk further."

Confused, I followed him to a small white room barely furnished with a table and chairs I stifled a grin when I saw the huge mirror on one wall, I had seen enough cop television shows to recognise the two-way mirror. While waiting I began to think they could lock me up and no one would ever find me, I stood up and paced the room nervously, the door opened and the grey haired women looked at me without recognition, I thought her to be one of the hospital cleaners before realising it had to be Bridie. It shocked me we both sat down across the table from each other and for a while stared at each other.

"Hi Bridie how are you?" I started awkwardly. "Do you remember me, it's Hayden?"

Her eyes widened and she studied me carefully. No spark and as Raymond said cold, she shrugged her shoulders and looked down at her hands on the table.

I had an idea and decided to try something different.

"Maisie sends her love she cannot wait to see you." I waited for some sign.

The reaction was slow at first like a fuse burning

until it blew.

"Was she released, what was she doing, how can she come here, you're lying?" Her voice had a smoker's gravel to it.

"Bridie, I thought you were once friends," I touched her hands, I was out of my depth, she brushed me aside stood up walked over to the door and started banging to be let out, a male Nurse let her out and I went in search of Raymond.

"How did you get on?" I felt he already knew the answer.

"I didn't, I don't quite know what I expected, who was the woman because I don't believe its Bridie?"

"Desmond said much the same, but who else do you expect it to be?"

"Raymond something's odd, I met the first true love of my life after 50 years and I am sure I was once hers, but there was no recognition at all even if she didn't know my face because of time she should have reacted to my name."

"She in a strange place the Cheadle Royal has been her home for twenty years or more and here she is struggling to cope."

"No it is more, she didn't recognise the significance of me being there and I agree she was emotionally cold, but angry too like she was making me get out of there, she was uncomfortable by me being there, more to the point when I mentioned Maisie she reacted." I played the scene in my mind.

"I'm surprised she reacted at all, probably because she didn't know you."

"She knew who I was, and wanted nothing to do with me, why I wonder?"

"Perhaps you're the one person who can get through to her.?"

"More likely I am the one person who will see who she really is and wants to avoid it at all costs."

"To me as her psychiatrist she's reverting to type, after my meeting with her brother and sisters she behaves as I would expect for someone locked up for fifty year's." He was dismissive of my concerns.

"It cannot be her, has she met her brother and sisters?"

"No they ducked out before I could arrange it."

"It's a pity, it might have told us something."

"Spoken like a true psychiatrist," we laughed. "You asked what the problem was earlier, well one you've seen for yourself and two if anything happens to Desmond his children have made it quite clear Bridie will not be supported."

"Which means she will have to leave private care and move to Abington and thus never be able to get back a normal life," I interrupted.

He nodded.

"Forgive me not being in any way medically inclined, I read through Bridie's medical notes at Desmond's during this last weekend I stayed there with him."

"And?"

"And I have got some questions." I decided to tread slowly and carefully not wishing to damage our relationship.

"Fire away Hayden, in the nicest possible way I'll make allowances for your ignorance." He laughed aloud at me.

"Let us start with why she was put into an asylum in the first place instead of a regular hospital?"

"This was purely, to contain the very real contagious disease, within her own body the tuberculosis had taken control and had a severe impact on the brain she had to be isolated so it was the best place short of a prison." He was not ready for my next question.

"If she was cured why did it take 50 years until now to arrange for her release?" For the first time since we had met he was lost for words, I guessed he knew them, but did not want to tell me.

"It was the sign of the times." He was struggling.

"An unacceptable answer Raymond and you know it, I have read her notes why give her an ECT which is electric shock treatment within days of her arrival?" Given only to mental patients to cure severe depression.

"She would have been depressed at the time."

"Because of leaving her family and having tuberculosis not because she had a mental issue, I remember her back then and she was a normal young girl."

"It was a mistake I admit, not being there I cannot speak for the reasons at the time."

"But the consequences are severe, it induces seizures and she would have been rendered unconscious and the notes suggest she suffered confusion and memory loss."

"Yes, you've done your homework." He confirmed.

"I also read after this treatment a drug therapy course was introduced over and above the treatment for her initial illness." He cringed in front of me knowingly. "What is strange is she was given clozapine and I looked this up too Raymond, this drug was only discovered in the 1950's and licenced for clinical introduction in the 1970's."

"What of it the Doctor's at the time would have felt she needed the drug." He was becoming defensive.

"Raymond, don't you see this drug was given to her in the early 1960's meaning she had been part of a clinical trial for mental patients when she wasn't one." I recalled what Desmond had told me. "Therefore as a result she suffered a movement disorder and extreme weight gains."

"Mistakes were clearly made."

"From what I can gather the potential effects could be Parkinson's or at the very least tremors, Dystonia which is muscle contractions causing repetitive movements and abnormal postures, my God your profession really has done a number on her." I searched my memory for more issues. "Oh yes there's more, stroke potential, thrombosis and pancreatitis."

"Fortunately Bridie has not suffered any of this, with the future looking brighter for her." He is trying to pacify me, but I was not going to let him or his profession off the hook so easily.

"By giving her an ECT and the antipsychotic drug the side effects meant the Darenth Park Sanatorium turned an innocent young teenager with her whole life ahead of her into a mental patient!" I stood up because it is the first time I had put my feelings into words to a professional, I was angry. "It's disgraceful, this could happen in my lifetime. "You mentioned there are about a hundred patients across the country currently being put through assessments how many were like Bridie?"

"I would suggest the majority would not have arrived in quite the tragic circumstances of Bridie London's." Raymond clearly trying to defend his own profession.

"But you don't really know do you?" He shook his head. "What form is the current assessment of her taking?"

"We start with simple things like the history of the patient, any medical issues currently affecting her at the moment, talk to her about likely anxieties, what drugs are currently being prescribed even mental patients get high blood pressure for example." He seemed more comfortable talking of life in his world. "Mostly we observe the patient, general appearance, skin, dry or coloured could mean anaemia, jaundice maybe, eyes, are they focused, body movements, weaknesses, does she cooperate, what are her moods or speech like, attention span, memory, judgement and knowledge."

"Quite thorough." I observed.

"It has to be, she gets a full physical examination, we do an EEG which detects abnormal brain function and a CAT scan which detects abnormal anatomy in a patient, mainly though as said at the start we observe."

"What of Bridie?"

"But for the fact Desmond or you have not recognised her and vice versus she is good to go so to speak, but I think we will hold on for a little while longer." It did not surprise me and it would give me more time.

"Thanks Raymond, I have kept you long enough." We both had enough for now, I noticed him looking at his watch.

"No problem Hayden, let me know if I can help further." He looked relieved I expected to be back soon.

"Now I'm beginning to understand the urgency." Desmond needed me and unknowingly so did Bridie, I was not sure she was my old Bridie, I hoped in time I would find her again.

"I don't think you quite do Hayden."

"What don't I understand?"

"Why do you think Desmond is so anxious to get you on board quickly?" I shook my head.

"He wants Bridie out before he dies."

"Yes that too," he said dismissively. "The other reason being, this is a government led drive as I mentioned earlier."

"Yes."

"Well there is a time limit of two years across the country as a whole and we are halfway through to the deadline with under half the patients assessed."

"I don't get the implications of what you're saying?"

"Those who are not assessed will automatically be moved to Abingdon forever. Meaning, we must get all assessments done with each patient, using our limited resources. There is also a timescale set for every patient and Bridie is rapidly reaching the end of her time."

"So if I or Desmond believe she is not Bridie the person I have seen will end up at Abingdon, whether it's Bridie or not she will be lost in the system forever?"

"About the size of it."

Chapter 9

The amount of documentation I had received weighed heavily on my mind and knew it was time for me to begin trawling through all I had received. By now, Desmond had sent me a dozen of the thirty diaries Bridie had written. All the requested information from each of the three hospitals Darenth the largest, Cheadle Royal next finally the Maudsley had come in. No amount of summarising for me by Claire could ever help with the volumes of notes received on one girl or woman fortunately I had the opportunity to read the medical notes at Desmond's, while he was engrossed with Cedric Bartholomew's journals. I had Cedric Bartholomew's six journals to read written during thirty years of his life at the Darenth Asylum, up to its closure in 1988, as he saw it throughout his career there. I appreciated his son's trust by letting me browse the journals before he writes them as part of a biography of his father for the future generations of the Bartholomew family to enjoy and be proud of, notably hoping he thought of him in such vain sometime in the near future. I had to wrestle them from Desmond who made me promise to return with them the next time I visited him.

   As someone who could barely concentrate on a paperback novel the task of reading the piles of medical notes and journal volumes together with the diaries received so far was daunting.

I had set aside or at least Claire did it for me, a full week free of meetings and the managing of my team, I was ready maybe not necessarily willing but determined to break out of my malaise and get on with it, there was much to learn.

I decided I would first start with Bridie's diaries, pretty much as Desmond had skimming over the more mundane aspects of her hospital life, in particular what she had for breakfast, lunch, tea and dinner, how long it took her to wash and brush her teeth morning and evening, along with the clothes she wore. I wanted to concentrate on the effect the hospital had on her, who she interacted with and attempt to understand her personally and hopefully referencing the main points trying to verify them within both the journals and the medical records.

Although initially Claire had begun copying the diaries, Desmond is now sending the original notebooks to me, Raymond had told him she did not seem bothered they were diminishing so he had not been returning them.

Picking up her first diary I noted scratched on the cover of the first hard cover of the A5 notebook were the words HOME, HOME, HOME. To an untrained eye, she must have been angry when she did it. I could imagine Bridie breaking down in floods of tears pushing her towards sleep.

I pulled the grey blinds down in my office, grabbed a large cup of black coffee and with Claire standing guard I wasn't to be disturbed it was time I let Bridie tell me her story.

Diary one 1963-1964:

Dad's brown raincoat flowed behind him as he strode from the building hurrying to the car park I watched him from my window leaving in our car it brought the pair of us here three hours ago. I screamed after him, I did not want him to leave me here.

"I'll will be back soon Bridie," Papa said. I begged him not to leave me here alone. I have never seen him cry before his shoulders hunched lower than I had ever known.

"It's for the best my darling!" he would not look at me, but kept pointing to the notepads and pens on the bed. I wanted him to take me home with him there and then, not tell me to write when he was gone. I loved him so much, but I could have hated him the moment he left me. The Nurse explained to me, he was doing what he believed was the best for me and loved me very much. It did not feel like it.

"Use them wisely as your personal diaries, one day I'll read what you write," he told me. I watched our black Austin 7 car move slowly crunching on gravel, turning left toward the outer gate of the hospital. He was not hearing me scream after him or chose to ignore me. Papa stopped the car and glanced back up at me. I had a fleeting memory of me and Angela who lived next door to Hayden across the road standing on the back bumper as Papa drove slowly around the block of streets near our home.

I had finally started to read the diaries, but I was not prepared to read my name within the first few pages, I felt myself concentrate harder as it had suddenly become personal.

Waving, screaming and thumping on the window, I was so desperate for Papa not to leave me. He drove out through the hospital gates leaving me, not knowing what will happen next. I saw, briefly, doubt crossing his mind, Papa's grim face raised a smile, a hand gesturing goodbye, we both knew today would change the rest of my life, I felt he didn't want to be my father anymore, I didn't know what I had done, I am only ill.

How I wished he had turned back for me. I wondered if I would ever see him again, people in the grounds below were gawping at me, but I did not care.

Looking at the medical notes, they simply recorded Bridie Beatrice London had arrived on Tuesday 9th April 1963 she was distracted by emotion it read.

I knew from what Desmond had told me during our weekend together he was broken hearted, he had stopped his car outside the asylum gates, out of her sight. He could not drive on because of the tears streaming down his face, an hour passed before he finally drove away from the sanatorium and his dear Bridie, he too had not a clue what to do next except to go back home and comfort a distraught Josey.

I picked up her diary and began reading again.

I have been here for three days now and the commotion from the corridor woke me in the middle of the night, I quickly pulled on my nightgown and looked outside of the door surprisingly it was not locked. I saw a young girl screaming, struggling within the grasp of three Nurses, one by his hands around her back and chest underneath her arms and the other, his hands locked around her legs as she was writhing trying to break free. The female Nurse with them attempted to placate her as she forced her knees down to try and keep them straight, by gripping her legs tightly, they marched her out of sight through the double doors leading to another corridor of the building, presumably back where she had escaped from. The lights dimmed, odd I think we are in prison and not in a hospital, it does feel this way, I must try to escape and see what happens. Where would I go? How far is it to get home? How would I get there? I wondered where they were taking her, I thought of following and I started to when a woman I had never seen before brushed past me.

"Return to your room Miss London nothing to be seen out here," she barked, it was the first time I noticed the sea of faces peering out of their own rooms, I wasn't alone in watching, I smiled at them, nervously they all began to retreat into their own spaces they seemed frightened. The lights went out, the hall in darkness, but I watched the stout woman in a navy blue jacket and light skirt disappear into a room further down the corridor a Nurse and Doctor followed her, she had a fat bum.

Papa suggested I write everything down, I have nothing else to do I will hide the diary somewhere. I hate it here, I have been stuck in this room since I arrived, I only go out of it when they want to do tests, and they have been sticking needles in me.

My room is green, light green. There are no pictures on the walls although there are marks where two might have been. I started to imagine what they were like, vegetables, fruit or flowers or like Papa's he has a world cup Chile 1962 football poster in the garage, reminding me of children in the road playing football. Some of the wall paint in one corner of the room is gone it is like a face looking down on me. I will call it Toby Papa has a beer jug at home he takes it down to the pub each Friday, looks just like it, can be my friend, I have drawn a circle around the chips on the wall and added some ears.

A wooden wardrobe contains my blue raincoat, brown jumper and skirt hanging up and on the shelves changes of underwear, white socks and my black flat shoes, I wore them for school. There is our old brown suitcase I wondered what is in it I will look later. I wonder if I can go out.

Desmond and Josey had packed her suitcase with clothes and photographs in the hope he may be able to remember the family.

There is a washbasin with a small crack to the right side edge with soap, toothbrush, paste and a brush on top in between the taps. The white toilet is in one corner, a toilet roll on the table, I hoped no one could see me going to the toilet it would be rude. There is a peephole in the door, which is not wooden like at home. The bed is made of iron and has a thin blue stripe mattress, one pillow and a heavy blue blanket. There is a small table to write on and chair to sit on. There is a light bulb swinging from the ceiling with a loop in the hanging cord, no shade and no switch inside the room, but one in the hallway for each I have noticed. A brown patterned rug with small red blocks it looks dirty to me. A window with a dozen foot square windows the top three open but it is too high for me to see out of, with bars to stop us getting out. The locks on the door are big it has a sliding door opening at the bottom I did not know why wonder if I could get through it?

They keep telling me I am very sad and needing

help, they took me into another room along the corridor, and a big round light at the centre hurt my eyes. The Nurse, I don't know her name she spoke foreign, said they would give me an electric shock to help me, I was scared, Papa once had a shock when he plugged in our television, he said it hurt him.

I have been asleep for a couple of days, the girl next door told me, it's the first time I had met her, Deborah I think her name is. I cannot remember she looked familiar. Not sure how long I have been here, it seems an age. Nurse Rhona said I would need an operation to help cure me perhaps I can go home soon.

Toby I am so sad and taking loads of pills, I keep getting dizzy I have to go to the toilet a lot, do not look it is rude.

I judged several weeks had passed by as the diary filled with the food she ate, what she liked or not in her sandwiches, overall it appeared from her writing she was mentally deteriorating. The next set of writings seemed different probably because she had been there a while her first operation had been, according to her medical notes, six weeks after she had arrived at the sanatorium.

They're taking me today Toby for an operation apparently I have water in my head, I didn't think I drank a lot of water, it causes my headaches, I'll tell you all about it if I remember, I cannot seem to speak properly.

I noted she was talking to Toby through her diaries. She had highlighted an ECT I spoke to

Raymond about it and her 'shunt' which Desmond described to me guessing the drugs made her slur words.

Although feeling frustrated for Bridie, I recognised she wrote the words over 50 years ago. I wondered if the Deborah she had described in the room next door was the same person Harry had known.

Cedric's first Journal mentioned the incident in the corridor Bridie had written of, the journal opening page showed a letter from Cedric to his family:

Cedric Bartholomew
Personal Journals
Volumes 1-6
Period 1963-1988
Darenth Park Mental Institution (Asylum) Kent
　In January 1963, I began my career in Psychiatry as a Junior Doctor and by August 1988 had progressed to an experienced Consultant Psychiatrist as head of my own department. The intervening years although regarded as career progression on my behalf have led to a catalogue of emotions, ranging from the extreme difficulties of the patients, trauma faced and inflicted onto those staff caring for them and the overall commitment by both staff and I, in an attempt to pursue the wellbeing for as many patients possible. Only for the majority of times to end in much sadness and tragedy, with those rare occasions when the reuniting of families produce sheer joy is success achieved and thus moving some way into feeling the overall approach, is in fact, worthwhile.
　To my family, especially Andrew my son, who

found it in his heart to follow in my footstep's medically, I thank you from the bottom of mine. The support shown to me by my family in my life and for the writing of these journals leads me to hope one day, they will provide an aide memoir for the future good of care in this field.

While I wish to have been a better family man and in particular a better father to Andrew, I can only hope the devotion to my chosen field and patients will mean you will at least think kindly of me in my passing.
Cedric

Browsing the journals I realised this was more a history of events, for patients and their stories rather than pure medical detail, I was grateful.

Then the young Doctor was passionate about working with patients who are "mentally challenged," I discovered he had highlighted at the beginning of his tenure at Darenth the contrasting nature of two young girls to make his points on the diverse nature of the institution. One already in the asylum cold as an ice pick and one who had arrived within his first few months, a gentile, kindly soft natured girl. Both I would later discover to be Maisie and Bridie respectively.

He painted a picture of bleakness and despair amongst staff, whose efforts futile and hopelessness in the levels of care achieved, the dictatorial way the administrators ran the asylum and one administrator in particular, called Jennifer Granger whom he described as 'a brute force of nature'. This led to a high turnover rate in staff numbers and as if in response a high number of patient issues.

"What the hell was that all about?" Jennifer

Granger, the hospital's administrator was angry and looked hard at the young Doctor Cedric Bartholomew and Staff Nurse Jackson standing before her.

"This type of spectacle does nothing for patient morale except to unnerve them and thereby promoting the idea they cannot leave the place." She referring to the manhandling of the distraught young girl carried away by the three Nurses in full view of the rest of the patients on the ward.

"Which they cannot Miss Granger!" Cedric stated the obvious.

"I do know Doctor, but why do they need to know?" she emphasised.

"Why not, if they're staying here for the long term surely it's kinder for them to know?" He long suspected Miss Granger did not want any more letters going out to their families describing the sanatorium as a prison. At times she would censored them quite heavily making sure the way she ran the asylum could not be questioned in any way.

"Is this what happened, which one of you spoke to her and what did you say?"

Nurse Jackson nervously shifted in front of her.

"Well?" Jennifer Granger had the look defying anyone not to tell her the truth.

"She was trying to pull at the window to open it and it was banging against the bars in the middle of the night, so I tried to placate her." Nurse Jackson owned up.

"What did you say to her?" Granger grew impatient.

"I said if she carried on her mother would not be able to come and see her." She did not see anything wrong with trying to get the child to behave better.

"What do you know of her, both of you?" she looked from the terrified Nurse to the young Doctor who did not appear to care much for the administrator.

They both shrugged.

"Evelyn's mother is dead, she died soon after Evelyn became sick, which caused her to be frequently upset, her only real comfort is she believes her mother visits each night and kisses her when she's asleep. Guess what you've told her, her dead mother will not be allowed to come, how is this caring for the patient?" Jennifer Granger made it her business to delve into every facet of each child; she was determined to understand the very fabric of every child in her care it is what made her so good at her job.

"I didn't think, sorry," the young Doctor Bartholomew bowed his head realising their error, he had learnt a valuable lesson and was determined to be more careful when dealing with the administrator in the future.

Nurse Jackson offered a similar apology.

"No I doubt you both don't think get out of my sight the pair of you." Jennifer Granger softened towards her Nurse as she was leaving. "And Rhona, do we really want to tell the girls and boys, they can never go home or their families have abandoned them because they've become too ill or become so disruptive at home? My dear girl they'd all try to leave!" She hardened towards them again. "So let's not, have any more nice little chats with our charges do I make myself clear?"

Both of them nodded, Cedric had never forgotten.

"Now go and sort out Evelyn," she dismissed them with a wave.

Jennifer Granger ran the hospital and loved it but it was becoming impossible when Doctor's, Nurse's and patients thought they knew better, the girl would have to be put into a straightjacket for a while, until she calmed down. What the Doctor, Nurse and patient never knew, is beneath her hard exterior she really cared for Evelyn. Once she was back calmly on the ward, Jennifer would wait until she was asleep and then kiss her goodnight, as her mother would have done, unknown to the administrator Cedric had spotted her going into Evelyn's room and seen her do it. She had been doing this on a weekly basis for the months the girl had been in the asylum. Gradually she would phase it out by suggesting her mother was gradually departing from this life, but for now, she acted as the girl's surrogate mother. Cedric had seen another side of the hard nose woman.

Bridie spoke out loud as she wrote, she had heard the raised voices coming out of the room at the end of the corridor everyone did, then through the small crack in the door she had left open, watched the Doctor and Nurse pass her room walking towards the corridor from where the screaming girl had been taken. She heard them say how angry the woman had been and how the Nurse had made a mistake, she closed her room door and picked up her diary to write.

"What shall I write about now Toby?" she looked at him in the corner, about me then, "I am 13 and my name is Bridie Beatrice London, nice to meet you Toby my middle name is Granma's, Mum and Papa have a greengrocer's on the corner of our road in Peckham. Mum's name is Josephine Papa calls her Josey, not us, my brother and sisters. Papa's name is Desmond, he doesn't like anyone to call him Des, keeps saying he refuses to be compared to the famous crooner of a singer, they're both old, but not as old as Grandma was, she died suddenly last year why or how? Not sure, we were all very upset.

   I met a very pretty girl today she has been here longer than I have, she said she saw me arrive some weeks ago her name is Maisie Belling someone said we look alike. I hope we become friends.

   I think I'm skinny, there was a horrible girl in the restaurant today who is a real bully, she keeps pushing around the smaller girls, she pushed me when I was putting my breakfast tray onto the metal trolley shelves causing me to drop it, one of the dinner lady's shouted at me. As I bent down to pick up the dropped bowl and spoon she shoved me to the ground laughing calling me a stick insect, Maisie ran to me picking me up which I thought was nice. The bully girl laughed at us, I was frightened of her.

   Maisie went over to her and hit her face with her forehead causing blood to pour from the girls nose, Maisie punched her in the stomach and the girl fell to the floor and then kicked her hard warning her never to pick on me again, Maisie became my friend today. The bully, Deborah, ran away crying, I hope she is not too hurt. I thought she was my friend she was in the room next door for a while and they moved her.

   I realised I had my answer about Deborah.

What do you think Toby am I skinny? Papa used to say I am tall for my age, I hope Mummy's stopped crying now she didn't want me to come here, before I left she shouted at the Doctor. Mum and Papa had been arguing, Papa said I had to go for the sake of the others and customers, I did not know what he meant. All he said was it could be catching, I did not understand why can I not go home now?

I am in this place, because they said I am very ill, something to do with my brain they said? She could not spell the word so looked at her notes clipped to the end of her bed, she wrote down Tuberculosis.

I imagine Mum's at home above our shop right now with Emma and Susan, they are my two younger sisters and Joseph is my brother, Mum probably would be combing and brushing my hair or one of my sister's now. Emma has light hair and is fat she eats all the cakes, only comes into my room when hungry to eat my sweets, she is as high as my elbow and four.

Susan is a bit bigger and six, according to Joseph she has mouse coloured hair, she's a beanpole eats vegetables all the time, Joseph is ten as big as I am but stronger, he pushes me around a lot I love him. I miss the smell of the earthy vegetables especially the potatoes we used to eat from the shop.

I used to go to the market in Papa's van to pick up the vegetables and fruit for the shop, best of all when we would buy the flowers, he used to let me choose some to sell in our shop, mostly I chose lilies I like them.

Something contagious they said it was the Doctors, who agreed with Papa surely they could catch it, so what, we could all be here together. I hope Hayden is missing me, Angela who lives next door to him, will try to tempt him away from me, she had better be careful or I will bash her when I leave here, I hope it will not be long. I love him, I remember, we watched the first television appearance of the Beatles together on the 625 show with Jimmy Young a few months back on the BBC. We were watching them in his house with his Mum, Dad and Sister, it was so romantic he put his arm around my shoulders while we watched them sing my favourites 'From me to you', 'Thank you girl' and 'Please, Please me'. His mum made us tea and sandwiches, we kissed and cuddled, I wish it could be more, It was Easter Saturday April, we ate our chocolate Easter eggs. If I closed my eyes, I can see and feel him cuddle me, it's going to be his birthday soon I think, I want to buy him something, I hope Papa will let me see him when I leave here, I'll write him soon, perhaps he can come and visit. I used to watch him from my room delivering papers for the shop around the corner every morning, sometimes he used to wave up at me watching from my room. I wish Mum would come and visit me."

"The girl's extremely sick surely we should call her father?"
"Not for us to worry about Nurse Jackson I have seen many a girl react to the drugs we give them like this." Cedric Bartholomew was not going to involve the hospital administrator or the family, Bridie was his problem now.

I had come to the end of the first diary and even now, I had started to skim pages with Bridie discussing the daily food intake and its taste at some length.
As I finished the first diary I tried to put some perspective on the years it covered 1963 and 1964,

the Beatles released 'Please, Please Me', there was Profumo, a cabinet minister had an affair, would we care these days I doubted it. The Great Train Robbery happened and John F Kennedy the American President assassinated.

I opened the next diary.

Diary Two 1965 – 1966:

I quickly grabbed this blank notebook for my new diary, I have not written for a while; Toby has been quiet lost a piece of his ear I noticed. Been sick a lot and the Nurses said I have been asleep for a week or more, I passed out and they have been quite worried, I told them I did not like the pills they gave me but they would not listen. I stopped taking any after the first horrible ones, washing down the sink. They have not found the first diary I hid behind the ridge on top of the old brown wardrobe along with the other notebooks.

They said today, I might be able to get up. I am stopping now I cannot think of what to say and am already so, so tired. My head hurts, painful to touch. I heard the Nurse say something to the Doctor about me catching poor Mary's tuberculosis as well but who is Mary?

Coughed up blood today I am not going to eat. I am tired and it is late, have to stop writing for now, night Toby. I am not sure what the day is, but I have been asleep for a long time and while my bedding is changed, I am sitting in the hallway on a metal chair; watching the corridor, which leads to the common room where everyone meets. I am cold I hear loud voices they told me to stay outside of my room and not to move.

My head hurts, my hair is shorter it's been cut why I cannot remember, when touching my head it's got a bandage around it, it feels sore, I need a mirror to see there isn't one in my room I'm very sleepy and slow in walking. I saw Maisie and waved at her, she blew me a kiss and went in the common room. I love her.

I turned to check the journals for any mention of this.
Cedric's Journal: Apparently, a disturbance broke out in the common room, the instigator said to be Bridie London by one of the girls involved, suggested she had been acting crazy. Bridie, during the commotion, hit her head against a protruding corner of a framed wall painting hanging on one of the walls. She promptly passed out and when waking she could not remember anything. Prior to this, she had been told to sit outside in the corridor while her room was being cleaned she disobeyed and followed other girls into the common room.

During the following day's Bridie complained of severe headaches, she was continually vomiting and upon examination rather than bruising there appeared to be severe swelling to the back of her head, clearly intracranial pressure, edema or swelling inside the brain. The concern is because of her previous condition of Meningitis Tuberculosis it may trigger infection, which could be fatal.

The decision was made to intervene surgically Cedric's team monitored her closely providing Oxygen, IV fluids and medication to reduce the swelling this did not have any effect so the decision to use a procedure called Ventriculostomy involving a small incision in the skull to insert a drainage tube. This did appear to resolve the problem and the patient although feeling very tired, depressed and with some movement challenges was progressing well.

This corresponds to her medical notes; I turned back to Bridies second diary, halfway through it:

The hallway is green same as my room, more voices, my head aches, catching my breath the room next door to mine opened, a girl dark haired peered out waving to me, I drifted in and out of sleep. As I waved back to her, my Nurses had finished my room. The girl disappeared back into her room. The name on her door is Florence Mason. I had a fit today.

Cedric's Journal: "Come on Bridie, time to get back to bed and put your oxygen mask back on you're looking breathless," this was Cedric's first real patient since arriving at the asylum, he was determined to look after her as best he could.
Diary: I like Nurse Rhona she has ringlets in her hair I would like mine to be like hers she is nice to me.
Toby I heard today about Eve, you know the girl who was struggling in the corridor she has left us. The rumour is she died, but nobody is too sure, I hope not.

Cedric's Journal: Evelyn Marchant died today, it is my first patient loss here or anywhere in fact, I do hope there are not too many going forward. She was kept sedated unfortunately this day there was a delay in administering the follow on medication. Of course, there will be an enquiry, the nightmarish screams reverberated throughout the corridors and the sounds will live with me forever. She dropped to her knees as Nurse Rhona and I flung open her door clutching her chest, a kind of peace spread across her face as she fell forward into my arms, no amount of resuscitation would ever bring her back she was where she wanted to be.

As I walked through Cedric's Journals something odd struck me, I flipped through the pages quickly confirming my find. Randomly I noticed there were numbers, likely referencing further notes separate from these. Andrew had mentioned Cedric's notes, five pages towards the end of journal six the number 32 discreetly appeared at the bottom left corner. Did this mean 32 incidents he could not put in the diaries for his family to see, I began wondering more about what was missing from the journals rather than what was in them. I wondered if Andrew realised and Desmond had noticed.

Diary: I met the girl in the room next door again, Florence, she is 16 same as me, I think everyone in the ward has the same size of room.
I spoke to Maisie today in the common room she is a bit older than I am, I think 17 and she has been here longer in another room down the next corridor, said she does not like it here. I am not sure if she has a Mum and Dad, she never speaks of them and they never visit her. She told me she watched me arrive and saw my dad leave. I remembered her helping me with the bully and thanked her she said she would always look after me. I do love her she is so beautiful.
I said I thought it was a hospital, but she said this was a 'menial animal' don't know what it means, I know they call it Darenth Park, and in some place

called Dartford in Kent.

Maisie said she had been here a long time and there were 14 other's, we were all 'Kwanteened'; unsure what this means either I did not ask in case I looked stupid, but I think we have to be left alone. Maybe it is why Mum and Dad never come.

We had our food together in the common room, met some of the other girls and boys, I wonder what they are eating at home vegetables from the shop I bet, tired now, I'm going to rest, will write again soon. Toby is looking after me.

Diary Three: 1967 – 1968

Maisie and I are spending most days together we try to fool everyone and put our hair the same way and wear the same dress we are like twins; people seem frightened of us except for Harry he is dishy and got muscles. He is the hospital gardener we try to keep him talking in his shed, he gives us tea and biscuits Maisie has a crush on him, he tells her she is too young. We think he likes Nurse Rhona. When she comes to find where we are, she is always flirting and giggling with him.

Maisie and Deborah had a fight today and I got the blame because I look like Maisie. Sometimes, I am not sure I like being her twin.

Maisie nearly stabbed Nurse Rhona I am glad she put down her knife.

Deborah hurt a boy today she kicked him because he called her fat. She cannot come to the common room with the rest of us for a week.

Maisie had an operation today she has had a bad back for a while. She walks like an old woman sometimes.

Unsure how long I have been here it has to be years I have almost finished this diary. I must hide it and start a new one. I asked one of the Nurses the date. She said its 1968 and it is nearly Christmas. I wonder if Mum and Dad will visit and bring me presents.

Unfortunately, I could not check on the operation Maisie had.

Medical notes/Event recording: The common room, the hub of the sanatorium gave rise to all the emotions and Nurse Rhona Jackson sitting in the far corner of the room away from the tables in the middle, liked to listen to the chatter of the girls as they swapped stories of their families and friends. Today they were talking of the boys who were walking in a line in the gardens out on their nature walks, the girls had been waving to them from the common room windows. Once or twice, she had to warn them about falling out of the open windows they were in the only place where bars were not at them. Segregated from the boys made the fascination all the greater, so each girl chose a particular boy as their fictitious boyfriend. The problem Nurse Jackson realised is what started out as harmless fun amongst them turned into something quite violent when two girls singled out the same unsuspecting boy.
As tempers began to rise she called out to them all to calm down, but under the surface there became an angry couple of girls at the centre.
"Calm down the pair of you," Girls turned around as if noticing her in the room for the first time. "Yes you Deborah and you too Bridie."
A push by Deborah to Bridie escalated the issue, the shoving became a show with the others girls in a circle, within a split second egging on the two girls

to fight, dinner plates, cups and cutlery spread on the floor as a table was up ended. She tried to get through to the front of the circle of girls quickly. Only to see Bridie, had not only knocked Deborah to the floor, but she had picked up a plate, then looking around at the crowd who were edging her on, smiled at them and brought it down hard and squarely on her face, causing blood to seep out from the cuts above and below her left eye as she struck. Then seeing a knife on the floor she picked it up and pushed it down hard toward the injured girl's body, only stopping, when Nurse Jacksons screamed above the baying crowd of girls.

"Bridie, put the knife down at once, now this minute!" it was enough to make her hesitate, but not before she saw the shaking of the head and pleading look in the eyes of her close friend Maisie Belling as she came towards her. The coldness in the eyes of Bridie London sent shivers down Rhona's spine, as she was ready to use it and before deciding to drop it to the floor she stabbed at the girls shoulder.

As Rhona picked up Bridie's knife the room populated with staff, filling with security, Doctor's, more Nurses and the hospital administrator, who dispersed the girls back to their rooms including Bridie and tended to Deborah's cut face and the shoulder stab wound.

The medical records update: Bridie has been described a risk patient prone to violence. The records also show Bridie had become a very forceful child, prone to lashing out on occasions, without warning, this was unexplained.

I had my own theory, knowing how gentle Bridie had appeared to be within Cedric's journals so far and through her writings during the previous two or three years. According to what I read, together with my own memory of her, I truly believe any operation would not change her character certainly not to the extent into being violent, I did not believe it, Maisie and Bridie had swopped identities. It had to be Maisie who was the aggressor under the guise of Bridie's name, and Nurse Jackson had mistook the two.

Disturbingly, according to the medical notes, Deborah Wealdon intended revenge.

The writing became sketchy, Bridie had scribbled for pages and pages of, most of it about clothes, food, how Toby looked and, nonsense such as, who is behind a light switch to turn it on. How many bricks on a wall and thoughts such as why does a chair and table have four legs each when she has only two to stand. Much of the notes were illegible and by now, I realised her writing only improved when she had something, she thought Toby or the world ought to know, hopefully, the time will come when Bridie will tell me her own story without the need to read from the diaries.

Diary Four, 1969 -1970:
We hit another girl today Toby, I got angry she tried to steal my boyfriend, so we hit her, I am becoming frightened, they have locked me in. I became so angry and everyone was shouting for it to stop. I am sad today I have a headache, I wish Mummy were here. She frightened me today I am going to avoid her.

I did not understand this last line who was she talking about? I suspected Maisie or Deborah.

Diary: It has been days now since I have seen anyone, the food tray put through the sliding part of the door at the bottom where a hand appears and not opening the locked door itself. I have not seen a single face, they shout at me to wash and make sure the toilet is clean. I hate them.

Cedric Journal: Their parents would have to be informed and the girl needs moving, she was getting better until Bridie lashed out at her. I note here Ms Grangers refusal to involve any parents however, she did suggest we should isolate the injured girl until she overcomes her facial and shoulder injuries, she thinks she will be well enough for me to sign off to go home. I objected on the grounds, the injured girl presents a risk to others. Unfortunately, for her, this time she had met her match from a much stronger willed individual. Agreement between all staff is we will monitor the situation.

"Excellent Doctor no-one ever need to hear of the incident again."

"Trouble is I don't think this is a one off."

"What do you mean? Bridie has not done this before has she?"

"No but I'm aware she craves attention and there has been some suggestion by the Nurses they've been bullying the other children."

"What on earth for?"

"She tells everyone who will listen of her love for a boy called Hayden who will come for her one day, she gets upset when they laugh at her."

"Utter nonsense she should have forgotten him by now, but let's keep an eye on her."

My heart jumped a beat as I read this, I was grateful she had me firmly locked in her memories.

Diary: I have started to make friends again with the others since they let me go out of my room again, Maisie and I have met a couple of the boys, we went into their corridor, not supposed to. One tried to cuddle me I told them I was not interested as I expect my Hayden will visit soon, I wish he would, they laughed at me I became angry again.

Sorry Toby, I know it's been weeks since I have picked this up, no sign of Mum or Dad, or Hayden, he has forgotten me by now, I cannot remember what he looks like.

I could not find Deborah today I hope she is ok it was my 20th birthday yesterday they did not come.

Cedric's Journal: Deborah Wealdon is in one of the high-risk units today.

Diary: Maisie's idea was not working too well for me. She said I could have fun with the boys and Hayden would never know so I would not feel guilty we could play tricks on the Nurses. She said Deborah would do it if I decided not to.

I did not understand this diary note by Bridie either.

Diary: Several Doctors came to see us all today, I am no better, they have given me different pills, I could not see Maisie today she has not been very well lately. I think she is sleeping a lot I hope she has kept the secret.

All of us, except Maisie, went outside for a short time into the garden today, the freshness of air hit our faces and I felt cold, I looked across at the car park in hope of seeing Papa. The hospital gates were open.

I wanted to go back in and get my jumper but the Nurse would not let me. I wondered where Maisie was. I asked Nurse Rhona who said she was very, very tired.

One of the horrid boys called us skinny today and was making fun at us holding each other arm in arm he said Deborah and I were like twins. She hit him picking up a heavy stone, she kept hitting him hard, and he made her so angry I begged her to stop watching him fall down and hit his head, bleeding badly on to the ground. Two male Nurses put me back into my room and locked the door.

Later in the day Nurse Rhona came to see me as Maisie was in intensive care in another adjacent hospital, I hoped she would be back soon.

I had another fit today.

Noting the writing trivialities of a young woman together with medical records noting every cut, graze, hurt fingers, aching knees and growing pains. Cedric's Journal's, thorough as they were the majority of his notes had no relevance to Bridie at all.

As I read on through the extensive papers, disappointed as not one of the notes corresponded to the numbers I found in the journals with mostly mundane comments and very little reference to Bridie skipping over as much as I thought I could, keeping the journals and medical notes as reference points for the diaries.

Picking up the fifth one, I was tired of them, Bridie was now probably about twenty-one with the diary year being 1971, by now the writing although scant had developed into a more serious tone and took this as a sign of her becoming of age. I noticed every comment or sentence followed as if it was one long day. I kept reading, but although each diary normally covered two years, it was difficult to pinpoint the days or months when something actually happened.

Diary five 1971-1972
I do not want to write anymore today, I doubt I will ever see my family again and she has done this to me. I wish he would stop touching me.

At this point, I decided I would record short details at 5-year time points unless anything particular occurred. Bridie had turned 21 just as the age of majority was lowered to 18, the Conservatives won the General Election and Jimi Hendrix died, how much of this Bridie would have been aware of I could only guess.

I picked up on Bridie's despair at this time her teenage years all but gone, what bothered me was the last two comments 'and she has done this to me' I wondered who she was talking about? 'I wish he would stop touching me'. I did not understand both these comments and felt only Bridie could tell me, but I had to find her first.

Cedric's Journal: "I told you Jennifer," over time both Jennifer Granger and the young Doctor had become more familiar with each other.
"I know Cedric, what can we do?"
"We need to check her medication, it's either not right for her or she's not taking it."
"Don't the Nurses watch over her while she takes them?
"I very much doubt it, I'll check."

"We have to make sure we document every incident fully, down track there will be decisions to be made about our lovely Bridie." Jennifer Granger had seen this before, she knew with sadness, the girl was heading toward permanent committal.

Bridie's serious tone had continued and along with it her handwriting had altered imperceptibly, slight but I noticed it had changed nevertheless, I dismissed it as her growing up.

Diary: Florence Mason walked into my unlocked room yesterday, it is the first time she had been well enough to mingle with the rest of the wards patients she is very quiet and shy, I took her around the ward and showed her the garden outside, she told me she had no one who cared about her. An only child her Mother died in childbirth and her Father left when she started to get ill. She had been in foster care for as long as she could remember.

During the past week, six of the girls had visitors, and a few patients have gone home. I felt let down and very jealous of them. No one came for me I asked why I was still here. They said I was too ill to leave. I cried a lot today.

A horrid boy called me a zombie maybe because of the dark rings around my eyes I could not be sure. She hurt him for me.

The Nurses say I am not eating enough. "You'll waste away if you're not careful," one said, I am so tired.

"You'll never be able to leave if you never get well," I do so want to go home.

I fell over today and cut my head on the edge of the door, I stayed in bed. I have been hiding my pills, they are too hard to swallow they make me sick.

The gate screeched and made me jump, I looked out of my window nobody else had heard the noise. I remembered my father looking back up to my room on the second floor when he waved to me the first day he left me behind it was a long time ago.

I went out of the hospital doors and walked the path to the large metal gates walking through them I was expecting alarm bells to ring out today, but nothing happened, I remembered, I took a very deep breath and turned to my right as Papa's car did. I frightened myself not knowing which way to go. I went back inside quickly.

Allowed to go out again today, it is very sunny.

I started to walk around the gardens, underneath the trees toward the large open gates I walked carefully looking around to see if anyone had noticed me over by the outside wall of the garden, I touched it and followed its curve as it led to the wrought iron gates, the entrance of the hospital. I was able to hold on to the bars on the gate, it moved with my weight pushing past it. I met Harry again today.

"Hello again I know you don't I? Who is it today Bridie, Maisie, Deborah or Florence?" Harry spoke to me and treated me not as a patient but normal, he walked me back through the gate. People ran up towards us both and he assured them we were ok. They ushered me quickly back into the building but left me in no doubt, I could not leave without permission.

I turned laughed at him and went back inside with them.

They found out about my pills today as I was moved, they fell out onto the floor they were in my small wash bag. The Nurse said no wonder I was not getting any better, it could damage me permanently I am not sure what she meant.

I am feeling very weak my head feels like a lead weight. They are watching me take my pills now, I asked about Maisie and the Doctor said she was in the secure unit but I know they are there because I hear screams and shouts all the time. I wish they would let me see her. They keep saying not until I am better.

Diary six 1973-1974:

The Doctor came and said I may need another operation, I asked for my Mum, but he said Mum and Dad had signed already, didn't understand and don't think I like this Doctor Lavery, he is different to Dr Bartholomew. He does not come to this part of the hospital very often, he is always touching and prodding my head, it hurts when he does it.

They have dressed me in a flowered gown, the back is open I must be quick as they are coming back for me soon. I think I am going to have an operation today I am so very tired I must hide the diaries.

This diary was on my bedside table when I awoke from the operation, did I write this, could not remember my head hurts, got lots of bandages. I am in a different room where's Toby this room is yellow I miss him. Why I am here? Maisie is returning to us soon as Florence might be going home or being moved, lucky her.

I realised I had skimmed this diary as quickly as I could, because of the sameness I got through it by completing only half of it. I pulled them all together placing the six I had read together and flipped through all the other ones stopping periodically in the hope of finding something of note. I would take the time to read them all more fully later, right now I needed to glean information as quickly as possible.

Through each diary, medical notes and records I have worked my way through, gradually the girls, Bridie, Maisie, Deborah and Florence turned into women. Florence never went home having no family to support her. The girls constantly rotated through the assessment wards without changes to their lives at the sanatorium and as a group would meet in the common room most days.

The boys Bridie wrote about, the girls crushes, likes and dislikes of those they made boyfriends whether fictitious or real, those boys turning into men and with a different perspective offered on the growing ages of the boys now being older men. The girls jealousies and their arguments the same, I gauged their medical records would reflect their health approaching middle age. Even the food they ate hardly ever changed. How they viewed each other generally as women and Cedric's journal, which I read fully, reflecting the realities of each day suggesting a sinister under tone of progressive violence amongst the inmates. Particularly it appeared by the four women and significantly, what the staff thought of them for being the likely ringleaders for most of the disturbances taking place amongst and towards the other mental patients.

The records show an assessment had been undertaken by the National Health Service and as an outcome directed all patients in the sanatorium should either be officially sectioned or, to save costs be sent home. A single page risk assessment for each patient was completed. In order, to retain the funding for the sanatorium, if a patient deemed a risk or at risk to society, they had to be committed.

Despite Cedric's Journal notes describing the unfairness of the methods undertaken the four girls were each sectioned, only Bridie had any family who could question the decision, unfortunately, the London's were never consulted.

1980 saw Robin Cousins win the gold medal at the winter Olympics for figure skating, the Iranian embassy siege by terrorists in Knightsbridge and the Marlborough diamond is stolen both in London, sadly, John Lennon was shot dead in New York.

The girls were still living at the sanatorium.

1985, the first ever mobile phone call was made, BBC's EastEnders went on air for the first time and is still going today, Live Aid raises 50 million pounds. Bridie is 36.

1988, Bridie's final year at the Darenth Park sanatorium meant she was a year off her 40th Birthday, Comic Relief was born, as is BBC's Red Nose Day, Pan Am flight 103 explodes at Lockerbie killing 270 people.

Bridie's comment in her *Diary 13: 1987 -1988* about a violent incident occurring with Rhona read as follows:

I heard Nurse Rhona left us today I was sad she didn't say goodbye, I wanted to say sorry to her we were only playing with the knife we found in the kitchen area she only bled a little, when I left her to rest on the floor.

I am writing this now because they have locked us in our rooms.

I heard sirens today and an Ambulance came.

A police officer wanted to know what had happened in the kitchen, I told them we were playing with Nurse Rhona and she decided to see if it would hurt her, when she sat down on the floor she said she was ok.

She will be moving soon to another part of the hospital, I wonder what it would be like. She appeared strange toward me.

Cedric journal: Nurse Rhona Jackson left us today she has suffered another trauma today at the hands of one of the women in her care on the secure unit the person had stabbed her for little reason over some petty argument. I'm particular saddened as the women appeared to be improving since being back on the ward with the other women she is used to, unfortunately the woman in her care had also been doing well until this latest incident.

This was one too many incidents for her, I would be afraid for Rhona if she stayed, at least the person will be confined in the secure unit until she leaves for prison where violent patients are better dealt, with little trust of the individual. Following an investigation and in depth interrogation of her close confidants, patients and staff had suffered at her hands during the many years it was time to close the chapter and prepare her for the closure of Darenth Park Asylum.

Florence Mason died today although she once had parents they were no longer alive so no next of kin was recorded, a family existed somewhere although not established where, it was very sad.

I was surprised at the wording of Cedric's text he would normally name names it was the first time I realised he was hiding something it was unexpected. The number 16 written in the left hand corner.

I found myself feeling sorry for all the women who had been at the sanatorium including Rhona Jackson, however, my interest is with Bridie and her release.

Although skimming through her diaries there was no mention of Florence Mason's death or what had happened. Initially, I guessed, Bridie had not been involved this time, but I was surprised at no mention of her given they were close friends unless she was purposely told not to write about her, the next question raised would then have to be why?

I decided to put down the diaries, medical notes, Cedric's Journals and realised I needed time to think, I have been frustrated since I met Bridie. Not knowing quite what to expect I realised it was not what I expected by any means. I knew I had not found the Bridie I remembered, agreed she would never be the same as she was, but there was not a spark of recognition for me especially now I had read a number of her diaries from the early days.

Originally, I was consuming her every thought and yet now I no longer existed within them. The later diaries appeared not to have the same quality of writing about them, in the early years the writing was prolific; now, the writing is sporadic I couldn't understand it. With Penny at home being cold towards me and getting nowhere with Bridie, I dreaded seeing Desmond again I was failing him as well as myself.

Instinctively Claire tapped on my office window to interrupt me.

"What the problem? Come on talk! You been stuck in here best part of a week now immersed in papers and you look as if you could hang yourself," she knew me so well.

"Ok the fact is I'm getting nowhere." Thoroughly

depressed even by the sound of my own voice.

"Explain to me where you want to be, surely this is about you getting to grips with Bridie's story and to justify the support you give her and Desmond when she's released to Penny?" Trust Claire to provide clarity when I really needed it.

"There's more to it?" Claire decided to close the door and sit down.

"Like what?" She was ready to help me, I was grateful.

"It's difficult."

"Explain," she tapped heavily on my desk and made me jump.

"Alright I want more than to be a crutch to them both."

"You cannot be serious you're surely not thinking about happy ever after stuff? What about your wife remember Penny and your children? Not to mention how this sits with Bridie." Claire always pointing out the realities.

"This is why it's difficult, but it's much more." It seemed reasonable in my mind.

"Come on tell me," Claire was getting impatient with me.

"I'm not convinced it is Bridie, Desmond's daughter who is in the Maudsley Hospital being assessed certainly not the person I met anyway," at last, I voiced my inner fears. "Or I ever knew many years ago."

"You are joking, how can it be? It has to be, must be her, who else can it be? Of course she's different, you knew her 50 years ago and that time she has been institutionalised, been very sick, mentally unstable, had umpteen brain operations, she cannot be the same young girl you once loved, a shell maybe, but how can it not be her physically?" She shook her head at me disbelieving.

"I know it's not her."

"What makes you so sure?"

"A feeling I have."

"Hayden you need more than just a feeling you need proof." I knew she was right. "If you persist in this you'll destroy Desmond."

"I know, I know."

"Well you'd better start getting some proof quick before they let the wrong person out of the mental hospital." Claire trusted his instincts, even though she was in no position to judge whether he was right or not.

"How does Desmond feel?"

"I know he has doubts, I haven't broached my feelings with him."

"Then go and ask him."

Which is exactly what I intended to do, I liked the thought of visiting his home again, although having lost my father some years before he reminded me of him, I did not wish to hurt him.

Claire was right of course. More to the point if I was right where was Bridie and who was the woman at the hospital we had met?

What do I say to Desmond? I discounted this, for now anyway, there might be one person who could hold the key to unravelling this.

"Claire, please arrange a meeting for me with Mr Raymond Barnyard and Andrew Bartholomew preferably at the Maudsley Hospital and when you get in touch with Andrew can you let me speak to him as I have a favour to ask of him," I intended to ask Desmond to join us as well tonight.

"Oh there is someone else and Andrew should be able to help with his attendance." It was an afterthought but may turn out to be helpful.

"Who do you want?

"Harry Bates the gardener."

It was not long before she arranged everything for the following Wednesday in London and I had spoken to Andrew as well who promised to do all he could. Maybe I was clutching at straws but I doubted without convincing the group I would get anywhere.

Chapter 10

Arriving at Desmond's home late morning on Monday, ringing the doorbell produced a loud response 'the door was open' he was poring over two large shoeboxes as if he had secretly been hiding them for years, the contents were laid out on the coffee table, mostly Josephine's jewellery her rings, necklaces, earrings and broaches, he told me.

"My intention is for my eldest to have these." He smiled as he spoke.

"You mean Bridie don't you?"

"Yes, when you find her I want you to give these to her Hayden." He started to worry me.

"We will give them to her together Desmond," I assured him watching him return it to a corner unit drawer in the lounge. I have never liked to see an aged person sort out their lives, ever since I watched my own mother sort her life policies and determine who should have what of her effects. I had not realised it was a prelude for her to get ready to die which happened very soon after, I didn't want it for Desmond, I wanted him to have time with his long lost daughter.

"This second box I want you to take away with you Hayden, it contains my last will and testament and various property paperwork. I have arranged my funeral already Josephine and I will be together again," I noticed his tiredness. "There's information in here," he tapped the box.

"Getting a bit morbid aren't we Desmond?" I

refused to listen to him.

"I want you to look after Bridie's interests, will you do it? Promise me?" He looked directly at me.

"Of course Desmond I will be honoured." I had been right.

"I have arranged for the reading of my will at this home directly following the funeral and when the majority of people have left here, I have taken care of the costs including the caterers, my solicitors who are on standby hold a copy of my will, you now have the only other copy." I shook my head at him and realised I was close to tears, was it because of the memory of my own mother and father or was it purely for this sweet old man, who had touched my heart and seemed to have a premonition?

"Desmond, it saddens me we have to speak of this, I will not open the box until the reading is done although I would like to read your will now."

"Of course my friend but I have to swear you to secrecy." He handed it to me.

He left me to get us some drinks sitting in the conservatory on a wicker chair by the pool, personally in heaven. The contents of the will was not a surprise, however, if the bequeaths were to stand, I could sense trouble if he left them as it is.

"Desmond I have read your will," he placed our wine on the glass topped wicker table and sat in the adjacent chair looking at the will in front of me. "It concerns me given you have mostly left it all to Bridie although there is not much detail of the extent of your estate, what about Joseph, Susan and Emma? Should I look into the other shoebox and extract some jewellery for Susan and Emma?"

"I don't understand, surely you of all people would like to see Bridie well taken care of? As to the overall estate the solicitors will sort it out, they know what to do."

"Of course I would, but this home would have to be sold and the proceeds split into four, because I would expect your other three children to contest the will, dragging Bridie through the courts with a great chance of success, when they spin how one sided your attention has been towards her." He had not thought this through properly.

"Well I can dispute this because I loaned each of them a lot of money across the years without getting any return, they would come to me for every problem they had in their lives." I began shaking my head.

"Desmond I get exactly what you're saying, but you're forgetting the most important issue," he looked at me confused.

"What's wrong?"

"You will not be here will you? So how are you going to dispute with them about your past where no-one else can?"

"Oh yes," he began to smile which turned into a huge wide grin. "Better re-think my will had I not? Thank god I thought.

"I'm afraid so Desmond, I'll help you as long as you're prepared to share everything with me."

"What do you have in mind Hayden?"

"Let me go and see each of them and get their take on what they think they deserve."

"Good luck with that my friend," he had a twinkle in his eye, left to him I felt he would want to spite them as a parting shot, but it would not help Bridie. "Ok I'll find the numbers and addresses for you."

Luckily, a few short phone calls was all it took to arrange a meeting for Tuesday the following day. I would travel to the Goring Hotel in London's

Belgravia next to the gardens of Buckingham Palace, it was Susan's choice, we would have afternoon tea at 4.30pm, it was likely to be expensive I would stay the night at Desmond's and travel to London tomorrow afternoon.

For Desmond he welcomed the time for more reading of Cedric's Journal's, for me by the time the evening drew to a close I had picked over his estate and was satisfied should he die, his will was likely to be accepted by all. I enjoyed his company spending more and more time with him, we had our meeting together at the Maudsley Hospital the following day.

He called his solicitors the next morning emailing the revision to them and promised to forward the copy of his revised will to me as soon as he could I hoped we would not need it anytime soon.

I caught up with my office emails remotely and called Claire who would expect me in couple of days, Thursday, she sounded frustrated with me, I was not doing my day job and it was a strain for her.

When I arrived early at the Goring Hotel, I was not surprised to see the London family already seated waiting for me to arrive.

Our table backed onto the conservatory and gardens, the grandeur crying out of the very walls, the waiter offered us champagne with our afternoon tea, I hesitated, my three guests accepted readily, I nodded agreement.

"So what is important enough for you to lavish such sophisticated attention on us Hayden?" Joseph making it clear the bill would be mine. His sisters giggled, out of place in their surroundings.

"Would you agree I have some influence over

your father?" His face told me he did not like it.

"Yes and I think it is unhealthy, what do you want from him?" he growled at me.

"Nothing I can assure you except to help him find Bridie."

"What do you mean find her? Emma smirked as if I had made a mistake. "We know she's at the Maudsley."

"Your father and I have since determined it's not your sister." Both women looked to Joseph for comment.

"So we've been wasting our time." Joseph not bothered where she was.

"What are you going to do once you find her?" It was Susan's question this time.

"Did you know your father has made a will?" I ignored her.

"I suppose you helped him draft it so you can rob us of our rightful inheritance?" Joseph suggested cynically.

"Have you read it?" Emma's voice had an edge to it. "What is in it? What are we getting?"

"How sad your father has considered his will, he must be worried he is going to die, perhaps you all should visit him, spend some time with him or pay him back the money he has lent you over the years." I could see I had touched a nerve.

"You're being ridiculous; it's got absolutely nothing to do with you." Emma was furious.

"Problem is he has asked my advice on what he should give you if anything." This hit the spot squarely with them.

"You?" They chorused.

"When he leaves everything to Bridie what are you going to do?" If I was going to pay a fortune for afternoon tea, I was determined to enjoy myself.

"What do you think, I, we, will fight for what is rightfully ours, you can be sure." Joseph anger rising and I knew this to be true.

"Let me get this straight, if you each gained something of worth, likely to earn money for you in the future would you agree not to challenge the will?" This stopped them in their tracks.

We spent the next fifteen minutes working through the fine tiers of sandwiches and cakes without a word between us, the silence appropriately eating away at them, as they could not speak openly to determine between them what to do. I decided I could play the waiting game, I held all the cards and they knew it.

"Of course we would." If I believed them.

"You all give your word?" Time to get serious.

"We said haven't we?"

"Your father would need guarantees, you agree Joseph?" They knew I would fight them for Desmond if they reneged on any deal we struck.

"Yes." He said with resignation, I guessed he had no stomach for a legal battle he could lose.

"You agree Susan?"

"Yes."

"And you Emma?

"Yes." Both deferred to their brother.

"I will see what I can do, remember I will hold you to this and if you think of changing your minds don't!" I hoped they would take my threat seriously.

I paid the bill for the teas, cheap enough to get them out of Bridie and Desmond's lives. I left them at the Goring Hotel getting the most out of what I had supplied, probably asking for a second helping.

When I left the hotel, I called Penny to update her and suggested I would see her on Thursday after a rare day at the office. Calling Claire, she wished me luck for my meeting in the morning with the group.

The evening at Desmond's a quiet affair, with him finishing reading Cedric's journal's after I had updated him about afternoon tea with his children and he found another photograph album showing Bridie's first communion and the parade down Fenham Road with all the girls in their white full length dresses. I remembered the time it was such a big day for her.

We arrived at the Maudsley Hospital with some trepidation, there were at least four if not five people I had to convince of my theory and was not sure I was right myself.

"This is all very mysterious Hayden, what are you up to my friend?" Desmond believed in me no matter what.

"All in good time Desmond," I felt his confidence in me and hoped I could justify it.

"Hi both of you," Raymond Barnyard greeted us as Desmond signed us both in. "Three others have already arrived, I gather we are awaiting another?" he deferred to me.

"Yes, there will be six of us in all." Unusually I felt nervous.

My guests at the meeting were Raymond Barnyard, we were using his office, as well as him being there as Bridie's Psychiatrist. Andrew Bartholomew because he knew the history of the Darenth institution, his late father Cedric had treated Bridie and he was another vital sounding board as a Consultant Surgeon and a person for Raymond to discuss options with given his father's credentials. Desmond London Bridie's father of course, myself and I had invited Harry Bates the gardener, who knew Bridie as she was growing up, the other person I felt who could help arrived as I was thinking of her.

"Hello, I hope I am in the right place, I am actually looking for a Hayden Robbins, I was told to meet him here!" I noted a woman in tweed.

"Nurse Rhona Jackson, I presume?" Delighted to see her.

"It's Webber actually, I married and I am retired now, no longer a Nurse." She smiled warmly. "Oh yes and now a widow."

"Please let us all go to my office," Raymond ushered us along the corridor.

Red leather bound sofa's facing each other and standing in front of them were my other three invitees. With Rhona in the mix, the introductions went smoothly, she knew Harry, which helped relax him in what he saw as exalted company, she hugged Andrew as if he was his father knowing him as a boy and said he looked just like him. Andrew, pleased to be in the company of Raymond Barnyard, the respected Psychiatrist who had, in fact read numerous articles produced by his father. Desmond had met Rhona and of course Harry, who he already knew usually having tea as I did when he had made numerous visits to Darenth Sanatorium up to 1988 and Raymond from their earlier meetings, alone and with his family and had occasion to meet Andrew's father Cedric when Bridie was at Darenth.

"Hayden, this is your show, what's on your mind?" Raymond busied himself passing around the refreshments on hand.

I took a deep breath and waited for the backlash for what I was about to say.

"Firstly, let me say thank you for coming here

today and to you personally Raymond for allowing me to use your office like this," Raymond bowed his head. "Clearly this meeting is about Bridie London, whom you all know either having watched, spoken to her, heard about, Nursed her, been connected medically to her care or as I have, known her since childhood and finally as a relative, her father." I had their attention Desmond bowed to me.

"I became involved at Desmond's request, following his meetings with Raymond discussing Bridie's potential release and her required necessary future long term support once in the community at large. Sadly Desmond's own immediate family, his son and two other daughters have disowned her." The group looked with sympathy at Desmond who acknowledged what I had said.

"Thanks to Desmond, Raymond, Andrew and Harry, I have been fortunate to be able to take an overall view of medical records, Bridie's diaries, Cedric Bartholomew's private journal's and Harry's knowledge of Bridie and the hospital itself, allowing me to understand what has happened to Bridie, what her life has been like and what she thought about her life." The room in silence I continued.

"My reason to include Rhona is to add clarity to certain episodes highlighted in the documentation and to establish what led to her leaving Darenth."

"I don't see what good can come out of dragging up the history of one patient she's either fit to go out into the world or to be locked away for good." Rhona suggested dismissively, a tone unexpected from her.

"Raymond, is Bridie here and being evaluated?" I ignored Rhona's comments.

"Yes Hayden, you know that already," he looked

at me about to stifle a yawn I continued.

"Do you have any reason to doubt it is Bridie London whom you are evaluating?" As I said it, I looked at each one in the group and found the answer I looked for.

"Why would I?" Raymond looked puzzled.

"Desmond how many times have you seen Bridie since you left her at the Darenth Asylum in 1963?" I watched him deep in thought as if it was somehow a fatherhood test.

"Four times all here at the Maudsley Hospital during the past three to four months."

"What, in fifty years?" I was trying to emphasise my point.

"Yes."

"Do you think you have met your daughter again yet?"

"No, I haven't." This upset Raymond.

"Hold on a minute, what the hell is this about, of course you've met your daughter, Desmond I made it happen!" Raymond had lost his cool. "Surely this is because of what she has been through in the past fifty years we had spoken of this we have to bring her back slowly to be recognisable as your daughter again."

"Sorry Raymond I know I have ambushed Desmond's understanding of his daughter, knowing full well the feelings he had after he had met your Bridie." I tried to calm him down a little.

"I'm at a loss she must be my Bridie, she has to be Bridie!" Desmond shook his head confused and looking to me for clarification. "Surely she cannot be anyone else?"

"Again sorry, I think we're getting a little ahead of ourselves let me ask Rhona and Harry what they remember about the closure of the Darenth Asylum and what they believed happened to the patients." I purposely shifted the conversation to give Raymond time to calm down and for Desmond to have time to consider what I was saying to him.

"I left a short time before the closure due to an accident I had at the hospital however, I did keep in touch with the nursing staff and Doctors, some segregation occurred with the patients." Rhona recalled the time with sadness.

"Yes I knew, absolute disgrace if you ask me it should never have been allowed to happen." Harry spoke up for her in a misguided attempt to protect her.

I looked at both Rhona and Harry I had clearly missed something within the notes given to me.

"I think I can help here Hayden," Andrew interrupted. "My father has various letters addressed to and from the National Health Service and Government departments on this very subject quite heated some of them and although I was much younger at the time I do recall his anger and ultimate frustration at being powerless to help." I did not understand.

"You've lost me all three of you what are you talking about?"

"I believe I can help you Hayden I have some history to share," confused I looked to Raymond for some answers as he stood up to address the group.

"Imagine if you will an antiquated, badly maintained hospital, a mental institution, save for the gardens," he nodded toward Harry. "Which would cost a fortune to be put right and with an area or local community in dire need of proper hospital facilities, not just a mental asylum to serve all of the people, what do you do?" He looked at us all not expecting any answer.

"The NHS decided in its wisdom with government approval and this was the key, the Darenth Park Sanatorium should close in favour of a newly built hospital on the same site." I understood, but shifting the number of patients had to be a logistical nightmare.

"Makes sense I guess!"

"Oh it did, but then there was a segregation problem to solve."

In chorus the group bellowed, "Of course,"

"Any chance I could join in what you're talking about." I asked feeling left behind amongst the medical people, even Desmond appeared on their wavelength.

"Dispersing 1500 patients suffering at varying degrees of mental instability must have been quite a challenge." I watched, at last Desmond was included in the hospital discussions.

"Now I see, Rhona what did you mean about segregation?" I understood but sought some detail.

"We had to make choices as mental health places around the country were at a premium and only half could be accommodated."

"What happened to the rest of them?"

"They were sent to bloody prison!" The quieter voice amongst us spoke.

"Harry please!" Rhona scolded him for swearing.

"Is this true?"

"Yes Hayden, approximately 700 were found placements at other institutions and 800...." She was cut-off in mid-sentence.

"Were sent to prison," the anger rising in Harry again.

"The official figures were 723 placements and

792 prison confinements." We all looked at Raymond with Andrew nodding obviously knowing the answer too. "Sorry I checked."

"How were the choices made for who goes where?" I was horrified and ashamed a country I actually lived in and supported could treat the most vulnerable in our society this way, I was in danger of joining Harry's soapbox so bit my lip.

"In some of the papers of my father's apparently, and forgive the pun, but it was quite clinical, those who had families currently providing a percentage of the cost towards the care of the patients would receive a placement in a hospital or one in a secure sanatorium. However, being the figure was higher than places at around the 800 mark they had to consider who were or potentially could be a danger to themselves or others which brought down the figure to a more manageable level."

"You mean those who could be returned to their families to be looked after."

"Yes the same as in 1975 when cost cutting had led to the majority of patients being sectioned or released." Rhona stated as if she was going on record.

"Is this true?" The logic escaped me.

"Back then yes," I noted Harry muttering under his breath. "So because Desmond had been funding some of Bridie's care she was automatically chosen for a better place than others."

"Yes."

"Why couldn't she go home?"

"She was classed as a risk patient to herself and others at the time." Rhona stated.

"Did the patients know what was going to happen?" It was the turn of Desmond already knowing the answer to his question.

"I can answer," Rhona chose her words carefully. "Each family were informed and groups of the girls were brought together and told, but how many actually understood what was likely to happen, debateable."

"You said each family were informed, are you sure because no-one informed us?"

"Oh Desmond, I'm so sorry."

"Did they have any idea of placements versus confinements and why?" I jumped in quick before the conversation took another turn.

Again, Rhona answered. "It's possible, although I question whether many mentally ill patients would think to those levels."

"But it is possible?" Was this what all medical staff thought of mental patients, a little short on intelligence?

"I suppose so."

"What are you getting at Hayden?" It was Raymond, who was following my thread.

"I have been trying to understand how and why the swap could have occurred." I heard a quiet gasp of understanding from Rhona.

"Sorry Hayden, I don't understand what do you mean swap?" Desmond worried.

For the moment, I decided to ignore Desmond's question by changing the subject.

"Rhona would you mind telling us why you left Darenth Park Institution so suddenly, I appreciate it was a long time ago?" Her pained expression told a thousand stories of a life caring for so many mentally challenged people.

"I was scared, for the first time in all my years of working there." I could see the memory etched across her face.

"You knew the hospital was closing why didn't you wait and help with the transition or the, what was it called, segregation of patients, I don't understand the reason you left." I felt Harry bristling with impatience, a protective urge rising within him again. "Why were you scared?"

"There was an incident with a knife in the kitchen one day when I got stabbed, the girls were messing around with the knives and I had previously told them to leave them alone she came at me and was determined to cut me," she paused as the memory long since dealt with came to the fore. "This was a grown strong woman remember not the poor sick little teenager you all have in your minds and Desmond because I was sure at the time it was Bridie."

"You had a doubt?"

"No, no you're twisting how I am saying it, I knew it was her." I was not convinced.

"Who else could it have been Rhona?" I had picked this up in one of Bridie's diaries but she said we never meant it to happen and wondered who else was involved.

"All the girls, well women were involved, there was a lot of confusion, but I do remember Bridie tried to stop it happening as well."

"Now I'm confused Rhona, she either tried to stop it happening or she stabbed you which was it?"

"Stop badgering her Hayden." Harry had quickly come to her defence, too quickly I thought.

"Bridie was blamed at the time so you had to be right at the time surely?"

"I'll never forget those cold, evil eyes she had, I knew my time would be limited if I had I stayed." I felt she was lying, I decided to let it go it was over 25 years ago and Rhona's history not mine.

"People let's have a break and I'll arrange for more refreshments." Raymond looked at me lowering his hands flat towards the ground telling me to calm it down.

"Thanks Raymond, can I ask if we could see Bridie before we reconvene?"

"Too many of you all at once seeing her, I cannot allow it."

"No, not quite what I meant, do you have one of those rooms which have a two way mirror in order we could see her being interviewed by one of us?" I watched Raymond's brain working to find a solution.

"What are you up to Hayden? He eyed me with suspicion. I smiled at him. Surprisingly he had managed to arrange the interview quickly and suggested I would be her interviewer.

The group were ushered into a room no bigger than a broom cupboard with hastily arranged chairs in front of a large window looking into another room a table pushed to the corner held a camera presumably to record the reactions and mannerisms of patients. Today the camera is not on.

On the other side of the window the clinical pale green room housing as before the basic chairs and table and this time Bridie was waiting for me.

As I joined her nervously, I was conscious we had an audience. "Hello Bridie, do you remember me?"

"Of course I do Hayden."

"How are you Bridie, how are you coping with the assessments?" I planned a slow start to engage her.

"Ok, at least I hope so," she was more talkative, perhaps animated is the right word, I noted her coldness again, minimum emotion behind her eyes.

I noted a mannerism of stroking her nose ending with her pinching her nostrils, a nervous reaction it appeared not noticing this previously.

"You seem better than the last time I saw you Bridie," she nodded stroking her habit.

"Do you ever think of Toby anymore, you spent hours talking to him?"

"I don't remember him." I looked toward the mirror and nodded.

"What do you remember of our time together when we were young Bridie?" I looked closely for any reaction, she was thinking trying to work out what to say, I could tell she was clever and started to wonder why she was here, even if I found it hard to believe in her as Bridie.

"Why is it important to you, will it help my assessments?" Stroking her nose, her cold matter of fact voice startled me.

"I wonder what happened to Angela," I spoke softly to her knowing she was always jealous of her.

"Who is she?"

"I am surprised you can't remember her she used to be your friend and my girl next door at number 32."

"Oh yes, I remember her now, it was so long ago I would be surprised if I remembered anything from back then." She was giving me her stock answer excuse, she could be right of course, but I doubted it.

"Talk to me about Nurse Rhona Jackson and the knife incident, when you were at Darenth Park." Suddenly, I had lit a fire, her hand immediately touched her nose I stood up and walked toward the mirror. I wanted Rhona to look at her directly as she spoke.

"She was always telling us off, complaining,

ordering us about. We had enough of her." As if remembering her assessments she followed it with the comment. "But it was all Deborah's fault she wanted to hurt her." Her eyes shone brightly, reliving the moment.

"Nurse Jackson left the institution soon after, did it affect you?"

"Not at all, I was glad she went at the time." She shrugged her shoulders, dismissing the thought.

"You mentioned 'us' and 'we'?"

"It was Maisie and Deborah."

"What kind of people were they, Maisie for example, what was she like?"

"She was ok, she was kind mostly, nice to me." She reddened as she spoke her hands twitching her nose.

"Maisie was quite cruel she beat up Deborah didn't she?"

"Not true," telling a lie.

"Maisie was the leader, she forced you to make out you were each other didn't she?"

"No."

"Didn't you want her to take the blame for what you did when you hurt people?"

"No, she would never hurt anyone."

"Who are we talking about now, Bridie?"

"You're confusing me and it was so long ago it was Deborah who was violent!"

"Not you then Maisie?"

"No I mean it was Deborah."

"Are you saying it was Deborah who violently stabbed Nurse Jackson?'

"I'm not saying anything." She looked coldly at me.

I stood directly looking at the window, knowing

they would be listening, watching and this Bridie would be directly facing the mirror behind me.

"Have you heard of DNA testing Maisie, oops sorry Bridie?" With my back to her, I saw, as others did, a jerk go through her waif like body, I was not sure whether the testing would be a problem for her or the fact I called her Maisie. She nodded weakly toward the mirror, by the time I turned around to face her she had composed herself once again.

I knew Desmond would be ushered out of their viewing room by Raymond to carry out a DNA test which had not been considered prior to my suggesting there might be a doubt about the identity of the woman in this room, I might have finished my interview there but I decide to play for some reaction. I sat down facing her again the mirror to my right, her left.

"Please look at the mirror on the wall Bridie." She did so as if noticing it for the first time.

"Why?"

"Do you know what it is?"

"It is a two way mirror."

"Good, do you know what it is used for?"

"To spy on the patients here," she thought about this for a moment and consciously selected a right answer. Anybody watching would know this woman in front of me was as sane as anyone could be. "So the Doctors can assess our progress."

It was then I knew we were dealing with an intelligent game player at times she did let her guard drop because she could not maintain it. It was time for me to play.

"Who do you think is behind the mirror today Bridie?"

"Doctors and Nurses I suppose." She stroked her nose.

"Mr Barnyard is there, you know him?" She nodded, demonstrating her boredom with a wide noisy yawn, outstretching her arms above her.

"Andrew Bartholomew is also in the room behind the mirror."

"I don't know him."

"You might remember his father Mr Cedric Bartholomew and he knew you and the others well when you were at the Darenth Park Asylum?" she visibly jerked like a nervous tick, her face reddened attempting to stay calm.

"Mr Cedric is not here, sadly he is no longer with us, but Mr Andrew has all his notes." I tried to keep the pressure on. "Mrs Webber is also with us in the room."

"Who is she I don't recall." A frown crossing her forehead, she lied to me.

"Oh sorry, I forgot she's married now, you would remember her as Nurse Rhona Jackson." I watched the effect on her with amusement her head dropped into her hands covering her face. "What is wrong Bridie, I'm arranging for you to meet her again after all this time how would it be for you?" I watched her struggle to compose herself.

"Very good," quietly she muttered and coughed.

"Sorry Bridie I did not hear."

"I would like it," she said loudly nicely on edge, believing the shocks were over she started to relax.

"Although it is such a small room, your father is here as well," at which point she was instantly wound up and back on edge.

"Oh I nearly forgot shame on me, remember when you and Maisie were friends all those years ago and used to play swapping names?" she groaned and stiffened simultaneously. "Who was the one person you could not fool?" She shook her head at a loss, furiously trying to remember. "Of course you do, Harry, Harry Bates the gardener." I could have punched her directly in the face such was her jaw dropping surprise.

"Well he is also here Bridie watching you very closely." Her eyes, the coldest look on the planet shot directly at the mirror searching for any sign he was behind it.

Words failed her and she looked directly at me searching for the truth in what I had said. I stood up and suggested it was time for me to go and thanked her for speaking to me again, one more parting shot.

"It would be fun if Maisie was behind the mirror or how about Deborah." I paused briefly watching the crumbling effect my words had. "I'm kidding Bridie, just kidding!" I left the room, followed by the sound of a chair hitting the door, she had exploded, job done, at last some emotion. Now she knew I lied to her.

The group were moving from their small cramped now very hot room as I followed them down the corridor making our way back to Raymond's office, each one had been very animated, during my sessions with our patient. As we filed into the office taking sandwiches and drink laid out for us a visible sigh went through the room, someone uttered a 'wow', another 'unbelievable' alongside an 'OMG'.

Raymond started us off. "Hayden I take my hat off to you it was incredible," The group murmured in agreement. "If ever you need another job, come and work for us, what you did in there opened my eyes and means her assessment will have to be restarted, there is so much additional data to be covered."

"I'm sorry Raymond, you do get the woman I have been speaking too is not Bridie?"

"Nonsense, she has a recall issue maybe. Her years being institutionalised playing too many tricks with her memory." He still did not believe me.

"I recognised her, those eyes are etched in my memory never to be forgotten she stabbed me." Admitted Rhona, at least she was convinced.

"Rhona are you certain it was her?" She nodded.

"Oh yes I am, but I could not tell you if it is Bridie or Maisie." It was going to be my next question.

"One thing, I did find odd why did you say Angela, who lived next door to you Hayden, she lived at number 32, when you know very well you lived at number 63 so Angela would had to have lived at 61." Desmond was perfectly correct.

"I know Desmond, but our patient didn't even question it, if there has been a cover up or the swapping of identities, Angela and where she lived would hardly have been the top of Bridie's list if she was given one, whoever this person is the information about the real Bridie would have helped her recall it in an instance."

"Oh I see now."

"Who is Toby, she did not know him either?"

"I can answer Andrew," Desmond said proudly. "If you get to read the early diaries of Bridie she mentions Toby as being a fictitious face carved within the plaster in her first room or cell at the sanatorium."

"You mentioned me in there Hayden." Harry looked concerned.

"I was trying to gain a reaction."

"The thing is, I only used to make out I could tell

them apart so they would act naturally around me, they were literally like identical twins, dressing and with the hair the same."

"So how did you tell them apart?"

"Easy, one of them had a habit, a mannerism if you like. She used to stroke her nose when she was nervous, been doing it ever since I first knew her long before the two of them became friends." He became conscious everyone was listening to him and reddened. "Did you notice her doing it during your interview with her Hayden?"

"Yes I did so which one is it?" Everyone stared at Harry realising he had vital information. "You already know the answer Harry?"

"I guess I do." His quiet demeanour only heightened the suspense we were all feeling.

There was a knock on the office door opened by Raymond's secretary Michelle, she handed him a piece of paper, his eyes raising as he viewed the contents, thanking her she left as quickly as she arrived.

"Wait a moment I have also got some news," Raymond waved the paper he had just received at us. "Hayden while interviewing Bridie you mentioned a DNA test, which until now had not occurred to us to do so we rushed Desmond away and did one."

"I guessed you might."

"We carry many types of testing in our laboratory so a simple, crude though it is, paternity test, gives us a fair degree of accuracy, I have the results here," he waved the paper again.

"I thought DNA testing took several weeks?"

"Not any more, you can buy a kit for home usage; naturally a more accurate test has to be done if there is legal action involved, which we will do." The group were surprised at the technology advance.

Raymond embarrassingly looked at Desmond directly. "The patient we have been assessing and you have been meeting with and watching Hayden interviewing is not your daughter I'm afraid." Desmond visibly collapsed in his chair I rushed to his side.

"Any indication as to who you do have in there Raymond."

"Frankly, I have not a clue Hayden."

"Maisie Belling."

"Pardon Harry."

"I knew it was Maisie Belling, I could tell from her mannerisms I was about to say if you recall." Harry smugly reminded us.

"Boy, forget the computer frauds, this is taking identity theft to a whole new level," Andrew whistled.

"Wait a moment you're all assuming it is this Belling girl but we have no proof, yes it is definitely not Bridie London, Desmond I am extremely sorry," Raymond genuinely was. "Harry it's probably 25 years since you've seen both girls, well women.

"Well I am convinced she's not Bridie, DNA or not." Harry announced to the group and no-one argued with him.

"I'm going to sound like my own callous children, what you're saying is my wife and I have been funding someone else's care for the past 25 years," Desmond buried his head into his hands.

"Desmond, this should never have happened there will be a full investigation I can assure you, it also means I should never have got you involved in this case at all as this is not Bridie your daughter."

I tried to comfort him as best as I could, we all did.

"You don't get it do you Raymond, where is she, where has Bridie been all these years?" Desmond's voice had a desperate edge he was too old for this type of news.

"It is what we all want to know Desmond," There has to be an investigation. "We will find her I promise."

"I hope she's alive." Desmond started to cry.

We all tried to console him as best we could, but the group gradually dispersed, the positivity at first felt being lost within us. The way forward is for Raymond to conduct a full investigation, Andrew to search through his Father's papers in order we can try to establish what patients went where. There was little doubt we were looking for Bridie London and her name was Maisie Belling.

Before we left I called and arranged for Claire to speak to the Prisoner Location Service in Birmingham and gathered they have first to find the prisoner and then to ask their permission to be contacted, having no idea whether she was alive as Desmond hoped or she was mentally stable to recognise my name I was not sure. It concerned me after all this time she would be afraid of her version of the truth.

Andrew was sure the patients or prisoners were in prison by way of a set court order stating an 'indeterminate prison sentence' meaning there was no fixed length of time of release. There had to be a request to the relevant parole board. These types of sentences are if the prisoner is a danger to the public, I guessed at the time. The patients were defined a danger to themselves. I started to wonder how many of the 792 confinements back in 1988 had since been set free.

How Maisie Belling was able to switch her identity with Bridie's was unfathomable such must have been her hold over her she accepted her prison fate.

The Prisoner Location Service immediately took up the case in the spirit of the supposed injustice to Bridie suggesting it would take them a full two weeks to find her if she's in their system. I did not want to consider the alternatives.

The Service did find a record of her immediately, but only to a point, when the sanatorium closed in 1988 Maisie Belling was being described as a very dangerous mental patient in need of a fully secure environment.

For the next 11 years, she was in London's Holloway prison where she had been periodically assessed resulting finally with her mental status downgraded to non-dangerous, which prompted a further transfer and she had been was sent to Drake Hall in Eccleshall, Staffordshire another closed prison. She spent a further 5 years there before yet another assessment took place, this time not for a transfer, but for prison release by the parole board sitting at the time in 2004. There the Location Service records ended she was not actually released, but transferred to a secure hospital. They were looking further into their records as they did not have the complete picture.

With Bridie, now agreed not the person at the Maudsley and likely to be Maisie Belling recorded as being in a secure hospital, if Bridie had swapped places where is she now?

Chapter 11

By the time I arrived back in the office on Thursday, I could tell my team were getting concerned about my continued absence, I spent most of the morning talking through their work and generally sitting with them in the open area catching up on how they were and with the latest gossip. Claire was itching to drag me away from them, but being determined to spend the time 'at' the office and wandering around the building talking to other managers and staff she gave up on me. She booked time in my diary for the whole of the afternoon, despite this being the 17th day we had spent attempting to find Bridie; we were starting the search all over again.

Claire and I spent some time going over what had happened and what we could do now. She suggested we concentrate on the real Maisie Belling at the Maudsley Hospital. We needed to understand her background in case we ran into difficulties proving Bridie should be the one released and not her.

She arranged with Raymond Barnyard we have access to all information about her. He facilitated our journey into the files of social services, insisting it being important to help in providing the right psychiatric care. It worked, like the papers on Bridie there were extensive notes and although these were confidential, without a family of her own there was little chance of any objection.

Maisie Belling arrived at Darenth Park Asylum in June 1962 she was 13. At the age of 7 years, she was in foster care having witnessed the death of one of a long line of her mother's boyfriends who had choked on his own vomit after one of their drunken binges while her father was, once again, housed at her majesties pleasure for robbery with violence. The Belling family were notorious throughout the White Road council estate in Chatham, Kent.

Maisie learnt how to feed herself from an early age, regularly abused by her mother's drunken and drug addicted friends, she would steal from them as they lay in their stupor. Social services acted belatedly to put her into care, scared of the reactions of those who knew her and led to family members with their friends threatening and beating up on the numerous foster carers, social workers and teachers once they found out where Maisie lived or went to school. The count being an unhealthy 25 foster homes and 26 schools a failure by all who served her.

One day, Maisie a very ill teenage girl, had been captured back by her family at 13 from her current foster home in order she could be used for earning money to supply the booze and drugs. When the police responded to a tip off, an under aged girl was likely to be raped at the latest party in her mother's home. When they found her, they sent for the Ambulance Services, as she appeared extremely sick. It was later determined she had developed tuberculosis, the best for Maisie was the secure asylum unit at Darenth Hospital with warnings to all her family, having endangered her very life if they tried any contact they would all be locked up for a very long time, her mother later serving 2 years for child neglect.

Her constant physical abuse and near starvation generally meant as a young teenager she was mentally unstable, and she had a life threatening illness, her family unsurprisingly decided to give up on her.

The more I discovered about Maisie, while feeling sadness at how society could have let her down, it was clear to me the more I researched her background, she had turned into a first rate manipulator at every school, every foster home with the sympathy card having been played wherever she rested. In foster homes, she would become the ideal child to care for, a loving helpful girl, a little flirtatious with the man of the house perhaps, however the women usually thought of her as the daughter they imagined they would have themselves, if she went into a home with children she would become their perfect sister, a confidant, a friend. This way she gained many possessions intending to sell them on, knowing each families secrets large or small she would use these against them if they tried to stop her moving on.

Unfortunately, she could not play the game for too long a few months in and her façade began to crack. The social workers knew her of course, and through some misguided attempt to place her with the right couple, they let inexperienced foster carers suffer the most.

The cracks start to show in her patience soon enough, she would become violent, first to the children of the house and then nearly always to the woman of the house who tried to hide it while trying to understand what the girl in care had been through. The man of the home would not stand a chance with the occasional dropping of towels after washing leading to accusations of wanting more than to be her foster carer, the guard by the carers after months, slipping, mistakenly thinking they were finally getting through to the child and believing they had built trust into their charge.

Mum's spend during shopping times, secret treats, Dad's washing of their girls hair, innocent enough but ending with innuendo's of buying the friendships, or supposed incidents while in the bathroom. Unknown to each individual couple the social workers were fully aware of what goes on and let this it carry on at family after family, in the belief they were doing what was best for the child destroying 10 of the families I spoke to, with only a half a dozen now caring for children after the experience. The rest would not speak to us, suggesting the fostering system had let them down too not just the child, only two family's out of the 25 were still foster carers and they would only look after babies, never a teenage girl again.

Maisie's exit strategy would start with coming home late from school, wanting better clothes, the latest mobile phone, demanding the benefits normal children received, like pocket money and games and then only to sell on to other children at school. She would use the phone to contact old friends on the white road estate so she could meet the men who gave her money for the young sex she could offer.

Each care placing would end dramatically, the foster care family put through the worst ordeal imaginable, three weeks of abuse, with accusations of physical and sexual harm Maisie knowing exactly what she was talking about in order to make the social workers jump immediately to the tune of the so called young and vulnerable girl. In every case, the carers themselves had to fight through all the allegations only to be exonerated, but disillusioned with the fostering process and their own level of support received, innuendo used as a political tool to silence their complaints. A new placing would then be found for her and once again with the minimum of information supplied to her new care family. Suddenly, everyone is arguing about the television, console for games and bicycle, down to bedroom furniture and bedding she used to 'own' at her old placing generously bought for their dear sad Maisie. This way she continued to build her possessions and funds.

What hurt Maisie the most was after her capture by her family and getting ill she had lost all those possessions she had built up, social workers dispersed the goods for the benefit of all. Those I spoke to found Maisie accusing her own mother of stealing her money, social services breathed a sigh of relief the day she went into the secure unit at the Darenth Sanatorium.

The fact finding on Maisie had taken Claire and I most of the two weeks the Prison Location Service gave us if they were to find Bridie, sure enough they succeeded if it turned out to be her.

In 2004 following her assessment by Drake Hall the patient known as Maisie Belling had been transferred to Rampton Secure Hospital, a high security psychiatric hospital near the small village of Woodbeck between Retford and Rampton in Nottinghamshire, being the same hospital type as Darenth Sanatorium had been, a plus for the patient as it was definitely not a prison. The notes suggested her being a model patient and she needed to be in a more relaxed regime.

Although classed as a high security psychiatric

hospital, Maisie Belling transferred to Broadmoor Hospital, Crowthorne in Berkshire, where some of the facilities enabled a rehabilitation programme to co-exist. Quite what the rehabilitation would achieve, another prison, a better hospital, less secure or actual release, which I doubted.

Broadmoor has over 200 patients both men and women, most of the patients there suffer from severe mental illness; many also have personality disorders. Although the average stay is about 5 years, some have stayed for most of their lives Maisie Belling fell into this category if Rampton is included in the equation.

Although undergoing extensive renovation the hospital resembled a prison with its entrance a huge domed green metal doorway filling its archway between Grade II Edwardian pillars housing offices built in the 1830's.

Raymond drove both Desmond and I through the gates, Wednesday now the first week of August, the day dull and grey. He had insisted we set out early morning needing to be back before lunchtime. His car checked while the doors were closing behind us. In front of us high metal gates when opened led us to a courtyard and parking where we were ushered into one of the front facing buildings and escorted up to the third floor where the chief executive's office resided.

Desmond was ecstatic when I told him we were going to see Maisie Belling who we think might likely be Bridie, unfortunately he could not turn up at the gate saying he was her father demanding to see her, as there was no proof of whom she was or whom she could be.

Raymond had called in a favour or two and was

arranging a DNA test to be done in the meantime we had to hope requesting a meeting with the head of the hospital and asking if Maisie/Bridie wanted to see us would work, fortunately it did.

With both Raymond and I on our way to the Chief Executive's suite, Desmond went directly to a separate visiting centre for the patients who lived in their specialised Paddock Centre a high dependency and personality disorder unit.

Raymond had given a brief outline of why we needed to see the CEO of Broadmoor by involving the West London Mental Health (NHS) Trust responsible for this hospital. This Trust reports to the NHS Executive through the London Strategic Health Authority.

"Mr Barnyard, welcome Sir to Broadmoor you have some powerful friends in high places who insisted I spare you sometime today," looking suspiciously at me, whom he was obviously not expecting. I realised Raymond must have called in every favour known to man.

"My apologies Gerard, this is Hayden Robbins who is acting on behalf of the London family." I felt him appraising me, I hoped not for any designs as a potential in-mate.

"Hayden, Gerard Sheridon is the CEO of Broadmoor," I shook his hand, moist I desperately wanted to wipe mine while noting the deep set eyes observing me like a Doctor does to his patient beneath eyebrows busy and aiming for the sky's.

On this side of the gates, the panoramic windows of his expansive office deliberately offered a stunning view of the grounds and buildings enclosed by high walling, only further to be enclosed by wired fencing.

"Welcome to you too Mr Robbins, although we

haven't established Maisie Belling is in fact a London yet have we?" he said curtly.

"Let's hope the DNA testing solves it." Raymond explained how Desmond had gone ahead of them full of anticipation.

"Quite, given our Ms Belling agrees to it."

"Why would she not?"

"Gentlemen please, there may be at the very least a swap of identities it is obviously for a very good reason, why on earth would the women calling herself Belling offer herself to a DNA test only to be implicated in God knows what cover up." He had a point however, I also thought he was a pompous bastard and was glad I was not either working for him or a patient in his care.

"Would there be any opportunity for us to see her as well as Desmond London Mr Sheridon?" Asked Raymond sensing an atmosphere between the idiot in front of me and myself, a diplomat at work I mused.

"I understood from Raymond, you haven't seen her since she was 13, she would have changed considerably within the past 50 years, you're aware aren't you?"

Nodding in agreement, the hairs on my neck stood up, but I needed this man so I fought my anger, holding my tongue at his patronisation.

"Gerard I'll happily take responsibility should anything untoward occur, we would rather like to see her as well, having come all this way." Raymond was on a charm offensive.

"Very well, forgive me for the moment gentlemen I'll see what I can do for you." He disappeared out of the office.

Watching his back disappear out of the door, I

looked at Raymond who raised his eyebrows as if to confirm my thoughts about the CEO.

"Hold it together old man." I laughed.

"I'm trying Raymond, I am trying real hard."

Within a few minutes, he returned flanked by two prison guards.

"Gentlemen please accompany my officers to the Paddock Centre, where Maisie Belling, your supposed Bridie London is meeting with Desmond London currently." By his tone, having fulfilled our request he dismissed us, I worried Raymond now owed a favour to Gerard Sheridon. I positioned myself behind Raymond as we left his office waving my thanks to avoid shaking his hand again.

"Thank you Gerard we appreciate it, "I found myself nodding in agreement.

"I must ask you to each meet her on an individual basis as there are too many of you for her own good." We agreed.

"We will space out our time with her be assured Gerard." Raymond acknowledged.

We followed his officers down the stairway out into the main courtyard leaving the main office block behind us. I attempted to converse with the officers but all I got was a grunt and a 'keep walking this way Sir" Raymond a step behind mumbled something under his breadth and I started to laugh finding difficulty containing my giggles, it was all becoming too serious.

We arrived at the Paddock Centre, the starkness of bright yellow hits you at first making the unit sunshine bright it was intimidating. The officers ushered us towards a tea and coffee seating area where we came upon Desmond his hands firmly wrapped around a hot something in a plastic cup, shaking his head sorrowfully as if he himself were an inmate we had come to see.

"Good God man what is it you look dreadful?" I too was shocked at his appearance he seemed to be shrinking before my eyes I quickly sat down beside him placing my arm around his shoulders.

"Desmond my friend what is it, talk to us please." He looked very frail.

"Oh Hayden, it's not her, the woman I have seen is not my daughter and now I don't know what to do." He was so dejected, I knew the fight to find her had left him resigning himself to never seeing Bridie again.

Raymond tried to console him using every possible psychiatric technique within his arsenal of expertise to no avail Desmond simply slumped on the table in complete despair.

"Raymond, take Desmond over to the armchairs in the corner while I go to see her," I nodded to the officers I was ready to take my turn and followed them down a corridor towards a similar basic room I went into at the Maudsley.

"Hello, another visitor two in one day, I am feeling very important." Instantly I knew this was not Bridie, this woman was huge the chair creaked as she moved.

"Good to meet you Maisie, It is Maisie isn't it?"

"Who else would I be, you haven't told me who you are." Her eyes were bright, playing with me.

"Hayden Robbins, Bridie must have told you of me when you knew her during your time at the Darenth Park sanatorium."

"Such a long time ago, why would it mean anything to me?"

"Well you are not Bridie and I suspect not Maisie either because you took her place here, you swapped with the real Maisie Belling?" She laughed at me.

"You make a lot of assumptions Mr Robbins look around you," she emphasised my name. "Do you honestly believe I would choose to be here over the cosy hospitals Bridie's been at, she was fortunate to have a family to support her at the time I did not."

"Who is in the cosy hospitals as you call it?"

"Oh I get it no wonder the old guy came to see me, you think I am Bridie in disguise, very funny." She could not have cared less. "You've all gone and lost her, ha, ha."

"We know we don't have Bridie, because we have Maisie Belling instead and yes until we came here we thought we'd find Bridie in you, but if you're not her either which you clearly are not, we have to find her."

"I could be Bridie if you wanted me to be." She was laughing at me.

"Except you did not recognise your own father?" she laughed at me again. "But if you're not either of them who the hell are you?" I was appealing to whatever good nature she had, having spent a life in institutions.

"Something you need to work out isn't it Mr Robbins?" Emphasising my name again, treating it as a joke. "It's your problem not mine."

"Do you remember what happened to her?"

"As far as I know you have her, I had enough of this now I want you to go and no more visitors." She called out to the officers I was escorted out of the room. "I do hope you're not going to cause trouble for me, I can get out of here any time I like." Her threat all too clear.

I met both Raymond and Desmond out in the seating area, Desmond was putting on a brave face, but as I updated them both he dropped into a melancholy state again. Raymond accepted he was not going to see her, it would not have served any purpose, he vowed to push for the DNA test of the person calling herself Maisie to establish who she was.

Escorted from the Paddock Centre across the courtyard directly to our car, no second meeting with the CEO, we drove through the green gates licking our wounds.

The three of us spoke little on the way back Desmond was quite morose, Raymond himself deep in thought. I was at a loss where to turn although I knew I had to keep the momentum going. I decided I would go back to see Harry once we got back to pick up my car at the Maudsley Hospital and with Desmond needing some time on his own getting the train back to Sidcup, I drove to Dartford.

This swapping of patients did not happen without others knowing why, Harry was the best bet more for what he would not say rather than to tell me.

Claire telephoned ahead and arranged for me to see Harry in the afternoon at the Darenth Hospital and to see whether Andrew could search any records he could find for a Maisie Belling, Deborah Wealdon and Florence Mason in particular their blood types going back to 1963 and then to progressively confirm them up to 1988. I felt these three women held the key to Bridie's disappearance and for us to find her, someone within the group knew more than they were saying.

I walked through the now familiar grounds of the Darenth Park Hospital towards the large sheds to the rear of the main buildings, I imagined Harry on his prized motorised lawn mower, as the smell of freshly cut summer grass filled my nostrils I loved it. Instead, the smell of charcoal, sun beginning to shine from the mornings grey, with a gentle breeze conjured up the countryside for me in one straight hit and it was wonderful, one could put aside troubles and problems to begin relaxing in the warmth, as others will do once the morning itself moves into the lunchtimes of the working.

Harry, expecting me, welcomed me like an old friend as he fielded requests from a small queue of people who wanted the sausages and burgers cooking on his barbeque.

"Pass me up those baps," enlisting me in supplying lunchtime fare to the staff. We sat outside his shed on canvas armchairs taking in the atmosphere only summer sunshine creates while drinking tea and sampling his barbequed food it was delicious neglecting to charge me for the pleasure. "I do this every year when the sun decides to shine." He told me.

"Tell me more about Bridie and Maisie and the two others Deborah and Florence Harry. What were they each like and how were they set apart?" I had to try to find a hook, mannerism or even their attitude, which could set them apart from each other especially after all this time.

"The four girls go some way back in time, but as I remember Bridie was always different somehow above the rest, not ill in terms of her sanity like others at the sanatorium, she was in love in the beginning anyway, which made her special." He raised his eyes to the sky as if it were unthinkable for a 13 year old.

"She was in love, who with?"

"You're a bloody fool."

"Oh." I blushed, and at my age too.

"In the beginning, it was the two of them, Bridie and Maisie. They were like chalk and cheese in attitude and temperament but identical in looks and perhaps it is why they became such good friends. Early on, they made a pact to always be friends and to look out for each other and never do anything which could or would harm either of them and as far as I know they never have, they loved each other." He thought well of them I could tell.

I raised my eyebrows.

"No while it did go on with girl crushes on each other and the boys from a separate wing of the hospital between the two of them they were inseparable, thick as thieves and better than sisters could ever be, they respected each other, they were real friends with a bond I doubt anyone could ever break, even today." He emphasised.

"Strange, I never got it from her diaries they were so close."

"I guess it didn't need to be spoken of they used to walk arm in arm everywhere and personally, I don't think either would have survived the asylum without each other. I mentioned before they played games swapping identities and it worked so much so they were able to get Doctors and Nurses to treat them as each other down to their medication, they laughed all the time about it and turned their disguises into an art form. One drawback for both of them was the recognisable warmth of Bridie as opposed to the coldness of Maisie they had to act out their roles to perfection."

"How long did this last?" I was fascinated.

"As far as I'm aware it lasted the full 25 years they were both here, however, the coldness and steeliness of Maisie led to other patients being frightened of her as well as some of the medical staff, certainly Nurses and junior Doctors." He was pulling thoughts rapidly from his memory with a smile of contentment suggesting it was a good part of his life back then. "We called them the terrible twins."

"When did the other two girls come onto the scene?" I poured us more tea and helped myself to another burger and bun, noticing the grounds were filling up with the afternoon visitors, families with their relative patients enjoying the day out.

"Deborah had been around them all most of her time it was not until Bridie's attack she became closer to them both."

"What attack?" I was flabbergasted. "I haven't read anything about this." I found myself getting angry, having poured over the documentation, medical notes, Cedric's journals and Bridie's diaries and there was no suggestion of an attack. "Harry what sort of attack is she alright, did she suffer, Oh my God poor Bridie."

"Hayden, Bridie was violently raped and it was suspected by a male nursing officer." I was dumbstruck, how could I have missed this in the papers or diaries, I regretted skimming the diaries now.

"When was this?"

"I guess Bridie would have been about 23 so during 1972."

"Who was he, did the police catch him?" I was frustrated with myself for not knowing because of trying to concentrate only on snapshots every five years, samples of information from 1970, I was angry for Bridie and at myself for not reading all the diaries.

"Calm done Hayden it was a long time ago and it

has been dealt with by the authorities and Bridie herself I might add."

"Please tell me how and what happened." Harry offered a beer I accepted, this news would drive anyone to drink.

"The man's name was John Devlin, there had already been a number of complaints by patients and Nurses alike where he was being 'familiar' it's what they called it in those days, he was touching them inappropriately." Anger started to well inside me.

"Why was something not done about him?" I was pressing him, accusingly.

"Hey, I'm just a gardener I wasn't involved." He felt blame where none existed.

"I apologise Harry, do you think Desmond knew?" He nodded.

"I would have thought so being next of kin they would have to have informed him, what if something had happened to her as a result of it?" Harry doubted anyone would have bothered, but if nothing else, he was loyal.

"I suppose so." Strange he never mentioned it.

"Hayden, he is an old man with old fashioned ideas, perhaps he felt you wouldn't help her because of it maybe?" A fair point, but I did not believe it of Desmond not toward me anyhow.

"Why ever would it make me not want to help?" I was perplexed.

"Damaged goods perhaps?" I disagreed and said so.

"Rubbish," anger again rising within me, I felt it unlikely my dear friend thought this way of me.

"Just the messenger, old chap."

"Sorry Harry, please do carry on." The sadness

and my helplessness for Bridie distressed me but I could do nothing about it until I saw her once more.

"Remember we're talking early seventies the decade after a period of anything goes, today its different, you cannot judge life then with standards now, anyhow Devlin was I understood given various warnings and for a while the problem went away until one day Bridie was taken by him for a regular assessment session. They were alone together most of an afternoon. Following her assessment she had gone missing for several hours, Devlin said she had wanted to return on her own. When found, curled up, unconscious, bruised, beaten up and as tests confirmed violently raped. He said he was only guilty of leaving her alone nothing more."

"Where was this?" My anger mixed with sadness for her.

"There used to be an old ambulance garage with some offices attached behind the hospital unused as its original function for some years and only then for storage of equipment such as wheelchairs, walking frames and crutches. These days a different NHS company deals with storage within a separate company."

"Bridie woke up and pointed the finger at him yes?"

"No, several weeks passed before she was able to talk about the attack initially she told Rhona, Nurse Jackson, by which time Devlin had convinced many people of his innocence he presented himself as a perfectly sane nursing officer and she, frankly, is already classified as insane, no brainer." Sounded a perfect get out, too perfect.

"So what happened next?"

"Devlin went before a panel of so called expects,

there was no proof, DNA testing didn't begin in earnest until the mid-eighties and he was deemed the sane one. This coupled with the embarrassment it would bring to the sanatorium it was hushed up although thankfully at the time he was suspended for three months pending further enquiries but he was soon back even before Bridie's injuries were healed." I felt ashamed at the treatment she had received and I could tell Harry felt the same. "The fact she didn't speak about it immediately hurt the case against him, typically she believed it was her fault."

"What about Bridie's testimony did it not count for something?"

"Yes it did, the panel, the authorities, Doctors, Nurses and the patients knew he did it, but with no proof, no police prosecution and with the hospital wanting to keep it quiet she was told they would keep a close watch on him, which actually meant they would do nothing about it."

"What effect did this have on her?"

"For a while she became a recluse confining herself to the restaurant area and her room, the girls used to come to her rather than previously, where they would wander free around the grounds in a group, this was when Deborah became closer to her, as a sort of protector." There was something else, I could tell from his voice.

The afternoon visiting hours were drawing to a close, staff, patients and families began dispersing which highlighted how long we had been sitting on our canvas armchairs. Harry began clearing the left over burgers and hot dogs, cleaning his man made stove as best as he could and suggested we move inside his shed out of the late afternoon breeze now developing.

"What ever happened to Devlin," disgust freely entering into my voice, hardly bearing to give him the time of day within my thoughts.

"Here we come back to the girls in particular Deborah, we spoke earlier about loves and crushes amongst patients and staff which happened within any institution and this one was no different. Deborah had no intention of replacing Maisie in Bridie's affections, she was too afraid of her, probably the only other girl amongst the other patients, however she did have a massive crush on Bridie and had vowed to look after her as her friend and after the attack believed she had failed her."

"Harry I'm confused what has this to do with Devlin?" I was missing something.

"Six months after the rape attack on Bridie, John Devlin was found stabbed to death with his throat cut and the general assumption it was Bridie who was responsible." I guess I had this picture of a teenage girl fighting against a bully, but this was a grown woman with a violent history.

"My God, were the Police involved, was there proof of this? What happened?"

"Hayden you've guessed it already, the police had no help from the staff at Darenth, the place was full of the insane, it's the risk workers take."

"You're kidding right?" Institutionalised murder, it was a new one for me. "Don't tell me no proof?" My anger for Bridie slowly dissipating, automatically believing it to be her revenge attack on him, I felt not one ounce of remorse for Devlin. "Good for the administration, I suppose, takes away the problem of a bully and a rapist?"

"Right, Bridie began rehabilitating herself amongst the other patients again, two girls who were always together then became a band of three."

What do you mean who was the third?"

"Hayden, for someone appearing so switch on and smart," he left the sentence in mid-air. "Deborah killed him not Bridie."

"Oh I see," I struggled to get my head around this. "What of Florence?"

"Another crush I'm afraid."

"On Bridie again, she must have been very popular?" Knowing her back in the early sixties, I could see how popular an individual she was, a magnetism drawing people to her without even trying.

"Yes I believe she was, is, one of life's needy and people feel drawn to her and want to protect her, unfortunately with tragic consequences, not immediately but later on before the sanatorium closed for good."

"How so, this was in 1988?"

"Yes, three turned into four girls as Florence was introduced to the group by Bridie, they had known each other for quite a while, although she never made it into the group until the girls were beginning to understand what would be happening to them and the likelihood of them splitting up. I gathered Bridie wanted all her friends to be close to her up until the closure of the sanatorium and no one could come between them. Maisie was the boss as always, Deborah was the hard girl, Bridie and Florence the innocent girls."

"What about the tragic consequences?"

"This is not my story to tell, I can only say before closure Florence died."

"Was she sick? Who will tell me the story?" I was getting agitated again, suddenly the information not making me confident Bridie was alive.

"Mr Bartholomew probably knew all the facts only he is dead so I don't know now." I decided not to push him on this he had told me enough." He started to look very tired. "At a guess I would suggest Jennifer Granger the hospital administrator and she retired long ago."

"What became of Deborah?"

"I believe she became one of the few who went home, released." I was surprised, another question for others not for Harry.

Bridie supposedly ended up in the Cheadle Royal Hospital, and then onto the Maudsley for assessment, Maisie at Broadmoor, Deborah went home and sadly, Florence died, all four accounted for, but if it is not Bridie in the Maudsley then what other permutations are there? It seemed too easy at first glance, but now it had started to unravel, Bridie goes missing and it's clear identities have been swapped, what puzzled me is why the need for a cover up?

My mobile chimed loudly for me, it was Claire from my office, it was bad news Desmond had a massive heart attack and been taken to Kings College Hospital from Catford train station, the next one along the line from Denmark Hill the closest station to the Maudsley. Desmond had caught the train going to Dartford, but had collapsed just before the first station down his line. Harry and I drove in my car from Darenth Hospital in Dartford to Kings College Hospital opposite the Maudsley Hospital in Camberwell, London in silence. On the way I called Claire and asked her to inform the other members of the group, a shock to both of us especially as I knew of Desmond's depressive state of mind the last time, we were together. I told Claire I also needed an address for Jennifer Granger together with her summary of Bridie's 1972 diary.

We arrived at Kings late into the afternoon and went directly to their accident and emergency department. By the time, we had arrived Desmond had already been transferred to their intensive care unit. Luckily with Raymond across the road in the Maudsley Hospital he had laid some of the ground work for us in terms of, we all in the group being his closest personal friends if not relatives could see him, although he had informed Joseph, Susan and Emma who were already on the way.

Only one member of the group could not make it Andrew Bartholomew, he was operating in theatre at the time. According to Raymond, Desmond had suffered a major heart attack, his second apparently, now unconscious the prognosis not good. It was not known whether he had a stroke at the same time, which we were told although similar in threat to his life if he came through it, he would stand more chance of some normality of life if he only had the heart attack I doubted it despite their encouragement.

We all met each other as good friends congregating in the waiting area within ICU, our voices in hushed respectful tones, Raymond and I updated Rhona on our visit to Broadmoor, and Harry mentioned he and I had been discussing Bridie's attack, which I noticed was not news to both Raymond and Rhona.

"Rhona what happened to Deborah Wealdon?" Broaching the subject made me uneasy given we were here for Desmond, but it was on my mind.

"As far as I know she had gone home!" Out of character I thought, she was quite sharp in attitude towards me.

"Would you know where home is for her?" I had touched a nerve and I did not know why.

"I don't think now is the time or place to discuss this with Desmond lying in there close to death!" she answered abruptly.

What stopped me asking her what her problem was had been the arrival of Desmond's three children. Joseph shouting to all, who would listen, calling for a Doctor to tell him what was going on, it clearly worked with the nursing staff ushering the three straight to Desmond's bedside with promises of the Consultants contact shortly, their faces wanting to enquire what we were all doing there, they promptly disappeared from our view.

Rhona spoke first. "I don't think they should be party to what we're talking about or what we as a group have been doing to find Bridie, their concern should only be about Desmond." We all agreed but I could not help feeling she wanted to stop the search anyway.

Desmond's three children came back into the ICU waiting area the four of us stood up and chorused "Any news?"

Joseph looked at us with disdain. "My father is doing as well as can be expected, but unconscious," he looked at us as a group. "The only people I know here is you Mr Barnyard." He looked around at the rest of us. "I thank you for getting word to me, to us, about my father," he nodded toward his two sisters beside him.

He looked at Harry. "How do you know my father?"

"Let me help you there Joseph, my friend here is

the senior gardener at the hospital where your sister had been at Darenth." Raymond found this amusing and stifled a smirk.

"Bloody Bridie again it's all I keep hearing, probably what caused my father's heart attack? And who the hell are you?" he turned towards Rhona.

"I'm your sister's Nurse."

"Of course you are, why not let everyone in here, it's a bloody circus." So far, he had deliberately ignored me.

"Hello Joseph." I bowed to Susan and Emma. "You all know me of course we must do afternoon tea again soon." I goaded realising as I spoke, it was not appropriate.

"I thought you would be here." The contempt in his voice evident.

"You've no place here any of you. Please go you're not his or my family, I am sure Mr Barnyard will be good enough to inform you of my father's progress," he dismissed us with his sisters smirking at us behind him.

"Don't worry Hayden, I'll speak to Desmond's consultant and keep you updated." Raymond had this way with him ignoring Joseph. "Go home and I promise I'll contact you when I know more."

Taking his advice, it was exactly what I did, dropping Harry back to Dartford, I no longer would be going back to Desmond's without him it would seem disloyal somehow, I decided going home the better option. On my way back to Ashford, I telephoned Andrew Bartholomew to update him on Desmond's progress. I asked him to check his father's records for a rape attack on Bridie by a John Devlin during 1972 and further, how did Florence Mason die in 1988. Why was Deborah

Wealdon released into the community given she was suspected of killing John Devlin some six months after Bridie's attack, though this was 1988 and where was she now?

"You don't want much do you Hayden?" I could almost hear his grimace down the mobile.

"I'm sorry Andrew, I know Rhona is hiding something from me and I suspect she will not tell unless I can find some evidence pointing to a cover up which she and your father was involved with." I had to be careful about pinning any blame, as it will likely affect the level of information I get.

"If you're trying to tarnish my father's reputation you can forget it, my help stops right here and now!" He was upset given the help including his father's journals he had loaned to me.

"Andrew, please believe me my interest is in finding Bridie and to understand the circumstances surrounding her disappearance nothing more I promise you, I am now more desperate given Desmond is in hospital and suspect all this could have caused his attack, somehow I have to make all his pain worthwhile. I am so grateful for what you've done so far we wouldn't be as far ahead without you." I hoped I had convinced him.

"You're sure it wasn't Bridie in Broadmoor?" No I could not be sure, but I am convinced it was not Maisie either, even though I have never known her.

"Absolutely positive." I would spend a few days at home, so he could contact me there.

"By the way I have given Claire Jennifer Granger's details." I thanked him.

As I pulled into my drive I had not expected the lights to be on, Penny was here I hoped the children might be home too. I was too tired for more arguments, but I hoped they were at home to stay.

So much had happened since Desmond first came to me, hard to believe it was only five or six weeks ago.

My task now was to check out the medical notes for 1972 alongside Cedric's journals I had read them fully and skimmed Bridie's diary for the same time, although I had received the summary from Claire I decided I would read Bridie's version first.

Chapter 12

It was good to see the house lights on when I arrived home weary with the days travelling and worried about Desmond. As I opened the door Simon and Carrie rushed towards me from the kitchen, I had not seen them for a few days and realised I had missed them both very much.

Walking into the kitchen Penny was conjuring up something for the evening meal as if she had never been away at all.

"Hi, I wasn't sure whether you would be home tonight, have you eaten?" She acted as if everything was normal and I had arrived home from the office, which I appreciated. I kissed her cheek picking up the day's newspaper from the kitchen table, normality I thought such bliss. I asked how she had been this past week.

"I'm fine, really I am," she had noticed my raised eyebrows. "I'm missing you ok?" Her attitude quite conciliatory completely surprising me. "You can talk to me you know, I am ready to listen."

"I would like that," hoping she would help me make some sense of my thoughts.

Simon and Carrie joined us and blunt as your own children can be to you, egged on by Carrie, Simon asked.

"Are you and Mum splitting up?" he hesitated. "Getting a divorce?"

Penny and I looked at each other carefully gauging a reaction.

"Honestly, I don't know," I looked into Penny's eyes. "I sincerely hope not."

"Come on let us eat," Penny suggested, my answer appeared to satisfy them for now.

Dinner passed with the children talking of their lives, updating us on their friends and school days and what they believed was the current newsworthy gossip. When Penny and I had time to ourselves and they had enough of our parenting for one day by escaping to their rooms to play whatever the latest game was on the X-Box, so much for any studying.

I poured us some rose' wine a Zinfandel I found cooling in the refrigerator.

"Hayden, I'm sorry as I said I am ready to listen." She had mellowed since our last encounter I felt her acceptance of the situation I found myself in.

I decided, I would go through everything with her, from the advances made by Desmond initially, to visiting my old home street, then to talking with Bridie's Doctors and creating a group of all the parties involved. Getting to speak to Bridie except it wasn't her was important and visiting her friend Maisie in Broadmoor except I didn't believe it was her either again hoping it would be Bridie which it wasn't, clutching at straws, I tried to find two more friends only for one to be dead and the other disappeared. I was convinced there was a cover up. Finding out about her rape and the trouble getting an understanding of what the extent of what the cover up is.

The key for me was Cedric's journal's, medical notes and Bridie's diaries although I felt the later ones had been written for show and not quite being real, but I didn't understand why, and the way Rhona her Nurse had spoken to me I was convinced she was hiding something attempting to stop me finding Bridie. I was convinced Harry knew, but would not share it because of his loyalty to Rhona. A further complication was poor Desmond and his heart attack, his own children refusing to let us go anywhere near their father and all three wanting nothing whatsoever to do with their sister Bridie or us, if she could ever be found and I wasn't convinced if she was still alive. I was not sure if Desmond knew of his daughter's rape ordeal, I needed to speak to Jennifer Granger the old hospital administrator to find out.

"Wow, I'm totally confused, I hope you understood all you've told me?"

"I'm trying very hard to believe it myself." Unburdening myself to her felt good.

"Why has it become so important to you to find her, is it only for Desmond sake or your own as well?" It was a question I expected but did not want to answer.

"I will not deny my motives were less than true, when this all started I was flattered, I rolled in everything I felt could be a reason, including what might be wrong with our relationship. I wanted the dream of my first ever love to put right what I perceived to be the wrongs in my life whatever the consequences.

"Worst of all you knew or at least suspected part of me thought this way, which is why you were so angry you were right and I couldn't deal with it. So part of me chased the dream telling myself I was doing it for Desmond and Bridie when all the time it was for me, since then it has developed into much, much more."

"What changed?" she was listening to me with an unexpected calmness I had not seen in her for years.

"I started to pick injustices, her rape of course, together with if you imagine, the total loss of her whole life, fifty years of it at least, with what started as an illness and could be treated these days within weeks in the comfort of home. The unnecessary operations she has had and a sheer frustration of not finding her, despite our best efforts."

"You must be close, a patient surely cannot be lost in the system or hidden as you suspect without someone knowing what happened to her."

"You may well be right all I can do is keep asking the right questions." My problem is to find the right ones.

"What happens when you find her Hayden?" Her voice subdued.

"Penny, honestly I haven't a clue, it largely depends how I find her and what state she is in I guess."

"Whatever you want to do is fine by me, I hope you will consider the children in all this," an answer not necessary, there was a certain resigned acceptance once Bridie had been found, she would always play a part in my life, the question is how much? I knew Penny felt, for once, powerless to dictate events and for her it became unnerving.

After an early rise and having driven four hours to Lincolnshire, Jennifer Granger was expecting him as Claire had called ahead telling her I would be arriving mid- morning to meet her at her home. Nestled in Woodhall Spa a charming cottage, off the main high road where the tourists at this time of the year kept the tea rooms and small shops busy helping the village survive the next winter, I noted she had to be a wealthy woman to be able to afford to live here.

When she opened her door I was shocked, from all I had learnt about this strong willed forthright fully focused career person, Cedric described her as a 'brute force of nature' in his journals, quite a contrast between this sweet smiling wizened old lady stood in the doorway who had to be in her middle eighties.

"Hello my dear I have been expecting you." Her hair grey pulled into a bun she struggled before me welding her sticks trying to stride purposefully toward her living room couches as I towered above her. "Please do take a seat, it is so nice to see someone it's very rare for me these days, I don't get out much with my arthritis." She held a wistful glance out of the window as she sat down. I declined the tea she offered fearing she would harm herself if I accepted.

"Thank you for seeing me Mrs Granger, I hope my secretary Claire told you why I wanted to see you?" I knew she had.

"Please call me Jennifer or Ms as it would be these days, I have never married, my career you know," she took another wistful glance out of the window. "She mentioned Bridie London?"

I began the story with Desmond of how a father was so desperate to do the right thing by a daughter he adored, to Cedric's Journal and his son Andrew's help, Harry and Rhona, Raymond's involvement and now because Desmond had suffered a heart attack I needed to discuss Devlin and Bridie's rape.

"Oh, it was such a long, long time ago, I would hardly remember, back to 1972 I think."
"Was Desmond her father ever told of her rape at the time or since to your knowledge?" I ignored her memory lapse wary of the frail old woman act a

leopard doesn't change its spots, behind this old lady façade, there's a razor sharp brain, I could tell she knew exactly what had happened even to quoting the year.

"Why would we tell him she was in our care and would be forever?" She spoke dismissively.

"Surely the parents have some rights over their child?"

"They gave those up the moment the girl came to us, she was ours not theirs," harsh I thought.

"You make it sound as if they were your property." I was beginning to get the brute force mentality.

"Don't be so naïve of course they were ours, we could not have family emotions interfering with their minds." Her steely tone led me to agree with Andrew's father.

"So it was generally NHS Policy not to allow families to be involved in their child's hospital treatment?" Her face sharply turned to stone before adopting a patronising softness.

"It was up to the individual hospitals choice to make the policy."

"So it was your policy?"

"Yes of course I was the hospital administrator."

"Did you think it was in the best interests of the patient's care?" She appeared to grit her teeth.

"Absolutely, most if not all of the patients were there or in institutions for the rest of their lives and needed to forget the family left behind." She was deadly serious. "Family interference never helpful."

"Did the Doctors see it this way in particular Cedric Bartholomew?"

"Ah such a lovely man, no they could never quite see the bigger picture."

"Which was?" She was annoying me.

"We, I had to protect our reputation." Beginning to sneer at me.

"Whose reputation would this be yours or the hospital?"

"Both."

"What of the patients?"

"The 'mental' patients," she emphasised. "Have to be controlled if the sanatorium was to function effectively. "Have you ever dealt with the insane Mr Robbins?"

"No I haven't." Shaking my head in frustration.

"They're a different breed I can assure you, it is not a coincidence being called 'mental' patients." She patronised. "They have a way of looking at the world, in a different way to us, upside down, sideway or straight up."

"Childlike?" I offered.

"Yes, but dangerously with an adults focus, which can cause self-harm or harm to others."

"Is this what happened to Bridie London?" Attempting to focus on the rape.

"An unfortunate circumstance which righted itself in the medium term." It sounded like words I would hear at the office.

"You mean Devlin's death?" she nodded surprised I knew.

"What about the drug trials taking place at the sanatorium was it in the best interests of the patients?" I had touched a nerve, looking around at the home she lived in.

"I'm not quite sure what you're implying, the drug trials were carefully regulated and were tested on our patients for the greater good, in order cures could be found, this goes on today." Nervously she tried to change the subject. "So what about Bridie do you know how she is?"

"No, I'm trying to find where she is, what were the side effects of the trials?" Attempting to keep her focused on my points.

"My dear how would I know I was the administrator, the Doctors, Cedric perhaps would have more of an answer for you." She was condescending towards me.

"You do know he died?"

"Oh yes I'm sorry, I forgot, I am old you see, a nice man."

"Who arranged for company drug trials to happen in the asylum?" Not letting her off the hook.

"Are you looking for something sinister or suggesting any wrong doing as I can assure you, I, we had the board and NHS approval." I was not going to get any further with her.

"What of Bridie, how did you help her when she was raped?" the narrowing of her eyes told me all.

"We contained the situation it's all I can say." I did not care much for this woman.

"Devlin was murdered, how did you contain that one?" Sarcasm entered my voice.

"You may not approve of my methods Mr Robbins, but I did what I thought right at the time," for yourself no doubt I thought, I was almost done here.

"How about Florence Mason, how did she die?" This hit her squarely.

"How do you know about her?" She became nervous.

"It hasn't been reported anywhere, you did inform the authorities what happened didn't you?" I could see she was uncomfortable.

"I cannot discuss another patient with you it's

confidential, how do you know of her?"

"Because I have been investigating how the sanatorium was being run at the same time as attempting to find out what happened to Bridie." She looked worried.

"This conversation is now over I am unable to assist you further." She had enough.

"It's time for me to go anyway, thank you for your help." Barely meaning it, I stood up, I did not expect much more from her and began to feel I had wasted my time, unfortunately because of this woman Desmond had wasted his life.

"Before you go, when you find Bridie, she may not be the same person you once knew." The cover up came to mind, but she would not be the one to tell me.

"What do you mean?"

"Remember my words, goodbye young man." Laughing at me as she bade me goodbye. My first impression of her turned out to be wrong she was not sweet at all.

The following day, at the office saw me tiredly updating Claire and trying to get hold of Andrew at Darenth, checking on how Desmond is and making time to see Rhona.

There was slight improvement in Desmond's condition and as Raymond informed he did not have a stroke although his cardiac arrest had been as serious as it could be. He had been moved to the Sam Oram ward a 25 bed unit specialising in heart conditions, unfortunately Joseph insisted only close family be allowed to see his father, for now we had to settle for this, as Raymond pointed out until Desmond is fully awake and cognitive we would have to wait anyway.

Sitting at my desk, it was a relief to get some normality back into my life, spending time with Penny and the children over the weekend did us all good, although Claire had covered for me well, my work had been mounting up, it was important I concentrated on it. Desmond never far from my thoughts.

As my scheduled meetings began to grow again I found myself daydreaming between meetings looking out of my office window to the road below wishing I was elsewhere. Realising I had been enjoying the search for Bridie more than I thought being such a change to my normal routine after two or three days tied to my office, Penny picked up on my frustration when I returned home.

"You're worried about not seeing Desmond aren't you?" she is good at picking up my moods.

"Yes I am Joseph London won't allow visitors, despite Raymond suggesting his condition had improved." I was afraid for my friend's sanity with his uncaring children around him.

"Are Joseph and his sisters at his bedside all the time?"

"No I don't believe so however, the instructions to the medical staff are quite specific."

"Come on let go there now, it's Tuesday night I doubt he'll have visitors," she grabbed her coat and car keys waiting for me in the hallway shouting for Simon and Carrie to both join us. Their love of adventure propelled them from their rooms and games in seconds, within ten minutes we were on the M20 motorway with Penny driving us toward London and Kings College Hospital. All four of us over an hour later entered the hospital following the sign posting to Sam Oram ward within the hospital's complex I made the point despite being here I wouldn't be allowed in to see him.

"You leave it to me." Penny strode off purposefully looking for an argument I loved it when she was in this mood as long as it was not with me.

Although way past visiting hours, the four of us quietly arranged ourselves sitting around Desmond's bed with the blue curtains pulled and surrounding us so we and the other patients were not disturbed; we had 15 minutes no more. Penny had suggested she was his daughter by a previous marriage and not accepted by Joseph her half-brother and half-sisters, but she was entitled to see her own father despite what they ruled. It mattered not to the Nurse on duty she did not care as long as we were quiet.

Sleepily, Desmond aroused from one of the many slumbers he had throughout the past few days, his face showing surprise and delight at seeing me grabbing my arm and shaking it very hard in acknowledgement. He was very weak, his age bearing down upon him hard since his heart attack. Introducing Penny and my two children brought a beaming smile from him when she told him of the ruse of relatives, his daughter his previous marriage, coming a long, long way to see him and it was important for his grandchildren to see him. He enjoyed the conspiracy, with a tinge of sadness briefly crossing his eyes knowing both Joseph and Susan had children, the grandchildren he never saw, used invariably as bargaining chips Joseph and Susan would play up their needs for books, school trips, in order to obtain money from him.

I was proud of my children as they played their roles within earshot of the Nurses. Penny wisely pulled them back so Desmond and I could talk, updating him on our continued search.

"My dear, dear friend," he spoke with no more than a whisper. "I have been waiting for you to come, we have found her. Bridie came to see me again yesterday and spent most of the day with me." This came as a shock to me, someone else making him believe it could be her while he was on his sick bed, it annoyed me and I fought hard to go along with his belief for fear of upsetting him.

"Did Joseph see her?" It was all I could think of saying.

"No he hasn't been in to see me in the past two days." He seemed disappointed with his son.

"You have been on your own with no visitors?" I was disgusted with Desmond's family arrangements of caring for their father.

"No, no, it's alright really, because Bridie has been here, she knew we were looking for her and she forgave me," his words soft and peaceful, I knew it was what he wanted to hear from her.

"But Desmond how is it possible?" I didn't understand and began to feel his mind had been playing tricks on him, I looked at Penny who gestured for me to keep calm for his sake, I was glad she was there.

"Hayden please try not to concern yourself with the details, we have found her, you can stop looking for her," he could hardly contain his excitement I felt he was also asking, warning me to stop our search. "I know she's safe and at peace with me."

I told him because the 'real' Bridie was never at the Cheadle Royal it had to be the reason why she refused to see him. Fortunately for us, it was Sir James Carew CEO at the Cheadle Royal who recommended 'his' Bridie London to Raymond in the first place, this wouldn't have kicked off without him, the information seemed to help.

He detected I was troubled.

"What is it Hayden?"

"I met Jennifer Granger." He was concerned.

"I see, I know about the rape." I was relieved and surprised. "She never told me it was Raymond who did when I met him the one time with Joseph, Susan and Emma, I'm sorry I didn't tell you, I was afraid it would cloud your judgement." I had no way of knowing, but I was not going to argue with him.

"Thank God you knew I was afraid to tell you without causing you more stress."

"We're a right pair afraid of what might upset the other, like a father and son." He laughed.

"And proud to have you Dad!" We hugged each other.

"Bridie is fine, I'm fine." Smiling he gripped my hand tightly and thanked me.

Penny tapped my shoulder tapping her watch indicating we should go as time had run out and especially as Desmond began to drift in and out of sleep.

I suggested to him we had to go, he nodded pointing to the top of his bedside cabinet where there was a letter addressed for me.

"Do not open it yet my friend, we would not have found her had we not met again," I felt tearful, as I watched my friend wilting in front of my eyes, I knew then after this moment together we would never speak again, I leaned down toward him and kissed his forehead.

"Goodbye my dear friend, as any good father would say, you should be proud you have helped Bridie and me, God bless you, you have brought peace to my very soul." I knew I was about to lose my friend, I fought back my tears as Penny gripped my hand.

I pushed back the curtains surrounding his bed as Penny, Carrie and Simon left us alone to wait outside of ICU. He ushered me closer to him and whispered.

"Don't worry my dear friend, all is right I promise." He held my hand tightly fighting against the sleep enveloping him. "She called me Papa Hayden, she called me Papa." His hand went limp as he drifted into a deep sleep.

Penny held me tightly and ushered me away and out of the ward clutching the envelope in my hand, I no longer holding back my tears, the children silently walking behind us holding onto my jacket in support.

Penny muttered our thanks to the Nurses who must have seen such scenes many times over. Silently we drove home. I appreciated Penny more this night than ever before.

The following day I busied myself in my office and also spoke with Raymond and mentioned our visit to Desmond.

"I'm glad Hayden, I did not want to say but over the past few days he had been drifting away more and more, he would have wanted to see you believe me." I did not tell him of Desmond's hallucinations, believing he had spent the day with Bridie, not wishing to harm any memory we had of him. I wondered if it was his mind playing tricks on him at the end or Susan or Emma cruelly spending time with him playing out some sort of game, I hoped not, but in his confusion, he thought it had been her.

Like the first day Desmond and I met again since

my childhood, I walked out of my office and strolled to the Whatman Millennium Park nearby and sat on the very bench where we first discussed finding Bridie, I prayed for him crying as I did so. I pulled out from my inside jacket pocket Desmond's envelope addressed to me, time to read it. I was intrigued given he had written the letter before I had seen him in hospital he had been lucid enough to write about Bridie's visit.

My dear Hayden

Since getting to know you I have found you to be a decent, honest man.

I made a mistake when you were young keeping you from my daughter preventing you being part of her life, I do truly regret this. Your tenacity in trying to find her leads me to believe this situation would have been resolved far sooner than it has been were you involved from the very beginning.

I would be proud to have you as my son, unfortunately more than my own.

I do have some glorious news, which I had hoped to tell you about whenever you could have come to see me, but I know Joseph has kept you away from me.

She visited me Hayden, my beautiful Bridie, now an aged woman, with a good deal of personal scars to contend with, she still has her wonderful twinkle in her eyes despite the many years gone by.

Hayden, she forgave me my friend, forgave me can you believe it? I have never been so happy, as I am writing this to you.

It is my time now my friend, you have supported me well, please, please you can stop looking for her now as she is very close to you believe me.

My sincere thanks to the son I wished I had, who

has helped me rest in peace.
  Goodbye to you Hayden, you are my true friend.
  You have my respect
  Desmond

I could barely control my despair as I walked slowly back to the working part of my life where I really did not want to be right now.

Back in the office I pulled her *1971-1972 diary 6* from my desk drawer gauging where I had been up to on the previous read before beginning my skimming, turning a few pages towards the middle of the diary, I came to the notes on her rape.

Although I had forgotten about it, I asked Claire why she never summarised Bridie's rape for me.

"I didn't want it to put you off trying to find her."

"You sound like Desmond," guiltily we laughed.

Diary: I have taken so long trying to write about this as my head has been all over the place, but Nurse Rhona insisted I should tell it even if it is to my diary to act as therapy to get this episode of my life out of my head. I pray it works in order I may start to live with it better. It helps the evil Devlin has not been around and now others have come forward about his touching them and a couple even told of him attacking them and him threatening so they would not tell anyone. I wish they had he wouldn't have done what he did to me, but I am not alone Rhona says, I was raped and beaten by John Devlin in the toilets and left for dead, there I have said it.

Bridie went on to describe the assault in graphic detail from her demanding he leave her alone to stop touching, to her crying in resigned acceptance, believing this was something she had encouraged. He left her bleeding struggling even to walk when she was found.

I should have known and told someone, I feel responsible somehow, a touch here a touch there, I let it go on. He was always around wherever I would go and be talking dirty to me, he was stalking me I know it now, hitting me at times on my bum each time harder than before, goading me it was a game to him and when I told him to stop, he suggested we were only joking around together.

One day, he was helping a girl back to her room, seeing me he started clicking his lips at me and laughed, a grin spread across his face, sinister.

I went into the corridor toilet, no sooner had I closed the door he was there grabbing me from behind one hand on my breasts the other pushed in between my legs.

I felt powerless, I started to scream, he spun me around and hit me hard across my face splitting my lip and told me to shut up, inside I screamed but no sound would be heard. By now, I was on the floor scrambling to get up, begging him to stop and leave me alone my face throbbing, he pushed me back down on the hard tiled floor and dropped to his knees. Suddenly he was crawling all over me, hands grabbing urgently at every part of my clothing, pulling, ripping, button's popping, he wasn't listening to me at all, concerned only about his violent act upon me.

With his left arm across my windpipe holding me down, I felt my soul being killed, his right hand thrust between my legs, he hurt me, I was pushing and scratching him he used his arm to spread my legs apart I shouted no! Would anyone hear me, I could not hear myself I remember sobbing and saying not to hurt me please, but he continued I felt as if I was splitting in two the pain extreme.

He kept pushing into me I told him, begged him to stop I know I am not a virgin anymore. I passed out not sure how long it took I was found by other patients and then, I felt Nurse Jackson's arms around me gently talking quietly to me waving everyone away. My mind drifted back to the first day at the asylum when Papa left me here, she was the one who comforted me I had forgotten, she made me feel safe, as she has done now, and I will love her forever. She asked me who did this and I told her, some of the girls who heard gasped.

I wanted to go to the toilet it was why I was there I was bleeding badly it hurt to pee. The next I remember I was in the medical ward being told by the Doctor he had examined me and I would be ok, the person responsible has been dealt with, I did not understand what he meant. I drifted off to sleep I was so very sore.

Dr Bartholomew came to see me with Nurse Jackson and Miss Granger, they told me I would be looked after properly now, I could go back to my room whenever I wanted. Miss Granger told me I should try to forget all what had happened it was best for everyone concerned. I did not speak for a very long time.

My sadness for Bridie overwhelmed me I wanted to see what she had said about Devlin's return to the hospital and thumbed through to the back of the diary.

Diary: I have not seen him yet, but Debs told me she had seen Devlin back in the hospital, I did not believe it I thought she was trying to frighten me. I ran to Nurse Jackson who said Debs was right he had only been suspended for 3 months, he would be working in another part of the hospital and would not come anywhere near me. I shall not sleep tonight.

I picked up her next diary, to find out what she thought of Devlin's death.

Diary 7 1973 - 1974

He is dead, I wished I had the courage to do it, at first I thought it was Maisie, but Debs admitted it, I gave her a huge kiss and hug I know she did it for me.

Good riddance he was a bastard!

I will waste no more writing on him.

This really surprised me, It was then I realised Bridie had dramatically shifted from a girl to a grown woman, a hard pill for her to swallow.

Claire interrupted a meeting held in my office she had just heard, Desmond had passed away peacefully. I immediately disbanded the meeting and stood up to my window idly watching people walking by the office building my mind blank and without thought a curious emptiness in my head, my heart in despair fighting back my tears.

I struggled to fight the sadness welling inside of me at his passing, I will miss him greatly and felt nothing but kindness and love towards the man I knew and remembered. God bless you Desmond. I knew I would have to continue trying to find her despite his wish to leave her unfound, in order to make sure she was financially stable and for her to decide what to do with the Sidcup property

Desmond had left her. I suspected I would find out why in due course.

    Within a week Desmond's funeral had been arranged by Joseph, Desmond had made no secret he wanted, wished to be buried with his beloved Josephine who was buried at the Sidcup Cemetery in Foots Cray, Kent a couple of miles from their home together.

    Although Joseph took the credit throughout the day for the excellent funeral service at the arranged gathering following the burial in Desmond's home, with caterers attending to everyone's culinary wishes, I knew Desmond had already paid handsomely to the Funeral Directors covering everything.

    He had been annoyed as no-one was willing to say the few customary words about the departed individual, when I got up and told the group what a fine man I thought he had been, Joseph should have spoken but chose not to.

    Apart from offering my condolences for their loss, I had little contact with Desmond's children, odd calling middle-aged people children. Joseph sneered at me most of the time at some vain attempt to make me feel unwelcome. On one occasion I was able to corner Susan and Emma without his ever presence between them. I missed Penny's presence beside me.

    "Desmond had become a true friend of late it was so kind of you to spend time at his bedside before he died." I looked at each in turn.

    "Are you being sarcastic?" Susan's red flushed angry face, almost exploding, told me she was not joking, I had hit a nerve.

"I'm not sure I understand," trying to be polite as possible.

"What are you talking about?" Emma emphasised the 'you'.

"He mentioned he had a visitor, a woman, who had spent most of his final days with him, I naturally thought it to be one of you." I was puzzled realising they did not have a clue what I was talking about.

"Well it could not have been us we took a short break and went to CenterParcs for a week together, we had a great time." I was horrified at their callousness.

"You mean to say you never visited your father once while he was lying in his hospital bed dying?" I showed my disgust. "And went on holiday?"

"Joseph was there at the hospital most times," offered Emma. "Besides we were stressed out, what could we have done anyway?" Susan excused herself tired of the conversation closely followed by Emma.

Soon enough it was mid-afternoon and time for people to leave, which left Joseph, Susan and Emma, myself, Rhona, Harry, Raymond and Andrew and at my own invitation Mr Carlton a senior partner of Boniface, Carlton & Haver Solicitors at Law.

It was quite clear Joseph and his sisters were trying to get rid of everyone as soon as they could, including the group and myself, so they could ransack Desmond's home.

Mr Carlton tapped Joseph on his shoulder.

"Mr London, Mr Joseph London?"

"Yes, you know this is my father's funeral," he had lost his politeness now most of the guests had gone. "Who are you anyway?"

"Just making sure sir, my card sir I represent your father and his estate."

"What the hell do you mean?" His face showing concern, this was not what he was expecting.

"Your father left a will and as the executor it is my duty to see his wishes are adhered to." Desmond would have enjoyed watching their faces.

"Remember, we had a conversation about this!" I spoke to all three of them at the same time.

"We never found a will and thought he would not have had time before he was taken ill," Susan said, her face draining of colour. "We looked everywhere." I bet you did, I thought.

"Well sir, madam it appears he did." Carlton looked down his nose at them through the glasses perched on the bridge of his nose.

"Who invited you here?" Her sister spoke out, Carlton shifted a little unused to being challenged for carrying out his clients wishes I stepped in.

"I did Emma, your father gave me a copy of it and asked for me to arrange for the solicitor be present in order to facilitate a will reading." It was great watching them squirm.

All three of Desmond's children looked at me stony faced, I added." He knew how important it would be for you." Their moods darkened considerably.

Mr Carlton made for the dining room and started spreading out his papers on the large oak table, while people followed him inside. Pulling him aside, I thanked him for the Facebook search on me he had recommended to Desmond bringing us both together. He smiled remembering Desmond's excitement at the find.

Joseph was drumming his fingers on the table.

"Get on with it man."

As Mr Carlton walked us through the formal legalities, in terms of Bridie not being present, he had a separate letter from Desmond stating I would be her representative insofar as his estate is concerned. He informed us, the valuations of properties and goods owned had already been calculated, inheritance tax, capital gains, probate services had all been arranged and informed at the request of Mr London.

Susan's patience for the legalities ran out. "Tell us what we will get," She was disappointed there was not going to be a free for all, Joseph told her to be quiet.

"Starting with personal possessions, Desmond left all of his wife's jewellery to his eldest daughter." I thought of Bridie.

"It would be me right? Because she's nowhere to be found," Susan tried her luck.

"I'm afraid you're not the eligible party." Carlton knew his business.

"Where is the jewellery, anyway?" I asked.

"I'm not sure Mr Robbins, I would guess in this house somewhere," Carlton assured me. I drew out from under the table the shoebox I had retrieved from the lounge, the jewellery should have been inside it, I looked directly at the three of them.

"It's not in here anymore?" I lifted the shoebox onto the table I had previously placed on the dining chair beside me. "This was in the corner unit in the living room and Desmond previously showed me the jewellery set aside for Bridie inside this box.

"Well we don't have them," Joseph said automatically as he briefly looked at his sister's face, he was troubled.

"Mr Carlton, we should consider calling the

police as I can vouch for the fact they were kept in this shoebox where I saw them two weeks ago and now they are missing, the only keys to this house are mine and his three children currently present. As no-one has mentioned a break in we should act immediately." Unintentionally I lied, it had been a month ago, but they were unlikely to question it.

"Could these have been possibly taken by someone today?" Carlton enquired not amused. "Surely not at a funeral."

"Alright, alright, I have got them, I only wanted to look at them, they were my mother's after all," Susan removed them from her handbag placing them on the table.

"Of course my dear, I understand." Carlton looked to me. "Are we satisfied Mr Robbins?" I nodded deliberately picking up the jewellery placing them back into the shoebox. "I'll take care of these for Ms Bridie London."

"There are two sets of property to deal with and cash within two banks and one savings account which is expected to cover taxes and solicitors fees. This bungalow property is bequeathed to the eldest daughter Bridie to live in or sell according to her wishes." Carlton became official.

"Oh I guess were being shafted by our father again, everything is Bridie's it is disgusting." Joseph shook his head in despair.

"Please Mr London let me finish, let me read a statement by your father attached to this will." The room went quiet even I never knew this existed.

Hi Everyone
I am glad you could make it and hope it all went well.

If you are now reading this statement, it means I am dead, so I will say this to my three children Joseph, Susan and Emma. It was never my intention to leave anything to any of you in my will, because the amount of support I have given all three of you over the years has been extensive. In business, marriage, school fees, deposits on houses, as well as funding cars for each of you with promises of payback never materialising added together, I have supported each one of you far more than I have ever done for my unfortunate Bridie. In short, I do not feel you deserve anything at all from my estate.

The groan audible from the three, Carlton continued.

However, for three reasons I have left you each something in my will and my gift is not out of my love for you, as I know in my heart of hearts you are cold and uncaring and certainly uncharitable where Bridie your own blood sister is concerned. Bridie has led a life in the extreme by anyone's standards and her life could have been all so much better. It could have been one of you but for the grace of God, she went in place of you, since then you have vilified her as if somehow her predicament was her fault and a slight against each of you. I suspect she would have shown each of you far more compassion than you would have deserved. Even now, I can picture you all impatiently shifting from side to side saying to yourselves I wish this old fool Carlton would get on with it so you can find out whether I have left anything to you, am I right?

We all turned and looked at the three of them expecting a response, most of us found it amusing. Carlton coughed at his client's picture of him.

"Just get on with it please." Joseph was both furious and embarrassed at having unintentionally confirmed his father's thoughts.

Carlton coughed even louder and went on.

My first reason is, it is what your mother would have wanted, and secondly, the bequest will become void immediately, if you contest any part of the will. Thirdly, and most importantly, because my dear friend Hayden who I have grown to love as the son I would have liked, who has supported me during these past weeks, persuaded me to do so as he suspects, as do I, you would hound Bridie to her dying days for your perceived share.

My dear children, somehow you lost what your mother and I had tried to instil in each of you when growing up. You became bitter and jealous of the one person you could have helped.

The biggest regret is not having enough time getting to know my grandchildren you purposely kept away from me, finding this hard to forgive.

Unhappily, I have to agree with Hayden you would torment the life out of Bridie so I could not let this happen I want her to live in peace.

Be aware, if you were unfortunate not to make the most of your inheritance and decided to chance your hand and go after Bridie's inheritance, Hayden has promised he will sue you on my behalf in order to revert your inheritance back to Bridie. I am sure you will appreciate this will create a mountain of debt and will ruin each of you.

There is a second property, which although known to you being the site of your old home in Fenham Road, Peckham I give to each of you equally.

It may surprise you to learn I have never sold our greengrocers building and land where we all lived as a family believing it to be a sound investment and

I kept it because of remembering Bridie, so you actually have her to thank for your good fortune.

"Here we go again, good old sis again."
"Please Mr London we are wasting time" Carlton fast realising why Desmond disliked his son so much.

I have always led you to believe we only had a lease on the Peckham property and in the beginning this was true however, prior to your mother and I retiring and vacating the property and with the Landlord being keen to liquidate assets. He offered the site to me as a freehold property and I leased both the business and the property myself to a similar family such as ours, allowing us to afford to buy the home you are, at this moment sitting in.

When the lease ran out this past year for the tenants who decided to retire, with planning permission I commissioned builders to restructure the land and buildings into six three bedroom superior apartments designed for the rental market.

Joseph, Susan and Emma, it is this development which now becomes your inheritance, shared equally between you, will provide you each once let, an income to live comfortably on in the future unless you decide to sell them, Carlton has the necessary income projections.

Good luck, while a good deal of the time I have not liked you as people, rest assured I bear you no malice, I have loved all three of you equally as I loved Bridie, my dying wish is you truly accept my sentiment and find it in your heart to embrace your elder sister too.

Think kindly of me my children.
Your loving father

For a brief moment the room was silence my

thoughts were with Desmond.

"How much are they worth?" Joseph doing sums in his head.

He broke a tension hanging over the rest of us; making us laugh at him unfortunately, he was serious, his father's words not touching him at all.

"Rest assured Mr London you three have the lion's share of your father's estate." Carlton passed three calculation sheets to all three of Desmond's children and quickly wrapped up the proceedings and left hurriedly glad it was all over.

"One thing, I doubt we will see each other again." I offered.

"No we will not and that's for sure," Joseph said, the other two muttering something under their breath.

"Good, keys please."

"What?"

"The keys of this property," I held out my hand, they all but threw them at me I asked the group to stay while watching Joseph, Susan and Emma put on their coats ready to leave, already discussing who got which apartments the two top, middle or ground floor ones. They did not look back at us, as they ceremoniously slammed the door behind them. It would be the last we would ever see of them, I hoped they heard us laughing at them, I breathed a sigh of relief, hoping Desmond had seen all. With the slamming of the door behind Bridie's siblings, we all relaxed taking time to consider Desmond.

"How ever did Desmond manage to produce a son and two daughters like them, they are a disgrace?" We all agreed with Raymond.

Chapter 13

Andrew invited me to Darenth Park Hospital on the following *Monday*, the last week of August, he had reviewed most of his father's papers.

Arriving at lunchtime, Andrew and I walked the grounds until we came upon a previously laid out table presumably prepared by the hospital's restaurant staff. Andrew had also invited Harry for what appeared a typical business lunch, except in open air, with an array of nicely cut sandwiches on a large platter presented to us with another for samosa's and onion bhaji's. The weather was holding allowing both Andrew and I to avoid the inside of the smelly sheds, Harry's domain.

Harry started unwrapping cling film from the sandwich platter and poured us the soft drinks on offer. His huge hands no match for the quarter cut sandwiches. Andrew opened up his green folder of papers as we helped ourselves to the fare.

"I did find the papers pointed to the answers you sought, although some it appears were deliberately hidden amongst a whole pile of training course papers in my loft, I only found these because when I discussed this with my wife she suggested I look up there knowing we had stored some of my Father's old papers there. It is why it has taken so long, it was quite strange though." He was troubled we could both see it.

"What was strange Andrew?" I challenged.

"I like to think I knew my father as a straight, up

front type of person, he always had had a Doctors need to keep every record and this he instilled in me, impressing upon me the need to keep records properly organised." He was becoming melancholy.

"What's the problem Andrew?" I could tell he was uncomfortable.

"These were buried amongst papers which normally would never ever be looked at except by the person who put them there and he is hardly likely to now." He pointed to the black folder he carried.

I shook my head not answering he was clearly disturbed about his find refusing to accept this memory of his father being secretive or at worst dishonest.

"My father appears to have covered up or at best mislaid papers inappropriately, patients notes hidden within his own training course notes." His voice bitter. "Each of the documents are numbered."

"Yes I know up to number 32, am I right?" Andrew looked baffled.

"How did you know?"

"I noticed throughout the journals they were displayed like reference numbers."

"I never noticed."

"They were put discreetly, but randomly in the bottom left hand corner, presumably by the subject it referred to on the particular page." It shocked him.

"What I am realising is my father must have covered up 32 incidents he should not have done."

"How long was he there for, 26 years? Not bad going over one a year. Have you read them all in conjunction with the journals?" I knew the answer because I had them.

"No, not with the journals, but I have read the notes and I'm ashamed of him."

"Hold on there, Dr Bartholomew, the man was a saint in my eyes I knew him back then, he did so much good. You cannot convict him without the facts." Harry said defending his recall of Cedric Bartholomew.

"I have to agree with Harry, the journals are in my car and I have finished with them for now." He seemed satisfied he could limit any exposure. "Besides as I've told you before I'm only interested in finding Bridie, there are two numbers I would like to see the documents for."

"What are they?"

"16 and 32."

"Did you find the answers to my questions Andrew?" I had no interest in laying blame for anything.

"Yes I did, more importantly the notes about Bridie's rape which occurred in 1972 happened to be with the papers relating to 1988."

"You mean Florence Mason's death?"

"Yes."

We took a break to eat with Harry pouring us more drinks.

"Andrew, 16 deals with Bridie's rape and 32 for Florence Mason."

"What about the Wealdon girl?"

"Oh I found papers about her too," he was troubled, thumbing through his papers it was number 18.

"What's wrong Andrew, come on tell me?"

"The reputation of my father, the papers should have been destroyed a long time ago and no-one would have been any of the wiser." He looked across at Harry who had known his father. "He seemed to have put together a whole raft of problems and hidden them all together within his training manuals for one reason only, because he was mixed up in the issues and had not wished to be open about them."

"At least it can help explain what happened back then Andrew."

"I suppose so Harry." He was not convinced.

"To be blunt Andrew, at the very least your father was part of cover up's or at best he engineered them, but at the moment only you have the information which could tell us the extent and the implications legal or otherwise. It's your call to share them my friend, my angle is to find Bridie for Desmond and nothing more." I was stabbing in the dark, but I tried to get him to open up by giving him an impression I knew some of the truth."

"I should have burnt them Hayden." He meant it.

"Andrew, I'm certainly not in a position to cause you embarrassment, I guess we are only after the truth." I noted Harry had dropped the Dr Bartholomew in favour of his first name.

"Harry's right what purpose would it serve to destroy your father's name, are all the papers incriminating, I doubt it, I am only interested in the papers to help me find Bridie?" I felt his internal struggle, but all I wanted was the truth.

"I'm not sure they do," he made a mental decision to help and I knew it was not easy for him.

"Would it help if I prompted you?"

"No I'll tell it as I see it, he wrote notes on each paper as well."

"I knew your father and had tremendous respect for him, are you sure you want to do this Andrew?"

Harry's words helped him.

"Yes Harry I do, you knew my father well?

"One of the finest upstanding people I ever knew, I am convinced whatever he has been involved in or hidden it could only have been for the good of his patients, you must believe it of him." I could tell Andrew was comforted.

"In 1972, mid-summer I believe staff shortages had become chronic within the sanatorium. Most of the staff doubling up on shifts due to holidays and the influx of many more patients as economy cuts across the NHS had forced closure of a number of hospitals. In particular, where they had psychiatric wards within them and with Darenth Sanatorium picking up the shortfalls, unfortunately the checks and balances required in a place of the asylums size were sadly lacking." He checked the stack of papers in the black folder he had been carrying for reference.

"The rape attack of Bridie London had not been documented properly through the medical notes, neither were the suspicions levied toward John Devlin, unfortunately proof was hard to come by. My father wrote pages of notes of her injuries and the subsequent mental trauma she suffered as a result, in fact he turned it into a psychiatric case study." This troubled Andrew. "He never submitted it."

"A good thing isn't it Andrew?"

"I suppose so."

"Come on Andrew, times were different then, try not to destroy your memory of a great father he must have been, he could not take the blame for the fault of others, what happened to Devlin?"

"He was suspended pending enquiries he came back after three months, not quite exonerated, but near enough."

"Who was responsible for the enquiry?"

"Jennifer Granger the hospital administrator, the scandal all, but finished her career, the one chance she had to redeem herself was to write a full report dismissing any responsibility by the NHS, which she managed however it was also not submitted. I have both her report here and the case study," he waved both at me.

"Why was her report not submitted?"

"It was not required, she offered to walk away from the sanatorium after Devlin's death the board refused, and told her to tear up the report which cited too much politics, it's my guess is she knew exactly what she was doing." Knowing her, I had to agree. "My father writes, how she ran the sanatorium with an iron will, unfortunately, when patients in her charge were blamed she felt she had lost control." I had this vision of a little old woman screaming at everyone, pity; in my opinion, she needs to be in prison.

"Who was blamed?"

"Bridie, Maisie or Deborah, my father's notes suggest he believed it to be Deborah, who adored Bridie at the time. The moment John Devlin came back to the asylum, he was in danger from her, I think the current phrase would be 'dead man walking', within two weeks of his return his death sent shockwaves through all sanatoriums and controls were tightened overly so. Throughout his notes I felt my father had taken too much of a fatherly approach to Bridie believing her to be the weak member of the three, primarily led by Maisie heavily influenced by Deborah."

"I have not detected any wrong doing by your

father, so my apologies for suggesting it earlier." I tried to be sincere.

"Please wait on your judgement, the second question was how did Florence Mason die?"

"Yes."

"She was stabbed to death in 1988 by Deborah Wealdon according to my father who identifies her from fingerprints and saliva proving it was her and the high probability she was in the same unit where the murder took place."

"I thought she had been released?" The beginnings of the cover up.

"Do the papers indicate why she did it?"

"Yes my father has noted from the sessions he had with Deborah she was in love with Bridie completely, she was everything to her, she acted as her protector, guardian even her owner."

"What of Maisie?"

"Deborah was scared of her, probably the only person she was scared of, Maisie and Bridie had been together since the beginning, it was a bond which could not be broken by anyone."

"So what of Florence?"

"Florence was relatively new to the group and another weak member, younger than all of them who loved Bridie too." I was beginning to see a pattern emerge I dismissed it as being part of prison life. "It's likely she could have boasted to Deborah about Bridie's feelings for her."

"You're suggesting jealousy as a motive?"

"Yes plain and simple jealousy."

"So Deborah was tried and convicted of her murder, right?"

"Why should she be?"

"I don't understand."

"She was already in the mental asylum the justice

courts would have sent her to, given the sanatorium was closing soon in favour of prisons and secure unit hospitals what difference would it have made?" It felt like Jennifer Grangers controlling hand on the crime.

"Your father would not have been able to cover this up alone, as a Doctor I would suggest even in those days it was beyond his remit."

"It looks like he did it with our old friend Jennifer Granger." Andrew was fighting his emotions, realising he did not want to believe it of his father, but the truth did not lie, he confirmed my thoughts.

"Jennifer Granger is the one to blame for this not your father Andrew."

"Perhaps his notes were a record of events, peace of mind for the family perhaps." Harry trying to help.

"It seems she did not have any family."

"So how did it work?" We approached it pragmatically.

"Ok, with the exception of Bridie the other three women had no family."

"Why is Bridie or Maisie involved?"

"Let me finish," I raised my hand in apology, given his irritation. "The situation became far more complicated, as Deborah had passed her mental examination and assessment the panel had agreed her release already."

"So much for assessments," he ignored me I could not help it.

"She believed she could get away without anyone finding out, but on the other hand she didn't want to leave Bridie either, such is the warped mind of the insane." I tried to get this clear in my mind.

"So what you're saying is she loved Bridie so

much she killed Florence because she was jealous." He nodded. "And was also afraid to leave the sanatorium, which was closing anyway, because she didn't want to leave Bridie?"

"Yes."

"By committing the crime she would be able to stay near her, despite the fact she must have known Bridie was also going to be moved somewhere else and they would separate anyway." I was flabbergasted.

"I guess it was a chance she was willing to take."

"But she was caught?" Harry interjected.

"Yes, yes," he said impatiently. "However, it created opportunities, as a group we have discussed the closure of the hospital and the disbursement of patients."

I agreed not wishing to interrupt him.

"Florence had died, like a great deal of patients over the years have died, nothing new, the cause of death was the concern."

"Yes murder." I pointed out.

"Not quite!" Andrew shook his head at us. "A brain haemorrhage would fit the bill and it was certified as such."

"Your father signed her death certificate?" A direct cover up by his father.

"Yes I'm afraid so, anyway Jennifer Granger persuaded Deborah Wealdon she take Bridie London's name and stay institutionalised otherwise she would be tried for murder, she liked the idea of adopting her love's name." He referred to his black folder again.

"Blackmail, to what end?" He glared at me.

"Patience please Hayden, I mentioned the opportunities before, they believed Bridie had suffered a grave injustice through the rape attack and her being associated with Devlin's death, together with a string of offences in the early part of her time at the asylum. They caused her committal, where most of those were attributed to Maisie Belling it was felt she should never have been in the place at all. Unfortunately, it was doubtful the panel would see fit to release her despite assessment tests all passed by her which was why the plan was hatched.

"There was a plan then?" I doubted one had existed.

"I'm only going by the notes." Andrew stated pointing to the folder.

"So names were swapped, how does it help Bridie?"

"It meant she could be released as Deborah Wealdon." It began to dawn on me opening up a new train of thought.

"Unbelievable! You're telling me Bridie adopted a two time murderers name and everyone was happy with this arrangement?" Harry shook his head in disgust.

"So she was released?" Was there hope, I could not gauge it yet.

"Not quite, there was a complication." I thought so cynically.

"Which was?" I was getting impatient.

"Maisie Belling wasn't going to keep quiet about it." I was confused again.

"Do you remember the criteria for deciding which patients would go to a secure unit hospital and those to prisons?"

"Yes those with family funded means would go to hospital and non-funded to prison." I noted Harry had little to say, but I wondered if he knew more it appeared a good act.

"Correct, Maisie wanted hospital not a prison which she was earmarked for."

"So they changed Maisie's name to Bridie's to hospitalise her and Deborah went to prison as Maisie, what did Deborah have to say about it?"

"She was quite pleased she regarded Maisie as one to be feared, it gave her credibility in prison."

"Are you saying the person I saw in Broadmoor, a secure unit incidentally, with Desmond and Raymond was the real Deborah Wealdon?" I actually had a conversation with a two-time murderer.

"Yes, confirmed by blood test, Raymond called me this morning he said he left you a message on your mobile phone. Who knows what assessments have happened during the past 25 years in order for Deborah to be reclassified, I would suggest her pensionable age must have something to do with it."

"I haven't picked up my messages today," I wished I had I would have been clearer earlier. "Bridie was automatically released as Deborah Wealdon?"

"Yes," confirmed Andrew.

"Then where is she?" I suddenly had the feeling this was not news to Harry.

"Hayden, it's the one thing which eludes me from my father's notes." Andrew was apologetic.

"Does Raymond know about this?"

"Yes, but only a summarised version."

"I wondered what he was going to do about it." He shrugged his shoulders.

"I guess we ought to get the group back together again, unfortunately without Desmond." We needed to decide on our next course of action.

"Yes, a good idea." There was hesitancy in

Andrew's voice.

"Don't worry Andrew, 25 year old cover ups cannot be in the public interest surely." I assured him.

"I hope not."

It had been a long day, I promised to get Claire to organise for us all to meet in the next few days. Bridie was free at least, where I did not know, a few more days would not harm her at all, even wherever she is, cover up or not the search had taken an unexpected turn.

A plan was hatching in my mind and I needed time to think it through, I wondered how much of this Harry and Rhona knew already, I noted Harry not contributing much to my meeting with Andrew, a coincidence? Two people who were there at the sanatorium when this had happened and Rhona had left the sanatorium at the same time. I was lucky Andrew had a conscience and had shared this with us.

Once again, the group would meet at the Maudsley hospital and I found myself thinking of little else, I had detailed the whole story to both Claire and Penny who were overwhelmed at the mystery it had thrown up, all starting for me via a post-it note on my computer screen. I looked at the piles of paperwork created across 50 years and felt the end was closer now than ever, despite not having read as much as I should have and wished my old friend could have been alive to continue the journey with me. I pulled his letter from the file clearly marked Desmond, Claire's efficiency I thought and smiled, what would I have done without her.

I re-read the letter once again and realised if

Susan or Emma had not visited their father in hospital, now I knew she was free somewhere it had to have been Bridie who had visited him. I hoped I was right for Desmond's sake. It occurred to me someone within the group or close to us had to have known we were looking for her in order she knew what hospital he was in to visit.

Chapter 14

The familiar reception area of the Maudsley hospital and staff helped smooth the way to automatic entry to Raymond's office. It was early morning and I was the last to arrive, the others already helping themselves to the refreshments on offer, I was warmly greeted by all of them I now considered my friends.

Raymond told me Andrew had summarised the meeting we had together and his concern for his father's reputation. Harry dismissed it simply by saying what is past is past.

"In principle I agree with Harry," Raymond spoke solemnly. "However the records I feel must be put right in terms of the women's names before I would be comfortable with it." I worried bureaucracy would get in the way.

"What records?" Rhona showed a real interest, which surprised me.

"For example, I have a proven Maisie Belling called Bridie London, who I'm assessing for release into the community and she's already part of a cover up about who she is, which also means what she has been responsible for." I could see the doubts he had. "My problem is in all the records she has shown herself to be a violent human being, at least in the first 25 years at Darenth sanatorium and it worries me."

"Surely in the past?" Rhona seemed to be taking a

keen interest, I wondered why.

"Since being older she has a good record doesn't she? Wasn't she recommended to you as a candidate for release by the Cheadle Royal?"

"Rhona her past is relevant, I cannot in all conscience pass Maisie Belling based on Bridie's London's past, and I will not do it." Raymond was adamant. "Despite her current good conduct."

"What are you going to do Raymond?" From what Andrew had explained happened back then I worried the house of cards might fall down and start a reaction nationwide and no one would benefit.

"In normal circumstances Hayden I would recommend her release to the panel however, we have been assessing her as Bridie London with a separate background to Maisie Belling. This means her assessment is flawed she must have her real name back to validate it. Andrew without condoning what has happened, I will not be doing anything about what we know happened" he emphasised. "But I am not going to continue to perpetrate a wrong deed, well intentioned though it may have been some 25 years ago." I noted an audible sigh of relief coming from Rhona who was blushing as I looked directly at her.

"Let us suppose you change her name back to Maisie, what difference will a new background of 25 years ago have on her assessment today?" I could have hugged Andrew for asking the question, it made Raymond stop to think. I noted a smile spread widely across his face.

"I'm sure in a policy document somewhere it suggests assessments need only go back as far as the last ten years so I think we may well be covered." He had his solution.

"Hang on a minute, if you change Bridie London

back to Maisie it means you will have two Maisie Belling's in the system, one who happens to be called Deborah Wealdon for real, so you're going to have to change her name back as well right?"

"No you cannot do it!" Rhona said a little too quickly.

"Why not Rhona, it would mean a cascading effect, two Maisie's lead to two Deborah's meanwhile Bridie is still submerged." I focused closely on Rhona.

"You've lost me Hayden." Harry pronounced.

"Raymond, Andrew?" Both shrugged their shoulders not understanding.

"Where is Deborah Rhona? Or should I say Bridie?" The group focused on her too.

"I'm not sure what you mean Hayden?" The rest of the group's attention sharpened.

"Oh I think you do, all along you have been questioning the necessity of the name changing and questioning why we should be looking for Bridie at all. I automatically assumed you were trying to protect the reputation of your profession, your past and even Cedric Bartholomew's for Andrew's sake, but it was always Bridie you were protecting wasn't it?" She nodded, tears in her eyes. "Tell us Rhona please."

I watched Harry take hold of her hand protectively, I was right he knew what was going on.

Rhona began her story slowly; she took us through the time she first met Bridie when her screams rang out through the corridor on the first day, dashing to the sound finding Bridie pressing herself tightly against the window of her room watching a man driving away later established as

Desmond her father. From this moment, she vowed she would help her.

Rhona spoke of Maisie being a cold fish who befriended Bridie becoming a close friend of hers. There were many incidents where Maisie would protect Bridie forcefully, they used to dress and wear their hair identically, acting as twins and played on it fooling many including the Doctors and Nurses.

"I can vouch for it." Harry interrupted awkwardly.

She described there was a system of punishment when the women were young meted out to the patients if they misbehaved, got into fights or arguments, abusing the schooling regime by not doing work assignments or failing to attend. The punishments were not harsh and consisted of a reduction of benefits like television time, recreation outlets, treats lost such as magazines, chocolate, books, paints or drawing materials and favourite classes of learning, all would be withheld, together with any contact with others for periods of time including family, isolation usually working the best.

Maisie was the worst offender at flouting the rules she developed a reputation for it, so as twins they would share the burden of punishment and for them it became fun.

Another girl wanted to get involved with them both, her name was Deborah Wealdon, who when young looked as they did until she developed a thyroid condition and ballooned in weight as she aged. Unfortunately, she never played like Maisie and Bridie, Deborah was dangerous, especially when the other patients cruelly laughed about her size. Bridie or Maisie never once insulted her taking her friendship unconditionally and in response

Deborah vowed to protect them both. It was true she was frightened of Maisie's capabilities, but where Maisie's threats amounted to pushing and shoving other patients, Deborah would make sure she harmed, bones would be broken and cuts would appear. The three were close and classed as the bullies of the sanatorium, perhaps not Bridie, but Maisie used Deborah and chose to let her be the henchman for the three.

On more than one occasion, Rhona confirmed she was threatened and subsequently stabbed, once if Bridie had not stopped it she would not be here to tell the tales.

"Deborah loved Bridie and would do anything for her, I once made the mistake of arguing with Bridie over Maisie's continued influence over her, I was attacked." She struggled with the memory. Rhona skipped to 1972 when Bridie's rape attack happened. "Clearly Bridie was distraught by the attack up to then she had been a relative innocent of sex and life in general, although she was 23." She explained. "Both Maisie and Deborah were angry for her, there used to be a saying in the sanatorium by the staff, mentally disturbed patients are dangerous most of the time however, mentally disturbed patients with a purpose are lethal, it happened Deborah got to Devlin first." I realised this was the most Rhona had spoken since meeting her.

"Initially, on his return to work John Devlin had kept far away from any contact with the women in the Rosemary secure unit where Bridie, Maisie and Deborah were patients, the unit named in memory of a previous long-term patient, one of the first to enter the sanatorium when built in 1878. A whole range of practices and procedures had been named after her such was her notoriety, at a grand age of 75 she had spent sixty years of her life at the asylum dying in 1938." She continued.

"The promised changes of practices restructured to avoid another Devlin and London incident, started to be relaxed and were all, but reversed within a week of his return mainly due to him ingratiating himself with everyone he possibly could. A changed man or so we thought, gradually he started to develop his true colours" She paused for a second making sure we understood.

"At first Devlin bragged how no one had proved he had raped Bridie despite everyone believing it to be true, one or two of the male Nurses heard him suggest she had been asking for it, he was angry, his reputation was tarnished and swore she would not get away with it, he was determined to take revenge. Unfortunately for him both Maisie and Deborah were watching and listening, waiting for their own opportunity."

"You include Maisie in this?" It was Raymond with the assessment in mind.

"It was clear Deborah would never act without the approval of Maisie and while I had no proof she was involved it was right to suspect her involvement." Rhona went on. "Devlin's death was classed as a likely, inevitable, certainly a potential consequence of the way he personally approached his vocation to working with the mentally handicapped." The pieces were coming together at last, I wished Desmond could have been here to listen she had our full attention.

"The first time, since his return to work he appeared in the Rosemary secure unit and all the inmates froze. Deborah emerged from the kitchen area, stood in front of the group and warned him off, she was physically a formidable looking character, bearing in mind she was six feet high and 25 stone in weight most people stepped aside for her and he walked away an angry man."

"You were there at the time Rhona?" She nodded to me.

"Devlin made a fatal mistake his own character would not allow a woman to talk down to or humiliate him least of all an insane one, he decided to catch Deborah on her own within the restaurant one evening after dinner. He expected her to be afraid of him, later an investigation showed, far from being scared of him, his attempts to attack her, led her to defend herself in the most forceful way possible. One of the kitchen staff clearing the meal dishes reportedly heard the commotion from the hall Devlin had not expected Deborah to fight dirty, punching him on his face as she spread herself on the floor on top of him while suffocating him. Once grounded she dragged him by his white coated uniform into the kitchen, one of the staff members clearing dishes ran as soon as she saw her pulling an injured Devlin across the floor, apparently he was screaming at her to stop, she didn't."

"The kitchen staff got help right?" It was Harry's turn to ask.

"Why would they? Most were patients themselves and they were frightened of Deborah, anyhow, it would be conjecture from this point on, a blocked kitchen knife was found with Devlin's blood on it next to the body. His throat had been cut and by the time found he had bled to death, stab and slash wounds were found on the body suggesting he had been tortured." I whistled at the thought.

Rhona was struggling, we decided we should take a break for lunch, Harry comforted her, we knew there was more to tell.

Strangely, everyone needed their own space, Raymond left quickly saying he needed to check on patients his mop of hair way out of control, Rhona and Harry sat quietly on one of the sofa's, which left Andrew and myself.

"Come on Andrew you look as if you could do with a drink." He let me lead him to the public house my father used to use, the Stirling Castle a short walk away and we sat down with a beer and fresh sandwiches.

"How are you holding up Andrew?" The air had a chill to it as we walked.

"I'm afraid of what Raymond intends to do, from the way Rhona is talking, this is turning out to be far bigger than I imagined it would be." His family's reputation would take a big hit there could be no doubt about it. "I thought at most it might be about misplaced documentation, but we are talking a murder cover up, identity fraud and God knows what else, it is difficult knowing what to do Hayden."

"Right now Andrew, you or I cannot do anything we have to listen to Rhona." I looked hard at him. "We have to let this unfold and trust we know what can be done once we know the truth and the extent of the cover up."

"Raymond could ruin me and my father retrospectively."

"I doubt he would want to do it, the errors of judgement occurred a long, long time ago, we need to work together with him to find a solution to put it right legally anyway." He was not convinced and I was struggling with it myself, finishing our drink's it was soon time to go back and hear the rest.

The walk back to the hospital a sombre one, I had no words of comfort for him except a hope the 25 year old cover up would stay just that, covered up.

When we all settled down again in Raymond's office it was clear Rhona had been crying, Harry by her side.

"What's wrong Rhona?" We were all concerned, but it was Andrew's question.

"I'm worried this will affect Bridie's life again and I have tried so hard," her voice tailed off.

"I too am worried about how this will affect my own father's reputation." She shook her head and looked at him coldly.

"At least he is dead, she is alive it will destroy her!" She buried her head in Harry's shoulders sobbing.

Andrew was angry with her I shook my head at him placing my finger on my mouth signalling him to keep quiet.

Rhona broke away from Harry and went to Andrew falling at his feet in apology.

"I loved and admired your father and had no right to say that to you." Andrew graciously helped her up and gave her back to Harry.

"Rhona will you finish telling us what happened back then, then we can together work out what the best way forward will be." I looked at the rest of the group assessing the level of agreement given. Rhona agreed.

"When Cedric and I found Devlin's body, it was horrible we had no option but to send for Jennifer Granger. Once the body had been placed in the mortuary of the asylum we soon realised there were choices to be made, either to call the police and let them deal with the situation or as Jennifer suggested they could deal with it internally," the sweet old lady rides again I thought.

It was at this point Jennifer Granger, Cedric Bartholomew and Rhona Jackson decided to cover up a crime. Police arrived and Jennifer Granger led them to the scene of the 'accident' in the kitchen area, which apparently had involved some mentally disturbed patients and a nursing officer. While checking on the vast urns providing soups, vegetables and casserole dishes fighting broke out between four of the patients and pushed over one of the urns scolding John Devlin fatally, his hands, face and body were badly burnt, screaming and unable to see he fell and hit his head hard on the metal worktops. The senior physician can confirm the outcome appeared to suggest the events occurred as explained.

Devlin's blistered face and hands so gruesome the police attending could barely look at the corpse, traces of food stains splattered his body as did the blood staining drenching his uniform from his slashed neck. This being explained as an attempt made to save his life by opening up an airway in his throat, but unfortunately complicated by the severity of the burns suffered, he died shortly afterwards as the Doctor Cedric Bartholomew attending testified.

Tidying up the throat wound, covering the stab wounds and pouring scalding water on a dead man's face and hands to blister skin was relatively easy for a trained Doctor.

I noted Andrew had his head in his hands hardly believing his father could have been responsible for such an act.

Rhona continued passionately about the stress

both physical and mentally the rape attack had caused Bridie, who had never, at her age been exposed to anything physical with any man, let alone being attacked in such a violent way. The counselling at first did little good and she became angry when any male nursing officer approached her, the only person she trusted was Cedric Bartholomew, it took her some four to five years to trust people again, men in particular. Unfortunately, along the way she would lash out at those who would touch or even brush by her hence the cause of her sectioning in 1975. Bridie had spent a year looking inwards blaming herself as most rape victims did. Rhona had seen many cases in her time as a psychiatric Nurse.

    Surprisingly, it was one particular day when she started to change her ways, most of the other inmates would keep far away from her, scared mostly of her angry reactions to almost anything. However, Maisie tripped on some concrete slabs outside in one of the courtyards separating the internal wards and broke her left foot, ankle in fact, she had to have both ankle and leg plastered up to her knee. It had a profound effect on Bridie who looked after her totally, they were inseparable, like a Mother hen clucking around her chick pushing the wheel chair, helping with washing and going to the toilet, generally spending every moment with her, it was a chance to repay Maisie for the years of support she had given her.

    When Maisie after several weeks in plaster Bridie helped her with crutches and then onto a walking stick, you would see them walking arm in arm laughing and joking with Bridie always supporting her. From then on, the two women were never in trouble again and if anyone tried to harm either of them then Deborah Wealdon would step in and defend them.

"What happened to Florence Rhona?" I was getting impatient.

"I'm coming to it Hayden." The others signalled for me to keep quiet. "In early 1988, when the sanatorium was due to close in the summer, all four girls including Florence Mason were heartbroken, the incident with Deborah and Florence occurred after the patients found out about the hospital closure. Deborah believed she would stay at the sanatorium despite its closure with the other three women, Florence told her she was stupid and laughingly told her she and Bridie would be together forever and both Deborah and Maisie would be sent away without seeing her again, it was fantasy of course, but she believed her."

"Deborah's jealousy of Florence was the main reason why she stabbed and killed her. Unfortunately, Florence assessments showed she was eligible to be released on the closure of the sanatorium in the summer she had not known this."

"Are you sure she didn't know Rhona? I know its extreme but many of my patients are afraid of change, release is massive, she must have known by the simple fact she was passing the assessments, which could have caused her to realise and not wanted it. Did she have any family?"

"No Raymond, no family, but I hadn't, we hadn't looked at it this way."

"Wait a minute you're saying she deliberately goaded Deborah to get killed."

"It's possible Harry."

"Rubbish I don't believe it, no, no!

"In any event it happened, Jennifer Granger

refused to let the public or the authorities know or let Deborah Wealdon be released, her assessment failed she was a dangerous individual. It was another cover up, it led to the whole assessment process being placed under scrutiny, there were leaks and I know Miss Granger was held responsible." Thank the lord I thought.

"Which she was?" I would have sleepless nights about the woman. "And Florence?"

"Florence Mason without any family support had a religious service without fuss and buried without drama with as much respect as possible in the burial grounds behind the hospital."

I confirmed this from Cedric Bartholomew's papers the cause of death listed as a brain haemorrhage and signed off by him, both Andrew and Raymond were horrified how their profession had been guilty of two deaths they now knew about.

Rhona explained there was a problem. "The headcount was wrong with Deborah Wealdon at the sanatorium she could not be released and headcounts for transferring patients to other asylums, hospitals or prisons had to be precise."

"I came up with the idea to release Bridie in place of Deborah substituting Florence's assessment for Deborah's. We persuaded her to adopt Bridie's name for the records in order her 'crime' would be forgotten when she transferred to a secure unit on the closure."

"And Maisie?" Andrew shaking his head in disbelief.

"Maisie was destined to go into prison because she had no family. She threatened Jennifer Granger with telling the authorities about the cover up of both Devlin's and Florence's deaths, at the same time Bridie refused to leave if Maisie went to prison." Good for Maisie, one in the eye for Granger she continued.

"As agreed by both Maisie and Bridie, Deborah should rightly go to prison for Florence's death and take Maisie Belling as her name. Maisie herself would use Bridie's name and move to a secure hospital unit, already partly funded by the London family who would not be any the wiser for it. Deborah did not care she had no family and knew her immediate family of four in the institution had broken up and it was her fault, she shouldn't have believed Florence, her life would never be the same again. By killing Florence and getting away with it, this way she may one day earn a chance of release." This worried me, but I understood for Maisie, the change would be good avoiding prison and moving to a more palatable hospital environment and with Bridie's release, there was a chance they could keep in contact in the future.

When Darenth Park Sanatorium finally closed in the summer of 1988, Rhona decided it was time for her to retire. Cedric Bartholomew took a sabbatical while the new hospital was being built, he in part, took on the project of designing and implementing the psychiatric facility within the new hospital for outpatients only. The new Darenth park would not cater for the mentally insane patients as they would now go to Broadmoor or places like it, although Cedric provided advisory services to asylums all the patients transferred out to, from the sanatorium.

Andrew acknowledged his father within two years had decided to retire and write up his journals and confirmed his father had acted as an advisor as Rhona had said.

Raymond suggested we break again it was

turning out to be a very long day.

"Would be possible to talk to Maisie?" He went off to arrange it and in the meantime, I asked if I could use the telephone, a private one located on the adjacent corridor. He came up to me as I finished my call we were alone.

"Look Hayden, I will not be party to any further cover ups." He was greatly troubled.

"Raymond, I want no part of any cover up either, but it's done, it's your choice what happens from here, at the very least it is name changes all round. NHS scandals dating back 25 years or more, we can all see the newspaper headlines. Rhona is an old woman and so is Jennifer Granger, whom I believe to be the main instigator, without her there wouldn't have been any cover ups, she also decided the rules for family involvement which I have to say crushed the London family because of it, so I have no sympathy for her at all. However, there is the reputation of Andrew's Father and his own by association and do you really think Harry could take the interrogations?" For once Raymond was lost for words.

"Raymond, we also need to consider three other people, for sure the real Deborah Wealdon deserves all she gets, but there's the memory of Florence Mason to consider and what about Bridie, does she get locked away again after 25 years of freedom. Maisie Belling, the person in your assessment room whom you have gotten to know during the past six months and agreed, she should be released despite her real background, she will go to prison. Do you realise whatever you do if she does go to prison she is hardly likely to keep quiet, she threatened before when she expected to go to prison why not now.

Look at our Group Raymond can we all cope with the fallout. I am not asking for a cover up, its damage limitation."

"I am struggling with this Hayden."

"Your conscience is too high a price for them to pay Raymond, cause and effect is what you must think about, satisfying your conscience will devastate, maybe 1, 2, 3 probably 6 lives and their families involved." I was right and he knew it.

"You're suggesting I opt for the simple option and ignore what's happened?"

"I'm not suggesting you ignore it, but what is gained by you blowing the whistle, will you feel better Raymond? I doubt it, I doubt it very much." I had made my point it would be up to him to decide what to do. "You're not about to cover anything up, the way I look at this, you're actually putting things right."

A troubled Professor Raymond Barnyard walked me to the main hall area where the patient's relaxed in recreation, one of them was kicking a drinks machine until he spoke to the man, he pointed to the woman sitting in an armchair alone, who last time, was introduced to me as Bridie London.

I walked across the hall towards her as Raymond left patting me on my back she looked up at me in recognition unaware I knew her story.

"Hello again Maisie, you'll remember me its Hayden, I think this time we need the truth." I watched her face carefully shocked, but relaxed, I noted relief crossing her face as the twenty five year old secret was now out in the open.

For the first time, Maisie smiled, her coldness disappearing she looked at me keenly speaking softly.

"What happens to me now I am back to being

Maisie, will I have to go to prison?"

"I don't know Maisie it largely depends on Professor Barnyard and your overall assessment."

"I'm getting too old to worry anymore," she shrugged, her comment tinged with sadness. "There is lots I could talk about you know?"

"I do! You have to consider will it help or hinder you, if you bring up the past, you go to prison, Bridie then goes to Broadmoor and hurting Rhona will achieve nothing, Jennifer Granger will lose her reputation in retirement although I doubt anyone cares." She laughed. "A dead man retrospectively would lose his deservedly so but his innocent family would be tainted by the scandal and then there is the memory of Florence and the worth of her life surely it counts for something? What is it worth to you?" I looked hard at the woman in front of me, I had grown to learn of as being a dangerous, cold-hearted person who would stop at nothing to manipulate anyone and everyone except one person it seems Bridie. It was what we had in common.

She shrugged the implications weighing heavily on her mind.

"How is Bridie?"

"Oh she's fine I er, er, at least I think she is, I haven't seen her in a while," she stuttered I had caught her out, so I decided to press on.

"When did you last see her Maisie?"

"It's unusual to hear my real name after all this time, not since Darenth." She played for time, but I was not going to let it go.

"Well when was it Maisie?"

"I haven't seen her since we left Darenth, how could I have done when she too is locked up." The wry smile, did not work for me.

"Don't lie to me Maisie, I have spoken to Sir James Carew, do you know him?"

"No I don't."

"Are you sure? Only as the Chief Executive Officer of the Cheadle Royal where you have stayed for many years, he found out for me you had a frequent visitor at least once every two weeks, do you know who the person was Maisie?" She shook her head keeping quiet, scared of the implications if she spoke.

"Deborah Wealdon, she visited you all the time, very strange isn't it?" I watched her face closely, frantically finding an answer.

"What's strange about having a visitor?"

"Strange enough, considering Deborah Wealdon has been locked up in Broadmoor for the past 15 years," her face painted a picture as she realised the full extent of my knowledge.

"It is Bridie who has been visiting you isn't it?" She nodded. "Have you seen her in the last six months?"

"No I haven't, we felt it would be dangerous while I was being assessed." At last an honest answer.

"You mean the assessment of Bridie London?"

"Yes."

"What will happen to her, it was all my doing?" showing concern for her friend.

"Where is she now Maisie?" She shook her head determined not to tell me. "You have to Maisie, unless you tell me I cannot help you." It was a threat I had no intention of acting on.

"We don't want to be helped, leave me and her alone." She was upset seeing the world she imagined beginning to crumble, but determined to protect Bridie. "She, I had to be assessed then she would finally be free."

"I cannot leave it and you know it." I caught myself sounding harsh. "Surely you want what is best for Bridie?"

"It is not my place to tell you, I don't want to talk to you anymore." The other patients noted her anger and had instinctively, begun to move in her defence toward us. I raised my hand to them and stood up to go.

Back in Raymond's office, Rhona had grabbed some sandwiches from the hospital restaurant for me and plated them. He was discussing the name changes required for the three women.

"I have spoken to Gerard Sheridon at the Broadmoor Hospital about their Maisie Belling and to officially own up to an administrative error when she was first transferred from Darenth, all the records were correct, but the name was wrong."

"Was he suspicious?" Harry asked. "I would be."

"Yes I believe he was, his biggest problem is why Deborah called herself Maisie, I passed this off as both a perceived game and not wishing to get another patient, a friend, into trouble, placated by this he said and I quote: "Such are the vagaries of the mentally insane."

"So Maisie Belling has now simply been reverted to Deborah Wealdon and no-one will be any the wiser, with both Bridie and Maisie it will be different." We were all listening to the Professor intently he tugged his eyebrows in concentration. "If we change Bridie's name from Deborah it has implications from her own life aspects, national insurance number, tax office, social benefits and state pension and there is also a risk, granted a small one, to her freedom."

"But it is possible to resolve?" He nodded the relief evident among the group.

"Hey, let's all not get too cosy there is plenty of work to do, if I'm right medically she has never been assessed."

"But she has Raymond, haven't you currently been assessing a Bridie London for the past six months?"

"Clever, Hayden, very clever." I noted he never dismissed the idea out of hand. "Under the Mental Health act assessments should normally take 28 days and treatment if needed, should last up to 6 months which is how we have played it with Bridie or Maisie as is now, especially those with authority release priority status. Normally under section 2 of the act only a mental health tribunal comprising of a Judge, a Psychiatrist and a social care worker can agree to release a sectioned patient."

"What will you do about the real Maisie?" Harry showed concern for her.

"Relatively easy, I can change her name, as I asked Gerard Sheridon to do so at Broadmoor for Deborah Wealdon and the assessments already match her medical records."

"I'm right you were assessing her as Bridie in order she would be released into the community, and she passed all tests?"

"Yes Harry."

"So will you release your Bridie as Maisie into the community?"

"Yes again Harry, I may get away with it being a mistake."

"Solves two, what about Bridie?" I had to ask.

"Hayden, if someone has been living under a different name for a quarter of a century, it is going to be noticed. The name Deborah Wealdon is on a patient in Broadmoor, with the other two now cleared, Bridie London does not exist. The only way is if I can provide paperwork suggesting she had previously, been passed by a tribunal following her own assessment.

"Can you do it Raymond, will you do it?" All of us fell silent, knowing it was very much Raymond's call.

"Of course I can, and yes I will do it." The group visibly relaxed, somehow he had justified the process to himself and I was pleased. "It is simply a duplicate of what I offer up for the real Maisie Belling. The tribunal meets bi-weekly and discusses people on paper. The similarity of the details in patients, every two weeks is hardly going to notice, with the issue becoming only a headcount problem.

"Why, in what way?" Andrew was listening attentively.

"There are no costs involved to be queried as the headcount could have been wrong for years and no-one will question a departing number."

"Will it make Bridie free, Raymond?" I had to ask.

"Yes it does, she will need to come in and sign the paperwork."

"Does it ease your conscience?" I smiled at him being the only one party to our conversation.

"Yes I think it does," the group breathed a huge sigh of relief reputations and people's lives will remain intact.

"There is one other thing to cover." Raymond, Harry, Rhona and Andrew looked directly at me.

"Where is she now?" To a person they all shrugged suggesting they did not know.

"Come on one of you must know where she is,

Maisie admits she has been visited by Bridie. Sir James Carew at the Cheadle Royal said a Deborah Wealdon visited the old Bridie now Maisie, several times on a regular basis, most importantly it adds credibility to our dear departed friend Desmond's claims, she visited him in hospital enabling him to rest in peace and she forgave him."

"But it doesn't tell you where she is now?" Imperceptibly I saw Harry nudge Rhona.

"No Andrew it doesn't, but it does tell me she's close to us, how else could she have known Desmond was ill and what hospital he was in?"

"What are you saying Hayden?"

"I'm saying one of us in this room told her, how about it Rhona?" her face reddened not expecting my question directly aimed.

"Why do you think it was me?

"I have been to see Jennifer Granger," Rhona's face dropped, any pretence she had disappeared.

"You were part of the cover up, you had to be, you were her Nurse from the very beginning, from the time Desmond enlisted me the help you have given has been minimal, to the point of obstruction. I began to ask myself why because you are a loving, caring woman. The way you fussed around Desmond was great, so you had to be protecting something or someone, and I guessed it would be Bridie."

"Bridie's been free for some 25 years, are you saying she's at risk of being put back into a sanatorium." The idea was clearly bothering Rhona. "It's unlikely she would ever want to found."

"It was Harry who persuaded me to be honest with you and tell you about Bridie," Rhona sat down beside me on one of the red sofa's grabbing my hand tightly. "I never wanted to lie to you

Hayden believe me, but I had to see what you would find out first."

"So you know where she is Harry?"

"Believe me I didn't until halfway through Rhona's story, it made sense to me so I tackled her when you were seeing Maisie."

"Please don't blame Harry this is down to me entirely."

"And my father!" Rhona nodded at Andrew.

"Forgive me Rhona, so I can get it."

"Yes, Yes."

"Tell me what about Bridie?"

"Oh sorry, but I could not risk it for her sake in case she went to prison." At this point Raymond interrupted her.

"Hayden, it appears Bridie has lived with Rhona for the past twenty five years or so, since Darenth Sanatorium closed." I wondered if I was the last to know.

At last, the mystery was solved, it would have helped knowing this sooner for Desmond's sake. I had one question.

"Yes Hayden, it was Bridie who visited her father in hospital." Rhona confirmed.

"Thank you." Suddenly, it was as if a huge weight, had finally been lifted up from my mind, I was tired out, all urgency now seemed to leave me, I was so pleased she was alive and started to look forward to seeing her again.

"The truth is I begged them to release her, I wanted the cover up. She was gradually dying in there, she was losing her spirit, she would not have coped with another institution and with Deborah stifling her with jealousy over anyone who spoke to her including Maisie, I had to get her out of there.

Florence dying was the last straw. Like I promised myself when she first arrived at the sanatorium, I was determined to continue looking after her for the rest of my life."

"Mostly I was able to keep Desmond at bay but when you arrived to help him and set up the group, I knew you would work out the truth eventually. I started to look at my own vulnerability when Desmond died and her future care. My husband Jack Webber looked after her as his own daughter, she loved him. Sadly, he passed away 5 years ago. We were a family, she was the daughter I never had and Jack was her Dad, he became the only man she ever trusted again apart from Cedric." You could tell she recalled her husband fondly.

"What of Maisie?"

"Bridie hated to leave her, she wanted her with us, but I couldn't take her as well, the years passed and when Maisie moved to the Cheadle Royal, I felt it was safe enough for her to start visiting her there, they have stayed very close since the early days."

"It's a turnaround and no mistake."

"What is it Harry?" enquired Raymond.

"Their friendship surprised me at first, I remember her watching Bridie she appeared to be laughing at her enjoying the pain she had when her father had left her at the sanatorium."

"She was like this Harry, it was her way, but somehow she changed, she used to look after her on more than one occasion, she saved Bridie from choking when she had convulsions, they developed an unbreakable bond, without Maisie she would never have survived the whole ordeal which was her life.

"What made you suspicious about the girls not being who they were supposed to be anyway?"

"The mole Raymond," I had confused them all.

"What are you talking about Hayden?"

"It was the mole on Bridie's neck, look at these photographs Desmond gave me," I pulled them from my inside jacket pocket. "I assume you have all seen these four pictures?" They agreed they had.

"If you look at the first two photographs and carefully at Bridie, particularly her neck as she looks at the camera lens on the right hand side, in the black and white photographs she has a black dot which could be dismissed as a photo mark nothing more, the pictures are of course quite old." I spread the photographs out in front of them on the glass-topped coffee table. "Take a look at the two coloured ones, no marks on her neck."

"It could be the black and white pictures, if they were taken with the same type of camera, a Kodak Brownie for example, I remember my father having one many years ago." Andrew offered. "No thoughts of pixel densities in those days."

"I agree, except for one tiny detail, when I knew Bridie way back in the early sixties, I kissed her neck a few times as a teenager and it made her giggle as I recall," I felt myself redden as I spoke of us together. "She told me how hateful the mole was to her despite me loving it and her at the time. As I doubt the hospitals or sanatoriums would run to cosmetic surgery for any of their mental patients, it suggested to me the last two pictures had a different Bridie in them."

"Why didn't you say before?"

"Andrew, I had to prove it," I looked directly at Rhona. "You have all seen how hard it was to get at the truth."

"I'm sorry." I smiled at her.

"What bothers me is why Rhona? Why did you deprive Desmond of his daughter for the past 25 years I fail to understand, even when Desmond stepped up his search and enlisted me, you could have told us." She shook her head.

"You don't understand, we were scared, at best she could be dragged back into an institution and at worst be complicit in a cover up and possibly be blamed for a part in two murders once the investigations started how could she be released. I, we could not risk it." She looked directly at me, sincerely. "She had been already locked up for 25 years, raped and nearly died I couldn't let her go back." I understood.

"Rhona where is she?"

"At home Raymond, I will bring her to you after the weekend on Monday to sign any papers and I can introduce her to you all if you wish?" Rhona guilty at her protection of Bridie.

"Oh yes we do wish so very much." A sigh of laughter spread through the group.

It was time for me to go home, spend the weekend with Penny and the children and give them an update.

Driving home I found myself relaxing for the first time in months, I hadn't spoken to or seen her yet but Bridie had a decent home and a life with Rhona, for Desmond's sake I would try and make her future the very best it could be and I think I knew how. My sadness was for Desmond, I hoped he had been watching. What bothered me was each other's reactions when we finally meet again for the first time in 50 years.

Chapter 15

Ringing home as I drove we agreed I would bring in fish & chips, within minutes of my arrival we were all sitting eating, I spoke openly of the name changes for each woman and Bridie being free for the past 25 years and about her rape attack unsure whether Carrie and Simon understood. Penny never stopped me as I went through the cover up of the killing of John Devlin and Florence Mason and how, Deborah had gotten away with murder twice. The children surprisingly, were unfazed by it all, too much TV I guessed. It felt good to speak about this to someone not closely involved.

Following the meal Penny and I made ourselves comfortable on the sofa, Carrie and Simon went to bed.

"Do you think the children understood what I told them?" I worried I had been too honest.

"I'm sure they did they're growing up fast Hayden, it helped with you telling them openly as if it was not a secret, they will forget easily. They are killing people every day on their X-boxes I doubt they understand the difference?" My mind was at rest.

"What about Carrie and the rape attack?"

"Hayden she'll digest it and ask me about it when she's ready, don't worry it will be fine, when do you see Bridie again?" She corrected herself. "I mean the 'real' Bridie?"

"On Monday morning, Rhona is bringing her to the Maudsley, Raymond needs papers to be signed in order they can show she has been assessed prior to her being released in order she can be 'officially' released and lastly to meet us all." I was conscious she might have a typical sarcastic comment to make. To my surprise, quite the opposite.

"You must be worried about the feelings you will have when you meet her again?" I felt an underlying depth of concern in her demeanour.

"I think I' am more excited than worried, as you're well aware with Desmond, for a couple of months I have lived and breathed Bridie trying to find her and despite the fact I haven't, I guess I'm looking forward to putting it to bed."

"You do yourself an injustice, only by keep pushing did you make it all come out into the open." I appreciated the rare praise she gave.

"Only because she wanted to be found in the end," which I believed to be true.

"Now come on, you've done more for the London family than you realise. Bridie can finally feel free without looking over her shoulder, Desmond found his daughter at last before he died and her awful London siblings have gone away forever." Thank God and with their sought after inheritance.

"I wish I could have known Desmond for longer than I did."

"Then you should have married Bridie when you were twelve." We laughed at the thought.

"We have a good life together," this day I loved her more than ever.

"Yes I think we do."

"Will you trust me to do the right thing?" I was concerned for her feelings.

"Hayden, I do trust you, the children and I love

you, it would be wrong of me to expect you not to follow your heart." Stunned I felt her to be deadly serious she continued. "At the very least she will be your friend and I do accept it, all else is emotions."

"Thank you for being so understanding Penny, I'm surprised."

"I'm a realist, I don't want to lose what we have Hayden, we're real, your real family," at this moment she was so precious to me.

I spent the weekend tracking down Desmond's three other children and tried to arrange meetings with them either together or separately to discuss Bridie's future welfare which they all refused. I told them she had been living a normal life for the past 25 years and would likely want to see them. Although I had spoken to each of them separately, not one wanted to see her, but all three wondered how much it cost because their father's money funded a stranger's hospital care. I did suggest I would look into it, of course I never will, they did not ask where she lived or how she had been during those 25 years. I felt I had done my duty by them for Desmond's sake, I no longer wanted any further contact with them and it would be up to Bridie if she wanted meet them again.

Sunday afternoon, the day full of bright sunshine, we had lunch Penny and I, on our floral patterned garden swing facing the back of our home, sandwiches on plates on our laps swinging gently to the easy sounds on the CD player from David Benoit's Professional Dreamer album. The children playing in the small paddling pool and chasing each other with water pistols.

"Will she live with Rhona? Bridie not far from either of our minds, my stomach was tense with apprehension over what Monday may bring. My mind racing through the practicalities and likely turmoil it will bring.

"I would expect her to consider living in Desmond's home, after all it is Bridie's already, he wanted her to have it and it's a great place."

"You've already stayed there with Desmond haven't you?" I remembered my time with him fondly.

"Yes twice with him and I was there following the funeral as the will was read there." I thought about the London family, Bridie's brother and sisters especially.

"Do you want me with you tomorrow when you meet her?" I looked into her eyes realising she was suffering too.

"No perhaps later," I selfishly didn't wish to make judgements for Bridie based on how even a simple hug would look to Penny if she was there, we held each other silently, swinging gently. I doubted I would sleep tonight.

Monday morning like any other saw Penny busy preparing toast and cereal for Carrie and Simon, a school day turning my feelings into normality, my children blissfully unaware of the emotional strain Penny and I were both going through. Everyone grabbing coats and bags instinctively ready to face whatever lay ahead on the day. Going our separate ways, the 'have a good day', comments held much more meaning than normal. At the last moment with our two children seated in the car she rushed back and without a word, kissed my cheek, I touched the place on my cheek as I watched them drive away through the window knowing today could change everything in our lives.

I called Claire at the office to let her know my plans for the day, which did not involve me going back to work. I knew she would cover for me, the 'good luck' from her welcome.

The group had arranged to meet again in Raymond's office at the Maudsley hospital at ten, this time we would hope to have an additional guest. I arrived early and decided to walk up Denmark Hill to De Crespigny Park behind the Kings College hospital campus. I sat on the nearest bench to the entrance, my brain numb watching grey and red squirrels chasing nuts playing amongst the grass and shrubs beneath the trees, occasionally chasing people along the pathways causing screams from children and women alike as they threatened to run up their legs. There was no way to prepare for the day ahead, I was nervous as hell. I walked purposely slow out of the park and back the way I came giving more time to work out what I was planning.

When I finally presented myself at the Maudsley reception a little edgy and five minutes late, it was no surprise again everyone had arrived before me, Michelle waiting patiently ushered me into Raymond's office, she said something about the day's weather and asked how I was, not listening I weakly smiled at her, I felt sick deep inside. The first to greet me was Harry who rushed to me as I entered the room.

"Hayden, we have seen her, she looks beautiful," he too was so excited.

"Hi Hayden, it's a big day?" Andrew tapped me on the shoulder over Harry's exuberance, seemingly at peace with the arrangements, his father's reputation intact. "Raymond and Rhona are with

Bridie sorting out the paperwork for her 'official release' in the administration offices."

I wished Desmond were here, as the last one to arrive I helped myself to coffee, I drank while looking out of the window seeing nothing in particular, watching traffic passing by up Denmark Hill, I blindly watched a red London bus meander its way through the traffic lights.

The door creaked open, Raymond in his normal bulldozing action led the way coming directly to me as I turned, he welcomed me and shook my hand, Rhona raised her hand and mouthed the word 'Hi', I kissed her cheek, and there beside her stood a slim middle aged woman head bowed, smartly dressed. At first, I did not believe it to be her, until she lifted her head and looked directly into my eyes and there she was at last, instantly I knew it to be Bridie my heat skipped a beat.

Ages did not matter, I saw once again the 14 year old I had left behind all those years ago, eyes bright and green like saucers shining at me with warmth and sunshine as she always did, touches of grey in her brown hair, my heart filled with love for her, at last I had found her. The strain of my efforts drained from my mind. My Bridie, my eyes drifted to her neck and spotted the mole, my mind sad for Desmond, I saw him in her.

"Hello Hayden," she stood a little over five feet high and looked at least ten years younger than I expected her to be. The room alive with the connection we had, she stretched up to me as I leaned toward her she kissed my cheek, I closed my eyes in sheer delight at her soft and fragile touch, I was lost for words, her voice as soft and tender as I remembered, the years blew away from both of us.

"Hello again," I stuttered, my heart and mind

somersaulting together in harmony, she with a perfect smile, even the chipped tooth had been fixed, I could not stop grinning.

"Right, let me tell you what we have done," Raymond interrupted us in order to get back to the business at hand, with Bridie and I holding hands we found a space on one of his red sofa's, my heart felt strange, full for the first time in 50 years. Her gentle hands playing in mine, fidgeting with them as she used to all those years ago. I recognised Desmond in her mannerisms and knew he would be proud of this moment.

"Hayden, put Bridie down," a smiling Harry grabbed her shoulders and she immediately stood up to him wrapping her arms around him tightly. "It's so lovely to see you again, I swear you haven't changed one bit."

"Daft Harry, of course I have, I'm so glad to see you too," she was kindly toward him.

"Now, now Harry let her go," Rhona protective, as she introduced Andrew I could not take my eyes from her.

"Hi I have heard so much about you, my father would have been so pleased I have met you and you look very well," he shook her hand warmly. "I'm sorry about Desmond, your father." I watched her saddened reaction. We all took a moment of reflection for the man who had brought us all together.

"I remember your father well Andrew, such a lovely man and always good to me," her voice beginning to falter, I could see she was uncomfortable being here in a hospital again, particularly one specialising in mental care, she became fidgety Rhona looked directly at me and nodded she also recognised the signs.

Raymond told us how he had managed to get copies of the original release of Deborah Wealdon and it seemed the hospital administration had attached the assessment of Bridie London. He effectively changed the name on the papers and then went over how he had sorted the numbers within the NHS. I barely listened, watching my dreams coming true in front of me. I silently spoke to Desmond and hoped he was listening.

"Hayden, perhaps you would like to take Bridie out to the courtyard if it is ok with you Raymond?" Rhona almost begged him, he nodded aware of Bridies rising stress.

I held out my hand to her, she gripped it until outside in the corridor then we held each other arm in arm. I felt her relief as we walked from the office, the courtyard a few metres away. In silence, we sat on a wooden bench facing, looking at each other connecting. Bridie spoke first.

"I have had a difficult time, my childhood without a family, my memories were consumed with thoughts of you, as a child I expected you to come and take me out of the sanatorium as my white knight, I know now it would have been impossible, but you found me in the end and I love you for it." I suddenly felt aggrieved and was not prepared to let her off the hook easily.

"I have read your diaries," we were dancing around our feelings. "Well most of them, I assume the later ones had been filled by necessity by Maisie Belling acting as you.

"Yes I had left them with Maisie as she had assumed my name so I haven't seen them in 25 years." I always knew if she lied to me years ago when we were kids and today was no different I did not believe her.

"I know she has been very protective of them, I guessed approximately 25 of the 30 diaries I know there are, had been written by you and five by her, I am correct aren't I?"

"Yes how did you know?"

"I could tell from the handwriting of course, it was the interest level in what was being said which gave it away."

"I do not understand."

"It was clear despite the diaries being in Maisie's possession since 1988, some of the later diaries were written by you. Nothing of substance in them, but meant only to maintain the deception of Maisie being you, am I right?"

"Yes." Her demeanour apologetic.

"Bridie believe me when I say I was really pleased to find out you've been free since 1988, but why on earth put your father through all this. He had tried on many occasions to see you or get you released." I felt myself angry for the old man who had become my friend.

"I'm really sorry for him, earlier on I decided he needed to be taught a lesson for leaving me in the asylum and then it became clear by letting him believe I was still inside, it served to add credibility Maisie was in fact me."

"So what changed, you could have stayed hidden?" I was indignant.

"Two reasons, Papa had been getting nowhere and he would not ever have found me but for him finding and getting you involved. We knew it would not be long before you worked it out, Papa was blind where I was concerned and already beaten by the establishment, you wasn't, but frankly we didn't believe you had after all these years the passion and strength of feeling you've shown to find me. You must have loved me so much."

"When you say we do you mean Rhona?"

"Yes and lately Harry knew, although I never met him again until just now with you. We needed to find out what progress you were making, how close you were to finding me." I was not impressed at all and feeling manipulated, my rose coloured glasses were starting to fall away.

"You said two reasons?"

"When Dad had his heart attack, I could not rest when I heard and I would not let him die without him knowing I was free and forgave him." A picture of Desmond lying in his hospital bed came to me.

"Had you?"

"What?"

"Forgiven him."

"Oh yes over the years, I gradually developed as a normal person thanks to Rhona and Jack her husband, well, as normal as I am ever likely to be. They made me see the lack of choices he had back then.

"What had he done to you needing your forgiveness?" for Desmond's sake I was not going to let this go.

"Again I do not understand?"

"Well its simple enough Bridie, you've blamed him for most of your life and even when you were freed you felt it necessary to punish your loving father for the last 25 years. He has literally fought your brother and sisters for most of their lives, because it always appeared he was showing you the most favour compounding the problem by him paying a contribution for Maisie's care and not yours." I hoped she started to get a taste of the anger

I felt towards her. "Did any of you give any thought for a desperate old man trying to do right by his sick and as he believed the mentally challenged daughter who had been locked up for the past fifty years or more." I could not help myself.

"We did not want to draw attention to my being free," she mumbled, shocked at my outburst.

"Do you honestly believe you could not trust your own father to keep quiet about it?"

"He put me away in the first place." She reddened in anger as she said this. "Oh I did not mean it."

"So this is why you think he needed your forgiveness?" As a father myself and for Desmond I felt contempt for the way she had behaved.

"Yes."

"And did he forgive you Bridie?"

"What for?" She never had a clue.

"Your mother, she died 12 years ago, you were free?"

"Oh God, I truly never found out until it was too late." Her eyes welling with tears.

"Where were you for him? He needed you more than ever, you could have told him, shared his grief, Joseph, Susan and Emma weren't there for him, but you could have been." Disgust swept through me.

"I couldn't do it."

"It hurt him Bridie and you wanted his forgiveness. I felt myself sneering at her. "So you almost let him die before releasing him from his lifelong guilt over you, how does that work. Did you sit by his beside, tell him who you were and refused to speak to him until he begged your forgiveness?" No way was I going to tread carefully with her.

"Hayden, it wasn't like that."

"Then tell me what it was like and how any sane person and I really mean this, how any sane person could torment someone for over twenty five years or more, aided by Rhona and husband and then lately Harry."

"I'm sorry."

"It's too late to be sorry and not me you could have said it too, I am truly surprised at you acting as cold hearted as Joseph, Susan or Emma. I think you felt you had to do it because I was involved not for any thought about Desmond or your mother." I looked at her in a different light, ashamed of her. "Your parents had no choice as it was presented to them by the Doctors."

"I know now."

"Then why not get in touch with them, you could have included both in your life, whoever you were called."

"I was scared of him, of everything and anyone I was waiting for Maisie, for her to be released as me." She stuttered and felt my animosity, not expecting this reaction.

"She had to be free first, then, I wouldn't have to care about what I did."

"Because she had your name?"

"You must see, she had a chance to get out of prison at last she was being assessed as me and almost out, I had to wait for her to be released from here?"

"But this wasn't about your father it was about you and Maisie." I was furious. "Maisie had only started to be assessed during the past year, what about the other 24? You let him down and me too!"

"That's not true." I ignored her reply.

"Meanwhile your father was wasting away trying to find you."

Rhona and Harry came out into the courtyard to find us. Bridie burst out crying and ran to them, I left them to it I could not cope with her hysterics I went in search of Raymond.

"Everything ok Hayden?" Raymond caught me in the corridor as I was walking to his office, I confessed all.

"I have suggested to Bridie, she hadn't cared enough about Desmond."

"Institutions do strange things to people's minds." It did not convince me.

"How do you mean?"

He suddenly changed in my eyes and suggested we go and sit at one of the breakout areas situated in the middle as an alcove within every other corridor and grab a coffee to talk. I felt like one of his patients. We found an empty one three corridors away from the courtyard where I had left Bridie being consoled by Bridie and Harry.

"Hayden, institutions, they leave their mark even on those who work in them, something happens to the brain, a detachment if you like. We all compartmentalise our feelings, emotions, we see too much, hear too much for the coldness not to affect us."

"Bridie's been out for a quarter of a century, surely there is a point where a return to normal happens?"

"You're right, however in Bridie's case initially she lost you, then her family, she had to deal with strange surrounding, beaten and raped, lost Florence followed by the breakup of everything she knew with the sanatorium closing down." Raymond was driving home his points a couple of student Doctors eyed the breakout area and moved on.

"She was then out in the wide world having had no experience of it at all, she was thirteen when taken to the asylum, it's a big ask for her to be 'normal'." I was starting to feel guilty at my outbursts to her.

"Surely she can feel something for others like her father and mother?"

"You'll find emotions and trust are at a premium to her, only one or two people will ever get inside her. Clearly Rhona is a person she sees as a mother figure, a father and or a lover would complicate her thought process and she would likely shut them out."

"I understand, but she had been released for 13 years before her mother died and a further 12 making 25 when I started to be involved. Surely she must have felt something for them they were her parents for God's sake." I was not ready to accept the poor Bridie routine.

"Hayden I am a psychiatrist, I have all the right words to say to you and probably never will convince you, but consider this at 14 her parents and friends and loves were taken away." This I accepted he went on. "Rhona since the beginning has been her friend, confidant, mother figure if you like for the past 50 odd years and her husband Jack filled the role of her father for about 20 years. My question to you is who would you lean toward, those who gave up on you or those who have protected you, however understanding you were of why it happened?"

"I see," there is the logic.

"I hope you do, because you're the one person in the world right now she needs approval from."

"Will she improve any further?"

"I doubt it at her age and the people she loves

right now are probably it for her." Raymond thought hard about his next comment. "Truth is Hayden it is likely you, Desmond and Josey have long ago been replaced by others."

"I'm sorry I upset her."

"Tell her it will help, come on let go back to my office." For another couple of corridors I struggled to keep pace with the rushing man in front of me, being quite lost for breath when he swung his office open to a sea of faces waiting for us, especially Rhona who was as mad as hell with me. My hands went up to her in acknowledgement and went directly to Bridie my arms stretching tightly around her apologising profusely.

Lunchtime approached and suggested Bridie and I could go for a walk outside of the hospital.

"Fine by me, you're free to do as you wish Bridie it is 12.30 now, get back here by 2pm then we can wind things up." Raymond looked around the group apologising, he had to go and see his patients.

"Is it wise, it's been a traumatic morning for you Bridie, you don't need too much stress, sit down and have a rest my dear." I could detect Bridie's disappointment.

"Rhona I promise I will look after her, it's been so long I would like to spend some time getting to know her again." I begged her.

"Oh all right but be careful both of you and no arguments!" Before she changed her mind we skipped out of the room, down the corridor to the entrance and almost danced our way out of the hospital, I felt like a young boy again.

On the opposite side of the road outside Kings College hospital, I saw a number 12 bus.

"Come on, we've a bus to catch." I grabbed her

hand pulling her across the busy road and we both ran for it, giggling as we jumped on the platform like teenagers.

"Peckham Rye please, for two." I said to the ticket collector, we sat together on the bench seat for three, facing the outside window and platform holding hands.

"Where are we going Hayden?"

"Home."

"Oh." She was silent for the rest of the short journey, nervously gripping my hand.

We picked up a bag of chips from the fish shop by the bus stop where we got off, within minutes we were on the corner where the London's Greengrocers had once been, now without the surrounding railings the apartment block looked smartly finished. People were living in them. The façade blended in with the surroundings and as Bridie looked up at the bricked up window once her bedroom and I reminded her she was looking at her mother and father's legacy to Joseph, Susan and Emma, she began to cry. It was hard for her, the present and the past colliding after an eternity.

"I'm sorry Hayden I am being silly, I am so happy to be standing here, free at last and especially being with you." We strolled down one side of Fenham Road and then the other back towards her corner, as I had done a couple of months ago, Desmond had been alive then.

"Thank you for bringing me here." I bowed and she looked at peace.

"Let's go back." Tightly holding her hand.

"Have you met her yet Hayden?"

"Who?" We were arm in arm walking to the bus stop.

"Maisie, of course." Her eyes lighting up as she

thought of her.

"Yes I have."

"How is she?"

"Very well, you do know she's here at the Maudsley?"

"Yes but I haven't dare ask to see her." She was excited at the thought.

"Why not, if she agrees I am sure Raymond could arrange it for us?"

"Would he, it would be great if he did, will you ask him?" I could not resist those pleading green eyes. "I was afraid to come here."

"Tell me why?"

"I believed before I signed any papers I could have been kept in here, it was always a risk." I shook my head, not believing it to be possible.

"From what I knew, no-one suggested you had to be re-admitted, but I agree I can see how you would have worried."

"I'm glad I came to see you again."

"How very kind you are dear lady." This time I exaggerated my bow to her.

"It's a shame we're so old."

"Speak for yourself!" We laughed together.

"Do you feel you're cured Bridie?" She spent time considering her response.

"The problem is I never felt I was ever ill in the sanatorium sense."

"You were when this started though?"

"Oh sure, I had an infection, but I wasn't a basket case I don't understand why I was put in a mental institution." It was something I had trouble with and Desmond's words came to mind.

"You needed to be isolated such was the nature of your illness, Darenth had the facilities only you got caught up and treated like any other mental patient."

"But I wasn't mad!" I had no answer for her.

I needed to speak to both Raymond and Rhona separately.

On our way back to the hospital, taking another bus she asked what I had done with my life since she had left me all those years ago. Briefly, I described my working life and at length told her about Penny and the children.

"They could have been ours," she said with genuine sadness, it was the first time she had mentioned any hope of a different life. "I was raped you know?"

"Yes I read of it, through the Doctors notes although there wasn't much about it in your diaries." I watched her mind reliving the past painfully. "Tell me about it another day."

"Nothing much to tell, it's in the past and dealt with. A grubby man took my virginity and got away with it."

"More to it surely, what about Deborah?"

"Ah, you know all of what happened?"

"Yes, she killed Devlin for you!"

"Not for me, although it did help me get over it, but I wouldn't have asked her to do it."

"How do you feel about it now?" I could see she had shut this off from her mind.

"Still hurt, abused, violated, but a good thing came out of it."

"What?"

"Oh er!" she struggled to answer as if realising she had said too much. "My friends rallied around me, he wouldn't do it to anyone else and I stopped being frightened of people, men in particular." Her answer vague and indicated the conversation was over I dropped the subject, one day she might open up to me, but not now.

On our return Bridie told them where we had been and I watched Harry and Rhona fuss over her as if she was their daughter, which she probably was now. Rhona would have already assumed the role many years previously I wondered about Harry, I knew he had never married. Mostly he was a loner, which was a benefit for him being a gardener, but seemed comfortable being within this group, I worried now our search for Bridie being effectively over what he would do. I felt sad Desmond had left such a hole in what was fast becoming a part of my own family too. Bridie was unconsciously helping to fill the gap by her mere presence alone.

After talking to Raymond, he quietly left the room and I helped myself to a couple of biscuits and watched how Bridie's magnetism drew in both Andrew and Harry, her bubbly personality shining through. Occasionally she looked up at me smiling contentedly and melted my heart, she made me feel young again, but at the same time guilty as Penny, Carrie and Simon came into my mind.

Raymond walked back into his office with his usual flourish of an entrance and nodded knowingly to me.

"Bridie will you come with me I need you to meet someone," she stiffened causing her to nervously glance across to me and Rhona, both of us expressed our assurance all would be ok.

"Rhona shall we follow?" I held my elbow high to her, standing up she took it.

"What's going on Hayden?" she treated me like a naughty child. "You're up to her something."

"Wait and see," we followed briskly behind Raymond and Bridie, who nervously checked we were behind her, weaving through the corridors until we arrived at the room I had previously been in with Maisie, adjacent to the common room. Behind his back, Raymond pointed to a door on the left before the one he entered. Rhona and I went into a small room almost a cupboard where two plastic chairs faced a large picture window, a two-way mirror into the room Raymond had entered with Bridie.

We were watching both of them as Bridie sat down at his request she twitched uncontrollably. Raymond spoke quietly which appeared to relax her.

"Is she ok Rhona?"

"She's scared of this place."

"Yes she told me of her fear and it's understandable."

"She has a healthy suspicion as I do, what is happening?" I could detect her concern for Bridie. "I hope this isn't some sort of trick to put Bridie back into a sanatorium."

"Patience Rhona please, do you honestly believe I would do it to her?" As if on cue, the door gently opened with Raymond walking toward Maisie who entered. Warmly kissing her cheek.

"I believe you two know each other, I'll leave you both alone," he left them to join us standing behind looking into the room at the pair.

"Hello you, this is a surprise," Bridie moved toward Maisie lifting up her hands to hers, I could tell they knew they were being watched, but their emotions suddenly getting the better of them, they grabbed one another hugging so tightly screaming, jumping up and down lost in joy, I thought they would hurt each other.

Bridie kissed Maisie on her lips and together they

explored each other's faces close enough to find blemishes. They pushed away the table and pulled the chairs closer and sat holding and talking quietly almost to a whisper, Maisie stroking Bridie's arm, I realised their connection was far greater than my own with Bridie, a pang of jealousy ran through my veins, I shrugged off the feeling.

"They love one another Rhona?" I felt a tinge of sadness wanting it to be with me.

"They've known each other for 50 years and have been through so much together as well as looking out for each other." I conceded they had the memories of a whole lifetime together.

"Do you know Maisie well?" I watched them feeling intrusive to their relationship.

"Yes at times I would visit her with Bridie especially when like today she would become nervous in the environment, she mostly needed support they're very similar in nature." Maisie had come alive and was extremely animated wanting to talk and talk whereas, Bridie wanted to hold her.

"Are they a couple Rhona?" I needed to ask, I hoped not out of jealousy.

"No not in the way you're suggesting." She prickled toward me protectively for the two women. "They are truly great friends like twin sisters, two opposite peas from the same pod if you like."

"Rhona I am only concerned for Bridie's happiness, wherever and whomever she finds it with." I felt I had lost Bridie all over again, this time not to an institution but to a friend of her choosing, I was genuinely happy for her and sad for myself, hoping one day she might realise she has more than one friend.

Raymond left the room as Rhona and I continued

to watch the women laughing forgetting any inhibitions they may have had, it started to feel as if we were intruding on their space.

With Rhona and I alone again, it gave me an opportunity to discuss an idea with her, if it worked everyone I hoped would be happy.

There were tears between the two, as Raymond reluctantly had to break up the reunion, a sad Bridie comforted by Rhona. I held Bridie tightly before I left as she had with Maisie my head all over the place.

Before I left the hospital I phoned and updated Claire suggesting we arrange a party at Desmond's bungalow in Sidcup, I gave her a potential guest list and likely dates to celebrate the project of finding Bridie. I wanted to mark its closure and officially disband the group, although I hoped we could all remain friends.

My drive home uneventful, my emotions though were in tatters, I found myself saddened I had not meant as much to Bridie as Maisie did. Absence truly did make my heart go fonder unfortunately it was not reciprocated. I realised I had a strange kind of love for Bridie built around my own imagination which was not real anymore. I remembered Penny's words to me 'we're real, your real family' and she was absolutely right.

Chapter 16

"What are you up to Hayden?" My secretary looked at me with curiosity the moment I arrived back in the office. "You never invite me anywhere."

"Do you want to come then Claire?" My thanks to her long overdue and she would like to see it through to the end.

"I wouldn't miss it for the world I'll get cracking on the planning." We laughed and I watched her skip to her desk, no swinging of the hips this time.

As the party day drew near I was getting apprehensive with the group coming and the plans put into place, I hoped our guest of honour would enjoy it. It had been two weeks since I had last seen Bridie or any of the others. Life had returned to relative normality save for me appreciating what I already had a good deal more.

I had spent yesterday evening updating Penny, the children no longer interested. She looked forward to putting names to the faces of what I felt had become my family during these past months and seemed happier I didn't run away with Bridie as soon as I saw her. With my on a 'pedestal' memory of her destroyed and replaced by a more brotherly and protective love for her, I too felt happier.

Desmond's home centred within its 5 acres spreading out like tentacles across his land, designed to accentuate space in every corner.

Penny and I decided we would present the

bungalow in such a way to Bridie as if she was finally coming home and would want to live here, but for a few days while we prepared, we treated it as our own.

There was the gentle hum of traffic from the Sidcup by pass two streets away; it hardly interfered with the rustle of trees as the home backed onto Scadbury Park nature reserve with the birds singing at the top of their lungs in the morning tending to drown out any noise. I was grateful being able to stand and gaze at the view across the reserve.

The challenge was to gauge what a father would like his daughter to appreciate, without questioning her I found myself looking at Carrie for guidance. Both Penny and I had spent most of our time cleaning the bungalow, with me doing the handy-man stuff and she rearranging furniture, the place pristine, now we needed warmth.

The summer sun took care of outside making the most of the tidied gardens courtesy of a local gardener. The barbeque stove, put in place ready, for the planned feast for guests on Sunday, tomorrow.

Carrie had the idea of placing as many photographs around the home, family reminders of Bridie's childhood, her mother and father even her brother and sisters, it turned into a game searching for as many as we could, by setting ourselves an hour we laid our finds on the plain lounge rug. A framed young family showing a proud father Desmond and proud mother Josie with their four children, a young Bridie beamed at him from the picture we had enlarged and framed above the living room fireplace in happier times.

We found pictures in the local library archive of the Queen's coronation party with a good shot of

London's greengrocers.

The next and best was Desmond and Bridie holding hands outside their shop in Peckham, another showed a young girl in white in her holy communion dress, it was mesmerising.

"She was stunning back then." Penny took the picture's from me, I nodded realising I was spending too much time reminiscing. "I'll try and get these framed as well."

We spent the next hour picking the best shots of Bridie with Desmond and or her Mother, the odd holiday snap and minimised ones with her brother and sisters, we suspected they would have had these taken in a booth. Desperately I wanted to find a photograph of both Bridie and I, but I knew one did not exist.

We decided on 15 photographs and Penny dashed off to find a local picture framer in the hope they could copy them and frame them in the groups we thought best, I asked her to copy another one and enlarge it I wanted two, one for Bridie and one I promised myself I would give away. We hoped they could do them all today.

My next task was to set up the barbeque and check the food, my two children were busy setting up the tables and chairs, I so appreciated them both and hoped their journey through life, would never be as fraught as Bridie's had been.

I was grateful to Harry for suggesting he would act as our chef as he was always cooking something outdoors at the hospital, even when I visited him we would be interrupted by the Doctors and Nurses supplementing their lunches with one of his burgers on buns or sausages in rolls, I looked forward to his coming tomorrow.

Summer and lunchtimes, I guessed would never be the same at Darenth since he decided it was his time to retire. Lately, Harry and Rhona had become inseparable I hoped it was a good omen. I had set out a plan and trusted it would work out tomorrow on the big day.

The four of us, my 'real' family sat outside on the patio of Desmond home hopefully, soon to be Bridies if she wants to keep it and live here, a clear September evening the moon as bright as the stars it centred.

"Will we ever live in a place like this dad?"

"I doubt it Carrie, not now I am retiring."

"Are sure you want to Hayden, I know you love what you do." Penny kept surprising me, I thought she would be horrified at the thought, but it seemed she had her own dreams too for us as a family.

"Yes if there's one thing the last few months has taught me, it is what is important, and that's us." I was getting soft, there would be a shooting star next, and we all sat in silence looking out above the darkness until we drifted off to our beds content as a family.

The next morning again Penny fussed over the cleanliness of the bungalow and luckily the picture framers had worked their magic so Simon, Carrie and I could position them around the home ready for Penny's inspection.

The day warm and sunny became magical with each hour passing, as my new friends began arriving, Harry and Rhona the first with a crate of beer and several salad bowls prepared lovingly, he had brought his own tools for the barbeque not leaving anything to chance.

In part, we were here to celebrate the life of our good friend Desmond, but also to celebrate the future of his daughter Bridie.

I watched as Rhona fussed over Simon and Carrie like a surrogate grandmother in the garden throwing a tennis ball between them, Penny organising the food in the best layout, while Harry monitored the charcoal on the stove constantly, taking the odd swig of beer when he thought Rhona was not looking.

Andrew tried quietly to open the side gate entrance to the garden, but unfortunately, the hinges needed oil and immediately discovered by all. After greeting everyone, he took me aside and told me he had picked up our guest of honour and sent her through the open front door and she was in the lounge waiting for me there. I caught my breath, I expected her of course, but now she was actually here. Walking across to the tables of food, I took Penny's hand and whispered to her our guest had arrived, we both entered through the French doors from the garden to the lounge.

"Hello Bridie, welcome," she was looking at the photographs and she was crying, quickly I introduced Penny who rushed towards her placing an arm around her shoulders. "Welcome to your family home." She shuddered sobbing in her arms.

"I'm sorry, really sorry, I hoped, tried, not get too upset, but seeing these photographs the memories came flooding back. I had locked them away deep in my mind.

We sat down and Penny said softly. "This is your home now, she sobbed even louder.

"What's going on?" It was Rhona, peering into the lounge seeing her crying. "Oh my dear, don't upset yourself," she took over from Penny. "It's all over now."

"Isn't it lovely how Penny has found and displayed all the pictures," Bridie nodded smiling at Penny.

"I would like this to be my," she hesitated. "My home, will you live here with me Rhona, please you and Harry?" He peered in through the French doors wondering what the commotion was.

"Well I'll have to think about it my dear, now I have a hot stove to attend to." It caused her to laugh and she began to relax.

It was Andrew's turn to walk through immediately noticing the photographs, with Rhona and Penny fussing over Bridie I pulled him aside.

"Have you noticed the second of the black and white photographs the one with the 20 girls showing both Bridie and Maisie on the end of the middle row?" He nodded.

"I've seen this one before, the likeness between the two uncanny."

"Do you recognise the Nurse in the picture?" I held up a magnifying glass for him to look closely."

"Good grief its Rhona, she was very pretty."

"What do you mean was young man?" We laughed at Andrew's embarrassment not realising she was in earshot. "Did you think I wouldn't be?

"Have a look at the young man beside her, looks a little like you old chap." I patted him on his back.

"You don't mean it never occurred to me."

"Yes Andrew, meet your father Cedric Bartholomew as a young man." He could not stop staring at it running his index finger across the figure as if somehow it would come alive.

"I have very few pictures of him as a young Doctor, he was never around." He, saddened by the thought.

"Your father had been responsible for those 20

women and he did his best for them. The testament to his work is two women you know, the woman sitting over there," I gestured towards Bride. "And the other you saw at the Maudsley, they survived because of your father, this is his legacy of which you and us all can be proud of, nothing else matters Andrew."

"Thank you Hayden, it's important to me to hear this." A chorus of 'good man' from Rhona, Bridie and Harry in the doorway listening. "I'd really like a copy of the picture."

"Already done." I handed him a copy of the small original along with a blown part of his father and looked across at Penny who suddenly understood why I wanted the extras.

"I need a drink." Overwhelmed he strode somehow taller out into the garden, a huge weight lifted from his shoulders clutching the photographs to his chest.

"Will you and Harry live here with me Rhona, please say yes?"

"Well I'm not sure honey we'll have to ask Harry?" Rhona raised her eyebrows at me as if somehow she needed my approval, which she had of course.

I took Penny's hand and we moved quietly out into the garden, watching Harry wrestling with the chicken, burgers and sausages on the blazing fire, I walked across to him with a beer in hand for him.

"This is a fine place of Desmond's," Grateful for the drink he took a heavy gulp, his face flushed from the heat.

"Would you like to live here Harry?" He looked at me in surprise. "I'm not sure Hayden."

"Bridie has asked if Rhona and you would like to

live here with her, what do you think about it Harry?"

"I would love it, but it's up to Rhona nowadays." He looked directly at me with a twinkle in his eye, settled then I thought.

Turning I saw Bridie now in the garden her floral dress swaying in the gentle breeze of summer, her figure hardly changed with the years, Penny and Rhona dancing attendance, my eyes followed her as she went to join Harry at the barbeque, she kissed his cheek.

For a second I drifted away, my mind had been on edge ever since I first met Desmond, this time I did not have to worry about where Bridie was, or how Desmond is, my mind forcing its own needs upon me. Within second's I was jolted back to reality, Raymond shook my hand and he had brought my Claire with him.

"No way was I going to miss this?" She grinned and made eyes at Raymond, trouble ahead I predicted, as he went for drinks she whispered. "He is a hunk isn't he?" I kissed her cheek.

"Be careful young lady," I scolded her as a father would Penny joined us.

"Well boss, I had to see what kind of mess you've got yourself into," I hugged her again for all the help she had given me, Penny kissed her and started to point out who's who pre-empting introductions and went off to grab Andrew. At this moment, I feared for him if Claire liked him.

"Alright, alright steady on." Raymond scolded us laughing coming back with our drinks, watching us embrace, I detected a slight edge of jealousy, definitely trouble I confirmed. "The boys done good, where is your lovely wife?" I pointed to her and he waved, Penny skipped towards him dragging

Andrew along behind.

It was my turn to worry, Penny and Raymond looked like a couple being of similar age they laughed and joked about seemingly nothing they had clicked instantly and I felt a pang of jealousy, I introduced Andrew to Claire, her arm immediately locked into his and asked him to show her the gardens.

The group naturally moved closer together, except for Simon and Carrie who were playing ball somewhere, as Harry had the barbeque under control. Claire and Rhona either side of Bridie.

Raymond stood behind me and quietly spoke to me. "Maisie Belling is in the car outside. She has passed her assessment so is being released into the community. The panel has sanctioned a phased release with all the paperwork done."

"Bravo, truly you've worked wonders Raymond." My plan looked good.

"I'm uncomfortable with your plan I hope the idea works." I ignored a naturally cautious psychiatrist.

"Who have you left outside?" Asked Penny who had an inbuilt antenna seemingly stretching for miles, I put my finger to my lips for her to not to say anything.

"It is part of Hayden's grand plan," he was laughing it was time for a toast.

"Ok everyone, it is time to raise your glasses to a fine man whose home this is, was," I corrected myself. "And without whom we would not be here today." Everyone grabbed a drink, Bridie grabbed Harry's arm to stop her falling.

"Bridie, I loved your father very much, for who he was and what he stood for. He had spent a lifetime wishing he had done the right thing by you and I hope, finally you will agree he did. I raised my glass. "To Desmond London, God bless him." The cheer of 'To Desmond' rang around the garden and hung in the air for a few moments.

"I would also like to say how thankful we are as a group to have finally found Bridie and wish her well for the future here in Desmond's, sorry, her new home."

I spoke quietly to Andrew and he left by the side garden gate, my eyes on Bridie, I noted a tinge of sadness in those saucer like eyes of hers I remembered well.

Harry muttered something about his sausages burning and ran back to his barbeque shouting it was time to eat unless we wanted crisp black food we all fell about laughing at him. I spotted Andrew who nodded at me from the gate.

"One more thing, before we sample the delights of Harry's cooking." Everyone turned from facing the barbeque.

"Bridie, I know we loved each other once so much and because of this it was why Desmond was so easily able to convince me to help him, during our life's journey we both have tread a much different path, I have to say mine luckier than yours." Penny was by my side holding my hand tightly. "I have achieved much and I know you to have loved another as I have." I squeezed Penny's hand. "The one thing, I, we can all do for you now is to return love by way of acceptance of you and provide the love you so desperately crave for." She looked at me confused. "Bridie, Raymond has some news for you which I hope you'll be happy to hear."

As Raymond explained to the group, the final piece in the jigsaw with Maisie passing the assessment. Everyone cheered him knowing how hard he had worked to pull off the minor miracles, from correcting Deborah's name back from being Maisie to Maisie's back from being Bridie's to finally freeing Bridie from a continued life looking over her shoulder. Always wondering if she would ever have to return to a sanatorium and unknown to her how he had worked hard to release Maisie herself. I watched her closely, she looked sadly alone I hoped it would now change.

"One more surprise folks and then we can eat."

"About time were ready over here," Harry said struggling with the food.

"Bridie, one final gift your father, Papa and I can give you is your Maisie!" She stood out from behind me and both woman squealed with delight, rushing at one another, they would not let go of each other ever again. Everyone clapped.

"Will you live with me, oh please Maisie, please?" Maisie was dumbstruck.

"Of course she will my girl and Harry and I will look after you both here in your father's home." Rhona hugged them both, their own journey together about to begin.

Harry voice boomed across the garden. "Come and get the food now please!"

No tears now, the group complete save for the absence of Desmond, but he was in our thoughts and hearts. Penny told me she had packed our things ready for us to go home and she whispered.

"I'm proud of you." I knew it of course, but it was nice to hear it.

Sensing the day was closing around her, Bridie tapped her glass she had something she wanted to say.

"In a good way, it seems my life is mapped out now, I hope my father forgave me for all the years he tried to find me, especially as I had been already released." She bowed towards me remembering our conversation. "I couldn't tell anyone for fear I would hurt those who helped me survive my ordeal." She looked at Rhona and Harry. "I love my father's home and this day will be a part of its memory always. Maisie and I intend to live here with our 'Mum and Dad'. "I thank you both and all of you for what you've done for me," looking at Maisie she added.

"From us both and most importantly, to my first love who without him, we would not be here now or in the right order where at last I can finally be myself." I felt myself blushing. "A love I will cherish always and more than this I thank you from the bottom of my heart dear, dear Hayden. Thank you for giving me back a family, not quite the one I started out with, but as good if not better in every way." She raised her glass to me as everyone applauded, Penny on one side squeezed my hand tightly and Claire on the other stroking my arm.

It saddened me to realise Raymond and Andrew were unlikely to be part of our lives anymore but hoped we would come together on future occasions. We left 'Mum' Rhona and 'Dad' Harry with their two adopted daughters Bridie and Maisie in Desmond and Josie's home.

I hoped they were both looking down with approval.

-o-

Books by the same Author
Alan Baulch

Finding Bridie

As a young teenager in the 1960's Bridie London develops the life
Threatening Meningeal Tuberculosis.
On Medical advice and because of risk to her siblings and his greengrocery business, her father Desmond London delivers her to a mental asylum offering the isolation she needs.
Unwittingly he gives up his parental rights consigning her to a life in an institution. At last there is an opportunity to release her from the mental torture after fifty years, with siblings unwilling to help, Desmond finds someone who can.
The corruption found by Haydon Robbins would shock the nation, with the real Bridie missing he must find her before it is too late.

Love, Life, Fantasies & Poetry

A thought provoking first volume of 30 Short Stories, Tales and Ramblings with 20 Poems spread across different genre's.
From Love in New York, A Scare in the Dark to Something Crazy, Asylum Seeking, The Pain of Redundancy, Spine Chiller and a Spirit of Hope.
With Poems on Time, Friends, Work, Teenage Angst and Human Values.
A Collection to Enjoy.

Mind Trap

Samuel Thornton arrived as a patient at the Berkshire clinic direct from Shanghai. The grip on his mind total. More patients arrive the grip on their minds the same pure evil.

Without out the help of David Bareham an ex-priest they will all die and be used as tools for the pleasure of Kali Ma herself.

Friends rally and a group with David is formed. They have to tackle the spiritual evil attacking them.

The group are taken on a journey following past lives, death and business corruption. Their experiences cause them to fear for their very souls.

Death beckons, they become trapped in a fight they couldn't possibly win alone.

The Tracer

A gas canister explosion in a scrap metal yard leaves Michael battered, an Amnesiac without a past.

By a 'quirk of fate', he is left with a unique gift his mission is to trace the missing.

Struggling with his identity, he enters a world where kidnapping, murder, rape, robbery, hate and great sorrow are normal.

Single-handedly he offers the solution for driving terrorism into extinction while providing the answers for solving crimes across the globe.

He has to be stopped, the only question who will get to him first?

Printed in Great Britain
by Amazon